TRUE MERCY

TRUE MERCY

Idelle Kursman

LUCK CAN CHANGE

This book is dedicated to my husband, Michael,

and our sons, Benjamin and Kaleb,

and to my parents,

Stanley and Arlene Kaplan.

ACKNOWLEDGMENTS

A BOOK IS RARELY WRITTEN WITHOUT THE tremendous help and support of family, friends, and professionals. I would like to thank my developmental editor, Alida Winternheimer, for guiding me in the plot, character, and writing development of my manuscript. I would also like to thank my husband Michael for listening to chapters despite barely being able to keep his eyes open from working so hard, and also my son Benjamin for taking the picture of downtown Morristown, which is featured on the front cover. Finally, this novel would not have been possible without the members of my two writing groups for their encouragement, editing, and critiquing for the past two years: Joanne Flexser and Jacky Sheppard from the Word Lovers Writers Group; and Cindy LaPenna, Sue Rutan Donald, and Tammie Winkler of the Mount Olive Library Writing Group.

You guys were great!

PROLOGUE

The man, Sergei Moskey, nearly passed out right on top of Marina. The reek from his sweaty, oily body could not repel her; since being taken into captivity she was now beyond revulsion. After months on this voyage, she had become inured to any foul odor.

Despite the darkness, Marina Dobrin could see his glazed eyes looking over her body as she lay chained to a hard, flat rectangular surface that served as a bed. The man had pushed the needle only halfway into her arm when he slumped forward, unconscious. Marina could see the veins in her arms and legs. She was waiting to whittle away and be no more than a mere skeleton.

The door opened slightly.

"Sergei . . . Sergei, where the hell are you?" an impatient voice hissed insistently.

The girl chained to Marina's right moaned. Earlier, she had moaned hopelessly for hours. Marina wasn't sure what Slavic language she was speaking, but she could no longer stand listening to the cries pelting her right ear.

Finally, Marina shouted, "Stop! Stop! Shut up! Stop!" She didn't know if the girl spoke Ukrainian or Polish or something else. She just knew she couldn't listen to that sound anymore.

The girl's chain rattled a moment and then all was silent. Marina had heard the girls praying in their various languages for the duration of the journey. She herself had no religious upbringing, but it seemed as if their God remained steadfastly indifferent to their suffering.

The man named Sergei attempted to rouse himself but to no avail; he was struggling not to fall off of her. He finally fell to the ground. Someone would come to fetch him for sure, so she ignored the sharp pain while she worked on taking the needle out of her arm before one of her other captors noticed she did not get her drug injection.

"Sergei, where are you? Are you stoned or fooling around?" the man whispered again, banging on the door. He was in such a rage he could barely get the words out.

With little room to move while she was chained to her bed, Marina managed to pull the needle out of her arm, struggling to keep it steady and straight so as not to stick herself. Fortunately, she had just enough freedom of movement to place it under her dirty sheet as her other captor swung the door open so hard it rattled like a heavy drum. He waved his flashlight. The girls who had been crammed into the room months earlier turned away to shield their eyes. Many let out a gasp or rocked in their beds. The only one who didn't was the girl chained to Marina's left. She had been lying in the same position for a few hours now; her mouth was open and Marina hadn't heard her breathing. Marina inwardly mourned her, knowing that she would never taste freedom again in this world.

The other man kicked Sergei on his back.

"Owww . . . Wha . . . what are you doing, Igor?" Sergei snapped awake at the pain of the heavy boot ramming into his body.

Igor Agapov looked over at Marina and made a face as if he had tasted something rotten. He took out his small bottle of vodka and finished it off. Igor always had a small bottle on him and would often take a sip when he got frustrated. Whenever he spoke, his stale breath permeated the air.

"I can't wait to finish her off. But all in good time," he muttered, staring at her, instinctively touching the scar along the side of his face. He turned to Sergei and snarled in a menacing undertone, "But I have to deal with this idiot first or I'll never get to sleep tonight." Igor jerked him up by the rim of his shirt.

"It's late! We've got to get out of here and lock the door! I need to go to bed! The ship will be docked soon and we have to get up in a few hours," he bellowed, his spittle touching Marina's hand. She twitched slightly, praying he didn't see her move.

She lay with her eyes closed and her jaw slackened, fearing he would check to make sure she had her injection.

But he was too busy slapping Sergei around.

"All right! All right! Stop! Calm down! I'll lock up and we go to bed," Sergei said, protecting his head from the blows, and opening and closing his eyes in an attempt to get his wits about him.

Igor stormed out. Sergei followed. Marina peeked as the door closed. But when it did close, the key did not swing in the lock. Marina expected to hear Sergei fiddling with the key to lock the door shut, but he took his key out and took off instead.

She heard the engine slowing down, figuring the ship was moving toward shore. Amid the roar of the splashing waves, she noticed the moon shone like a glowing lantern in the air through a small porthole window. She shuddered, recalling the last time Igor had said the ship was docked, he meant they would be unloading the girls. Marina refused to allow her mind to think about the horrors that awaited them.

She had become so thin she was able to slip out of her chains. Marina waited until she was confident her captors were sleeping. Earlier in the day she had overheard them talking about all the work they would have to do soon. Since then she wondered where they were and how the girls would be tortured. She pictured a dark, dirty place far from where anyone could hear their cries.

Marina strained her ears to hear the approaching footsteps or smell the stale whiskey of the night guard. Nothing.

Is this my chance? she asked herself. Images of Igor's steely-eyed look of pure hatred assailed her. If she didn't escape now, any day he would wreak a terrible vengeance on her for scarring him with his own knife. She could tell every time she saw him that inside his head he obsessed over finding the right moment to finish her off.

CHAPTER ONE

BRUCE

"Adam, you'll start a fire if you don't watch the pot on the stove!"

Bruce Hitchens hurried into the kitchen and turned the flame off. He leaned on the counter for half a minute with his eyes closed and tried to drive away the images in his mind of the boiling water overflowing and the whole house burning down. He was a man of medium height and build, with intense dark brown eyes and black hair dotted with specks of grey. He ran a hand through his hair. When he looked at his hand, he noticed a grey hair had fallen out. At forty-two years old, he had been seeing a lot more grey hairs in the last few weeks. Ever since his son returned home, Bruce had neglected to dye his hair. He shut his eyes tight and his chin touched his chest. One more thing he couldn't find time for.

"Oooh!" Adam walked into the kitchen and put his hand over his mouth. "Daddy, I was just lookin' at the flowers outside! I love lookin' at the flowers I planted with Mommy."

"Adam." Bruce raised his head. Slowly and carefully he

turned around to face his son. "There's a time to look at flowers and there's a time to watch a pot so it doesn't boil over and burn the house down." By the time he finished his sentence he was gritting his teeth and balling his hands into fists. He then took out a potholder and removed the lid. He saw the limp macaroni popping up under the blackened cheese.

Thank God I remembered to buy antacids yesterday, he thought.

"I'm cookin' my specialty t'night, Daddy—mac 'n' cheese," Adam declared, holding his head high, seemingly oblivious to his father's agitated state.

Bruce nodded with his shoulders slumped, still leaning on the counter for support.

This moment was just one more of his many second thoughts about bringing Adam home. His son had resided in the Fairmount Home for six weeks, ever since his wife Maggie had passed away. Bruce sank down into the chair of his tiny kitchen, rubbing his temples as he once again weighed his options.

"Suppa's ready, Daddy," Adam smiled as he stirred the burnt dinner with a spoon already covered in cheese. "I can cook meals for you, Daddy, now that I'm back home." He looked over at his father and smiled.

Bruce groaned inwardly. A diatribe began in his mind with all the words he would never dare speak out loud.

Don't you realize what could've happened if I didn't walk in here at that moment because I needed a break? Do you actually think I want to eat a ruined meal? Adam, why do you have to be so dense? Where were you when brains were handed out?

Bruce immediately looked down in shame for thinking these thoughts about his own son. He prayed the day would never come when he let these words slip out in a moment of frustration. Adam couldn't help his disability any more than Maggie could help dying and leaving him to care for their disabled eighteen-year-old adult son alone.

"Adam!" Bruce yelled, his eyes bulging with alarm as he saw his son about to grab the pot barehanded.

"Daddy, I'm an expert cooker. Mommy said so!" Adam said as he opened the drawer where his mother kept the potholders, one hand flapping in the air. He had thick hands for a young man his size, also of medium height and build like his father. Only Adam had inherited his mother's wavy light brown hair and fairer complexion.

The twinkle in his big, round brown eyes and his generous smile reminded Bruce so much of Maggie that he briefly reminisced of when he first saw her nineteen years ago. His tender expression turned to a frown when he recalled telling her he wanted to wake up to her beautiful face for the rest of his life.

When the mac 'n' cheese was on the table, Bruce contemplated taking a bite or just moving the noodles and cheese around, pretending to eat. He slowly brought a few noodles to his mouth and was surprised to find the meal was still edible. But each plate had only small portions. "Didn't you make more macaroni, Adam?"

"Yeah, I did, Daddy, but a lot of the noodles got stuck at the bottom of the pot," his son said as he dug his fork into his plate.

Bruce heaved a sigh. *Burnt.*

His mind drifted back to the presentation he had to finish tonight and send to his team to go over tomorrow when Adam interrupted his thoughts.

"Daddy, let's go for a walk after suppa. OK?"

Bruce's last bite got stuck in his throat. He reached for

his apple juice to help the pasta go down, wishing it were a stiff drink.

"Actually, Adam," Bruce put down his fork delicately as he looked at his son, "this isn't enough. I'm going to have to call for a pizza delivery."

His son wasn't offended at all. He lit up and said, "All right! I love pizza!"

Bruce couldn't help smiling. "Good. You start cleaning up and I'll look over some notes. Deal?" He held up his right hand.

"Deal!" Adam slapped his father's hand hard. Bruce held back a yelp and stopped himself from snapping at his son. He massaged his hand to calm the swelling.

"Sorry, Daddy." Adam covered his mouth with his hand. "I'm just excited 'bout pizza."

"Adam," Bruce said through gritted teeth, "you're getting stronger. You've got to control yourself. Don't ever slap somebody's hand so hard." Bruce held out his right hand. "Just shake it, son. Shake it."

Adam gently shook his father's hand, studying his father's face.

"What is it, Adam?"

"But Daddy, guys are tough. They like to play tough."

His father's eyes narrowed. "It doesn't mean we're made of steel. Men can break bones." Bruce held out his right hand and then balled it into a fist. "Where did you learn about guys being tough and playing tough anyway?"

"From TV. They showed guys runnin' around wit a ball and gettin' dirty . . ."

"Adam, running is one thing and slapping is another."

Bruce closed his eyes, trying to control his temper. Hunger

and the burnt smell of cheese were trying his patience.

Adam looked down, his eyes sad. "Sorry, Daddy. I just wanna be the way boys are supposta be."

Bruce stared at him, his anger turned to sympathy, at a loss for words. If only life were fairer and his son had a chance.

He finally found his voice. "All right, Adam. I'll be going over my notes. You clean up and we'll call for the pizza."

◆ ◆ ◆

As Igor lay in bed, he couldn't sleep because he was too busy thinking, planning.

Surely I'll be able to find a weapon to do away with her once we get off the ship. His body trembled in anticipation of that event. He would explain to Andre how, in a fit of madness, she had attacked him once they arrived at shore. She'd lost her mind after she realized what they were going to force her to do. For a brief moment, Igor thought about using the excuse that she tried to escape, but he dismissed that immediately.

These women had no escape; they were completely under his control. They were simple girls who knew no English. The very sight of their malnourished bodies and dirty clothes would frighten any stranger away.

Igor turned to his side and felt his eyelids give way. After secretly bringing the women to shore, he would have the task of feeding them and finding them decent clothes. His insides got aroused thinking of all the power he and the other men had over them.

But that one girl, he thought. *Why did she seem sharper and more sophisticated than the rest?* Was it because they had taken her captive differently than their usual method? Unlike the others, they knew little about her.

Exhaustion finally swept over Igor; he welcomed the calm stillness of sleep, for tomorrow would be a busy and important day.

CHAPTER TWO

MARINA

THE SHIP HAD COME TO A COMPLETE STOP. THE other women slept, oblivious to this pivotal moment where their individual fates were to be determined by their kidnappers, who regarded them as mere merchandise to be sold to the highest bidder. Every limb of Marina's body shook as she crept silently from the ship to the dock. Her heart thumped with regret and guilt thinking about all the innocent victims she was forced to leave behind if her own escape was possible.

Am I being cruel and selfish, no better than Sergei and Igor, for abandoning them? Her guilt overwhelmed her so much that she almost took a step back toward the ship.

But then she spotted security guards scattered over the port. She also saw men busy hauling crates. Marina covered her mouth in time to silence her gasp. She crouched lower behind a post. Assuming these men were accomplices to the kidnappers, it struck her that if she escaped from here, she could possibly expose the human trafficking operation and save the other women, too.

Marina spied guards pacing the grounds of the dock, a few holding binoculars in towers, and several in small boats scouring the seas. She studied the kidnappers' ship. "Circova Wines" was written on the outside.

Though she tried to remain as hidden as possible, Marina kept her ears open for anyone speaking Russian or Romanian. She saw many cars coming from ships and being hauled into the biggest trucks she had ever seen. She closed her eyes and wracked her brain, trying to remember if her captors ever spoke about shipping cars. She could not think of one instance. Was there even a connection? Marina was too scared to even contemplate it. She bit down hard on her lower lip, trying to still her shaking body as she tried to figure out what to do next.

As she lay crouched behind the post, Marina's eyes traveled to the small bright lights dotting the night sky. She stared at the stars, pondering that this was her first taste of freedom in months. She prayed it would last and she would never experience such trauma ever again. While she studied the night sky, searching for clues that her prayer was heard and an infinite power would show compassion, an enormous steel truck drove in and parked ten feet away from her.

Marina huddled behind the post, so scared she heard her teeth chattering. She closed her eyes, waiting to be discovered and thrust back into the living nightmare, but all she heard were two men talking at a distance. One spoke American English, but the other spoke English with a heavy accent that she did not recognize. She finally dared to open her eyes; the back of the truck was open and faced her, and she faintly made out the sparkling silver of cars packed inside. The two men spoke with their backs toward her; they were concentrating on each other's words and did not look around.

"You've got to deliver these cars by seven o'clock in the morning," the taller man who spoke American English told the other man. When the shorter man gave no response, he asked, "Are you familiar with Morristown?"

"Yes, *sí*, I know Morristown," he answered. He had long, dark hair wrapped in a ponytail. Marina smiled to herself: she remembered when her brother used to wear a ponytail. He wore it for years while their mother constantly berated him that he looked much better with short hair. Months before she was kidnapped, her brother had cut his hair short, saying the school he wanted to attend would not accept him with long hair. Marina remembered how her mother had broken into a satisfied smile every time she saw him with neater hair.

But the men's conversation broke into her happy thoughts.

The taller man brought out and unfolded a piece of paper from his back pocket. "Here's the address," he said. "Help them unload half the vehicles in Morristown and then you immediately drive to Bound Brook and help them unload the other half." He stared at the other man. "I know you've been to Bound Brook many times. Use the GPS for finding both car dealers. You should have no problem."

The man with the ponytail took the piece of paper. "All right. I have a general idea how to get to Morristown already." He paused as he scanned the directions. "South Street. Is that near a restaurant or coffee shop? I been working two days straight and will need coffee and breakfast." He looked up at the other man. "And I haven't been paid yet. I've got no money on me."

The American looked down and put his hands in his pockets. Then he faced the other man again, smiling, and said, "I'll tell you what. Somewhere on South Street is a soup kitchen. You know, for people that have no money. Go have breakfast there. No one will bother you. They won't ask questions."

The shorter man nodded. "And do they serve coffee?"

The taller man's smile faded. He put his hands on his hips and bit his lower lip while staring at the other man. Slowly, he reached for his wallet in the back of his pants and took out two bills. Handing it over, he said, "And here's money for coffee. Just make the car deliveries on time with no problems, will you?"

The shorter man took the money and stuffed it in his front pocket. "No problems," he said.

The taller man nodded before he walked away. The shorter man with the ponytail looked at the paper as he made his way to the front of the truck.

Marina didn't know where Morristown was but realized this might be the perfect opportunity to escape and get something to eat. A soup kitchen? Free food? She looked up at the sky. The sun rose slowly in the distance; it would be light in an hour. Looking from side to side and seeing no security guards or anyone else, she slipped into the truck and climbed her way inside. The cars were compact, but she still worried that if one fell on her, she would be crushed.

I'll have to take this chance. What other choice do I have? She curled up into a ball against the side wall, trying to make herself as small and as far away from the cars as possible. She stayed in that ball until she heard the back door of the truck slam shut. Marina shuddered in the darkness and stared at the vehicles with their shiny surfaces and mirrors, praying they were securely fastened and none of them would crash down on her, killing her instantly. She bit her lower lip and tried to quiet her panic by thinking about getting something to eat. While forcing her mind to concentrate on this thought, anxious to be as far away from her captors as possible, the engine of the mammoth truck started and Marina felt the shaking of the truck slowly moving.

◆ ◆ ◆

Sergei heard a loud knock on his door. He rose instantly and quickly put on his clothes. Whipping his door open, he marveled at the port the ship had landed in.

America! A country full of possibilities like bars, beautiful women, and luxurious hotels!

The ship was docked in Newark, New Jersey, only miles from New York City. Sergei's mind was filled with the hundreds of things he could do and all he had heard about the city when Igor approached and interrupted his reverie. Bumping the side of his head, Igor barked in an angry tone, "Enough of your daydreams of America. We've got a job to do!"

Sergei stepped back. The smell on Igor's breath of vodka mixed with sweat assaulted his nostrils, vanishing his good spirits.

"We go check on girls, then we eat breakfast," Sergei responded, turning around and walking as far away from Igor as possible.

"Goodt," Igor said from behind him.

Sergei rolled his eyes but continued at a brisk pace. He heard Igor muttering behind him about the woman he intended to get rid of the moment he got the chance. Sergei ignored him. They had been stuck at sea for months. Raping and abusing the scared, drugged-up girls failed to arouse him anymore. He desired cheerful, easygoing women to go out drinking and dancing with. He wanted to be viewed as a handsome, available man, not a monster. At first, Sergei got a good laugh when the woman slashed Igor's face. But his partner's disposition grew even more repugnant and intolerable when Igor Skyped his girlfriend and she dumped him upon viewing the jagged lines of his scar. Now he was bitter and hell-bent on revenge. There had been numerous moments when Igor had vowed to kill her off but then changed his mind at the last moment. Igor always excused his backing down by claiming his method of killing would fail to appear to be an accident or the woman had the opportunity to kill herself. Sergei knew better; Igor was afraid of losing his job or getting killed for losing one of the girls. And every time he would berate Sergei as being the reason he could not pull it off. This was yet another reason Sergei relished finally getting off the ship; he would make it his business to separate from Igor and his abusive behavior.

They walked into the cabin where they held the women. They heard the usual gasps and chains rattling when they walked in. Today they would not be drugged; the girls had to get ready to be used for what they'd been kidnapped for. Igor and Sergei were responsible for waking up the women and herding them quietly to the dock. The women were usually too tired and drugged up to notice what was happening; in case a few of them made noise, they carried stun guns in their belts. When the women were on the dock, other men would take over, and Sergei and Igor could eat their breakfast.

CHAPTER THREE

ADAM

BOTH FATHER AND SON ENJOYED EATING THE fresh, hot pizza. As they ate their slices, Adam looked outside, staring at the familiar hills, the green swaths of grass, and the narrow roads, some paved, others dirt. His daddy insisted it wasn't a farm any longer because they grew only flowers. He didn't raise animals on it the way his daddy's daddy used to, but he liked the idea of living on a farm.

Adam stared at the blossoming apple trees standing tall and grand right outside their kitchen window. If he stretched his neck out enough, Adam could catch a glimpse of the flowers his mommy had planted. She had always told him that blossoming flowers in the spring were God's way of saying life has to go on.

"I wish Mommy would say that again," Adam sighed.

"Say what, Adam?" Bruce asked.

"That God said we need flowers in the spring to go on." Adam closed his eyes, trying to remember what his mother used to say word for word.

His father said nothing.

Adam stared at him, delighted to be back home. Even though he had to come home to an empty house after work and Daddy wasn't nearly as much fun as Mommy was, it was at least better than the Fairmount Home.

At the thought of Fairmount, Adam blinked his eyes to shut out the memory of that place.

"Adam, you can't go for a walk now," a hulky male staff member told him.

"Why not? I always go on walks wit my mommy after suppa." Adam stood up and stamped his foot.

"You're not at home no more. You have to follow the rules here. You know that," the man said as he wiped the face of another client after his meal.

Adam kicked his chair and it went tumbling to the ground with a loud bang. The kitchen became silent.

"Adam, you've got to go to the quiet room now," the hulky man stood up to full size and took a few steps toward him.

"No! I go out for a walk after suppa!" he said as he folded his arms in front of him.

"We need backup," the man told another staff member as he slowly approached Adam.

As the other staff member reached for the phone, Heidi appeared from another client's bedroom and laid her hand on the staff member's shoulder while he pressed buttons.

"I'll take you for a walk, Adam," Heidi said.

"Heidi, you're the best! You take me on walks just like my mommy did!" Adam said as he ran over to her and locked his elbow into hers.

They passed the big staff member as he shook his head at Heidi.

"Heidi, you're spoilin' 'im! We'll never be able to manage 'im

when you're always giving in to 'im." He scrunched up his face as
he shook his finger at her.

*"Dwayne, chill out! He just lost his mother!" Heidi said as she
led Adam out the door.*

*"He won't stay here if he thinks he can get his way all the time!"
Dwayne shouted after them as they walked out the door.*

*Adam wore a delighted grin and laughed giddily as they began
their walk. Even though Heidi looked nothing like his mother, when
he glanced at the young woman with blonde hair always pulled
back into a ponytail, he had the same warm, happy feeling he did
when he used to be with Mommy.*

"Adam! I'm talking to you. Look at my face," Daddy said.

Adam finally turned to his father even though he'd rather
be thinking about Heidi.

"Adam, don't forget to brush your teeth before you
go to bed."

Adam watched his father staring intently at him. He had
trouble returning people's stares and kept looking away, but his
father's eyes would not leave his face. He remembered working
with teachers about keeping eye contact when he was little.
Adam would always be delighted to earn a little piece of candy
or a sticker if he looked at his teachers' faces long enough.

But right now he noticed that his father had the
same scrunchy face that Dwayne always got when he was
angry with him.

"Adam, what did I just say?"

"What did I just say?" Adam echoed.

"No! What did I just tell you before? About brushing your
teeth," Daddy said as he massaged his temples and swallowed
even though he was finished with his meal.

Adam blinked and thought for a moment. Suddenly his face lit up and his lips curled into a victorious smile.

"Adam, don't forget ta brush your teeth before you go ta bed," Adam repeated. To add emphasis, he wagged his finger.

He sat up, waiting for praise.

But instead Daddy leaned back in his chair and said, "Let's clean up here, son, and then I've got to go back to the presentation I've got to finish on the computer tonight."

As they cleared the dishes and utensils and put things from the table back where they belonged, his father turned to him.

"And what will you be doing when I'm on the computer?"

"Let's go for a walk!"

But his father shook his head. "I told you I can't take you out for a walk every night after dinner. Tonight I've got work to do," his father said slowly, talking with his teeth pressed together. "Why don't you watch TV?"

"OK, Daddy." Adam stared down at the floor, clearly disappointed.

"Aren't some nature shows on now?"

Adam looked up and was smiling again. "Yeah, Daddy! They keep having that show 'bout butterflies."

Adam headed into the living room and turned on the TV. He placed the remote on the nearby table and plopped down on the couch. He watched his father cleaning dishes through the open kitchen door and occasionally shaking his head and blinking hard.

"Why you do that, Daddy?"

Bruce turned off the water, shook his hands of the suds, and turned around. "Do what?"

Adam looked like a puppet held up by strings when he

imitated his father blinking and shaking his head.

"Son, I'm just trying to stay awake while doing everything I have to do," he explained, turning red. "Working and taking care of you by myself is a hard job."

"I miss Mommy," Adam blurted out, his face turning into a hangdog look.

"I miss Mommy too," Daddy said softly. Then he turned around and started the water again. "Hey, Adam," he snapped, seeing the juice and a plate on the living room table. "Please put that stuff back."

◆ ◆ ◆

"What an ingenious operation this is," exclaimed Sergei as they entered the room. "It's so easy and we make so much money. I can't wait to spend it while we're in the states for a few days. Atlantic City? Is that the name of the place where they gamble?"

Igor, who took out his tiny bottle for a sip, waved away Sergei's comments dismissively. "It's too far away. We're not going to be here that long and we're going to be too busy. What? What happened? Where is she?" Igor stared, eyes bulging, at Marina's empty bed.

"What happened to her? What happened?" he yelled. He slammed his bottle against the wall. Some of the less-drugged women opened their eyes and tried to sit up upon hearing the tiny bottle shatter. He slapped the women's faces who did not stir and woke them up with that question.

"She's gone!" Igor screamed.

Igor shoved the woman's table into the middle of the room,

nearly hitting some captives chained to their makeshift beds. Women screamed, trying to sit up but unable to because their chains restrained them.

Igor's archenemy had disappeared.

Other men ran into the room, grabbed Igor, and held him down.

"You must be quiet!" one of them barked. "We look for her now!"

"Where is she?" Igor snarled, foam streaming from his mouth, his bloodshot eyes gawking furiously at the men.

"We look," another man said. "The only trucks that left here were loaded with cars, most being shipped to somewhere called Morristown."

Igor strained to turn his head toward Sergei. "If we cannot find her here, we go to Morristown! You and me, Sergei! We find her!"

Sergei's eyes bulged upon hearing his boss's command . . . His plans of going to nightclubs and partying were slipping away and turning into mere fantasies. He struggled to control the urge to shout at Igor, his boss, "No!"

CHAPTER FOUR

MARINA

Marina remained lying in a ball in the back of the truck surrounded by cars. She yearned to stretch out and lie flat but feared she had a better chance of being crushed by one of the swaying automobiles chained to its steel rack. Too uncomfortable to drift off to sleep, she huddled and waited with a pounding heart, wondering if this would indeed be her opportunity for freedom. Her body swayed every time the truck stopped for a red light, and pain shot up her knees. Her body nearly lurched back when the truck resumed driving or rode over the occasional bump in the road.

She felt her legs cramping and was about to take a chance with her life and lie flat when the truck slowed down, pulling into a driveway. It seemed like the ride had lasted for hours, but as soon as the truck came to a full stop, rather than feeling relieved, Marina held her breath, her body quaking in terror. Within a minute she heard the back door of the truck being hauled open. She silently covered her face with her hands as the light entered the back of the truck.

She overheard men talking outside, and when she dared to peek, she found them surveying the cars. She didn't dare breathe. Her body shook even more now at the thought these men were about to leap into the truck and find her. But no one entered, at least not yet. Marina shut her eyes hard, awaiting the end.

When she gathered enough courage to open her eyes, the men were gone. Marina took a long breath and sat cross-legged while she wondered where they were. Crawling to the edge of the back of the truck, she spied men exchanging papers a few feet away. They stood in front of a rectangular glass building that displayed similar cars inside and outside. At the center of the top of the building was a large sign reading Don's BMW. The men put away their papers and pointed toward the truck before they entered the building. Now was her moment.

Marina slipped out of the truck, careful not to make the slightest sound. The sun was just beginning to rise, so she hoped they wouldn't notice her. The men continued chatting as they left the building and approached the truck. Marina tiptoed silently to the front of the truck. Seeing no one, she proceeded to run, forgetting about the soup kitchen despite her empty stomach. Her only goal now was to run without anyone tracking her down.

Despite weariness and hunger, Marina kept running. She surprised herself by still being able to move despite the long journey being chained to a bed most of the time. Igor's words still rang in her ears. Often as she fell asleep at night on the ship, he would stare at her with pure, unadulterated hatred and mutter, "I will never rest until you pay for this scar you gave me." Hearing his menacing words in her head propelled her to run even though her legs resembled toothpicks without an ounce of fat or muscle. She felt her hair—so dingy and dirty, with so many knots she couldn't even run her fingers through it. Even though she was grateful she had no mirror to look at herself, she was sure she'd scare anyone with her appearance.

Marina had no idea where she was going, but she felt safer the farther she ran. She was risking her life, but she couldn't go through any more torture. Marina still felt heartsick leaving the other girls behind. She silently vowed she would do everything in her power to help the other girls escape. But for now, she ran. She had no idea how long she had run, but soon the sun rose.

Besides her appearance, Marina was relieved she hadn't seen anybody because she feared whomever she encountered may have ties to the human trafficking ring. Fortunately, she had mastered English in school, even winning several prizes for her fluency, so when she saw a sign that read Welcome to Morristown, New Jersey, she was relieved that at least it confirmed her present location. Marina hadn't seen any police cars, but she was afraid to trust even them with her newfound freedom. She had no food, money, or anywhere to go, but she felt exhilarated that she had regained her freedom at last.

She realized she was now headed toward a town center. As she approached, she saw the buildings were old but solidly built and well-kept. Many little shops and restaurants were clustered together. The signs on the buildings looked new and colorful, better than in any town she had ever seen in Moldova. Modern, mostly newer cars filled the roads, and people walked on the sidewalks, some carrying shopping bags, some carrying briefcases. Parents pushed baby strollers. A big park near the town hall was filled with people sitting and chatting. She noticed a cluster of men and women in fancy suits coming out of a restaurant and shaking hands with each other. Her stomach screamed—it was completely empty now. She tried to ignore it and keep going until her energy was totally depleted. Marina sought to blend in with the other walkers, hoping no one would notice her. She passed a bakery, the aroma of freshly baked bread wafting in the air.

If only I had some money! Marina thought as she grabbed chunks of her hair in frustration.

But she continued walking past a drugstore, a sub shop, a homemade ice cream parlor, and a clothing store. If she walked into a food store, Marina was afraid she'd break down at the sight and smells of the food. Most pedestrians were in a hurry, and no one paid attention to her.

Then, as she felt like collapsing in hopelessness, she spied two women with baby carriages get up and leave a bench on the sidewalk. One of them left a light blue bag with long handles. They continued walking in deep conversation and did not look back.

Finally! Marina approached the bench, praying the bag had food in it. She quickly snatched it, ran into a parking lot behind some stores, and hid near a garbage dumpster. She opened the bag, peeking around to make sure no one spotted her.

Inside the bag she found treasures! Little crackers, two juice cups, and a packet of damp wipes. Marina alternated between stuffing her mouth with crackers and washing them down with juice. She ate and drank more slowly as she became satisfied. The damp sheets smelled like perfumed soap. After she ate, she took the wipes and rubbed them over her face, neck, arms, and feet. Afterward, she fiddled with her hair. She still felt dirty from Igor's strong hands grabbing chunks of her hair and roughly grabbing her whenever he got the chance. He often tried to push her to the ground until her other captors warned him he would cause needless injury and problems if he kept trying to harm her.

Feeling better, she continued walking behind the shops and other buildings, her eyes darting everywhere for both anyone following her as well as a place where she could relieve herself and pour clean water on her hair.

After ten minutes of furtively walking and gazing around, she saw a large grey stone building on the corner. People of all ages walked in and out carrying books.

Could this be a library? she wondered.

Marina feared that someone would spot her if she stood still on the sidewalk, so she headed over to the stone building, wrapping her tangled hair in a bun so she wouldn't attract attention. Engraved in the front of the building were the words Morristown Public Library. Ducking her head and covering her face with her hand, she walked in. Inside were a vast number of books on shelves, a book check-out where staff scanned library cards into computers, tables with people reading books, and a row of computers near the long wooden desk where the librarian sat. Marina spotted a few men and women wearing old, dirty clothes with unkempt hair resting their heads on the tables.

So, she thought, *I'm not the only one homeless and in trouble.*

"Bathroom, please?" Marina asked the librarian at the long wooden desk.

Briefly glancing up from her reading, she pointed down the hall and said, "Go down there. It's on your right."

"Thank you," Marina said, grateful the woman did not look at her strangely.

She slipped into the women's room and relieved herself. She wished she could stay hidden there for a while, but with only two stalls, someone was bound to come in and complain she was taking too long.

Wishing she could lock the door of the whole women's room, she went to the sink, turned on the faucet's two knobs for both hot and cold water, and dunked her hair into the sink. It was still tangled when wet, but at least she felt cleaner. At the sink she found a rubber band and picked it up to put her wet brown hair with all its knots into a ponytail. Upon leaving the ladies' room, Marina looked behind her to make sure no one was following her. Satisfied she was safe for now, she walked farther into the library. Marina spotted another open room with the words Children's Library printed in bright bold letters. She sat down on one of the tiny chairs and watched the little children examining books with adults.

"Do you need some help?" a young woman with the name tag "Roberta" approached her.

"No, no I don't," was all Marina could manage, barely able to look the woman in the eye.

"You're welcome to look around."

Marina tried to smile but her mouth was stiff.

A woman with shoulder-length light brown disheveled hair and half-open eyes shuffled in slowly. She carried an infant and held hands with a toddler. She spotted Marina sitting alone at the little table and plopped down on one of the chairs. She yawned the moment she sat down and told the little girl to find a book while finding a comfortable position to hold the baby. She turned to Marina and asked, "Do you have children?"

"No, no children," answered Marina.

"Are you a student doing research?" she persisted.

Marina wasn't sure what she meant but responded, "Yes, I'm doing research, yes."

"I would love to go back to school," she sighed. "I was getting my Master's in elementary education when I found out I was pregnant. Big surprise. My husband and I thought we would both be earning a decent income by the time we had kids. I was teaching at a private school then and was making next to nothing. Now we gotta watch every penny. I was all set to continue going to school when April entered preschool. I was on the pill, but I got pregnant again," the woman kissed her baby. "They're wonderful but it's awfully hard to enjoy them when you're struggling and already worried about how you're going to pay for their college."

Marina listened and nodded. The woman's situation seemed much more manageable compared to hers. She had beautiful children and hope for an easier life. At least she didn't have to worry about her freedom and staying alive every day. The little girl came back with a book on kittens.

"Read this, Mommy," she said.

The woman smiled at her daughter and took the book with her free hand. She opened the book and squinted her eyes as she began to read. Then she glimpsed at Marina again. "I just want you to know that you're doing it the right way. Finish school and then have the babies. It will make life so much easier."

Marina wanted to cry. Instead she just smiled.

She thought about leaving, but as the mother read the story to her children, her melodious voice and the rhyming of the words were actually soothing to Marina. It took her back in time to when she was a little girl and could rely on her parents to take care of her. Her mind was comforted thinking about those days. She wished she could drift off to sleep in her warm little bed again after her mother or father read her a children's story. Marina couldn't keep her eyes open. She thought she heard the woman say bye but she continued drifting off. She had no idea how long she was asleep until the librarian kept trying to get her attention.

"Excuse me, miss," she kept saying.

Finally, Marina woke up. She lifted her head and looked around with her half-awake eyes at the unfamiliar place until she remembered she was in the children's room in the public library.

"Miss, I'm afraid we're closing now. We open tomorrow morning at 9AM."

"W-What time is it now?" Marina asked.

"It's 5PM. Have a good evening." The librarian named Roberta tried to smile but her arms were crossed and one of her shoes was tapping the ground.

"Good evening." Marina lifted herself from the tiny chair and rubbed her knees to get her circulation back. Then she walked out.

The air was chilly when she got outside.

She wondered whether she should have asked the librarian to call the police but had doubts if the police would in fact have helped her. Marina was convinced she couldn't take that chance. She continued walking, staring down and hiding her face with her hand. She spied an elderly lady sitting at a bus stop about twenty feet from the library, past a few small shops selling specialty goods.

Would you help me? Marina mentally pleaded to the woman as she approached her.

The woman's lips turned up in a smile and she wore a friendly expression. She was dressed in a long white coat even though it was warm outside. Her hair was impeccably styled and stiff, like she had just come out of the hairdressers. The lady watched pedestrians pass while she waited patiently for her bus to arrive. Marina put one foot forward toward her but stopped abruptly.

On the other side of where the lady sat, a familiar-looking man stood staring at Marina.

He held a Styrofoam cup in his hand. He had long black hair, a short black beard, and small, penetrating eyes glancing furtively around as if he were trying to observe without being observed himself. He was dressed all in black and looked to be in his late thirties. Marina watched him reach into his jacket for his cell phone while sizing her up. Searching the recesses of her memory, she suddenly remembered where she had seen him.

Her body shivered and her jaw dropped the instant she remembered.

This was the man who had injected her and the other young Slavic women with drugs to sedate them. They had been chained to beds that were nothing more than boards with no pillows and dirty sheets. He was one of the men who would help watch over the terrified young women, slapping any who tried to resist. She remembered how trapped they all were and how they would be violated according to the will of their captors. Marina shivered as she recalled how he would leer at the women, displaying his enjoyment of watching them helpless in their miserable bondage.

Sergei. This was Sergei. Not as brutal as Igor, but he clearly enjoyed manhandling the women.

She tried to move as Sergei hung up his phone and tossed out his black coffee. It splattered on the sidewalk as nearby pedestrians stared at him in disgust. The elderly woman in the white coat moved as far away from him as she could on the bench, examining her coat for possible stains.

He was only twenty feet away.

Marina instantly forgot about her hunger and asking for help. She felt an adrenaline rush through her entire body as she bolted in the opposite direction, narrowly missing bumping into two teenage girls who were carrying shopping bags as they strolled and chatted happily down the sidewalk. She prayed she would be able to will the police to suddenly appear so she could flag an officer down. But then she pushed away that thought.

Who knows what kinds of connections this Russian ring has? Someone's allowing them to operate freely. It could be the police.

She kept on running, too terrified to look back, wondering if she could possibly lose him.

Marina spotted a crowded restaurant and slipped in. Inside were immaculate hardwood floors and high ceilings. Colorful paintings adorned the light grey painted walls. The booths were made of a high-quality imitation leather.

"How many, please?" the host, a middle-aged man with a balding head and a beer belly asked before looking at her. When his gaze rested on her, he surveyed her up and down and wrinkled his nose.

"I'm, I'm wondering if you're looking for help?" Marina said the first thing that popped into her head.

"I'm not hiring right now. Sorry," the host answered, staring at her torn, dirty clothes.

"Uh . . . please, may I use your bathroom?" she asked with pleading eyes.

"The restroom is for customers only," he answered, moving away from her.

"But . . . but I am a customer. Can I sit down?" Marina asked him, forcing herself to scan outside the window.

She didn't see the man anywhere.

Did I really lose him?

"Sit there," he ordered her to a table in the back. "I'll get you a menu."

She slid silently into the back table as the host handed her a menu.

"Where you from?" he asked.

Marina tightened. She stared at the man but no words would come out.

"Just so you know, this is a high-end restaurant. People come in here with nice, clean clothes. You don't look like you belong here, much less work here," he sneered as he walked off.

Knowing she couldn't stay, she abandoned the menu, leaving it on the table as she got ready to leave the restaurant. She passed a large tray of meals on a stand and stole a few french fries.

Stuffing them in her mouth, she walked closer to the window to get a better view of the street, her heart trembling at every step.

She froze.

The man was getting out of his parked Mercedes. He scanned the street in every direction.

I can't go through there.

"Ex-Excuse me," she asked a passing waiter, a young man with a face full of pimples carrying two jumbo steaks with fries.

Marina resisted the urge to grab more fries.

"Yes? May I help you?" he inquired, surveying her torn clothes.

"Is there a back exit?" she asked, breathing deeply and holding her hands to her sides to calm her rising panic.

"Down there, past the restrooms," the waiter said, pointing his chin in that direction.

"Thank you."

As she turned around, she spotted a plate of small cookies at the cash register. The cashier was busy talking to a customer, so Marina swiped three as she hurried to the back exit, searching in all directions inside and outside the restaurant while dropping each cookie into her mouth whole. By the time she got to the door, Marina fought the urge to scream and cry for help.

She opened the door and gingerly stepped outside.

Sergei, the man in black, was nowhere in sight.

Marina walked through the town, attempting to blend in with the crowd. It was now approaching early evening and it was getting dark. She had no idea where she was going or what she would do next. She squeezed her eyes shut and brought her hand to the side of her head as she weighed her options. The sun had gone down while she was in the restaurant. Marina looked up at the sky: soon it would be nighttime. A chill swept inside her as she imagined kidnappers hiding behind buildings, waiting for her to come near. Marina crept in the shadows, careful to avoid nighttime lights from stores and street lamps. The large traffic of people walking on the sidewalks had whittled down to a handful, making it even more dangerous for her. She continued to make sure no one was following her.

As she stopped and stood still on the sidewalk away from any lights, paralyzed in indecision, she saw a tall man with long dark hair and a dark beard walking toward her.

Was this man Sergei?

Marina blinked. Was her mind playing tricks on her? Was she only imagining him walking toward her?

She wasn't sure but was too scared to find out. She hid her face and stayed hidden between two store buildings as the man passed. She could barely make out his features as he passed her hiding place, but she was fairly certain he wasn't Sergei. As she sighed in relief, her eyes grew wide and her head shot up at another fear: perhaps more men were searching the streets for her. Was Igor out there too? Her legs shook; she was afraid she would collapse. Marina leaned against one of the building's walls as she held her breath, afraid to move, but after a few minutes she slowly returned to the sidewalk.

In the distance, she spotted a massive stone church on the corner across from the library. She only now realized she had been walking in circles around downtown Morristown. Taking in the imposing structure with its large sign in front with the quote, "He who trusts in the Lord shall be surrounded by kindness" right above the schedule of prayer services, Marina prayed the doors would open. Dizzy from hunger and fearful of losing her balance, she stumbled around the building looking for the entrance.

When she finally found the church's entrance, she staggered up the steps, hoping to find the sanctuary she craved. Finally making it up the steps, she found the doors bolted shut. She fell to the ground with her hands clinging to the dark wooden door. Her legs simply gave way from under her and slowly she fell to the ground and silently wept, her energy totally depleted.

I can't go on. I am ready to die tonight. What's going to happen will happen. I've done my best.

Her eyes drifted closed with this thought. It was getting colder out and she began shivering but was helpless to do anything about it.

Respite was brief. Her eyes popped open at the sound of a menacing growl.

From across the street, a large, grey German shepherd baring razor-sharp teeth barked in her direction. As she lifted her head, the barking grew louder. Marina's whole body shook and she stifled the urge to scream. In her terror she found the sudden energy to stand up and run. The growling dog ran after her. Marina was so scared she thought her heart was going to leap out of her body. But then someone down the road whistled and shouted, "Get over here, Brice! Now!" By this point the dog had almost caught up with her but retreated at the sound of his owner's voice. When she had the courage to look back, she saw the huge German shepherd running in his master's direction.

Marina was relieved but couldn't stop shaking. She thanked a Higher Power. She'd never had any religious training in her life, but she remembered neighbors attending church on Sundays and coming home with expressions of peace and contentment. Marina realized intuitively that a Higher Being was more in control of events than any human was, but she'd never had the inclination to reflect deeply on this.

Passing the church, she now meandered in front of houses. Lights were on, and she saw the bright, colorful screens of televisions inside the windows of several homes. At one house, a whole family was gathered around the flat-screen television drinking hot drinks and munching on popcorn. She wondered if these people had any inkling how much more fortunate they were than she had ever been. Marina had grown up in a three-room apartment with her parents and brother. It was always cold in the winter and hot in the summer. Their TV rarely showed a clear picture. Her parents worked many hours and never had time to gather around the television and watch as a family. A few people stared out from their houses, probably to find out what the dog had been barking about. Most shook their heads and one said loudly out the screen window to no one in particular, "That animal is a menace. One day I'm going to call animal control."

Cars occasionally drove by, no one even glancing her way. Marina's initial fear of the dog propelled her to run, but she now lost steam. She stopped and breathed deeply to fill her lungs with air, but she was too tired. Then she had another stroke of luck—a truck carrying a cargo of oranges sped by with a loose door in the back. After hitting a bump in the road, two oranges fell out. Without thinking of safety, Marina hurried into the street, grabbed them, and tore into the fruit. She had never tasted such fresh oranges in her life. She was torn between devouring the oranges and enjoying the sweet fruit. While relishing the fruit's tangy sweetness, she felt orange pieces caught in her throat.

Then, in her eyes, another miracle occurred. A few houses farther up and across the street was an apartment building. On the front grounds lay a sprinkler with six nozzles watering one side of the front lawn in unison and then revolving to the other side. The water rained down high, covering the large property. Marina crossed the street, watchful of speeding cars, and sped to the sprinkler system. She opened her mouth and stuck out her tongue to consume as much water as possible. Water enveloped her whole body in the process. She got drenched but didn't care—her throat cleared and her thirst was satisfied.

She soon shivered uncontrollably but, strange to even herself, was reluctant to move as she waited for the nozzles to return to where she stood. The water occupied all of her attention, so she failed to notice one of the building's residents staring at her from a top-floor window. He had long white hair that stuck out in all directions like Albert Einstein's. His small, beady eyes bored into Marina.

The man finally opened the window and yelled, "Hey, what do think you're doin' there? Get outta here!"

Marina broke out of her trance and jumped. She almost slipped on the wet, slick lawn.

"Oh, sorry!" she yelled up at him before running away.

She ran again but couldn't stop shivering. The longer she ran, the less she shivered. Marina spotted a park ahead and raced over. She saw a playground and benches. She ran to a bench and fell asleep as soon as her head rested on the wood. Marina told herself she had no choice but to succumb to her captors if they found her. She had nothing left to resist them.

◆ ◆ ◆

Sergei kept cursing under his breath. Where had she gone? He walked up to the corner where he was supposed to meet Igor. Igor stared at him, awaiting some news. They kept hearing about trucks near the ship traveling to Morristown, so Igor decided the two of them would scout the area.

"Did you see her?" Igor demanded.

"No," Sergei responded, attempting to meet his partner's eyes. He wouldn't dare confess that he was certain he saw her but then lost her.

Now Igor was the one cursing under his breath.

Sergei felt like punching the wall of one of the buildings.

All he wanted was to get the girl and be rid of Igor.

The men walked silently back to the Mercedes.

CHAPTER FIVE

ADAM

In the midst of his dreams Adam heard his father's voice telling him he had to get up soon. He nodded as he always did, but this morning, instead of forcing his eyelids to open, he drifted back to sleep. Eventually the alarm clock rang loud and insistently, but rather than reaching out to turn it off, he shot out of bed and threw it across his bedroom. He then settled back underneath the covers. Images of taking walks with his mother at home and with Heidi along the vast property of Fairmount Home occupied his dreams. Whenever he saw one of them, Adam's hand reached out to grasp theirs, but he was unable to reach them. He pictured himself crying tears of frustration and shouting, "Lemme hold your hand, Mommy! I need you!" or, "Heidi, come back! I need to take a walk with you!" But both only smiled and did not respond to his cries.

Finally, Adam sat up, awake. His face was wet from crying and he was all sweaty. He didn't know what time it was and he didn't care. He tried to lie down and go back to sleep but couldn't; those images came back as soon as he closed his eyes.

Seeing but not being able to touch or talk with Mommy or Heidi was too much. Adam knew he was supposed to get ready for work, but he didn't want to think about it.

He finally rose out of bed and dressed in the clothes his father had left out for him on the chair. He decided that after breakfast he was going to take a walk, hoping that if he pretended Mommy or Heidi walked beside him, he wouldn't feel so lonely.

Adam carried his mother's picture to the breakfast table and stared at it while he ate. After he finished, he noticed the clear blue sky from the kitchen window. The leaves on the trees were blowing slightly. Mommy would have called it ideal weather for a walk.

Grabbing his sack that had his water bottle, he decided to take a walk. But when Adam pushed the front door open, the sadness of walking all by himself was too much. Instead he closed the door and turned on the TV.

"Aw right!" He jumped up and raised his fists in the air as if he won a sports event when he saw a nature show was on. Even though he knew he wasn't supposed to, he bit his shirt as he watched a group of elephants trudge along, lugging their heavy bodies toward a stream. When they arrived to the water, they dipped their huge grey trunks in. Some drank while others sprayed themselves like people do when using a hand-held nozzle over their heads in the shower.

Adam's eyes kept switching from the TV screen to the window. He crouched forward on the couch to be as close to the TV as he could.

"Look, Mommy, look at the elephants!" he cried, pointing his finger at the screen and bouncing up and down.

"Mommy, I wanna see elephants. Can we go someplace

and look at elephants?" Adam said as he flapped his arms and bounced on the couch. He turned to his right. But his mother wasn't sitting next to him.

He was all alone.

Staring down with his hands on his cheeks, he lost interest in the elephants. The thought occurred to him again that maybe he was supposed to go to work today, but he brushed that thought away. All he wanted was to be with his mommy.

He started thinking about when his mother used to take him to folk dances. She always tried to teach him how to do the steps. Sometimes he would accidentally step on his mother's toes. She would yelp in pain, but she never got angry with him. He was so afraid of stepping on her toes again that he kept stepping back.

"Hey, watch it!" a man once said to him. "You're pushing me!"

"Sorry," his mother would reply.

Adam would often receive glares from people he would accidentally push, but Mommy continued to smile up at him as she tried to help him make the right steps to the music.

Tears streamed down his face. Even though the elephants were raising their trunks and sounding like horns as they continued their journey in the wilds, Adam sobbed in his hands. Only when a stream of mucus covered his nose and hands did he get up and wash himself.

As he covered his face with a towel near the bathroom sink, it occurred to him that he missed his bus—he was supposed to be at work now. Adam removed the towel and hit the right side of his head. Why didn't he catch his bus for work? Charging out of the bathroom, he paced the hallway while flapping his hands, occasionally hitting his head. Adam walked up to the phone and stared at it, trying to remember what he was supposed to do. He had never missed his bus to work before and since this was out of his routine, he was simply stuck and directionless.

He continued staring at the phone as if it would magically tell him what he was supposed to do. "I'm supposed ta press a button," he thought aloud as he rested a fist on his cheek with his elbow on the kitchen table. He studied the buttons, trying to remember his father's directions. Four buttons were pictures—one of his father, one of his boss, and the other two pictures were of a policeman and a fireman. He stared at them until the four blended together in a blur.

In the midst of his confusion, he turned his attention to the window. Since he was at a loss over what to do, Adam stepped outside and watched a butterfly travel past him.

"Hey, butterfly," he called out. "Here to gimme company?"

But the butterfly flew off into the distance.

"Awww, butterfly, thought ya were gonna stay wit me. Don't got my mommy no more. Daddy's at work. I gotta be here all alone."

Adam knew he was not supposed to go outside all alone except if he just walked around the house. So he decided to do just that. Then he would go inside and maybe then he would remember what he was supposed to do. As he walked, still carrying his sack with water, he looked at the street in the distance and recalled the memories of his mother greeting him when he came home from school.

The special little bus for Adam's school dropped him off. Twelve-year-old Adam looked uncertain as he made his way off the bus, but his face turned into a huge grin upon seeing the reassuring smile and wave of his mother.

"How was your day, sweetie?" she asked as she kissed her son's forehead and waved to the bus driver. As Adam reached for her hand, he noticed she had her apron on.

"Whatcha makin', Mommy?"

Mommy broke into a smile. "I'm making chocolate chip cookies. I just rolled them into little balls and put them in the oven. I saved the mixing bowl for you to lick."

"Aw right!" Adam raised his hand as if he had just won a race. "And what's fer suppa?"

She gave him a little squeeze. "That's my boy! Always wants to know about three things: food, walks, and nature shows. We're going to have pancakes tonight. Daddy is working late again and he's having his supper at work."

"Why?" Adam asked, and when he looked at his mother, she was no longer smiling.

"Daddy has a lot of work to do this week. He'll just be home to sleep and eat breakfast."

"That means we can take longer walks after suppa, Mommy. And then we can watch nature shows since Daddy won't be here."

"That's right, Adam," his mother said. She wasn't smiling anymore and fixed her gaze down as she spoke.

As soon as that memory disappeared, Adam became aware of where he was, walking all alone. His thoughts turned to a memory from the time he had spent at the Fairmount Home:

All the clients were in the living room watching TV or playing with toys. Only Adam sat and stared at nothing out the window.

He shut his ears with his hands because one of the boys kept making noises. Only when a staff member removed the boy from the living room did Adam unblock his ears. Every time someone turned on the TV, Adam insisted they watch nature shows, but he had only gotten his way once. Cartoons held no interest for him.

Neither did movies unless there were animals in them.

"Hey, Adam!" Heidi said as soon as she walked in. "Look at those kids on the TV. Looks like they're havin' fun!"

Adam couldn't help but turn his head upon hearing Heidi's enthusiastic voice. He gazed wordlessly at the TV screen.

He then pointed his finger at Heidi and said, "Where's my mommy, Heidi?"

Heidi stood up and reached out her hand to him. "C'mon, let's go for a walk."

The other clients didn't even look up. They were so absorbed in what they were doing that they didn't notice them quietly leave the room. The other staff members saw and said nothing.

Heidi and Adam walked arm-in-arm outside. After a little while, Heidi pointed to the sky. "Do you know who's up there?" she asked him.

He shook his head.

"Your momma," Heidi said, gazing right into his eyes. "Your momma's up there in heaven and she's watching over you."

Adam gazed up at the sky. "Hi, Mommy," he said, waving his hand at the sky. "Mommy, come down and be wit me."

But Heidi shook her head. "Your mommy can't come down, but she's watching over you always. She takes care of you from the sky now. She's always there watching you so you're never ever alone."

Adam continued strolling on his own near his house. Hoping he would see his mommy, he kept turning his eyes up. Without realizing it, he walked on the grounds farther and farther away from his house. He waved, hoping that would bring out his mother. It didn't, but it somehow made him believe she was nearby.

Adam glanced to his right. Fifteen feet away he saw the other houses on his street. A woman pushed her child in a stroller. An older woman swept her porch. She didn't see Adam, but when she would see him, she would stop and stare. Sometimes she waved; other times she looked at him and shook her head. Adam didn't understand her, and when he asked his mommy about her, his mommy would shake her head and wave a dismissive hand. That left him confused. He shrugged and kept on walking, lost in his memories.

◆ ◆ ◆

Sergei struggled to keep his eyes open but had finally given in to an uncomfortable sleep. He must have slept for an hour or two because when Igor woke him up, daylight approached. He still felt groggy but could not fall back to sleep.

"How? Tell me how did she get away?" Igor ranted while driving. He kept slamming his fist into the driving wheel.

"Stop! You're going to get us killed! You've been driving all night like a madman. We need to stop and rest," Sergei barked at him. His joints hurt, as he had been sitting in the car the whole night. He couldn't wait for the car to stop so he could get out and move his body.

Igor glared at him. "I do not stop until I find her!"

Sergei lay his head back and groaned, cursing his fate. He tried to figure out how to convince Igor to stop when the gas meter light came on.

"See? We are almost out of gas. You must stop now." Sergei couldn't hold back a smile.

Sergei could almost see steam coming out of Igor's nostrils as he looked at his partner's face contorted in rage as he turned the car back and headed toward town.

CHAPTER SIX

BRUCE

Bruce kept glancing at his watch, something he had begun doing since Adam had returned home. He constantly worried about his son catching his bus to the factory, wondered if everything was going well for him at work, and hoped Adam was following directions. Adam's supervisor discouraged it, but he couldn't stop himself from calling to make sure his son was all right. Today, though, he made a conscious decision not to call. He needed to focus on his own job and getting ahead, despite the fact that he would no longer be able to get the satisfaction of making Maggie happy.

He smiled at two coworkers who passed by his small office. He didn't want to appear lost in his own thoughts.

"Getting ready for the presentation today, Bruce?" Gwen stopped at his desk. She was a pleasant-looking, slightly plump woman in her mid-thirties who never failed to dress and act professionally.

"Just about," Bruce told her. After taking a sip of coffee, he forced himself to smile and look more relaxed. "I think this will finally seal the deal."

"Great! How's Adam getting along?"

He automatically tightened his grip on the coffee cup at the mention of his son.

"We're getting there slowly but surely," he said. "I'll e-mail you my notes for the presentation tonight."

Gwen smiled and tossed her shoulder-length bleached blonde hair. "I'll be looking forward to getting them. I'm feeling good about this presentation too," she said.

She bit her lip pensively and Bruce stared at her, wondering what she was going to say next.

"Um . . . maybe there's a day this week we could go out to lunch?"

Bruce blinked hard and raised his eyebrows. "Oh . . . I . . . ah . . . I'll have to check my schedule and . . . and get back to you."

Gwen's eyes shifted to the large calendar on his desk, but Bruce's eyes did not leave her face. He felt a blush creep into his skin.

"Get back to me," she said, winking.

She then walked away to say hello to somebody else.

Bruce hid a smile as he remembered joking with his wife about Gwen. She always appeared to be on a "manhunt," flirting and dressing as attractively as she could. But her number one priority was work: she wanted to eventually become a branch manager, and that took precedence over her personal life. It was whispered in the office that every time she got serious with someone, she would tell her boyfriend that their relationship had to take a backseat to her job. The relationship would soon fizzle after that.

Bruce rested his chin in his hand as he contemplated what Gwen on the fast track saw in a man who had a special-needs child.

Thinking about his son, his attention turned to the phone once again.

It's better that Adam's living at home with me, he reminded himself.

He remembered when he used to come home to a dark, empty house with no one to talk to except the conversations he held with himself in his head. The garbage was always full with leftover cartons from takeout meals. Washing the dirty utensils and plates by himself only increased his depression and feelings of isolation. Now he would come home just as Adam would begin cooking his simple meals, trying to remember the steps.

He recalled his conversation with Adam when he arrived home yesterday.

"Hi, Daddy. How was your day?" Adam always said cheerfully upon Bruce entering the house. He always put on his mother's apron, but he couldn't tie the string behind his back. So the apron always hung half on and half off.

"I'm makin' mac 'n' cheese, Daddy. How'd you like that?"

Bruce concealed a smile as he said, "Mac 'n' cheese is fine, Adam. How was your day? Did you make the bus on time?"

"Yeah, but they made me work all day today."

"Well, that's what work's all about."

Stampin', stampin', stampin'. My hand hurts." Adam shook out his hand for effect.

"Do you rub your wrist like I showed you?"

"Yeah, but it still hurts. Mr. Price said he'd work on gettin' me ta do somethin' else sometimes so my wrist won't hurt so bad."

"Mr. Price told me you're stamping too hard. You've got to take it easy, Adam."

Father and son sat down and talked more about Adam's day. He never failed to add too much of an ingredient to a meal. Whenever he made mac 'n' cheese, Bruce's mouth felt glued together from the extra melted cheese throughout the pasta.

Bruce shook his head and got his mind back to the office. He had to demonstrate his presentation to his team.

But before he got through a paragraph, Bob Pell, a client from Auto. Inc., walked over to his office.

Bruce froze for a moment and spotted index cards on the corner of his desk. Those cards contained his notes for Pell's issue. He had worked on it a few days ago. Did he forget about a meeting this morning?

"I'm sorry for walking in on you like this, Bruce. I was in the neighborhood and thought I'd stop in to find out if you were making any progress with my problem," Pell said as he coughed into his hand. He tried to smile while clearing his throat.

Bruce knew Pell was nervous because his company's production was being held up by a technical problem in the new system he had recently purchased for his company. The men were supposed to meet later in the afternoon, but Bruce understood the man's impatience.

"Have a seat, Bob." Bruce stood up and shook the client's hand. "Since you're here now and I have some time, I'll show you what I came up with."

Pell sat down, glancing furtively around him. He had recently taken over his father's company, and Bruce could tell he struggled to appear competent and professional.

As Bruce explained his findings, Pell's face brightened and

he sat up taller as he realized Bruce had thoroughly researched the options and come up with the most practical solution.

"We'll get on it right away, Bob," Bruce said as he stood up and shook hands with him.

"Thanks, Bruce. I always know I can count on you." Bob smiled as he shook Bruce's hand warmly. "Because of you, I can sleep at night."

Pell walked away, smiling, and Bruce savored this feeling of accomplishment.

Unfortunately, his euphoria was brief. His cell phone rang. Bruce felt an ominous shudder pass through him as he grabbed his cell phone.

"Hello?" Bruce answered.

"Mr. Hitchens, this is Mr. Price, your son's supervisor at the Hutton factory," he said with an aristocratic British accent. "Your son wasn't on the bus to report for work this morning. We thought he was possibly sick and you would call to let us know."

"Adam didn't go in at all today?" Bruce felt his heart beating faster. His coworkers, seeing his eyes bulging through his glass office window and hearing his voice rising in alarm, stopped what they were doing and looked at one another.

"No, Mr. Hitchens," Mr. Price continued, seemingly unaware of Bruce's panic. "We must be informed if Adam is sick or cannot come into work for any reason. We impress upon all our workers from this program that a job is a serious responsibility."

"Wait! Let me call home and then I'll call you right back!"

Bruce felt himself sweating. Adam was proud to have a job and he was always on time for the bus.

Riddled with anxiety when he took his son out of Fairmount Home, he felt sure something like this would happen without Maggie watching him. If something did happen, Bruce would never forgive himself. He admitted to himself his willingness to bring him back home was due to the loneliness he felt when Adam was away.

This is what you get for being so selfish, Bruce! he reprimanded himself. *Fairmount tried to tell me he would eventually adjust to his new surroundings.*

He hung up and called home immediately. The phone rang. The message came on.

"Adam, where are you? Call me right away!"

He did not care at this point that everyone on the floor heard his panicked voice almost screaming into the cell phone. His fellow employees on the floor stared silently at him, but he simply sat at his desk staring at the phone, willing it to ring.

"Something wrong, Bruce?"

Bruce looked up, shaken from his imagination of worst-case scenarios. Steve Vick, his boss, stood outside his open door.

Bruce always tried to maintain control at work, but he couldn't get the panic out of his voice. He told himself then and there that once this was resolved, he had no choice but to hire someone to keep tabs on his eighteen-year-old son without considering whether he could afford it or not.

"Steve, my son is not at work or home. I need to find out where he is," he said, looking his boss in the eye.

"Sure, Bruce. Do what you have to do. Just tell Dave what you were about to tell your team so he can cover for you."

All the vitality left Bruce. He deflated like a defective balloon.

If this happens again, not only will I be denied that promotion, but Dave will replace me.

But he had no time to worry about that now. After hunting down Dave, Bruce hurried to his car. His legs were weak and his whole body was sweating. He didn't know where to look for Adam besides home. Bruce's mind and body were so paralyzed with fear that he had trouble putting his stiff hand into his pocket to reach for his car keys. To his horror, they were not there. His eyes bulging, he fumbled in every pocket of his clothes to find them.

"Dammit! Where are they!" he yelled out loud. *Were they lying in his office?*

Damp with sweat and cursing uncontrollably, not caring who heard him, he searched the interior of his car through the window. When he couldn't find them, he shut his eyes: he did not want to take time going back to the office while he was steadily losing control of his emotions. Plus he dreaded encountering coworkers seeing him in this agonized state. They would question him and offer help or simply stare. Invariably they'd slow him down. He let go of the car door and, head bowed, worked his way back into the building. Fortunately, on the ground near the door he spotted his keys. He must have put his hands in his pockets so fast that the keys slipped from his grasp without him even noticing. He snatched them up, breathing more regularly now. He glanced at his watch; he had wasted five minutes looking for his keys.

As he started his Buick, memories flooded his mind about being told what his son could and could not do. Social workers had repeatedly reassured him that his son could stay home alone for a few hours and perform up to four-step tasks if he practiced following directions. These tasks could take up to four months of repeated practice before he could perform them independently. Bruce was thankful Maggie did everything she could to get Adam's teachers to prepare him for as much independence as possible even though he would never be able to live completely on his own.

Still, he kept imagining the worst. Had Adam burned himself at the stove like he did the other night? Did Bruce accidentally leave the wrong medications out? Was he lying comatose on the kitchen floor? He was as careful as a pharmacist to leave out the correct pills and dosages, but since he'd had to leave for work earlier than usual this morning, could he have made a mistake? What would he find when he finally arrived home? He hit the gas pedal, driving seventy miles an hour in a forty mile-per-hour speed zone.

◆ ◆ ◆

After filling up the tank, Igor and Sergei ate a quick breakfast at the Morristown Diner. Sergei drank three cups of coffee and tried to get nourishment, but Igor guzzled down his meal and kept looking at his watch.

"Let's go already!" Igor angrily coaxed his partner. "Aren't you finished yet? We don't have all day for you to finish breakfast!"

Sergei almost choked when a piece of toast got caught in his throat. He gulped water, looking around the diner to see if anyone noticed Igor's unreasonable rushing. Swallowing invectives he yearned to hurl at his partner, Sergei quickly finished his meal.

They soon left and were back in the car. Igor drove and studied all the people he saw, paying little attention to the road.

Sergei kept glancing at him nervously and shaking his head. He'd always known Igor was crazy, but now he was dangerous because no one was telling him what to do. Igor kept craning his neck when he saw any woman that resembled the one he was searching for.

All of a sudden, another car stopped short and the driver's honking pierced the usual sounds of traffic. Igor slammed on the brakes. He and Sergei would have gone through the front window if they hadn't been wearing seat belts.

"Hey, whatcha doin'? Watch the road, buddy!" the driver shouted.

Igor gripped the wheel and grabbed the Smith & Wesson he kept in the front of his pants.

"Igor, no!" Sergei said, grabbing his arm.

Igor slammed on the gas instead, raising his middle finger at the driver.

How the hell are we supposed to find this woman in this busy town? Sergei thought. *I'll have to find another time when Igor is away to contact Andre. But he slips around so quietly, appearing as if out of nowhere, like a ghost,* he thought ruefully. *For now I'll keep quiet so as not to anger him, and the moment I get a chance, I'll make that call.*

CHAPTER SEVEN

MARINA

THE TWEETING BIRDS WOKE MARINA FROM THE park bench. She tried to remember what had happened last night that had led her to wake up on a bench outside. She observed the park was green and well-kept with new benches and playground equipment, but her thoughts were more focused on how famished she was and how dirty and gross she felt. Marina noticed two white plastic structures. She got up from the bench and saw they each had the words "Portable John" written on the front. She remembered reading in an American story in school that john was used to mean bathroom.

Anxious to relieve herself, she opened one but screamed when she saw a dirty, unkempt man with ragged, smelly clothes sleeping in a sitting position on the toilet. He stirred upon hearing her, but she slammed the door with shaky hands and approached the second john with her heart thumping. It took some time to steady her hands before she knocked on the door. Hearing nothing, she gingerly opened it and peeked in. Inside it was dirty, but no one was there. Marina quickly locked the door, and relieved herself. She then scrubbed her hands with hand sanitizer from the dispenser, wishing there was water to splash on her face and neck. She exited the john, still trying to piece together how she had gotten here in the first place.

She sat back down on the bench and recalled her escape from the port via the truck carrying cars in the early morning hours. She got up and walked until she reached downtown Morristown again. The familiarity of the downtown area calmed her to a certain degree but her sense of relief proved fleeting; ten feet away she spotted a man leaning on a car. He had a pale face, short black hair, and large sunglasses. He was thin except for a disproportionately large beer belly. When he turned his head, she spotted the scar on the side of his face.

Igor. Marina was forced to lean against a building, her knees buckling under her. When she regained her bearings, she turned around and walked as quickly as she could in the opposite direction. She continued walking for a long time before daring to look back.

The Mercedes was still parked in the same spot, but Sergei had joined Igor, and the two of them kept surveying their surroundings as they drank coffee and conversed.

Marina walked hurriedly, and when she couldn't see them anymore, she broke into a run. She sped so fast and so far that when she turned around, the town was no longer in view. Instead she approached residential streets with large, majestic-looking homes, well-manicured lawns, and new luxury cars parked in the driveways. As she kept running, she entered a neighborhood where the homes were older and not as affluent. She turned on a street with more modest homes.

She dashed toward a wooded area with countless trees that seemed to break the cycle of homes lined up. She spotted deer along the way eating flowers and plants. Rather than entering what looked like a field, Marina spotted a small house in the distance standing far apart from the other houses on the street. Out of breath but too afraid to stop, she stumbled upon some branches lying on the ground. Luckily, she landed on her hands on a bed of dry leaves. Only then did she realize how winded she was. Her body protested when she tried to get up and start running again. Overcome with exhaustion, she found she couldn't move her arms and legs. Despite hunger and cold, Marina drifted off to sleep. She thought she must have been running for hours. The only things she knew were that they'd be searching for her and she was not safe. Marina prayed they would not come looking for her here, wherever here was. She passed out for a time.

Upon regaining consciousness, she forgot what had happened. For a moment she thought she was back in Moldova with her family. Then the cold, harsh reality of her escape descended on her and her whole being shivered. She searched to see if anyone was coming to capture her. Trying to ignore her screaming stomach, she struggled to stand and start running again, but she couldn't recollect which direction she had come from. Covered with dirt and scratches from branches lying on the ground, Marina worried briefly about what kinds of animals wandered around but shook off that concern. She had too many other worries. If her captors caught her, she knew what would happen: they would savagely beat her, take pictures, and then leave her to slowly die. Her pictures would serve as an example to other girls who thought about trying to escape.

Marina attempted to get up but was too weak from hunger. She forced her head up and gazed around for a stream in the hopes she would at least have water to drink. Finding none, she dragged her body, searching for bugs, ants, anything to get some energy. She was dizzy, and the effort to drag herself proved too demanding. She managed to crawl to a nearby cluster of trees and bushes but collapsed and fainted—too weak to even try to catch an ant.

◆ ◆ ◆

When he finished his coffee, Sergei crushed the Styrofoam cup in his hand. He wished it were Igor's body he was crushing instead. He turned to his partner and spat out, "So what do we do next?"

"We ask around," Igor responded, not even looking at him. He surveyed his surroundings. "We talk to people who may have seen a crazy-looking woman."

Sergei dunked his cup into a sidewalk trash can and ripped open the passenger side door of the Mercedes so hard, the door scratched the edge of the sidewalk. Upon slamming the door shut, Igor, oblivious to Sergei's anger, murmured more to himself, "We go now."

CHAPTER EIGHT

ADAM

IN THE MIDST OF HAPPY MEMORIES OF LICKING THE chocolate chip cookie batter while his mother checked the cookies baking in the oven, Adam spotted a woman on the ground.

He was afraid she was dead. On nature shows he occasionally saw an animal lying dead on the ground, still and lifeless. But before he panicked, he saw her thin, delicate fingers move. He craned his neck to stare at her, never having seen a person so thin. She had long brown hair and wore old jeans with holes everywhere and an old paper-thin, short-sleeved brown shirt. He saw marks on her upper arms because her sleeves were rolled up, but he didn't know what they were. He stood staring at her, shaking his sweaty hands in the air and looking around. He was told to never touch a woman except to shake her right hand. When he was at the Fairmount Home, he was allowed to walk arm-in-arm with Heidi when they took walks. That was it. He shuddered as he remembered what had happened when he was younger.

He was in a restaurant with his parents. A woman sitting at a nearby table smelled like the flowers from his mother's garden. She smelled so good that Adam kept looking over at her. While his parents were busy discussing what was on the menu, he inched closer and lay his head on her breast because he loved smelling the flowers.

"Ahhh! Oh my God!" the woman gasped, jumping up.

Adam looked up, surprised. "You smell like the flowers in my mommy's garden!"

The woman screamed.

"Adam!" said his parents together. He remembered their faces were all red.

"Leave that woman alone!" the manager came running out. "Get outta here!"

His father ran over and grabbed Adam's arm.

"I'm so sorry! My son has autism. He loves to smell flowers! He didn't mean to touch you inappropriately," Mommy told the woman.

But the woman rushed away, her high heels click-clacking on the tile floor as her hand reached into her pocketbook to pay her bill. Adam always remembered that it looked like she had seen something scary by the look on her face as she sped away as quickly as her high heels allowed her. He had scratched his head, following her with his eyes, not understanding what he'd done wrong.

"I'm afraid you'll have to take your son out of the restaurant," the man said to Mommy and Daddy. "He's scaring my customers." Adam remembered the man didn't talk mean, but he wasn't talking nice either.

His parents took him and left. Ever since then, his teachers and his parents would tell him he could never touch a woman except to shake her hand. By the time he entered the Fairmount Home, the teachers and staff were teaching him to shake the right hand.

Now both his hands shook, which always happened when he was nervous. Should he just leave the woman here until his daddy came home? Daddy would know what to do. Adam walked around in circles, hitting his head with his hand while mumbling, "What should I do? Should I call Daddy? Do I look for a doctor? What should I do?" He stared at her as if trying to will the woman to wake up on her own.

He paced until he grew dizzy, then sat down on the grass and leaned on a nearby oak tree, still keeping one hand waving in the air. This spring day had become unusually warm. Not a leaf moved on the ground. He loved to sit in the sunshine; the winter had been bitterly cold and sad. Adam looked over at the flowers and thought of the new beginnings Mommy had always talked about. Finally, his hand stopped flailing and his overwhelming panic gave way to happy thoughts about being with Mommy. Adam felt drowsy, and as he calmed down, he drifted off to sleep.

◆ ◆ ◆

Sergei watched Igor talking to some children. They shook their heads when he showed them a picture of Marina. Sergei, who was sitting in the car parked on the street, closed his eyes and sat back.

Waste of time. He is wasting valuable time, Sergei thought. *I could be making more money if I managed some of those girls we brought over. I could have slept with some American women. Then I would have gone on the ship back to Moldova. But here I am with this idiot, searching for this one girl who escaped. Bah! Forget about her!*

He opened his eyes and looked at his companion as he got back into the car.

"Any luck?" he asked.

"None," Igor replied tersely, staring straight ahead.

"What did you tell them? Why did you say you were looking for her?"

"I told them she's my sister."

Sergei let out a loud laugh. "Sister, huh? You need to find your sister to kill her," he chortled.

Igor was silent.

"Give it up already, will you? There's money to be made. We're wasting time," Sergei reprimanded. He added, "Andre will be furious when he finds out what you've been doing, not to mention putting me through all this."

"I don't give a damn about Andre!" Igor retorted loudly and angrily, startling Sergei. "She knows too much and she's on the loose. She could bring down the whole operation, you idiot!" He turned to his companion, instinctively touching his scar.

Igor started the engine. He said nothing more but kept observing Sergei gravely.

"Igor, you know, getting rid of her will not take away that scar," Sergei said gently. "And we make no money chasing after her. Who knows? She could be somewhere else by now."

"I'm going to ask more people," Igor snapped, pulling out the car.

CHAPTER NINE

MARINA

Marina tried to open her eyelids but could not muster the energy.

They will find me!

As she struggled to awaken, she gaped at the unfamiliar terrain. She was lost. Her stomach growling with excruciating hunger, Marina remembered the hard candy. On the morning before she escaped, she had not been able to will herself to get up from her hard bed, and another girl, pitying her and realizing she would get punched if she refused to get up, slipped her a piece of wrapped hard candy. Marina searched the recesses of her memory, trying to remember where she had set it down. Was it lying near her bed? No, she'd never taken it out of her pocket. Now she remembered: it was in a front pocket of her jeans! She weakly lifted her limp right hand to feel her pockets. Her empty stomach screaming, she reached her right pocket: nothing. Marina cursed under her breath. Now she would have to move her stiff arm over to the other pocket.

As her eyes became more focused, she noticed cuts on her hand, most likely from collapsing on branches. She pushed her arm to continue moving. She felt her left pocket and wanted to cry tears of joy; she felt the hard candy, and after a few tries, she finally lifted it out. The candy was grey. She couldn't tell what flavor it was but she didn't care. Making a concentrated effort to steady her shaking hand, Marina brought the candy slowly to her mouth, turning her head sideways so she wouldn't swallow it whole and choke. The candy was sticky in its clear wrapper, so she carefully pulled it out of the wrapping with her teeth and popped it in her mouth. Its gummy substance stuck to her top front teeth, but to her, it was the most sumptuous food she had ever tasted. As she dislodged the candy, Marina managed to lift herself into a sitting position as she finished chewing, feeling a sudden spurt of energy from the candy's sugar.

While wishing she had some water to rinse her mouth, she turned and spotted a man sleeping against a nearby tree. Her body shook as if an electric current had run through her.

Was he there earlier?

She would have screamed if she had the energy. Unable to stand, Marina struggled to crawl away amid the branches and twigs. When she looked back at him, his head stirred and his arms moved.

When he opened his eyes, he shook his head in bewilderment and opened and shut his eyes. He spotted her and leaned forward to get a better view.

"Hi," he said.

Terror filled Marina's oval-shaped blue eyes. She backed away. When a large oak tree prevented her progress, she leaned on it, using all her strength to rise. She panicked when she looked back, for the young man had now risen to his feet.

"No! No!" Marina screamed. She wished she had something heavy to throw at him and then run for her life.

"Whatsa matta? Why're you mad? I didn' even touch you," he said, staring at her while she struggled to remain standing and leaning on the tree. He approached her and lifted his hand like he wanted to shake hers.

Marina searched around furiously. She didn't know how many people were there. She breathed so heavily she thought she would faint. What if she were trapped? She stumbled to the ground as she tried to run. Realizing escape was impossible, she started crying.

"Why're you cryin'?" he asked, turning his head slightly in curiosity.

Marina didn't hear him. She slumped on the ground and lay sobbing, her face closed in resignation, awaiting the worst. After awhile, she realized the man hadn't come closer. She stopped sobbing and breathed heavily. Slowly, she looked up.

The man approached, extending his right hand while his left hand waved near his head. She noticed he had large hands for a man with a slight build.

"I'm Adam," he said slowly. He had a blank, innocent expression in his large, round, brown eyes.

Marina studied him. He wore faded light jeans with a broken belt loop. His red T-shirt was half tucked in and half tucked out. It appeared washed although it had dark stains. Little holes of different sizes dotted the top front near his shirt's neckline. He appeared normal, but he struggled to get his words out. His eyes met hers for short periods of time and then he continually shifted his gaze slightly away from her. The man looked clean, but his wavy brown hair was rumpled with a few twigs stuck in it. It was obvious that he shaved but didn't do a very good job. Small tufts of hair stuck out of his beard.

She couldn't take the chance of being caught and sent back to the hell she had escaped from. She wobbled as she tried to flee. Marina stumbled while Adam still held out his hand.

"My name is Adam," he said again, taking a moment to form his words. "I jist shake a woman's hand."

Marina could barely get words out. "Who are you? Where am I?"

"You're at my house," he explained. "I live here. I missed my bus for the first time today. I couldn' get up this mornin'." When he said the word "first" he lifted his thick right index finger.

She didn't know how to respond. She stared at him and then scanned her surroundings to see if anyone else was there.

Was she dreaming? Marina closed her eyes and shook her head. When she opened them again, he was still there.

"Do you know Heidi?" he asked.

"Who's Heidi?"

"She's the lady from the home who took care of me. You know 'er? Did she send ya here?" Then his eyes brightened as some realization came over him. "D-Did my mommy send you?" His eyes grew wider and his expression was awash in happiness.

Marina's fear ebbed away. As she rubbed away her tears, she was silently thankful that she'd always paid attention in English class in Moldova. In fact, languages were always her best subject. "No one sent me here. I'm lost. If you can tell me how to get to the nearest town, I'd appreciate it."

Adam regarded her quizzically, and she feared her Romanian accent was so strong he didn't understand her. Fortunately, that wasn't the case.

"The nearest town is a long ways from here. You need car or bus. If you wanna bus, I can show you where ta gettit," Adam said, pronouncing each word slowly.

"I can't get a bus. I have no money," Marina answered, her shoulders drooping and a pained expression on her face. She peered around and jumped when she heard a rustling noise behind her. She swung around fast, only to find a bird flying from one tree branch to another.

"I can give ya my bus an' candy money," Adam offered. "I was gonna go to the drug store and buy candy bars when I'm at work, even though my mommy would'of gotten mad at me. She don't like me ta eat candy, but she's not alive no more. I'm here all by myself 'till my daddy gets home," Adam hung his head. Both his hands were above his head and shaking in the air. "My daddy's gonna get mad at me 'cause I missed the bus." He looked up, and Marina saw his eyebrows shoot up with fear, thinking about his father's reaction. "Oh no!" he exclaimed. "I hope my daddy's not gonna put me in the home again. I don't wanna go back there!"

"What's wrong with the home?" Marina asked, suddenly intrigued.

He shook his head in horror. "Oh, it's terrible! I can't watch my own TV shows. I can't go out when I want ta. And I hate those group walks! Only Heidi lets me go out fer walks wit her and nobody else. Like the way I used ta with my mommy."

Tears formed in Adam's eyes. He bit his shirt. She realized the holes had come from bite marks.

Adam could never be part of the trade. Unless he's a brilliant actor.

Still she looked around, fearful someone would appear with a gun. She was hungry and weak. She had cuts all over her body and yearned to wash up. She stared at Adam and rubbed her stomach. "I'm so hungry and thirsty. Is there water nearby where I could get something to drink?"

Adam shook his head. "I got water and drinks and food in my 'frigerator, but my mommy told me never ta let strangers in our house," he said sadly and shifted his gaze. Then he brightened and lifted his right index finger. "But I can bring ya breakfast outside, if ya still wan' it."

"That would be perfect, Adam!" Marina said, her body getting more relaxed once again.

What choice do I have but to trust him?

"How about I walk you to your house?" she suggested slowly and carefully, adding, "But Adam, you cannot touch me."

"Oh, I learned that already. I can only touch your hand," he told her.

"My name is Marina. Nice to meet you, Adam," she hesitated but reluctantly extended her scraped right hand.

"Nice ta meet ya. I'll shake your hand but then that's it," he said somberly, apparently not noticing her unkempt appearance. He swiped his arms in front of him as if they were scissors to emphasize the point.

Adam smelled like the outdoors, but she detected the smell of soap on his hands. They were rough and red like he washed them a lot.

He walked on his toes, as if hesitant about the feel of the ground he walked on. She scanned the landscape in every direction, searching for danger over the tops of bright marigolds, tulips, and blossoms. When no danger appeared, she noticed the colorful blooms and couldn't resist a moment of appreciation. The trees stood tall and provided shade as they passed. Marina wished they were fruit trees. She still felt dizzy and unsteady. Her stomach screamed, demanding food. She felt her throat; it was so parched. As if reading her mind, Adam took out a bottle of water from his little sack.

"Oh wait! I got some water. Wan' some water? I didn't opennit yet. My mommy always said ta never share a bottle 'cause you can git germs." He continued, struggling to get out the words as he handed it to her. "I've got lotsa water in my house. My mommy and daddy always wan' me to take lotta water when I go out fer walks. You want?"

"Oh yes! Thank you, Adam!" Marina clutched the water bottle as if she was in possession of the most valuable commodity in the world. She guzzled it so fast that some of the water went down her windpipe. She bent over, hands on her thighs for support, and spluttered and coughed at the ground, splattering her shirt and wheezing from taking too much water too fast into her parched throat.

"I'd hit yer back, but I promised to just shake yer hand, and a promise is a promise," he said, looking stone serious and raising his thick finger. He breathed hard after making the effort to get his words out.

Fortunately, Marina stopped choking and took deep breaths. "That's OK, Adam." She smiled for the first time. "I'm not choking anymore."

Marina then drank in smaller gulps. The tightness and fear enveloping her body ebbed. She hadn't felt this relaxed in a long time. She felt like crying from relief.

Then to Adam's surprise, she poured the remaining water on her face, hair, and arms.

"Uh . . . as you can see, I am very dirty and cut up," Marina responded to his staring eyes and open mouth.

He nodded. "My daddy makes me get washed up every night, but I think that's too much! I only like to take a shower when I git dirty."

Marina smiled.

He led her to his white ranch house with green trim. It was small but well-kept, and in the front and back were more flower gardens, which brightened the house and the grounds surrounding it. The sun was out and there was now a slight breeze.

◆ ◆ ◆

Unbeknownst to either of them, a Mercedes was driving about ten miles from Adam's house. The car stopped every mile, and two men, all dressed in black, got out and peered around, passing the binoculars to one another.

CHAPTER TEN

ADAM

ADAM LOOKED UP AT THE SKY, GRATEFUL HIS MOMMY had sent him Marina.

Heidi said Mommy is watching me. Mommy must've brought Marina to him. He sat on the front grass under their large oak tree watching his new friend enjoy her breakfast. He couldn't stop smiling and putting his head down slightly, his shoulders shaking when he giggled like a delighted little boy.

Marina loves Cheerios as much as I do.

She seemed to finish her toast instantly.

I musttave toasted them real good fer her and put on jist enough butter. And she looked so happy drinkin' the orange juice. Mommy told me how many times I need ta shake the bottle. Mommy said I made the best breakfasts.

He sat up taller as he watched her, remembering that Mommy always told him he was a smart boy.

"You wan' somethin' more?" he asked her.

Marina nodded and looked down.

"Adam, do you . . . do you, uh, think I could take a shower

in your house? Maybe? I'm . . . I'm very dirty and I must look horrible and scary."

He saw she was dirty, but when he watched nature shows, animals appeared out of the woods and they usually were dirty, too. That explained why they often traveled to a river or lake and washed themselves.

Since Marina came outta the woods, she's dirty, too, he reasoned.

"That's . . . that's 'cause you came outta the woods," he explained.

"Ah, sorry?" she asked, peering at him with wrinkled eyebrows.

"In nature shows, the animals come outta the woods dirty and they need to take a bath in the lake," he said, pronouncing each word slowly and carefully.

"Oh, yes," Marina responded, her brows shooting up in understanding. "But I cannot bathe in the lake, you see. I need to take a shower inside a house."

Adam looked from her to the house. He knew Daddy didn't let him bring strangers into the house.

But even his daddy pointed out that people should not act like the animals.

He gaped at Marina. Since Mommy sent her down so he wouldn't be all alone, how could he not let her take a shower in his house?

Mommy would say yes, he thought.

"Mommy said yes," Adam blurted aloud.

"Sorry, Adam?" Marina asked, wrinkling her brows again.

"Yes, you can take a shower in my house," Adam said, smiling at the sky as if he had just received his mother's approval.

"Oh, Adam, thank you!" Marina said. He thought he saw tears in her eyes. "And I promise you that as soon as I finish, I will leave and you won't have to do anything more for me."

At this, Adam frowned. "Oh no, Marina. You're my new friend now! Then we can take walks and watch nature shows, and . . . and . . . make chocolate chip cookies, read books, and even make lemonade!" Adam said the last part with emphatic enthusiasm. He flapped his hands as he got up and boomed, "Let's go!"

◆ ◆ ◆

They had been driving all over Morristown. Igor wanted to slam the binoculars against the Mercedes. He jerked his head all around so the scar that glistened along the right side of his jaw and down into his neck pained him. As if he needed another reminder why he wanted to take that woman down. Massaging the scar was useless, but he instinctively did it whenever he moved his neck too much. He turned to Sergei, seated in the passenger seat, staring at him with steely eyes.

"You know, you're wasting time, and it's only going to get us in trouble. Andre would say to forget about the girl. We don't always get a profit on every woman we kidnap," Sergei said, tired but trying not to sound too exasperated. He wanted more than anything to convince Igor to change his mind about finding this woman.

"Andre said you listen to me and I know what I'm doing," Igor retorted, his voice louder than necessary. He added, almost defensively, "She ruined my life and you know it."

"I know you are going to get us both killed. That I know."

Igor's eyes gazed ferociously into his companion's. Without warning, Igor punched him in the face. While Sergei grabbed his nose and moaned, Igor got out of the car and paced. He touched his scar lightly and took out his small bottle for a sip.

"She will pay," he said to himself. "She will pay for making me look like a freak."

CHAPTER ELEVEN

MARINA

Equally enthusiastic, Marina rose up and carried the plate, bowl, and glass. She knew this was risky, but she was caught up in the excitement of getting clean. When she left Adam, she knew he would be devastated, but she couldn't worry about that now.

Upon entering the house, she saw the rooms were small and the house was spartanly furnished with old furniture, but it was clean. She stared at the two identical vacuum cleaners in the living room.

"My daddy likes to vacuum the house. He's always telling me ta vacuum too," Adam said. "He don't wan' no crumbs on the floor 'cause he don't want mice."

He continued slowly, "Here's the TV where I watch nature shows, and here," he said, opening a drawer, "here's my nature tapes. I watch 'em a lot when I can't find nature shows on TV." He threw the tapes back in the drawer and said, "Wanna see my kitchen? I got lots of different cereals!"

"Oh, I don't need to eat any more, Adam," she said, patting her stomach.

"Here!" he said, pulling out a tape he found near the TV. "Here's a tape on butterflies! I love butterflies! They're so pretty the way they fly in the air. Let's watch this tape. OK, Marina? OK? OK? You'll love it too!"

How could she say no? His eager eyes and delighted expression made it impossible.

"All right, Adam. If you think it's all right," she said, sneaking a look outside the windows.

"Sit there!" he enthused, pointing to the middle of the couch. "That's where my mommy always sat when she watched TV wit me."

Marina hesitated. "What if someone comes over and wants to know what I'm doing here? What if your father comes home?"

"Nobody comes." Adam shook his head. "Daddy's at work. He comes home later. Now that you're here, I have a friend." He pointed up at the ceiling. "Mommy must be smilin' in the sky 'cause I'm not alone no more. Mommy always said she wanted me ta be happy. That's why she sent ya."

All of Marina's hesitations melted upon hearing those words. Her mother always told her the same thing: her biggest wish was to see her children happy.

For the moment, she felt surrounded by the warmth of love and care, the direct opposite of her feelings among the sex slave traders.

So Marina sat down while Adam put in the DVD and then sat next to her. His face glowed with happiness. Marina couldn't believe her presence could give this young stranger so much joy. She no longer feared he would harm her—he even brought out her own maternal feelings.

Marina asked slowly, "Adam, I just need to take a shower. Would you please show me where the bathroom is?"

"Oh yeah! The shower," Adam said, banging his head and flapping his hands.

"I'll show you the shower and then we can watch the tape."

Marina followed him to the bathroom. There was soap and shampoo in the shower stall and a stack of towels on an old, rickety vanity.

"Tell me when you done," instructed Adam, who beamed with happiness. "I'll make peanut butter 'n' jelly sandwiches, and we can eat 'em 'n' watch tape 'bout butterflies."

He skipped down the hall toward the kitchen.

"Uh, Adam," she asked timidly.

"Yeah?" he turned around. "We can watch another nature show if ya don't wanna watch tape 'bout butterflies."

Marina quickly shook her head and raised her hand. "No, no! The tape is fine, but . . . I'm sorry, do you have clean clothes for me, maybe?"

Adam's eyes raced as he thought about it with one hand waving above his head in the air. Then he shot her a triumphant smile as he said, "My mommy has clothes in her bedroom."

"Adam, I don't know . . . ," Marina started to say, but he had already entered his parents' bedroom.

Marina fiddled with her tangled hair as she waited. He came out carrying an evening dress, a polka-dot skirt and matching top, and a pair of jeans and a red T-shirt. The evening dress dragged on the floor.

"How 'bout these?" he asked her.

"I'll take this." She gingerly took the jeans. "And this." She pulled the long-sleeved red T-shirt.

"Take all of 'em!" Adam handed them to her, one hand flapping upward.

"No, no. Thank you. Um, Adam, one more thing please," Marina asked, her brows tightening and her mouth twisting as if in pain.

"What is it, Marina? My mommy's in heaven now. She don't need these clothes no more," Adam responded sadly, his voice breaking as he looked upward.

She bit her lower lip. *I hope he understands this.*

"Adam," she whispered conspiratorially, leaning her head toward him. "Does your mommy have underwear? Do you know what I'm talking about?"

"Underwear? Sure, my mommy has lots of underwear," he exclaimed as if this were the most natural topic of conversation. He returned to the bedroom and came out with a handful of bright yellow, pink, and orange underwear.

"I need just one. Thank you again, Adam," Marina said, smiling, her shoulders relaxed. "I am all ready to shower now."

She locked the bathroom door and breathed a sigh of relief. She tested the shower's water temperature and peeled off her dirty, sweaty clothes that were so worn they weren't strong enough to even serve as cleaning rags anymore.

◆ ◆ ◆

Their car was parked at a local gas station in town. Igor was in the restroom. Sergei opened and closed his cell phone.

We shouldn't be searching for her. We should have finished our business with the girls we brought over here and then gone to clubs and bars. Then we would go on the ship back to Moldova to find more women to make more money. If I call Andre now, he will agree with me.

He opened his phone and dialed. Just then he felt a prickle on his neck.

"What are you doing, Sergei?" Igor was behind him with what was most likely a pocketknife.

Sergei dropped the phone. His eyes darted from side to side, trying to think of something.

"Who were you calling, Sergei?" Igor said slowly. He moved the knife slightly into his partner's skin, causing a trickle of blood to form.

"I-I-I call my friends in Moldova," he stuttered. "They expect me to be back in a week."

"The ship wouldn't have come back so soon. You weren't calling Andre, were you?"

"Of course not! I wanted to call friends to tell them I would not be back for a while."

Igor fought his impulse to cut the carotid tissue in his partner's neck. Instead he put the knife away and looked around to make sure no one had seen.

Sergei let out a deep breath. His whole head was damp with sweat. He put his hand on his neck to stem the bleeding and fished around his person for a handkerchief.

CHAPTER TWELVE

ADAM

WHEN ADAM HEARD THE SHOWER TURN ON, HE skipped into the kitchen to make lunch.

After washing his hands with globs of dishwashing liquid, he hummed while spreading the peanut butter and jelly on sliced bread. He tried to spread them on evenly and neatly, but some still splattered on the kitchen counter. He cleaned the counter with a damp paper towel with one hand while the other was flapping, when he heard the sound of a speeding car approaching the front of his house.

He stared open-mouthed with his eyes bulging. It was his daddy's car.

"Oh no!" he blurted out.

Turning around to look at the bathroom door, he heard the water still running in the shower.

"What . . . what . . . what am I gonna do?" he asked himself, banging the corner of his head. He paced the kitchen floor, waving both arms upward. "What am I gonna do? What will Daddy say? I don't wanna git in trouble. Daddy will like Marina.

I'll tell Daddy she's nice. Daddy'll like her. He will, he will."

The shower stopped running. But before he could do anything, he saw his father jump out of the car.

He gulped as his daddy stormed in the front door.

◆ ◆ ◆

Sergei watched as Igor paced around the field far away from the residential neighborhoods. The only structure nearby was a ramshackle old building that looked like it was ready to fall apart. Sergei had no interest in it. His eyes were focused on his partner, pacing back and forth in front of it. Igor always paced when he didn't know what to do. Sergei sat and sighed. He also didn't know what he should do. He always knew Igor was unstable, but he didn't realize how obsessed he could get once he made up his mind on something.

Why the hell hadn't Andre realized that about him? he wondered, closing his eyes and shaking his head. *I thought he carefully screened his men.*

His eyes turned back to his partner. *Andre must have some need for men obsessed like Igor, but this has gone too far. Andre needs to know what's going on before Igor jeopardizes the whole operation.*

Sergei shut his eyes and craned his head back. Even though Igor crept about in a stealthy silence, he had to find a moment to call their boss before Igor could cause more trouble. The sooner the better.

CHAPTER THIRTEEN

BRUCE

"ADAM!" BRUCE SHOUTED ONCE HE STEPPED inside the house.

"Hi, Daddy." Adam stopped pacing, his hands still up. He tried his best to smile, but all he managed to do was expose all his teeth.

"What are you doing here? Why aren't you at work?" Bruce's heart calmed down as soon as he saw his son.

"I couldn't wake up this mornin', Daddy." Adam looked down and resumed flapping his hands.

"You couldn't wake up this morning?" Bruce stared at him, his face now hot with anger. "Adam, when you have a job, you have to get up whether you want to or not!"

Adam slumped his shoulders. "Daddy, I was too tired ta catch the bus."

"So did you call Mr. Price and tell him you weren't coming in?"

Adam hung his head lower and slowly shook it.

"Why not?" Bruce demanded.

"I forgot. I forgot how to do it."

Bruce put his hand on his hip, faced the ceiling, and shook his head.

"Adam, you just have to push a button on the phone with the picture of Mr. Price."

"I forgot."

"Why didn't you call me? Did you forget my picture on the phone, too?"

That would have been close to impossible. His picture was taped to all the phones, and his son only had to hit a button to call him as he had done many times before. Adam was also supposed to wear a bracelet with his name, address, home phone number, and Bruce's cell phone number.

To his chagrin, Bruce noticed that his son was not wearing it.

"I was tired, Daddy," Adam said softly, struggling to get the words out.

"Tired? Adam, you're eighteen years old. You have a responsibility to call Mr. Price and me if you can't get to work. If I did this at my job, I'd be fired."

Adam stood staring at the ground, waving his hands and occasionally hitting the corner of his head.

Bruce felt his face grow redder. "What if I didn't wake you up and set your alarm clock? What if I was too tired? That doesn't go, Adam. I've got responsibilities. You do too. You're an adult now. You've got to act like one!"

"Sorry, Daddy," Adam said quietly, a tear forming in his eye and biting his shirt.

"Sorry?" Bruce shot back. "I was about to get to an important meeting together when Mr. Price called and said you weren't on the bus this morning. Adam, this can't go on! I've got to make a living or we won't have food to eat. I won't be able to pay our bills!"

"Sorry, Daddy," Adam said again. Tears ran down his cheeks.

Bruce pointed his finger at his son, gritting his teeth. "This absolutely cannot happen again, Adam! If it does, we'll have to make other arrangements. I can't stay home to make sure you catch your bus!"

Adam nodded silently. More tears streamed down his cheeks.

"I know you don't like the Fairmount Home, but there are people there who can watch you at all times. That may be the only solution."

Adam's face turned white.

"Daddy, I won't miss the bus 'gain. I promise," Adam said, shaking his head fervently.

Now Bruce felt bad. But what else could he do?

He reflected that this was now an impossible situation to live with.

"Come on," he told his son, breathing deeply to calm his temper. "I'll call—I mean, you'll call Mr. Price and then I'll drive you over to work."

"But Daddy, it's lunchtime. I'll go in tomorrow," his son protested.

"Call Mr. Price now and ask him if he needs you to come in today." Bruce took his cell phone out of his jacket pocket and dialed Mr. Price's phone number.

Reluctantly, Adam reached for the phone. His father made sure the speaker phone was on and handed it to his son. He kept staring at him while tapping his fingers on the counter as they waited for Mr. Price to answer. He noticed the peanut butter and jelly sandwiches on the kitchen counter and wanted to ask why Adam had made two instead of the usual one, but his son's boss picked up the phone.

"This is Mr. Price," he answered with the tone of a CEO of a big company.

"Hi, Mr. Price. This is Adam Hitchens. Sorry I couldn't get outta bed this mornin'. My daddy can drive me to work."

"No, Mr. Hitchens. I brought someone in to replace you for today. If you don't call in when you're sick, then you'll have to find work elsewhere."

Adam gulped. Bruce shut his eyes and shook his head.

"This job is not your right, it's your responsibility. If you can't live up to this responsibility, then out the door you go, Mr. Hitchens."

Bruce made a face. Stamping labels all day an important job?

"Yes sir," Adam said, the little cell phone trembling in his hand.

Mr. Price went on. "So this won't happen again, young man?"

"No, next time I'll be sure ta get up when the alarm clock goes off. I couldn' fall asleep last night. I'm angry my mommy was taken away from me. I miss my mommy."

There was silence on the other end. Bruce's face was etched in pain upon hearing his son's admission. Then Mr. Price spoke quietly.

"What's that, Mr. Price?"

After a pause, his boss said, "Then I'll see you on Monday, Mr. Hitchens."

"See ya, Mr. Price," Adam said cheerfully before hanging up.

Adam breathed a sigh of relief.

Bruce spoke as soon as Adam hung up the phone. "So I take it you're not going into work today."

"Mr. Price says I don't need ta go in t'day," Adam said, smiling.

His father said nothing and stared at him for a long time.

Finally he spoke. "I need to go back to work, Adam. I promise we'll talk when I get back home tonight." Bruce spoke more gently now. He looked into his son's eyes. "Will you hang around the house so I don't have to worry about you?"

"Oh yes, Daddy. I just met . . . ,"Adam stopped himself.

"Who did you just meet?" Bruce looked quickly back at him, his eyes growing big and his eyebrows raised.

"Nobody, Daddy," Adam responded quickly.

Now Bruce's eyes narrowed as he said slowly and quietly, "Are you sure about that, son?"

Adam glanced back and forth and his hands were swinging rapidly upward. Every time he opened his mouth to speak, he closed it again. Finally he said, "Yeah, Daddy."

His father spoke gently, almost smiling. "You can tell me anything, Adam. Who did you meet?"

"I just met a butterfly," he answered, putting his hand over his mouth.

Bruce's eyes narrowed again. "A butterfly?"

Adam nodded vigorously. "Yeah, Mommy always said she loves ta see butterflies in the spring and welcome 'em to our garden. I just met one."

Bruce continued staring at his son. His shoulders slouched and he then closed his eyes and sighed.

"Adam, I've got to get back to work. Promise me you'll stay in the house the rest of the day. Watch TV. I'm going to call you every hour to make sure you're all right, but you have to stay in the house to hear the phone ring. Promise me you'll do that," His voice sounded as if he were begging.

Adam straightened up and brightened. "OK. I promise. Have a good day, Daddy," Adam said, his hand already waving his father good-bye.

Bruce reached for the door handle. He hesitated. "Wait, I'm just going to go to the bathroom," he said.

"No, Daddy, wait!" Adam shouted, reaching his hands forward to stop him.

"Is there a butterfly using the bathroom now?"

"Yes!" Adam shouted. Then he put his hand over his mouth.

"What?" his father demanded. He shook his head and did not wait for an answer. He tried the door but it was locked.

"What the hell's going on?" he turned to face his son.

Adam's mouth hung open. One of his hands waved in the air, more vigorously than usual, and the other one kept banging the corner of his head.

Bruce turned back to the bathroom door. "Who the hell's in here? Open up now!" His eyes were filled with fury as he pounded on the door. "I'll break this door down if I have to. Open up in there! Now!" The door unlocked and Bruce pulled the door open so hard it ricocheted against the wall.

Inside stood a young, very thin woman with his wife's clothes on.

◆ ◆ ◆

Sergei glanced at his watch and then up at the sky above the parked car. It would be dark soon. Igor spoke to a family taking a late afternoon stroll. Sergei failed to notice the young son pointing to the picture and eagerly talking to Igor.

I'm not good at texting yet, but I'll try it now, Sergei thought, stealthily pulling out his cell phone.

He awkwardly tried to type in the words to Andre. He cursed under his breath when he kept hitting the wrong buttons.

Why the hell do they have to make the keys so damn small?

But when he looked up in frustration, he found Igor staring at him. Taken by surprise, Sergei dropped his phone at his feet.

His companion got into the car but said nothing.

"Anything?" he asked Igor, glancing at him nervously.

"Maybe," was all he said.

"I go to a gas station and pee," Sergei said, opening the car door. "Then we go to eat."

Igor said nothing. When they found a station, Sergei left and headed for the bathroom.

Igor saw the cell phone on the car floor. He opened his car door and threw it on the ground. Then he got out and stepped on it, cracking it.

CHAPTER FOURTEEN

MARINA

THE MAN WHO ORDERED HER TO OPEN THE DOOR stared open-mouthed. She cowered at the sight of him and instinctively raised her arms to prevent him from coming nearer. She froze, and no sound came out of her throat. She trembled, wondering what was in store for her and whether Adam would defend her or, if he was possibly in collusion with him.

"Who are you and what are you doing in my house?" he demanded. He started at her and she instinctively jumped back.

"I . . . I . . . ," she began.

"Daddy, this is my new friend, Marina," Adam said, his whole body quivering. "We're gonna eat peanut butter 'n' jelly sandwiches 'n' watch TV."

Bruce stared at his son as if he didn't recognize him.

"Adam, what the hell's going on? Who's this woman and how did she get into our house?"

"My . . . my name is Marina and I can explain. It's not your son's fault."

Bruce looked from Marina to his son.

"What do you mean? Adam, you're not supposed to let strangers into our home! Don't you realize you're putting us in danger? You can't stay home if you're going to do things like that!" He turned back to Marina. "And you," he said, pointing to her, "get out of here before I call the police!"

"But Daddy . . . ," began Adam, whose face turned red and tears fell down his cheeks. He jumped up and down and flapped his hands.

"I'll go. It's okay, Adam. I'm sorry I caused a problem." Marina edged down the hall, trying to get as far away from Adam's father as possible.

"And what are you doing in Maggie's clothes?" he demanded and stepped toward her like he was going to tear them off.

Marina trembled and backed away.

"Daddy! Daddy! She's my new friend! I gave her Mommy's clothes 'cause she needed 'em!" Adam shouted.

"No, no! I'll go! Adam, it's okay! It'll be all right," Marina consoled him. She saw this as her opportunity to escape.

But Adam jumped in front of her, blocking her way. Snot slid down his nose, he smelled of sweat, and his hair stuck out in all directions. She backed away, fearing him, too.

"No, don't leave. Stay wit me, Marina. I don't want you ta go 'way, too! You can't leave me like Mommy and Heidi." Adam turned to his father. "Daddy, Mommy sent her to me!"

Marina's focus on self-preservation melted upon hearing his words.

Bruce lost his angry composure for a moment and stared at his son, dumbfounded.

"I've got to go, Adam. Thank you for helping me."

Adam screamed and pulled his hair. He became so hysterical

that Marina feared he was about to lose control of himself.

Then Bruce stunned everybody when he shouted, "Wait!"

Marina gripped the wall as she waited to find out what Adam's father would say next.

Adam looked at his father with his red, tear-stained face, removing his hands from pulling chunks of hair and now flapping them furiously at his sides.

Bruce gulped, looking from one to the other as if deciding what to do next.

As if answering his question, his cell phone rang. He took it out from his jacket pocket and answered it. The volume was turned up on the cell phone and Marina could hear the whole conversation.

"Bruce, is everything all right?" the strange voice asked hurriedly. Bruce straightened up, eyes wide with alarm. Marina guessed it must be his boss.

Before he could answer, the voice said, "The presentation's in an hour, Bruce. This meeting is crucial. Did you find your son?"

"Yes, he's here, Steve . . . ," Bruce began.

"Oh, good! I'm glad you found him and he's safe. You'll be able to come back to the office now? We need you, Bruce."

Marina could hear the pleading in the boss's voice. Bruce closed his eyes, seemingly at a loss how to respond.

"I'll . . . I'll come in as soon as I can, Steve. I promise," Bruce said, his resolve deflating.

Adam's face changed into a wide smile, and he bounced up and down. Instead of his hands flapping vigorously, they now shook up and down like an excited puppy. Marina stared at Bruce with large, grave eyes.

Bruce put his hands on his hips and stared at Marina. "What

were you doing with my son?"

"We were havin' a great time, Daddy," Adam spoke for her. "I gave Marina breakfast 'cause she was hungry, and she was all dirty so she took a shower."

"How did you get here?" he asked her, ignoring his son.

"I . . . I had to run away." Marina bit her lip to keep from crying.

"Are you in trouble?"

She hugged herself as she answered. "Some people tried to hurt me and I had to escape."

He took a moment to look at her. She was so thin and drawn, her legs were like sticks. Her eyes were hollow and even though Adam had given her food, she still looked weak and fragile.

"Daddy, me and Marina are goin' watch a nature show," Adam announced happily, oblivious to the tension in the room.

Bruce stared open-mouthed. He turned his gaze from his son to Marina. Finally, he settled his stare on Adam.

"Adam, will you promise me that you'll call me every hour if I go back to work?"

"Sure, Daddy," Adam said, bouncing and waving his hands in delight.

"I'm going to call you too, son, to make sure you're all right," his eyes went in the direction of Marina. "I want to make sure everything is all right here."

Marina stared. She didn't know what to do with her hands so she just kept them limp at her sides. She did not try to speak.

Bruce slowly picked up his briefcase and headed to the front door, steadily watching both of them.

"And you," he said, pointing his finger at Marina. "Please do

me one favor. Just one favor. Take off my late wife's clothing."
He waved in the direction of his bedroom. "Take any of my
clothes," he waved to his son's room, "take anything of Adam's."
He stopped short. "And please change in the bathroom with
the door closed."

She nodded vigorously.

"Oh, Daddy," Adam said, coming to tug his father's sleeve.
"It's not nice to change in front of somebody else. Mommy told
me that," he shook his head.

Bruce swallowed. His body alternated between sweating
and trembling. He needed to run back to work and yet he could
not leave the house.

He stood there, unable to make a move.

At a loss for words, he stared at Adam and Marina, took
out his cell phone, and walked out the door.

Still cowered against the wall as if she were paralyzed; Marina
didn't know if she should be relieved or fearful. *What will his
father do when he gets back?* she wondered. She was certain he
would not turn her in to her kidnappers, but what if he called
the police and the police tipped them off? She shuddered at
the thought.

"Marina, my daddy's still out there." Adam interrupted
her thoughts.

Marina looked outside and placed her hand on her heart.
Is he waiting for the police?

The minutes went by like hours. She gaped at Adam's father
in the car. Before she could decide what to do, Adam said, "I'm
gonna go outside and find out why my daddy's stayin'."

She couldn't breathe. Adam looked out the front window
and waved at his father. With his back turned, she considered

finding the back door and running away, but her legs refused to move. He had his hand on the doorknob, but his father drove away. Still trying to move a step forward, Adam announced, "My daddy left."

While she was processing this, he interrupted her thoughts.

"Let's watch TV." Adam came uncomfortably close to her. "Whaddya wanna watch, Marina? Cheetahs, whales, elephants, beavers?" Adam opened his DVD drawer and cradled a stack in his arms. "Wanna watch beavers build a dam? Dam's a bad word, but my daddy said we can use dam wit beavers 'cause that's their home." His eyes entreated her. After swallowing a few times, she found her voice.

"Any . . . anything you want to watch is fine with me, Adam. Anything at all," she said, trying her best to smile but wishing she could burst into tears instead.

What is going to happen now? she wondered.

She took a deep breath as she followed Adam skipping into the living room with a big smile on his face. His whole body radiated happiness.

"Wait, Adam, wait." She suddenly stopped. Adam turned around, his mouth forming an O.

"Your father wants me to change these clothes," she said, looking at what she wore. "I don't know what else you have, but I don't want to upset your father."

Adam shrugged his shoulders and bit his shirt. She guessed he was trying to think of what else she could wear. He glanced at the ceiling and then down at the floor as if searching for an answer. He put his hands up in desperation.

Aside from going to a store, how would I find something else to wear? The clothes I came with are dirty and thin with holes in them, but what other choice do I have?

On her way to the bathroom to pick up her dirty rags from the garbage to put them on again, an idea hit her.

She stopped. "Adam, do you have a robe?"

"A robe?" Adam asked. "What's that?"

"It's what you put on over your pajamas when you get up in the morning, before you put on your clothes to wear during the day," she explained as she wondered why he had never heard of it before.

"Oh, a robe," he said, raising his eyebrows. He shook his head. "I don't like a robe. I don't like how it feels on me."

Marina slouched her shoulders. *Now what am I going to do?*

But his eyes lit up. "My daddy wears a robe. I'll git it." He let go of the DVDs on the living room table, making a small racket, and ran to his father's bedroom.

Marina winced at the noise and hoped none of the DVDs had gotten broken.

He came out dragging his father's dark blue robe.

"Oh, thank you, Adam. I'll put it on in the bathroom."

She closed the door and examined the robe. It was too long for her. She looked in the mirror. If she took off her clothes and put on this robe with its belt in the middle, her breasts would be exposed. She would most likely trip because it was too long. What to do?

She decided to keep the clothes on and cover them with the robe. When she walked, she had to pick up the robe as if she were wearing a long, elegant skirt.

Marina walked into the living room holding the robe up. As soon as she sat down on the couch a few feet away from him, she noticed some of the DVDs were cracked.

"Which one you wanna watch, Marina?" he asked eagerly.

"Ah, you know, Adam," Marina said, rubbing her neck, "I've always wanted to see what American television is like. Are there any nature shows on the regular TV set?"

"We can look, Marina. Wait'll you see what TV's like!" He grabbed the remote from the table and bounced back on the couch. His face was all smiles. "I love watchin' TV with someone. We can talk 'bout the animals."

Adam pushed a few buttons and then stopped. He sniffed. Turning to Marina, he sniffed again, and to her horror, he put his head up close to her shoulder and kept his face there. Marina was so surprised and frightened she didn't know how to respond. Slowly she inched away on the couch. Adam didn't try to grab her; he just followed her with his nose near her neck.

She stayed silent, trying to gauge the situation. His nose nearly touched her neck.

Finally he spoke. "I like the smell of soap. It smells good. Sometimes I like to go into the bathroom and just smell the soap. Daddy don't like when I do that. One time he bought soap with no smell," Adam told her in a shocked tone as if his father had left him at home with no food. "I told Daddy he can't do that, and he didn' do that again."

Marina blinked and listened, not knowing what to think.

Adam continued, "My mommy and daddy told me not to go near people wit my nose, but I like to smell different things. They say I scare people, but I just like to smell."

She nodded and inched away to the farthest end of the couch.

"I like ta smell lots of things," he explained, appearing oblivious to her moving farther away. He moved his head slightly closer to her, lowered his voice, and said conspiratorially, "I also like to smell feet. Mommy would laugh whenever I smelled her feet, but Daddy would git mad. He'd say, 'That's gross!' Adam mimicked his father's stern tone and narrowed eyes. "The people at the home would git mad too. You won't mind if I smelled your feet, would you, Marina? Would you?"

Marina swallowed and stared. Her eyes shifted to find the front door and contemplated bolting from the house.

Adam went on. "Sometimes I fart a lot. I can't help it, but my mommy got all upset, and Daddy said I gotta control mineself 'cause I got my mommy upset. They gimme pills that taste like candy. I chew it like I'm eatin' gummy bears whenever I need to fart now. Daddy says I'm much better, but I like to chew those candy pills," he told her.

"Adam," Marina said loudly, "I so want to watch a nature show." Her eyes were pleading.

"OK, Marina," Adam said brightly and smiled. "We both love nature shows, so we gotta find one."

Marina couldn't begin to process what she had just heard.

She guessed Adam must be seventeen or eighteen. She concluded he was retarded, but what did his fascination with smells mean? That he kept repeating he couldn't touch a woman? Waving his hands whenever he got excited? Chewing the top of his shirt? But Adam interrupted her ponderings.

"Sometimes I watch nature shows wit my daddy when he comes home, but lots of times he falls asleep. So we're not watchin' the nature show together then, are we Marina? You won't fall asleep, will you, Marina? Will you?"

"No, I'm not going to fall asleep, Adam," she said with the utmost seriousness.

A smile encompassed his face. "Yeah, 'cause you love nature

shows just like me, right?"

"Absolutely." She couldn't help smiling.

"My daddy says he likes 'em, but I don't believe him 'cause he falls asleep all the time. But we both love nature shows," he said, pointing to himself and Marina. "We don't sleep." He picked up the remote.

Marina forced herself to smile and tried to settle back on the couch, but her trembling prevented her. Her mind raced about what would happen once Adam's father came home. Would she be on the run again?

Adam pushed lots of buttons, but he couldn't find a nature show. When he channel-surfed, he found a show that caught his eye.

He sat, his elbows resting on his knees and his hands on his face. After a minute he began chewing on his shirt again. A beautiful and stylishly dressed young woman and a handsome, muscle-toned young man in gym shorts and a muscle shirt were arguing on the TV screen. Adam looked sideways at the TV, shaking his head, obviously not understanding what they were talking about.

"They keep talkin' 'bout a baby. Where's the baby?" He looked all around the screen but didn't see one.

Marina sat still with her eyes wide open. She looked from Adam to the screen.

"They're talkin' a lot about 'im but I don't see 'im," he said again.

The woman kept rubbing her belly.

"Does she hava stomach ache or somethin'?"

Then the woman started to cry and the man went over and hugged her.

Tears welled in Marina's eyes. She had not encountered a tender moment between a man and a woman in what seemed like years. Her recent memories were filled with nothing but brutality. She was so absorbed in the scene that she didn't hear Adam's questions.

"Where is the baby, Marina? I don't see no baby," Adam said as he was still searching for the baby on the screen. "I can't find the baby."

Marina forced herself to pay attention.

"Excuse me?"

"They're talkin' bout a baby, but I can't find 'im." Adam was now frazzled as he sat directly in front of the screen, searching. "A man is huggin' the cryin' woman, but where's the baby, Marina? Do you know?"

She hesitated, not sure he would understand, but she had to try. "Adam, they're talking about a baby who isn't born yet."

She wasn't sure she should be the one to educate him on the facts of life.

"How da they know a baby's comin' if it ain't born yet, Marina? How?"

Marina took a deep breath. She wondered if his father would be furious with her for trying to explain to him about pregnancy.

"Adam, right now the baby is in the woman's tummy."

She turned to the DVDs on the table to find one that wasn't cracked. When she did, she said, "Adam, I'd like to watch this show. Could we watch it now?"

Her hopeful expression was met with Adam's delightful smile.

"Sure, Marina. Let's watch this show 'bout beavers." He grabbed the tape and put it in, seemingly forgetting all the pregnancy talk. About a minute after he placed the DVD in, the phone rang.

◆ ◆ ◆

The sign on the restaurant read The Morristown Deli: Voted Best Deli Restaurant in Morris County. Sergei couldn't wait to eat. He looked forward to a delicious end to a grueling day with Igor. He searched his memory, trying to figure out what had happened to his cell phone. Igor shrugged when he asked him. *How was he going to contact Andre now?* He shook his head—he hoped his memory would be clearer after he had eaten a good meal.

They were seated and got their orders right away.

"After we eat, we go back to the hotel. Perhaps we give up on this search for this woman and join the others," Sergei told him.

To his surprise, Igor nodded and took a large bite out of his sandwich. Food hung out of his mouth as he chewed.

Sergei took his eyes off his gluttonous partner and focused on his own sandwich.

I can never watch that pig eat, he thought disgustedly. He put his napkin down. *I need a few minutes away from him.* Out loud he said, "Let me go to the bathroom."

Igor nodded and continued eating. When Sergei was gone, he put liquid droplets in Sergei's sandwich, covering his hand with a napkin. Looking around, no one appeared to notice. They were too busy talking and enjoying their own double-stacked deli sandwiches.

Sergei exited the restroom and returned to his seat. He took a healthy bite of his pastrami sandwich. Before he could sit back and relish the taste, Igor told him, "I think I've found her."

"How?" Sergei asked impatiently because now he had to delay enjoying his sandwich.

"I asked a family questions while you sat in the car and slept," he answered with a Cheshire grin. "I ask if anyone saw a young woman in rags wandering around. At the gas station, a boy saw her while walking to school." He added with a sneer, "I do the work while you just sit and complain." With that Igor took another bite of his corned beef sandwich.

Sergei decided to completely ignore him as he savored his pastrami sandwich. He ended up thoroughly enjoying it. He loved American deli with the coleslaw, potato salad, pickle, and a glass of Dr. Brown's soda. Truly a feast. Now as he sat back to contemplate what a satisfying lunch he had experienced, he glanced at his partner sitting across from him. Igor scraped the plate with his finger to pick up every last morsel of food. Sergei looked around the restaurant, embarrassed to be seen with this brute. Fortunately, the other diners concentrated on their own food and conversation and didn't appear to notice Igor's piggish manners. By the time he turned back to him, Igor was studying him.

"What? What's wrong now, Igor?" Sergei asked.

Igor opened his wallet and took out some bills, keeping his eyes on his partner. Sergei felt drowsy. After awhile he had trouble keeping his eyes open. His partner continued to stare.

"Why am I getting so tired?" Sergei said out loud.

The waitress came and took the cash. Igor left a tip a lot bigger than she usually received.

"Thank you," she gushed. "Have a wonderful day."

The waitress left the table so happy she failed to notice Sergei having trouble keeping his head up.

"Come," Igor said. "We go to hotel and I plan what to do next. You sleep."

Sergei nodded, using all his strength to get up from the booth. He couldn't understand why he was so tired so suddenly, but his brain was too sluggish to think about it.

He stumbled to the car like a drunk.

CHAPTER FIFTEEN

BRUCE

WHEN BRUCE LEFT HIS HOUSE, HE KEPT TURNING back as he took out his cell phone and dialed. While the line rang, he considered calling his boss and telling him he couldn't go back to work today. He reluctantly called the only person he could count on in an emergency but whom he dreaded to bother

"Hello?"

"Judy, I'm sorry to bother you. Are . . . are you busy now?" Bruce gripped his phone so hard he had to remind himself he might break it.

"No, Bruce. Not at all. What's wrong? Is Adam all right?"

"I just came home and found a woman in my house with Adam," Bruce said out of breath, hurrying to his car. "She's real skinny and looks weak. I'd call the police but Adam got hysterical; he says she's his friend. I need to go back to work, but I can't leave him here with a stranger. When I told her to leave, Adam went ballistic. Oh, Judy, I don't know what to do," Bruce heard his own voice choking as he confided in his sister-in-law.

"I'll come over, Bruce," Judy said with no hesitation. "When you come home from work, we'll figure this out together. Hang in there. I'll be over in twenty minutes."

"Judy, I don't know what to say. Maybe I should just call the police . . ."

"You don't want to set him off. I'll come over and see what I think. What does she look like? Does she look dangerous?"

"No, just the opposite. She's underweight and weak. I don't know where she came from or how she finds the strength to even stand up."

"Listen, Bruce," Judy said. "I am in my car and on my way over. You go back to work."

"But . . . but . . . ," he began.

"You go to work. I'll be there as quickly as I can."

"Drive carefully," Bruce raised his voice, but she had already hung up.

Once he was in his car, Bruce contacted Steve.

"I'm coming back to work now," he told his boss in a low voice. As much as he wanted to, he could not drum up any enthusiasm, something his boss always valued from his employees.

"That's great, Bruce! I'm glad to hear everything is fine with your son," Steve exclaimed.

Bruce turned back to the house again. His son watched him from a front window. His eyes were lit up as if all was right with his world. He waved vigorously to his father with one hand while he twisted the other at a steady, even pace in the air.

"Everything's fine, Steve," he lied. He rotated his shoulders and breathed in. He used his other hand to rub his eyes. "I'll be there in fifteen to twenty minutes."

"Your team will be seated in the presentation room waiting for you. Gwen bought you a turkey sandwich for lunch. She wants you to know she ordered it just the way you like it," Steve told him in a cheery voice.

Bruce rolled his eyes. "Great," he said flatly.

I'm leaving my son at home with a stranger who has problems and I'm supposed to make a crucial presentation and be excited about a specially prepared deli sandwich.

He turned his attention to starting the car's engine, still clutching the cell phone. After looking at his house, he put his phone away.

He sat in the car, fumbling through all his pockets for his keys. When he finally found them, he stared at them until he finally placed them in the ignition and started his car, reluctantly driving away.

Upon arriving at the office, Bruce walked into the building, clutching his phone to his ear.

"How's everything going, son?"

"Great, Daddy! We're watching TV and now we're gonna watch a tape 'bout beavers," Adam said.

Bruce could hear in his son's voice how thoroughly happy he was.

"That's great, son," Bruce said, relieved. He tried to word this as tactfully as he could. "Ah, where is Marina now?"

"Sittin' on the couch wit me. She loves TV just like I do."

I'm sure, he thought with a smile.

"Adam, Aunt Judy is coming over soon. To keep you two company."

"All right!" he roared happily. Bruce could tell from his voice that he was jumping up and down. "Wait'll I tell Marina!

She'll love Aunt Judy!"

"It'll be great," Bruce said, trying to muster up some enthusiasm. "I'm heading into work now, but we'll keep calling each other. Wait, Adam, how about I don't call you unless there's a problem. How does that sound?"

"OK, Daddy. That'll be great."

"I'll see you in a little while, son. If there's any problem at all, call me. Remember that. Adam, what did I just say?"

"I'll see ya in a little while, son. If there's a problem, call me. Remember." Adam parroted his father's words back as best as he could.

"Bye, now. Be careful." Bruce closed his cell phone and hesitated before moving forward.

I can't risk Adam calling me during the presentation, but how am I going to get through this? he wondered, massaging his temples with his free hand.

He thought about how frail and helpless Marina was.

She's in no position to harm him, he thought. *She's alone and scared. Adam must be safe.*

He took out his cell phone to call his sister-in-law again but immediately closed it. He knew she'd arrive as soon as she could.

I can't be a pain-in-the-ass brother-in-law all the time.

He checked his watch. If he didn't hurry, Steve would call to find out what was taking him so long. He reached the elevator and went up to his floor.

He felt light-headed when he walked in the company offices. Could all this be happening so fast all at the same time? He had just overcome the nightmare of losing Maggie. He hoped things would eventually settle down into a normal routine with Adam home. Now he stiffened at the thought that perhaps he was entering into another nightmare. He leaned against the wall, trying to breathe deeply and calmly, telling himself he had to be strong and not give way to panic. He was an adult and he needed to shoulder all these responsibilities. As much as he hated relying on his sister-in-law, he was grateful for her support. He wasn't alone.

As Bruce steadied his nerves and began to feel more normal, Gwen spotted him.

"Oh, thank God you're here, Bruce!" she exclaimed with a ready smile. "Hold on, I'll take your sandwich out of the refrigerator." She hurried to the kitchen, clicking the floor with her high heels. Bruce wondered how she was able to move so fast. Maggie could never wear high heels. She used to say it was like walking on stilts.

As he smiled to himself at the memory, a hand grasped his shoulder.

"Good to see you. Just in time, Bruce. The client's coming in fifteen minutes. While you're eating your sandwich, go over with your team what you're going to say."

Bruce smiled weakly. He had hoped to contact Adam again before the presentation. No time.

"Let's nail it, Bruce." Dave came over with a closed fist as if he were coaching a football team. "If we get a contract, we're all goin' to move up the ladder."

Gwen shot past Dave to give Bruce his sandwich. She tripped as she was about to give it to him. Bruce caught her just in time. Fortunately, the turkey sandwich was still wrapped and it only got a little crushed between their bodies.

"Oh, sorry, Bruce!" Gwen giggled slightly, accentuating her blood-red lipstick and batting her eyelashes with heavy black mascara.

"It's OK, Gwen. Thank you," he said. In an effort to make a show of commitment, Bruce said, "Now let's roll up our sleeves and get to work, shall we?"

◆ ◆ ◆

Igor watched with satisfaction and relief as Sergei lay slumped on the passenger seat. He was so groggy that Igor almost had to carry him to the car after they finished lunch.

He drove to a deserted part of town that had a dilapidated building with boarded-up windows. There he stopped and checked Sergei's pulse.

He was dead.

Goodt! Igor thought. His feeling of accomplishment quickly turned to fear. *How will I dispose of the body?*

Pressing his forehead against the steering wheel, he concentrated on his options.

Bury the body in the ground? No, it would take too much time and someone might see him, especially in broad daylight.

Drive to the shore and throw his body into the Atlantic Ocean? Igor slapped his head. *Someone would certainly spot the body or it would wash up on the shore.*

He tilted his head back and thought. *What about the abandoned building? Who goes in there? It's in an isolated location and far enough from the road where no one will smell the rotting body. At least not for a while.*

He slapped the steering wheel, this time in triumph.

Tonight I will break into that old building and dump the body.

Looking in all directions until satisfied no one was around, Igor drove behind the building and waited.

I wish I could buy a bag to put Sergei into, but I can't risk it. So I wait.

Finally, night fell. It was pitch black outside. Alternating between sitting on a large rock and walking around the car for hours made Igor bored and cranky. He swore and grabbed the side of his cheek where the scar was imprinted. Whenever the weather turned cooler, it was as if his scar came alive with a throbbing pain. Only about a dozen cars had driven on the road. Confident no one would spot him, he took a hammer and flashlight out of his trunk and approached a board that sealed off a window in the back of the abandoned one-story building. He kept hitting it. When it finally gave, there was dusty, dirty charred glass in the window. He turned on the flashlight and surveyed what he could see inside the building. Dozens of rats scurried all over.

Goodt! Igor thought as his lips curled into a victorious smile. *His body will rot away and the rats will finish him off. Perfect!*

He turned off the flashlight and opened the passenger door of his car. Sergei's body felt cool by this time. He appeared as if he were in a deep sleep with his head resting on his chest.

"Goodt night and good-bye, Sergei," Igor chuckled as he unceremoniously dumped his body into the building. He returned to his truck and took out duct tape. As best as he could, he resealed the boards on the window.

Hopefully, no one will come by here anytime soon.

But unbeknownst to him, a teenage couple had quietly driven up and parked twenty feet away. While they made out, the boy glanced at Igor resealing the windows. He made a mental note of it and decided he wouldn't think about it further until tomorrow.

CHAPTER SIXTEEN

MARINA

THE BEAVERS WERE ENTERING THE DAM ONE by one. Adam's eyes were transfixed by the screen. He turned to her and was about to talk about it when the phone rang.

"Wait a minute," he told her, his forefinger pointing up as he lumbered to the phone. Marina sat up, wondering who that could be. It was probably Adam's father. Could it be the police? Her kidnappers? Marina was so engrossed in her fears that she was startled by Adam's cheerful tone. When he returned to the living room, he wore a big smile that encompassed the lower half of his face, and his hands waved. "Guess what, Marina? This is the greatest."

She forced her jaws to loosen and smile, "Oh, what is it, Adam?"

"That was my daddy. He told me my Aunt Judy's comin' over," he declared like a little boy about to receive Christmas presents. "You'll like her, Marina. She's the best aunt in the whole wide world." He put his arms out for emphasis. He plopped on the couch next to her and declared, "I'm so glad you're here and

Aunt Judy's coming over! I hope we can do this every day!" His eyes grew more serious and Marina detected fear in his eyes. "Please don't leave me, Marina! I want you to stay and not leave me like my mommy and Heidi did."

She stared but failed to come up with words to respond. When the TV show's narrator said the word "dam," he turned his head immediately back to the program.

He turned to Marina. Her eyes grew large as she waited to hear what he wanted to say.

He lifted his forefinger. "Mommy always told me not to use the word 'damn' 'cause it's not a nice word," he explained soberly. "But when you talk 'bout beavers, you can say the word 'dam' 'cause that's what their homes are called."

Marina's eyes looked more normal. "I understand what you mean, Adam. Of course."

"My mommy don't like curse words. She says it ain't nice," Adam said, but he put his hand near his mouth and whispered in her ear, "But sometimes my daddy uses curse words. Mommy says he shouldn't. It ain't nice, but sometimes he's real angry when he comes home from work. Mommy says when Daddy gets angry, she'll allow it."

"I see," Marina said, grinning despite her fears.

They continued watching the show. Adam turned his gaze to her and noticed Marina looking down and rubbing her palms together. He watched her and when she saw him staring, she spoke.

"Adam," she said slowly, "what are you and your father going to eat for supper tonight?"

"Mmmm," he said, putting his hand on his chin. "I don't know. Last night I made mac 'n' cheese." Suddenly, his eyes brightened. "I think I'm gonna try psghetti and sauce tonight."

"You make supper, Adam. I'm impressed," she said. "What kind of meals do you usually make?"

Adam looked at her sideways. It appeared he wasn't sure what "impressed" meant, but it sounded good. "I make mac 'n' cheese, grilled cheese, and psghetti," he said, sitting taller as he named them on his fingers. "And peanut butter 'n' jelly and bagel 'n' butter."

"What about meat? Do you eat meat?"

"Nah. We go to restaurants if we wanna eat meat. My mommy knows how to make meat, but we don't."

Upon hearing his words, Marina wracked her brain trying to think of dishes she used to make. She always made quick meals for herself. She wasn't fond of cooking and most often she did not have time to follow recipes. But what could she make for them tonight? What did they already have in the refrigerator?

"So, Adam, you don't keep meat here in the house?"

"Nah . . . but we do now 'cause Daddy likes to grill out in warm weather."

"Can I see what you have?"

"Sure."

While the beavers nestled in their dam on the river, Marina, picking up her robe so it wouldn't drag on the ground, got up and went to the kitchen. Adam followed her. In the freezer she saw a big chunk of hamburger. Frozen solid.

"Adam, let's see what I can do with this meat," she said as she turned to him. "Is that all right?"

"Sure," Adam said with a wide smile. "We can make somethin' together."

Marina took the hamburger out and placed it on the kitchen counter. While staring at it, she grabbed chunks of her hair in despair. *What nice Moldovan meat dishes does my mother make? What recipes have I tried on my own? Damn! If only I could retrieve that recipe book my mother gave me one Christmas from my apartment in Chişinău.*

She looked over at Adam. He returned to watch the show about beavers, and now he lay on his stomach on the couch trying to mimic the beavers when they swam to their dam. She was relieved he didn't see her distress.

The phone rang.

"Adam, pick it up. It must be your father," she told him.

Adam untangled himself and lumbered to the phone.

"Hi, Daddy," he said. His eyebrows creased and then he burst into another wide smile. "Hi, Aunt Judy. It's my Aunt Judy," he exclaimed.

Marina tried to smile, happy she had a momentary distraction from thinking about recipes.

I might as well wash the meat in warm water, she thought. *That much I remember.*

"Wow, Aunt Judy. That'll be great!" Adam exclaimed, bouncing and raising his fist before flapping his free hand. "And you can meet my new friend. Her name's Marina," he explained as she took a break from trying to defrost the frozen meat. The shock of cold on her hands was too much. "She's living with us now. You'll like her a lot, Aunt Judy. She likes nature shows too."

Adam listened on the phone, then said, "I dunno her last name."

He listened one more minute and then said, "See ya tonight. I love you."

He hung up the phone and bounced in excitement. "My Aunt Judy's comin' here in a few minutes and she's bringin' her meatloaf. It's delicious. You'll love my Aunt Judy, Marina."

Marina felt an incredible weight lifted off her shoulders. There would already be a meal! But she felt obligated to do something. "Ahh, Adam, do you have lettuce?"

"Lettuce?"

"I would like to make a salad . . . for tonight, you see."

"Yeah, let's make a salad."

After the show about beavers was over, Adam sat at the kitchen table and observed Marina washing the lettuce in the sink. She washed each leaf separately and then placed it in a paper towel before putting it onto a plate. Adam forgot about helping and instead kept turning around to glimpse out the window to see if his daddy's or Aunt Judy's car was driving up near the house. "You and my Aunt Judy are goin' be here for suppa," he exclaimed as he turned from the window and turned toward Marina. "It's goin' be so much better than when just me an' Daddy are here." His smile turned to sulking while he was watching Marina cut up tomatoes.

"What's wrong, Adam?" she asked, studying him.

"I don't wanna go back to work and stampin', stampin', stampin'," he said, making the motions on the kitchen table. "Why can't every day be like this?" he whined as he placed one elbow on the table with his chin in his palm and his other hand waving in the air. He bit his shirt as he thought about this.

Behind him he heard a car driving up.

"It's Aunt Judy!" he announced, jumping out of his chair so fast it jolted back and forth like a seesaw. He opened the front door and reached his arms out wide, ready to enclose them on his aunt, but she was carrying a large Pyrex loaf pan.

"Hi, Adam. I'd hug you but I've got a lot in my hands."

"I can help, Aunt Judy."

"No, no," she said with widened eyes as she clutched the pan tighter. "I'll just hold this straight so nothing topples over."

"You can meet my friend now, Aunt Judy. Her name's Marina," Adam said, bouncing up and down and flapping his hands.

"I'm so anxious to meet your new friend," Aunt Judy said. As Adam led her into the house, Marina noticed the aunt's face was frozen in worry.

"This is my Aunt Judy, Marina," Adam said when he held the door open for her. He closed the screen door too quickly and it hit his aunt's bottom as she walked in. Instead of saying hello, Judy just stared open-mouthed.

"Hello. Nice to meet you." Marina lifted Bruce's dark blue robe and came over to greet her in an attempt to break the ice.

Judy remembered her manners.

"Hello, I'm Judy Hitchens. It's so nice to meet you."

"Let me . . . let me take the pan and put it on the counter," Marina said. She looked scared and she was awkwardly holding up the robe. "Adam and I were making a salad for dinner."

"My, that . . . robe is too big for you," Judy blurted out.

"She's wearin' Daddy's robe 'cause he doesn't want Marina to wear Mommy's clothes," Adam explained.

Judy stepped back, her mouth open in shock. She was still holding the meatloaf.

"What . . . what did you say, Adam?"

"Aunt Judy, don't be upset. Marina came here wit dirty

clothes and she needed some new clothes. I gave her Mommy's pants and shirt, but Daddy did not want her to wear them," Adam smiled, looking at his aunt and expecting her to understand.

Judy recovered herself to hand Marina the pan and said, "How's this, I also made a salad, a spinach, egg, and onion salad, a different one than you and Adam made. It's in the car." Her hands gestured to the Mercedes SUV parked outside. "I'll bring it in. I also have an outfit that I picked up from the dry cleaners for my daughter. Why . . . why don't you change into that? You two are about the same size. You'll be much more comfortable."

"Are you sure that'll be all right?" Marina asked as she looked at the expertly crafted meatloaf and perfectly mashed potatoes with a pool of brown gravy at the top.

"Absolutely." Judy crossed and uncrossed her palms for emphasis. She turned to Adam. "Adam, will you help me bring in the dress?"

"Sure, Aunt Judy." He was about to run out the door when his aunt said, "Wait, honey."

He stopped.

"It's covered in plastic, but try not to get it on the ground. Carry it with both hands like this," she gestured as if she were carrying a toddler.

"Sure, Aunt Judy. Let's go."

Marina loved the simple yet elegant black dress. She whispered a prayer of Thanksgiving: sparkling gold buttons dotted the top of the dress, which had sleeves that covered her elbows sufficiently to conceal the patchwork of injection marks on her upper arms. Anyone who saw them would be shocked; Bruce and Judy would be convinced she was a drug addict. Changing in the bathroom, Marina kept examining the sleeves until her mind was at ease the marks weren't visible. She wanted to twirl around, but there was not enough room in the bathroom. She was still so thin that she could almost see her veins sticking out. The dress would have fit perfectly if she were her normal weight—it was now a little too big. But nevertheless, she felt reborn wearing it—more like her old self when she used to wear attractive clothes and feel confident. She remembered the compliments she used to receive whenever she dressed up.

Will those days of normal, everyday living ever come back? she wondered as she stared at herself in the mirror. *Or will I forever be damaged?*

As she was engrossed in these thoughts, Marina absent-mindedly opened a drawer in the bathroom. She found a wide-bristled brush still in its package. She rubbed her hand against the bristles, something she hadn't done in a long time. She couldn't put it down. Marina couldn't resist: she opened the package and felt the bristles without the plastic cover. It relaxed her; a normal part of her old life before being kidnapped was brushing her hair every morning. She delicately tried brushing her straight brown hair and unknotting the many strands. She looked back in the mirror. Marina looked more like herself now.

She felt guilty but she opened still another drawer. She found toothpaste. Her captives made sure she brushed her teeth and her breath smelled like mint, particularly before sleeping with men. As she squeezed toothpaste onto her finger and rubbed it against her teeth, she felt liberated knowing she was brushing on her own accord; no one was ordering her to. Marina rinsed her mouth when she heard a knock at the door.

She stood up straight, startled. "Yes," she said hurriedly.

"Marina, my daddy's here, and Aunt Judy said suppa's almost ready." She heard Adam's voice behind the door. "Aunt Judy wants to know if the dress's OK."

"It's perfect, Adam. I'll be right out."

She took one last glance in the mirror, not looking quite like her old self yet but a definite improvement.

As she came out of the bathroom, she heard Adam announce, "Aunt Judy, I'm gonna wash my hands."

"Oh, I'm so glad you want to be clean. I always have to remind my kids to wash their hands, still," Judy told him. Marina could hear her setting the plates on the table as she took silverware out of a drawer.

When Marina walked into the kitchen, she looked up from setting the table. "Much better," she surveyed her with approval. "Is it comfortable? It looks too big."

"It's wonderful. Thank you so much for letting me borrow it. I feel so much better," Marina answered, trying not to look down in shame. She knew the woman did not mean to be hurtful when she remarked it looked too big. She had no idea what she had gone through.

Adam was at the sink. Judging from the almost-empty dishwashing liquid and the big ball of suds on his hands, he was spending too much time washing his hands.

"Adam, Adam, whoa. Enough with washing the hands," Judy told him gently as she took silverware out of the drawer.

"Let me finish setting the table. Please." Marina hurriedly walked over and Judy handed her the silverware.

❖ ❖ ❖

Moscow

The city of Moscow had become more cosmopolitan and upscale over the past few years. Russian millionaires launched businesses, mostly in the technological field, which made many feel they had a chance at improving their lives for themselves and their families.

But not all the populace of the city of Moscow enjoyed the fruits of prosperity. In different sections were still those who had a long way to go. These areas were filled with seedy bars, rundown apartments, and garbage everywhere. Most Muscovites chose to ignore these areas when extolling the virtues of their city, hoping these parts would transform sooner rather than later.

Here lived those who did not have the luxury of skills training, education, or the benefit of connections. These unfortunate ones wandered the city in search of menial, low-paying jobs. Those who managed to find them struggled in substandard living conditions. Adding to their difficulties was the ugly old problem in Russia: alcoholism. The bars were always full in the late afternoons and evenings where those who felt disenfranchised and left behind poured their frustrations out into numerous glasses of vodka, which damaged their wallets as well as their livers. There they found the solace of companionship. Many people, particularly the young in the prime of their lives, would wander the streets during the day searching for work and toward the end find their way into one of the many local bars.

In an abandoned warehouse, a basement contained hidden rooms which housed a full-fledged organization led by the notorious Andre Sokolov, head of the largest human trafficking ring in Moscow. He and his men had managed to evade the authorities for many years. Right now their most pressing concern was the absence of Igor and Sergei in New Jersey.

"What are you worried about? They're just two nobodies who disappeared," Vladimir Bok, Andre's right-hand man, told Andre.

"Everyone has to be accounted for," Andre snapped. "Every employee and every girl we kidnap! The smallest mistake could bring down my whole empire!" He turned to face his employee. "Any moment the authorities could discover us and have our heads!"

Vladimir gulped. He knew Andre was right. "So we need to send someone to find them."

Andre nodded.

"I will assign one of our most capable men."

At this Andre faced him with his dark glasses and shouted, "No! We need some fresh blood to do this. Our men have gotten too complacent, too comfortable." He pointed his finger up. "Go to one of the bars," he ordered. "Someone strong, someone desperate, even a little crazy. He'll do the job for us and then we decide whether we'll keep him or kill him."

CHAPTER SEVENTEEN

BRUCE

BRUCE COULDN'T STOP SMILING. HE FELT LIKE dancing. He was making a comeback.

Maybe I should think of myself as "the comeback guy," he thought giddily.

The presentation was such a success that the client made an offer immediately. Dave just sat there. He couldn't even get a word in.

Serves him right, that greedy young upstart! He thought I was down and he made a stab for my job. Not so fast, Davey boy!

"Excellent job, Bruce. Are you back on track!" Gwen came over and gave him a wet kiss as she enfolded her arms around his shoulders.

"Congratulations, Bruce. Way to go! I'll remember this when I give out Christmas bonuses!" his boss Steve said, shaking his hand warmly.

Other people congratulated him and patted him on the back. He hadn't felt so happy in a long time.

When the crowd dispersed, Steve came up to him. "Hey,

Bruce. Let me take you out for a late lunch—Il Michelangelo."

Bruce's eyes lit up. He was about to say yes when he remembered Adam was home with the woman his son claimed was his friend. He looked at his watch with a downcast face and said, "Can I have a rain check on that, Steve? I've got to get home."

"Ohhh," Steve said, shaking his head. "Of course, Bruce. I almost forgot. You get home to your son."

After Steve shook his hand again and returned to his office, Bruce headed for the men's room to call Adam.

His dialing was interrupted when Dave entered the men's room.

"Great job, Bruce," he said, flashing his white teeth in a boyish grin.

"Thanks, Dave." He tried to smile.

"You know, we're all real happy for you."

Bullshit, Bruce thought.

"Why, I appreciate that, Dave."

"No, really. You've gone through the ringer lately and I admire your ability to perform so well when you're under so much stress."

"Have a good dinner, Dave. You did a lot of fine work yourself. I can't take all the credit," Bruce said.

"Thanks, Bruce."

With that, Dave left.

Maybe that kid isn't so bad. So what if he's always complaining he'll never be able to pay back his student loans? Maybe I was just imagining him dropping hints that he needs my job to finally be solvent.

As he thought about this, he remembered to take out his phone again.

"Allo, Daddy?"

His eyebrows furrowed and his jovial expression turned serious. "Is everything all right over there, son?"

"Yeah, it's great, Daddy. Guess who's comin' over and bringin' meatloaf?"

"It sounds like your Aunt Judy," Bruce said, cracking a smile.

So I'll get a delicious meal after all, Bruce thought, amazed at his good fortune.

"And how's Mary?"

"Who's Mary?"

"I mean . . . I mean Marian," he stammered.

"Marina, Daddy. Her name's Marina."

"Of course. Marina. How's Marina? I-Is she still there?" Bruce asked as he closed his eyes. *How did my life get so complicated?*

"Yeah, Daddy, she's still here. And guess what?"

Bruce froze for a moment in sheer terror. "What, Adam?" he demanded.

"We made a salad for suppa," he declared proudly.

Bruce let out a deep breath. He smiled in an attempt to regain his light mood. "That's great, son. I'm coming home now."

"Okay, Daddy. Seeya," Adam said before he hung up.

Bruce slowly put his cell phone back in his jacket pocket. On his way back to his office, Steve was standing by his door.

"Bruce, this was such a success that we must celebrate a little now. Come into my office and we'll share a drink. A vintage wine I only take out on special occasions."

Bruce's mouth curled into a smile. "OK. A small celebration would be nice."

Everything's quiet at home. Judy's coming. I'm entitled to a little celebration.

Steve held the door to his office for Bruce. "Take a seat." He pointed to his brown leather couch. "It's a Bodegas Contador I bought in Spain a few years ago. Sound good?"

"Sure," Bruce said as he loosened his tie a bit.

"You know, this deal is going to boost the production numbers of the company," he told Bruce as he poured two shot glasses. "Our investors were getting worried there. The heat was on. You know what I mean?"

"I sure do," Bruce said as he took a glass. "Thank you."

In my life the heat is always on, he thought.

Steve raised his glass. "To my always dependable manager, Bruce Hitchens. May his star and the star of this company go higher and we all enjoy better times ahead."

"Here, here," Bruce said, raising his glass with bright eyes and a smile expressing an inner joy he hadn't experienced in a long time.

Steve drained his glass, then sat down comfortably on the couch.

"We need more people like you, Bruce," his boss told him. "You have thorough knowledge of whatever you're explaining when you make your presentations. It grabs our clients and makes them feel respected when you clearly explain your reasoning and patiently answer their questions." Shaking his head, he added, "And man, do you have a way with words!" He looked up in the air for a moment and said, "From what I remember, you were a business administration major. How did a guy like you end up with such writing talent?"

"My minor was English." Bruce's eyes sparkled and he couldn't help feeling his cheeks turn red. He clearly enjoyed the praise, particularly since he had always felt overlooked. "The year after I graduated college, I was writing what I thought would be a best seller while looking for a job."

"And what was the book about?" Steve asked, staring intently at Bruce. He was genuinely curious.

"Technology. I wanted to combine my passion for technology and writing. I had plans to try to get published, but when I found my first job, I became so consumed with it that the book was left only half written." Bruce felt an inner satisfaction, remembering how his younger brother Matt and his father used to scoff at the idea of Bruce making money from writing.

"Forget your romantic notions about being a writer!" His father gritted his teeth as he pointed at Bruce. "You'll never get anywhere! You'll end up in a homeless shelter!" His father shook his head. "My son the writer, living in the sewer!" He chuckled at his own joke.

"I only develop my writing skills for business purposes," Matt chimed in. "Bruce, how many people have told you that the odds of getting published are slim to none?"

"That's right." His father nodded his head approvingly at Matt. "Just try to get a good job and a regular paycheck. No woman's ever going to marry a man who wants to get rich from writing a book. Hah!" He laughed at the thought of it.

"You don't understand," Bruce was almost pleading with them. "I want to go into technology, but having a book under my belt will improve my job prospects!"

"Ahhhh . . ." His father waved his hand and shook his head in disgust.

"What career, Bruce? You're looking for an entry-level job! It's time to check back into reality, brother."

"Writing a book is a huge potential asset!" Bruce insisted, but his argument sounded hollow even to his own ears.

"I'm interested in seeing your writing. If it's anything like your presentations, I'll be bowled over," his boss interrupted Bruce's thoughts.

"Ahhh, yes, but . . . ," Bruce started.

"Did you save your work?" his boss asked, eyebrows going up as he leaned forward to hear his reply.

"Oh, yes. I just have to look for it." Bruce went through the house in his mind, trying to remember where he had left it. He glanced up at the clock.

"Ah, Bruce, you need to go now. Sorry I kept you so long. If you have time and can find your writing, please bring it in. I'm curious to see what you came up with." Steve put his glass down on the nearby table. "We may be able to update it and use it for the company."

"All right, Steve. No problem." Bruce attempted a weak smile.

He had always thought about throwing the manuscript away but never could. Maggie had always encouraged him to write and loved hearing him practice his presentations in front of her. She would sit and listen to him with a wide, girlish smile, as if she had nabbed the star player on the high school football team.

Steve rose, signaling their short celebration was over. He reached out his hand and Bruce quickly stood up and shook it.

"And just do me another favor, Bruce?" he asked.

Oh no! What could this other favor be about? I should dig up a report from high school?

"Sure, Steve. Name it."

"You and your son—Adam, that's his name?"

Bruce nodded, trying to ignore his rapidly beating heart.

"You two have a relaxing evening—and then look for your writing," Steve said, winking.

"Will do, Steve. You have a great evening yourself."

As Bruce headed toward his car in the parking lot, his mind reverted back to those images of his father and brother dismissing his plans for the future. Even as he savored the fruits of his recent achievement, the past claimed a stranglehold on his confidence.

The bumbling, troublesome big brother.

He wallowed in these self-defeating thoughts for a moment when his head shot up again.

Adam is alone with Marina now. I'd better get home and think about past discouragements another time.

When he pulled up beside his house, his shoulders relaxed upon seeing Judy's Mercedes parked in the driveway.

Bruce walked in, looking around. Marina caught his eye. She wore a striking black dress that he didn't recognize. He brightened when he saw her; he saw her as a person now rather than a potential danger. Bruce nodded to her quickly and then turned his attention away to Adam and Aunt Judy.

"Adam." He went over to his son and examined him. "Is everything all right?"

"Yeah, Daddy." Adam was bubbling over. "Marina and Aunt Judy are here and we're all goin' to eat suppa together. Aunt Judy's made a meatloaf, and me an' Marina made a salad."

"Hi, Bruce," Aunt Judy said as she took the meatloaf out of the oven. "Just in time for dinner. How was your day?"

As Judy spoke, she kept glancing at Marina.

"Today was great. My presentation went really well." He grinned. Then he glanced at Marina. "Judy, you've probably met Marina."

"Oh yes, I did," she said, smiling at the young woman.

"Adam told me she's his new friend. I'm anxious to hear how they met."

Bruce's body tightened up. "To tell you the truth, so am I. I trust they'll explain it all to us at dinner."

"Sure, Daddy." Adam bounced and smiled, flapping his hands.

Bruce was grateful for Judy being there and making dinner, but he wished she wasn't there while he was finding out about Marina's story. At the same time, Judy provided him with a buffer of protection—he would later ask her what she thought about all this and what he should do. He didn't want to be the only one to witness her story.

He looked at the perfectly set table. "Adam, did you set the table?"

"I was gonna, but Aunt Judy said she'd do it." He pointed with one hand to the living room and flapped with the other. "I made the tapes on the table nice 'n' neat, but Aunt Judy says some of 'em broke." He breathed heavily as he spoke to his father. "What're we goin' do, Daddy? What're we goin' do?"

Bruce waved his hand in dismissal. "I'll buy you new DVDs … um, tapes, Adam. Not a problem. How did they get broken?" He tensed suddenly.

Adam shrugged his shoulders and there was silence. Finally Marina spoke up.

"I think Adam may have dropped them on the table accidentally. It's my fault . . . I asked him for something and he got distracted."

Marina's voice was grave.

"It's OK," was all Bruce said, but he wondered if the table was damaged as well.

I've got too much on my plate to worry about that, he thought.

There was an uneasy silence for a moment. Then Judy broke it by announcing, "Everyone, sit down for dinner."

Bruce sat across from Judy, and Adam and Marina sat on the remaining sides. As Bruce sat down, he remembered Maggie voicing her disappointment that they didn't have a dining room. He looked at them squeezed in tight at the kitchen table. Only the meatloaf could be on the table. The salads and other sides had to be placed on the counter because of lack of room. It struck him that Maggie was completely right.

He forced himself to brush off that memory as Judy served him meatloaf, mashed potatoes with gravy, her spinach salad, and Marina and Adam's green salad.

"It's my Dutch meatloaf," Judy said as she continued serving the others. "I hope everyone likes it."

"I love Aunt Judy's food," Adam said as his eyes seized upon the plate of food in front of him. His arms were flapping.

Bruce put down his fork. "Judy, did you make this for your family and bring it over here instead?"

"To be honest, I did. But my kids called me and told me they were staying late to watch a football game, so I brought it over here. Don't be upset, Bruce," she told him as she touched his arm. "They're not crazy about my meatloaf anyway. I just felt like making it to give myself something to do. So you," and she looked at Adam and Marina, "and everyone else enjoy."

"We couldn't get better food in a fine restaurant," Bruce declared, slowly picking up his fork again. The success of the presentation buoyed his spirits, but he knew he had to get to the bottom of how Marina had come here. He decided everyone should eat first, enjoy, and then talk.

Adam told everyone about the beavers while he quickly ate.

"Slow down, Adam." Bruce touched his arm. "The food's not going anywhere."

Everyone finished and complimented Judy and Marina. Marina looked down in acknowledgment of their praises while Judy flushed from the joy of hearing her cooking so highly thought of.

"I wish my own family would bother to pay me a few compliments on my cooking once in a while," she said in a bittersweet voice as she played with her fork. Looking up, she said, "I only wish I had time to make dessert."

"Aunt Judy, you're the best cooker in the world, and I can hug you because you're my family." Adam got up and enclosed his aunt in a bear hug.

Bruce opened his mouth to add to his son's praises, but a fast-approaching car interrupted his train of thought.

A BMW sedan came screeching to a halt in front of the house.

Marina froze open-mouthed and ready to bolt.

Bruce stood up. "What in the world?"

Getting up to glance out the window, Judy turned to Marina. "Now you'll get to meet my children."

"Oh, I'm looking forward to it," Marina said as she recovered from her shock.

Sarah, David, and Danielle all got out of the car. They all looked hot and tired, their lips in a thin line.

They all look like Matt when he's pissed. Bruce chuckled to himself while keeping an outward serious demeanor.

One rang the bell continuously and another pounded on the door as Judy got up to answer it.

Before she could say a word, Sarah spoke, "Mom, you forgot to bring your cell phone with you again! We had a feeling you'd be here. The football game ended early. And Dartmouth College called. You didn't put down a deposit for me and the deadline is tomorrow! And I couldn't find anything to eat." She was tall, slender, and perfectly coiffed, wearing light makeup, a sleeveless white T-shirt, and a tailored yellow miniskirt. She wore her hair in a ponytail with virtually no hairs out of place.

"And Mom, why didn't you make supper? There's nothing in the refrigerator," David added in a huff.

"But you said you were all going out for pizza," Judy protested.

"I spent all my cash gassing up my car and there's no money left in my bank account! Sarah didn't have enough in her account either." He wore designer jeans with holes in them and a white shirt with Ralph Lauren printed on the front. David wore expensive designer sunglasses, but Bruce didn't recognize the brand.

"Here's where all the food is." Danielle pointed with her chin at the remainder of the dinner on the table. She turned to her mother with veiled eyes. "It looks real good, Mom." Danielle put on a friendlier face when she realized everyone at the table was staring at her. "We tried to find Uncle Bruce's phone number but couldn't." She was slightly pudgy in rather plain, loose-fitting jeans and shirt. The only makeup she had on was lipstick that was too dark for her fair complexion. She wore her long brown hair loose with a headband.

"Sorry, kids. My number's unlisted." Bruce barely got his sentence in.

"And Dad called," David said as he leaned his slender frame

on the hallway wall, ignoring his uncle. "He's coming home tonight. Late."

Judy's jaw opened wide. "Tonight?"

"Hi, kids. Nice to see you." Bruce smiled and waved.

They all stared in his direction. Finally, they mumbled, "Hi, Uncle Bruce."

"Hey, Adam." David touched his back. "How's my main man doing?"

"I am fine. I watched a show 'bout beavers with Marina," he said enthusiastically, unaware of the tension in the air. "Can all of you and Uncle Matt come over for suppa tomorrow night? We'll have a great meal."

"If my mom's making it, I bet we will," Danielle sneered and Sarah elbowed her.

Then all eyes focused on Marina.

"This is my new friend, Marina. My cousins Sarah, David, and Danielle," Adam proudly pointed to each one.

"It's so nice to meet you," Marina said, trying to smile.

"Wow. Where did you two meet?" David opened his eyes wide in surprise and grinned. "I'd like to meet a friend like that, too." He tousled Adam's hair. "Good job, cous."

"I have a black dress just like that," Sarah remarked, studying it.

"Marina needed something to wear and Aunt Judy let her borrow it," Adam declared. "Aunt Judy is so nice."

Sarah and Danielle stared open-mouthed while David smirked and said, "Whah! I'm hanging around with Adam from now on."

Before anyone could say anything more, Sarah's cell phone buzzed. "Hi, Dad. We're all at Uncle Bruce's . . . Yeah, we know you're coming home in four hours. Here's Mom." Sarah handed the phone to her mother.

"Hi, honey. I wasn't expecting you back for a few days. How was your trip?" Judy said cheerfully. Her smile disappeared as she listened to her husband.

"Don't worry, Matt. I'll have something whipped up for you by the time you get home . . . Yes, yes . . . I know you're exhausted. You have all of tonight and tomorrow to rest . . . yes, yes, see you later." Judy closed the phone and sat back in the chair, closing her eyes. "Matt says hi to everyone."

"Where did he go this time, Judy? Was it Thailand?" Bruce asked inquisitively.

"South Korea," she replied, her eyes remaining closed. "Getting the account didn't go as well as he expected, but they agreed to a smaller amount."

"Well that's good. That was a big trip." Bruce turned to Marina and explained, "My brother has a big company. He travels all around the world." *Unlike me, he's a somebody,* he added to himself.

"Yeah, and now he's tired and cranky, Mom." Sarah looked over at Marina. "Did you give her that? If you did, I'll have to buy another one."

"Oh, no! I will clean it and give it back to you. I'm so sorry." Marina turned red and looked like she was about to cry.

But Sarah softened and waved her hand. "Don't worry about it. I'll buy another one."

"It actually looks real nice on you," Danielle added upon seeing her distress.

"Thank you," she said gratefully.

"Well, I really enjoyed our dinner together." Judy opened

her eyes, sat up, and attempted to smile. "It was lovely meeting you, Marina."

Judy got up to clear away the dishes when Marina took them from her. "It's OK. I'll clean up. It was nice meeting you and your wonderful family."

Judy gave her the dishes, gratified.

"Thank you, Judy. You came through, as always, but we really have to stop bothering you so much. You have a family of your own." Bruce got up and gave her a small peck on the cheek.

Judy waved her hand. "Call me when you need me, and if I can help you, I will."

"Say hi to Matt for me."

"Aunt Judy, you're the best. I wished you lived next door," Adam said, bouncing up and hugging his aunt.

Despite being initially bothered their mother was here, Judy's three children couldn't help smiling. David shook Bruce's hand, and Sarah and Danielle kissed him on the cheek. The girls shook Adam's hand—they could never get it straight when it was all right to hug and kiss him or not.

"Slap me five, buddy," David said.

"Ah, David, wait . . . ," Bruce began.

But it was too late. Adam slapped David's hand so hard he almost keeled over in pain.

"Adam," Bruce said through gritted teeth, "how many times do I have to tell you to stop slapping so hard?"

"Daddy, I forgot," Adam said, looking frightened and biting his shirt.

"Adam, what do you say?"

"Sorry," Adam said dolefully, staring at the ground.

David rubbed his hand and flexed it in and out. "It's all

right," he replied. "I should have remembered what a strong dude you are."

A smiling Judy kissed Bruce, Adam, and Marina, and said good-bye, her kids trailing behind her.

◆ ◆ ◆

Hearing Vladimir walk down the creaky basement steps of his secret office, Andre reached for his phone and checked his messages for a third time. Nothing from either Igor or Sergei. He looked around at his sparsely furnished office with wood furniture and aqua blue mosaic floors. He tapped his gold pen on his gleaming natural wood desk. He took off his big dark glasses for a moment; he concealed his face whenever anyone entered his office. He always wore impeccable, top-of-the-line suits: Gucci, Versace, Brooks Brothers. On his left arm he wore a Rolex watch. Finding no new messages, he hung up.

Sergei would not desert him—he loved the travel, the money, raping the victims. But Igor was a wild card, especially since one of the victims slashed him and he was left with a scar. Andre had planned to eliminate him after this last venture; he sat back and sighed. He should have gotten rid of him as soon as that incident occurred, but he had been too concerned about their voyage and the sale of the women. He now realized he had no choice but to hire someone new to find them. His men and resources were already being maximized all over Europe. He had to wait.

Vladimir arrived at Andre's office as soon as he was summoned. Vladimir was physically Andre's smallest employee and appeared nonthreatening to the casual observer. But appearances could be deceiving, particularly in his case. Beneath his long, thick, dark sweater and pants, Vladimir had muscles of steel. He had served Andre the longest of all his employees and was by far the smartest. If there was anyone Andre relied on the most, it was the unassuming short, thin man who stood before him.

Vladimir stood before Andre's desk in his dark, well-hidden office that resembled a dark, ominous cave. Even he did not sit down until Andre told him he could. Once seated, Vladimir got right down to business.

"No word about either one," Vladimir said in his clipped Russian.

Andre waved his hand in disgust. "Igor is dead, or soon will be, once we find him." He paused. "How is the search going to find them? Once they are found and done away with, let's hope that same man is competent enough to replace the two of them." He leaned his tall, massive body toward Vladimir and fixed his concealed eyes on his employee. "You haven't told me about possible candidates."

Here Vladimir was at an advantage. He had tried unsuccessfully to convince Andre that neither Sergei nor Igor was a good fit: one was a good-time lightweight while the other was just crazy. But Andre could not be persuaded; he hired them because he owed favors to some contacts who helped him in a pinch. One of them had insisted on him hiring these men. In a rare occasion, Andre failed to keep in mind that the weakest employees had the potential to bring down his entire operation. This time he allowed Vladimir sole authority to make the hiring decision; Vladimir's instincts were usually right on target.

"I have carefully screened potential men. Anyone with serious charges on their record are immediately dropped from consideration—we don't need any potential conflicts with the police. I also test how strong they are emotionally—what are their idiosyncrasies, their weaknesses. I don't want any more screw-ups."

Andre winced at the last statement. If anyone but Vladimir would have criticized his choices so blatantly, they would have lived to regret it, depending on how useful they were. A less important employee may not even be allowed to live but would instead be "discovered" dead in another city for insulting the great and mighty Andre.

"There is someone I'm considering," Vladimir continued. "He is brave, at times recklessly so. He is physically strong, no question, and is known to get along with others. He also has no trouble inflicting pain upon others whenever necessary. And," he added, raising his finger, "he also possesses something most of our men lack."

Intrigued, Andre asked, "And what is that?"

Vladimir smiled confidently, as if he had just made a crucial move in a chess game. "He doesn't look like a mean, ugly thug. He can be quite charming. He's a sharp dresser and a handsome man. These traits can prove to be useful for us."

By now, Andre sat back stunned by this man's description. He asked the obvious question, "So why does he need to get involved in human trafficking?"

"Ah," Vladimir said as if he were impressed by an unusually sharp student. "It is well-known that his father terrorized his family, raped his daughters, and abused his wife." Vladimir leaned forward. "The father is dead, but his son is alive and well. And also a psychopath."

CHAPTER EIGHTEEN

MARINA

MARINA PROCEEDED TO PUT ALL THE PLATES, silverware, glasses, and pots in the sink and got ready to wash everything.

Bruce stood behind her.

"Marina," he said softly,

She turned around.

"I'm going to get Adam ready for bed and then we can talk."

"All right." Marina nodded. She turned around and began washing the dishes, her body tensing up again, not knowing what would happen now.

What will he say? Will he try to get rid of me? She looked outside. It was already dark. She tried not to shake as she washed, but in her head she yearned to scream in panic.

She turned around quickly as if she felt someone right behind her.

"Good night, Marina," Adam said, waving at her. "Today was a fun day. Will you stay here tomorrow?"

His head bobbed forward as he stared at her earnestly.

He began waving his hands in the air while he waited for her answer.

Staring helplessly at him, Marina didn't know what to say.

"Son, you'll see Marina in the morning. It's time to shower and get ready for bed," Bruce said as he came over to collect Adam. He did not look at her. Her shoulders relaxed as she realized he would not throw her out tonight.

"Good night, dear," she said to Adam like an affectionate mother to her child. "Thank you for everything. Sleep well." She felt tears well up in her eyes in gratitude to this man-child who had rescued her. She felt like enwrapping him in a bear hug herself. Instead, she smiled and waved as he waved again.

"Adam, I'm waiting," Bruce called from the bathroom with restrained patience.

Adam walked backward, still smiling and waving as he left the kitchen.

Marina finished washing the dishes and then sat down at the kitchen table. She was tense and exhausted as she waited to find out her fate.

"Wash your arms," she overheard Bruce instructing his son in the shower. "And don't forget your feet."

A few minutes later Bruce helped him brush his teeth.

"Remember the back teeth. Brush the gums, too. Here, let me help you."

Soon she overheard the sound of the razor.

"I want you to shave me, Daddy," Adam whined.

"You know you have to learn how to shave yourself, son. Let's do it hand over hand."

"OK, Daddy, but don't hold my hand too tight," Adam complained.

"I'm only guiding you, Adam. The more you try to shave yourself, the less I'll have to guide your hand. Eighteen-year-old young men have to shave their own beards."

Marina could hear the exasperation in the father's voice.

After spending many hours with him, she concluded that Adam had autism. She remembered seeing an article and hearing discussions on autism in Moldova, but she had never really paid attention. She figured she would look into this more when she got married and thought about starting her own family.

She realized tears were flowing down her cheeks. She looked for tissues as she tried to erase thoughts of having a family of her own. Once she was back in Moldova, Marina would be forced to confront this issue, but right now she was emotionally unable.

I'll need lots of help trying to navigate my way after all this. Images assaulted her of the many months on the ship.

"How did you wind up here?" another young Moldovan woman who had been chained to the bed beside her asked. The woman was sluggish from the drugs and no longer offered resistance when their kidnappers stuck a needle in her arm.

"I was walking to the train in the early morning hours. It was a Sunday morning," Marina recalled. Black and blue marks covered parts of her arms and legs. She was newer and still fought the injections.

The other woman's eyes widened. "You were not promised a job overseas? You were going to meet them?"

"Not at all," Marina replied. She paused a moment, remembering talking to other young women. All were tricked into coming by thinking they were going to be nannies or waitresses overseas.

"My family lives in the country," the woman continued. "Both my parents had been seeking work for many months. They

couldn't find anything. When a neighbor told us about this job for me, it sounded too good to be true," she said bitterly. *"We were so desperate we never bothered to notice the way he always gaped at me up and down, especially my breasts."* She seemed defeated, yet her eyes were dry.

"I can't cry anymore," she said, directing her eyes right at Marina. *"I have no tears left."*

Marina was so lost in thought that she did not hear someone enter the room.

Clearing his throat, he said, "Ah, Marina, can we talk now?"

Marina jumped and nearly fell off her chair.

"I'm sorry. I didn't mean to startle you," Bruce said, backing away, his face turning red.

Still shaking, Marina nodded. When she was finally able to speak, she said, "I'm sorry. I was lost in thought."

"That's OK," Bruce said gently. "Why don't we sit down and you can explain to me how you ended up here with Adam."

Marina nodded and steadied herself. "I suppose it's going to sound crazy."

Bruce took his seat on another chair. "I'm listening. A lot of crazy things happen in this world."

Taking a long, anguished breath, she began, "I was in Chișinău, in Moldova, visiting my boyfriend, who originally came from Moscow . . ."

Bruce held up a hand. "Forgive me for interrupting, but I've never heard of Moldova. I was never good at geography," he admitted. "It must be somewhere near Russia?"

"Yes," Marina responded, choking the words out. "We share a border with Ukraine. We used to be part of the former Soviet Union."

"Ah, now I understand. An Eastern European country." He glanced around. "Let me get you a glass of something to drink. What would you like?" Bruce stood up and headed for the refrigerator.

"Cold water is fine."

"Do you want something stronger? I have wine and beer," he offered.

"Yes, wine would be good," Marina said, brightening at the thought of a drink relaxing her.

"Here you are," he said as he handed it to her. "Go on."

"Thank you." She took the proffered wine and took a few sips before continuing.

"My boyfriend and I had broken up but thought we'd try again. It wasn't working out." She gave a mirthless smile. "He was more fond of vodka than he was of me, so I left him a note at his apartment early, like five o'clock in the morning. We had met his friends at a café the night before and he was still sleeping off a hangover. The morning I left, I decided to walk to the train station alone. I needed time to think and convince myself I was better off without him.

"While I was walking, a man in a black Mercedes got out of his car so fast it was as if he magically appeared right next to me. He spoke in Russian. I speak Romanian and Russian.

Those are the two official languages of Moldova," she explained. "He tried to take my travel bag and offered me a ride. I told him no, but he came nearer and showed me the gun hidden in his coat. It was early in the morning and no one else was out. I tried to resist, searching around for someone to help me, but there was no one.

"Then another man got out of the car with a long knife.

I tried to run away, but the one with the gun said, 'If you scream, you're dead.' I stupidly tried to hit the one with the gun, but he pushed me to the ground. Then the man with the long knife ran over and stuck a needle in my arm, and my body became paralyzed. I couldn't speak, and they quickly carried me into the backseat in their car. By the time they drove off, I was unconscious."

Bruce stared at her while she told him her story. His eyes grew wider in horror as she told him the details. He said nothing. She hoped he believed her and did not think she was making this up. She thirstily drank more wine before she continued. Marina stared at the empty glass of wine and took a moment to savor its calming effect, dulling her senses before going on.

"Do you want something more to drink?" he asked, leaning forward.

Marina shook her head, fearful he would think she was also an alcoholic. She sighed, took a deep breath, and closed her eyes.

"When I finally woke up, I was chained to a bench in a room with about twelve other women. I heard the lapping waves of the ocean outside. We were on a ship. I was still dressed in my street clothes, and the other women wore old, torn shirts and clothes that were too big for them. No one had pillows or blankets. Just dirty, ragged sheets under them, many bloodstained. They were all chained. Some slept, others had blank stares, and the ones that had the strength moaned. Two were dead. The chains were so tight that none of us had much room to move. I kept hoping this was some sort of nightmare and I would wake up and everything would be normal again. I kept closing my eyes and shaking my head to escape this nightmare, but this was reality. Men with alcohol on their breath came in periodically to check on us. They carted off the dead women like trash."

Her lips quivered as she struggled to tell him the worst. She couldn't even look up at Bruce. "Whenever the men came in, all of us were afraid of being taken out individually. That would mean they would rape that woman." She choked on this last sentence, unable to continue for a few moments.

Marina's eyes remained closed. The next part was even harder to talk about. She heard him get up and come back with a small box he pushed toward her. When she realized it was a tissue box, she smiled in gratitude and reached for one to blow her nose.

"They'd bring in pails and brown toilet paper to use when we had to go to the bathroom. Whenever somebody had an accident, the men would slap that woman so hard that she rarely ever had another one. There'd always be a foul odor in the room." Her tears streamed down but she plowed ahead.

"The ship docked in Turkey. They decided who needed to be more drugged and who needed to be unchained and brought out. We screamed and whimpered whenever they came in. At first, I didn't know what was going to happen to us. In about a week, I found out what we were being used for. Before men came, they would take three or four of us out at a time. They would unchain us and give us food to eat—stale bread and cheap, sugary food to give us strength. The kidnappers watched as we took a group shower, soaping our bodies and washing our hair. Then we would brush our teeth. Our kidnappers would have to help us stand up. They even brought out makeup and promised those who put it on would get extra food.

"We became like ravenous animals, doing everything possible to get more food, sometimes even snatching food from other women. We were cleaned up, sat in chairs, and waited as strange men came in and decided who they wanted to sleep with. They spoke as if we weren't even in the room." Marina choked up and had to stop. Her stomach heaved. Wordlessly, Bruce got up and placed more wine in front of her.

She continued, "When the ship docked, I saw my chance to escape. I did not realize they had brought us to America. In the early morning hours, I fled the ship and hid in a nearby truck. The truck began moving and it arrived in Morristown . . . I kept running . . . I didn't know where to go. I ended up outside your house and that is where I met Adam. I must have fainted near your house. . . . When I woke up, he was sleeping against a tree close by. He gave me breakfast and said I was his new friend. After I ate, he let me use his shower and that's when you came home."

Marina stopped, getting choked up. She blew her nose again.

"That's enough for tonight, Marina," he whispered. "I'm going to make up my bed for you. I'll sleep on the couch. You can tell me the rest in the morning."

"Oh, that's all right. I can sleep on the couch," she protested, but he had already risen and headed for his room.

Too drained to protest further, Marina tried to collect her thoughts as she played with the rim of the wine glass.

Was he really allowing her to stay for the night? What'll happen tomorrow?

As she tried to think of what could happen, she fought to keep her eyes open, too tired to even lift the delicate glass. She did not want to fall asleep here on the kitchen table—that would be awkward.

"The bed's ready," he announced. "On the bed there's an old T-shirt of my father's—he was a bigger man—anyway, it should be long enough to be pajamas for you," he said. After a pause he added, "There's a new toothbrush for you in the bathroom." He held sheets and blankets that she guessed he would use to make up the couch. He stood by the door, appearing unsure of what to say or do next.

"I don't want to take your bed. I'll sleep on the couch," she offered, struggling to keep her head up.

When he didn't respond, she gazed up at him. He stared at her.

"It's all right. I don't mind a bit. Good night."

"Good night. Thank you for letting me stay." She stood up and walked past him, smiling at him briefly and then facing the ground.

He continued to stare at her for a moment longer before smiling and readying the couch in the living room.

◆ ◆ ◆

Igor woke up and faced the bathroom mirror in his hotel room with its old, dusty frame, staring at his scar. He turned off his cell phone because Andre kept leaving him messages, telling him he was needed elsewhere.

I can't stop until I find and kill that girl. It will be a slow, agonizing death for her for making me look like a monster.

No matter how much he tried covering it up, that ugly patchwork scar shaped as a half-moon managed to expose itself on his face, up to his jawbone and extending to his neck. Igor had to be careful not to chew much on that side. Even though he was thirty-seven years old, relatively thin and muscular with the exception of his gut, and had retained most of his jet black hair with thin wisps of grey, he was convinced everyone was repulsed by the scar. He felt his only opportunity to be with a woman now was to rape kidnapped women. The women struggled and their eyes were seized with fear, but it was all he could get.

Now that I've gotten rid of Sergei, who was going to turn me in to Andre, I can finish this woman off. It will be easier and quicker now.

On the worn counter beside the bathroom mirror was the name of the street a boy had mentioned where he had spotted a thin, raggedly dressed young woman with straight brown hair. Igor picked it up and examined it.

"Speedwell Avenue," he said out loud.

Time to get this over with.

CHAPTER NINETEEN

BRUCE

Man, o Man, what did you get us involved in now, Adam?

As Bruce lay on the couch thinking these words, he couldn't get Marina out of his mind. She was so fragile, yet trying so hard to be strong and hold herself together. He didn't know how she could survive after all she'd been through. How could he help her? He had enough trouble taking care of Adam. What more could he do?

He turned to his side. Sleep would not come. In his mind, her story turned over and over.

Human trafficking. Sex slavery. Could that really exist? In the twenty-first century? He searched the recesses of his memory. A few years ago he remembered going to a movie with Maggie. In the movie, a man's daughter went to France with a friend and they ended up being kidnapped by an Eastern European mafia. What was the name of that movie? He searched his memory before finally coming up with the movie's title. *Taken.* That was the name!

On the way home from the theater, he remembered them discussing whether it could actually happen or if it could only be a made-up situation nowadays. But their discussion had ceased when they saw Adam's tear-stained face in the window as they drove into their driveway. Adam clapped his hands and smiled when he saw them. His babysitter told them he had gone to sleep and then woke up crying for his parents a few minutes before they arrived home. Maggie rushed over to him, kissing his forehead and cuddling him. Bruce viewed their interaction with consternation. He thought she babied him too much. He didn't realize then that autism and mental retardation were not something he would eventually outgrow. Adam would remain childlike for the rest of his life.

Bruce checked his watch on the table near the couch. One o'clock in the morning. As he pulled more covers over himself, he realized Adam sought that maternal nurturing ever since Maggie died. He had never even considered the thought of dating or remarrying. Contemplating such a move overwhelmed and exhausted him. He had reached the limits of what he could handle. Mulling this over in his mind, sleep finally overcame him.

He opened his eyes to the light. He shot up. It was morning. He found his watch. Six o'clock.

Thank God I woke up without my alarm clock. He sighed. But his head fell back on the pillow as he remembered it was Saturday.

He considered staying in bed some more when he heard Adam running to his bedroom.

"Adam!" he whispered insistently.

Too late. He heard Adam ask Marina, "Where's my daddy? Are you still asleep, Marina?"

"Adam!" he whispered again, getting off the couch. "Adam,

I'm right here. Let Marina sleep."

"Oh, there you are, Daddy," he said loudly. His pajama shirt was full of holes of all shapes and sizes randomly spread out along the top. His pajama bottoms barely covered his diaper. His anxious expression transformed into a delighted smile.

"Shhhh. Come on, Adam. Did you go to the bathroom yet?"

"No," Adam said, shaking his head.

"You go to the bathroom. Flush the toilet and wash your hands with soap. I'll help you with breakfast," Bruce said as he forced his reluctant body out of bed.

"Daddy, whatrwe goin' do today?" Adam whispered loudly.

Bruce said nothing but pointed toward the bathroom. Adam bowed his head and slowly headed there.

Bruce stretched. The sofa was not as comfortable as his own bed, but once he fell asleep, he had been fine for the rest of the night. He hoped Marina would stay asleep while he took care of his son. He heard the toilet flush and the sink water running. And running.

"Adam, enough with washing your hands," he admonished as he made his way into the bathroom. The water stopped running in the sink. Bruce walked in and saw lots of lather still on his son's hands.

Bruce closed his eyes. "Rinse off the soap," he sighed as his hands covered his face.

Adam turned the water on, and as soon as the lather dissolved in his hands, Bruce turned off the faucet. He took out a toothbrush and toothpaste. "Son, you've got to try to do these things for yourself."

"I don't wanna," Adam complained.

"Nobody does. But you have to do it unless you want to

look like a bum." Bruce held out a hand to his son's chest to prevent him from leaving the bathroom. "Marina's still sleeping. Let's do this quietly. You understand, son?"

Adam pouted as he nodded, then lowered his head.

Bruce closed the door, reached for the toothbrush, and squirted toothpaste on it. He attempted to guide his son.

Adam kept taking his hand off the toothbrush. Growing impatient, Bruce brushed Adam's teeth himself.

After he guided Adam to brush his hair, Bruce led his son to his bedroom.

"Now what decent clothes can we put on you today?" he said out loud, rubbing his chin. "Do you have any shirts left with no holes in them?" He opened his son's drawers.

When Bruce finally found a shirt and jeans for him, he said, "Look at me."

Adam struggled to make eye contact with his father. His natural tendency was to look away, but teachers had worked with him for years on focusing his eyes.

"Here are some clothes for today. I'm going to get washed up and dressed. Try not to wake up Marina. And, son," he held Adam's chin to make sure he got his attention, "you can eat cereal and milk while I'm getting ready. You must be very quiet. Then we'll make toast. OK?"

"OK, Daddy." Adam nodded.

"What do you do now while I'm getting dressed?"

"Eat cereal and milk."

"And be very . . ."

"Quiet!" Adam said a little too loudly.

Bruce winced. He put his finger to his lips. "Be very quiet. Shhh."

Adam copied him.

Bruce tapped his son's arm and winked. "You got it, kid."

As he walked out of Adam's bedroom, his son asked timidly, "Daddy?"

"Yes, son?"

"Can . . . can I smell your feet? Please?" Adam waved his hands and stared earnestly into his father's eyes.

"Adam," Bruce turned his eyes up to the ceiling and threw up his hands in the air, "you know the answer to that. It is not . . ."

"Allowed," Adam finished the sentence, looking down and sullen.

His father rubbed his temples. "But if you're real good and quiet this morning, I'll let you smell my cologne."

Adam broke into a grin, bounced, and clapped his hands. "Yeah, Daddy. OK."

He turned around when Adam said, "Daddy?"

Bruce closed his eyes as he turned. "Yes, son?"

"Don't forget."

"No, I won't forget, Adam," he said, and he quickly left the bedroom.

Bruce retrieved his second set of clothes from the living room and went into the bathroom. More awake this time, he noticed two damp shower towels instead of one.

Did Marina already take a shower this morning? He shrugged, thinking this was probably the case. Afterward, she may have gone back to bed.

He always enjoyed these few moments when he was by himself and wasn't attending to his son. He hoped Marina would sleep. He had no idea what this day would bring or what he was going to do about her. But instead of thinking about the problems, he kept thinking about Marina.

He ducked his head under the shower nozzle.

Life has a way of working itself out, Maggie used to tell him.

He expected a phone call from Matt today. Bruce had spoken with Judy briefly last night, telling her Marina's story before he went to bed. He was probably wondering what the hell was going on now. This would certainly be a novel problem.

Bruce came out of the shower and dressed. When he opened the bathroom door, he smelled pancakes. His eyes widened in fear.

What the hell's Adam doing in the kitchen now? He ran in there, silently praying there wasn't smoke and chaos in the kitchen and he would not have to call the fire department.

Hurrying to the kitchen, he saw Marina flipping pancakes near the stove. She wore the same black dress she'd had on last night.

"Hey, Daddy! Marina's making strawberry pancakes and they taste so good!" Adam exclaimed. He wasn't paying attention to how much syrup he was pouring. His pancakes were drenched. Bruce's jaw dropped when he saw syrup landing in the small holes on Adam's shirt.

Marina turned around, and Bruce noticed she had large, expressive eyes, delicate features, and a rosebud mouth. He thought for the first time she must be beautiful in normal times.

"Adam, don't pour so much syrup," she gently admonished him.

"Marina's the best," Adam declared, smiling brightly with his mouth covered in syrup.

Bruce squashed his impulse to snap at his son and instead smiled in spite of himself.

"Um, I'll make pancakes for you. Do you like strawberries?" Marina asked shyly, turning slightly red.

"Strawberries sound great."

"It's delicious, Daddy. It's much better now that Marina's livin' wit us. Right, Daddy?" Adam's eyes twinkled. He was clearly enjoying breakfast.

Seeing his son so happy, Bruce couldn't help smiling also.

"While Marina's making the pancakes, let's change your shirt, Adam. I'm definitely going to have to buy you more shirts," he said, waving his son to come with him to the bedroom.

By the time he returned, Marina had put a plate of pancakes out for him on the table. "Thank you," he said. "But you need to eat too."

"I already ate," she said quietly, her eyes down.

"You must've gotten up while it was still dark," he exclaimed.

"Yes, I'm used to it," Marina said as she abruptly turned around to avoid expanding on the subject. She then quickly added, "I woke up, got showered and dressed, and then went back to sleep."

"Adam," he said to his son, "Marina made the pancakes. Now will you clean the plates and the pan once it cools off?"

"Sure, Daddy," Adam chirped.

I'll have to keep an eye on him to make sure he actually does it, he thought, knowing his son could be forgetful. *I'll clean my own.*

To his surprise, Adam began cleaning where he'd just eaten right away.

"Adam, you do such a nice job cleaning up," Marina remarked, seated at the table. "My brother never cleans dishes."

Bruce noticed her expression was awash in maternal tenderness.

"Really?" Adam asked while he squirted more dishwashing liquid into the sponge.

"No, he always leaves them for me and my mother."

Bruce observed their conversation while he savored the buttery pancakes with strawberries and powdered sugar.

"What a feast." Bruce managed to pause from the delightful meal to praise the cook.

Bruce noticed Marina had an alarmed expression on her face.

"What is it, Marina?" Bruce asked.

"I must contact my family," she replied, studying the floor. "I know they will be relieved to hear from me, but how will they feel when they found out what's happened to me?" She shut her eyes and drew in a breath.

"What do you mean? They'll be ecstatic to hear you're safe!"

Marina nodded with her eyes still closed. It appeared as if she were fighting back tears.

As soon as he finished, Adam took his plate and silverware. Bruce, anxious to change the subject, said, "Adam, when you're done, why don't you watch a nature show while Marina and I talk."

"But I wanna watch a nature show wit you two too." He stomped his foot.

"We'll be in there before you know it," Bruce tried to reassure him.

"And after nature show, we all take a walk," Adam said as he pointed his finger.

"Right," Bruce replied. More than anything, he wanted Marina to continue her story.

Hearing Adam channel surfing in the other room, he turned to her and for the first time, he noticed several ugly welts on her arm in various shades of red. She sat across from him at the table. She had rolled up her elbow-length sleeves to fry the pancakes, and jagged lines were exposed. Marina put her arms underneath the table and locked eyes with him.

Bruce's eyes bulged. *Is she actually a dangerous drug addict?* he wondered. *Have I been putting Adam and myself in danger?*

Marina seemed to read the concerns on his face.

"My kidnappers kept injecting me with sedatives," she said quietly, staring at the floor. Her eyebrows creased and she appeared as if she were about to cry. He hesitated asking her this, but he felt he had no choice.

"Marina," he said as he looked into her pained eyes, "did your kidnappers inject you with drugs often?"

She nodded, her eyes never rising to meet his. Her lips trembled as she tried to speak.

"Every day . . . ," she began.

"Here's a show on cheetahs." Adam lumbered into the kitchen, waving his hands. His hair stood up, most likely from rubbing it against the couch. "Daddy, you said cheetahs are the fastest animals." He walked up to his father. "Daddy, you and Marina watch it wit me. Please. Please."

Bruce closed his eyes and restrained himself from snapping. "Son, give us a few more minutes . . ."

He approached Marina and said enthusiastically, "Marina, you wanna watch the show 'bout cheetahs, right?"

Bruce noticed his son's eyebrows furrowed when he saw her pained expression.

"Marina," he said quietly, "don't you like cheetahs? Daddy says they're the fastest animal in the whole world."

"Oh, Adam. Of course I would like to watch a show about

cheetahs." She gazed at him affectionately. She reached out to touch his arm but quickly pulled back. "I just need to speak with your father a little while longer. Then I would so enjoy watching the show with you."

Adam nodded, smiling and waving his hands again. "OK. When you come to watch the show, I'll tell you what you missed." He turned to Bruce. "Daddy, are you goin' come in too?"

Shuffling in his seat while he tried to hide his growing annoyance, he smiled and said, "Sure, son. I'll be in there too."

"Great!" Adam held his fists in the air as if victorious before he returned to the living room.

Bruce noticed the expression of adoring affection in Marina's eyes as she watched him leave the kitchen.

"He's so sweet," she said, turning to Bruce. "He's such a gift. When my brother was his age, he always walked around angry and moody, but Adam brightens up my life."

Bruce wanted to quip that she must still be feeling the effects of the wine she had drunk last night but soon realized he'd never taken a moment to consider his son's sweetness and innocence. He would often hear Judy complaining about her kids never giving her respect, but he always told her she was lucky they were normal and they would soon grow out of their rebellion. He turned away, remembering Judy gazing at Adam with the same adoring eyes.

Bruce did not dwell on these thoughts. There was a more pressing subject at hand. He turned to Marina. Glancing in the living room, he said, "Marina, we'll watch the show with Adam and then we've got to get you to a hospital to check you out."

She stared open-mouthed at him as if he suggested she return to her kidnappers. "I can't!" she shook her head and hugged herself. "Oh, no! I can't!"

"Why? No one at the hospital will hurt you. I promise," Bruce said as he yearned to reach out to comfort her.

Marina looked pale but said nothing.

"If they injected you with so many drugs, you've got to get checked out right away. I'll call the police . . ."

"No! Not the police. Please," she begged him. "When I get to the hospital, I'll tell them and they will call the police." She turned to the living room. "The police will scare Adam. Let's watch TV with him and then you can drop me off at the hospital. I need to handle this by myself."

"Marina, you can't handle all this by yourself after all you've been through. Please, let me help you. The sooner you get checked out and the police get involved, the sooner you can go home and be with your family, leading a normal life again."

After he said these words, he realized when she returned home, he would never see her again. But he brushed aside these thoughts, thinking he was being selfish. Her well-being was the top priority.

"Daddy! Marina!" Adam came in and dispelled the tension in the air. "They're showing a whole family of cheetahs! Look at the babies! Come! Come!" Adam announced, oblivious to the serious expressions on his father and Marina's faces. Marina tried to smile and unexpectedly touched Bruce's arm.

"Come, we can't miss this," she told him, rising.

Glancing at his watch and realizing the show would probably be over in fifteen minutes, he rolled his eyes and followed them into the living room.

◆ ◆ ◆

Dispatchers notified patrol officers Juan Rodriguez and Mark Smith about a suspicious-looking incident at an old building in Morristown. It had been called in as an anonymous tip early in the morning.

Smith gulped down coffee when they reached a red light. "Man, it's too early in the morning for this. On a Saturday yet."

"I hope we don't have a murder scene. It will be all over the papers in this town, and the reporters will be camping out at the police station," Rodriguez said, thinking out loud. He had already loaded up on coffee.

"They should have torn that building down years ago. What do they need it for? It isn't even a historical landmark," Smith said, shaking his head.

"From what I heard, people kept expressing interest to buy the land but the offers always fell through," Rodriguez answered.

"With that ugly, boarded-up building, I'm not surprised. The city should've torn it down," Smith said. He pointed his forefinger to his head. "People, they just don't think."

They spotted the house and parked in front. They got out of their police car and looked around.

"Hey, look at this, Juan!" Smith said after they searched the grounds for five minutes. Rodriguez came over and found Smith pointing out footprints. "It looks as if there's one set of footprints here. We're lucky it hasn't rained in a few days."

"It leads to that badly boarded-up window," Rodriguez observed.

As they stood there, a foul stench assaulted their nostrils. They glanced at each other.

"We gotta go in," Smith said. Rodriguez nodded and took out a flashlight. Both men drew their guns.

Smith banged on the window. "Police! Anyone in the building come out now!"

Silence.

Rodriguez nodded, and Smith tore off the boards with a side-handle baton. Both raised their guns to the window.

"Come out with your hands up!" Smith ordered. More silence. Rodriguez's flashlight glowed while he kept his body away from the window.

Their guns still drawn, Rodriguez and Smith entered the door in a flash. The smell grew even stronger now that the door was open. They took out handkerchiefs to cover their noses and mouths before walking into the dark, dusty, moldy building. They heard tiny squeaks as rats scurried around. Many had attached themselves to a rotting body. The men looked at each other in horror.

"I'm calling for backup!" Rodriguez told his partner as he grabbed his phone.

Smith, meanwhile, pricked up his ears and scanned the room with his flashlight to detect any hint of movement or noise.

Within a half hour, the old dilapidated building was sealed off as a crime scene. Police officers scanned the rooms with flashlights in search of a murder weapon. A medical examiner carefully examined the body. After taking pictures, Sue Fant, the crime scene investigator, joined the medical examiner. She was prepared for the grisly site, viewing the body full of cuts and abrasions. The body was also bloated and still warm. Maggots crept all over it. Sue swept a net that was normally used for skimming pool water so she could collect flying insects above the body; an officer put a number of crawling insects in jars for later examination at the lab.

Sue shook her head. "There's no sign of struggle. My guess would be he was already dead. But we'll bring him over to the lab." As she said this, Fant took out her cell phone camera and took pictures of the victim as well as the surrounding area. She then circled the body, searching the scene for evidence with her flashlight.

Using latex gloves, the medical examiner took out a small plastic bag filled with hairs. "Hopefully some of these hairs I found on the body will be the murderer's. This is the only evidence I can find so far. It looks like the murder was committed somewhere else and the body was dumped here." He looked up at Fant. "But it's so dark in here. So far no one's found blood or a weapon."

"What about a wallet or a watch?" Fant asked him.

The medical examiner shook his head. "Nothing."

Rodriguez, Smith, and other police officers continued scanning the outside of the building as well as the inside with flashlights.

"If only we could raise this roof and let the light come in. Then we just might spot something," Rodriguez muttered to Smith.

Smith nodded. "It may be the only way. It's just too damn dark in here and the walls are rotted out."

More police came. They took out giant flashlights and continued scanning the whole house.

CHAPTER TWENTY

MARINA

On the way to the hospital, Marina sat lost in thought. Bruce spoke about the sterling reputation of the area's hospital, but she couldn't focus on his words.

"Daddy," Adam chimed in from the backseat. "Are you goin' hold Marina's hand at the hospital? You always hold my hand when I go."

"Uh, I'm . . . whatever she wants to do, Adam," he replied awkwardly.

"Afta we go ta the hospital, are we gonna go ta the store and you'll buy me more shirts, Daddy?"

"Maybe," Bruce answered, looking at his son in the rear view mirror.

"And at the store you'll buy me a candy bar?" Adam asked hopefully.

"We'll see, son."

"And afta that, we'll all take a walk?" he persisted.

Bruce grabbed the steering wheel tighter and responded curtly with gritted teeth. "Maybe we will."

Marina smiled briefly to herself, but she couldn't stop her body from trembling.

I'll tell them I can handle it myself. They need to go buy Adam more clothes. Then I'll have to find a way to escape.

Bruce turned on the street of the hospital. Large office buildings stood on green, manicured lawns. She saw professionally dressed people walking in parking lots and on the sidewalks. Cars of all shapes and sizes drove by and most looked new and luxurious. Marina peered beyond the bend and saw large homes farther down the street. She looked at her clothes—she was still wearing the black dress Adam's aunt had given her. It was still clean, but she wondered if everyone would stare at her emaciated body as soon as she exited the car. She took pains on her appearance and tried to reassure herself she was looking more normal. But on the inside, she was still a mess. Judy had looked at her strangely last night, but that was because her presence in Bruce's house had surprised her. *She didn't look repulsed, even though I wore that long, blue robe.*

Bruce turned into the parking lot of a large building on the street. In the upper middle was a large aqua glass window with Morristown Memorial Hospital in large lettering. It was a large, sprawling brick building with white shutters—by far the biggest building on the street. She bit her lip upon seeing security guards stationed around the hospital.

Unexpectedly, Bruce squeezed her hand. "It will be all right," he reassured her.

He parked the car. Marina's wobbly legs refused to move and she remained sitting in the car, but when she turned, she found Bruce's hand reaching out to help her out of the passenger side of the car.

"Thank you," she said unevenly as she silently cajoled her legs to move while she clutched his hand.

"See, Marina," Adam said a little too loudly and pointing his forefinger. "Daddy holds my hand when I have ta go ta the hospital." He then knitted his brows and peered at his father. "Daddy," Adam said quietly. "How come you can hold Marina's hand?"

Bruce looked dumbfounded for a moment. Then he said, "Uh, son . . . it's like this . . . I'm . . . I'm an adult, a lot . . . older than you. So that's why I can hold her hand."

"Oh," Adam said, nodding and waving his hands, seemingly satisfied.

They walked through the hospital's main entrance. Right away Marina noticed the walls were painted a soft blue and white. Plants adorned the lobby. It resembled a hotel more than it did a hospital. In Moldova, hospitals were old and worn, all in serious need of repair. All of them contained wobbly old furniture. Here in Morristown, she felt like they were about to check into a luxury hotel until the sight of a hospital staff worker pushing a patient in a wheelchair brought her back to the stark reality.

Biting the front of his shirt, Adam straggled behind, staring at the gift shop.

"Adam, come on," Bruce called to him.

Adam enthusiastically pointed his finger at the gift shop. "Look, Daddy! A candy shop! Daddy, can I get a candy bar? Please! Please!"

People close by stopped and stared.

Bruce turned red as he said, "Adam, it's too early in the morning." Seeing his son look crestfallen, he said, "Maybe I'll buy you a donut later. Maybe."

His son's disappointed expression transformed into a delighted smile. Bruce repeated, "Maybe."

Marina regarded Adam warmly. His comments and questions helped her relax and stop obsessing over her fears, but as they approached the receptionist's desk, her face turned pale and her legs felt weak again. She kept darting her eyes, looking to see if anyone noticed her extremely thin frame or if people whispered and pointed toward her.

"It's OK. Take it easy," Bruce said as he tightened his hand around hers in a strong yet gentle grasp, which steadied her nerves and helped boost her courage.

Marina tried unsuccessfully to relax her body. She took deep breaths.

"May I help you?" a stout woman with a grey bun peered at them.

"This lady, uh, needs to go to the emergency room."

The woman eyed her. "The condition?"

Bruce turned to Marina, but she just stood there wordlessly, pale with fright.

The woman turned her eyes from Bruce to Marina and waited.

Bruce took a breath. "She's been hurt."

"How has she been hurt?" the receptionist asked not unkindly.

"Yeah! Marina came to our house. She had no food and nothin'. I made her food and she watched TV wit me," Adam told her proudly.

The woman lifted her eyebrows as she stared at him. Then she looked at Bruce and Marina as if waiting for an interpretation. When none was forthcoming, she shook her head, obviously perplexed, and said, "Let me call a doctor."

Marina looked at Bruce, who stared from the corner of his eye at his son. Adam smiled wide.

When the woman got off the phone, she said, "Go down this hallway and turn to the right."

"Thank you," Bruce said as he led the wordless Marina. Adam, who kept glancing at the gift shop, trailed behind.

"Adam, stay with us," Bruce admonished.

Marina struggled to breathe. She fought images of being kidnapped once again as she walked. She searched for the familiar faces of her kidnappers. She clutched her stomach, fighting the rising nausea that rose from her stomach to her throat. She prayed her anxiety wouldn't cause her to vomit her breakfast, especially in public.

Bruce gave her hand a little squeeze. "It's going to be all right."

As they headed toward the emergency room, a nurse approached them. She was a young woman with a chubby face and red hair.

"I'm Ann Donald, your nurse for today," she said in a pleasant voice as she put out her hand.

Marina nodded and shook her hand.

"Please come in with me and I'll take down your information," the nurse continued and indicated Marina should follow her.

Her heart dropped. *What was going to happen now?*

"We gotta go in too," Adam said in a reprimanding voice to the nurse. "She's our friend!"

Nurse Ann's calm demeanor was interrupted as she stared at Adam and tried to conceal her amusement. She asked, "And who are you, young man?"

Bruce smiled weakly and patted his son on the back. "We're going in too. Don't worry, son."

The nurse's expression was a question mark as she led them to her nurse's station. She pointed to the chairs near her desk as she sat down in front of the computer.

"First, let's begin with your name," she said to Marina.

"Marina Dobrin."

"And what are you coming here for?" Fingers still on the keyboard, she watched Marina and waited.

"I-I w-was kidnapped from my native country and my c-captives injected me with drugs," Marina exhaled as if she were holding her breath the entire time she said this sentence.

"And when was this?" Nurse Ann asked, her eyes opening wide.

Marina stared at the ceiling. *When was I taken captive? How long ago?*

"Six months, I think."

"How did this happen?" the nurse asked quietly as she gazed steadily at Marina.

Once Marina began telling her story, the nurse kept typing, her eyes returning to the computer screen.

"I was walking to the train station in Moldova and I was kidnapped with other women. We were in a boat for about a week before it docked in Turkey. A-And for some reason the boat o-only stayed there a little while before it moved on and we eventually ended up in America." Marina's voice broke a few times and she felt tears come to her eyes. The nurse handed her a box of tissues while Bruce took her hand and gave it a reassuring squeeze.

She heard footsteps walking briskly behind her.

Marina held her breath and slowly turned around. A man and a pregnant woman passed by.

"Have you called the police?" Nurse Ann asked, her eyes steadfast on Marina.

Marina squeezed Bruce's hand and shook her head with a woeful, fixed expression.

"Do you know the name of the drugs you were given? How did they give them to you?" the nurse persisted.

"I don't know the name of the drugs. They just kept injecting us," Marina whispered in a childlike voice.

"We need to call the police," Nurse Ann said, reaching for the phone.

"No! No! Don't do that!" Marina looked at her in alarm.

Adam, who had been sitting quietly and rocking his body while listening the whole time, stood up with his arms flapping and angrily told the nurse, "Don't you hurt my friend!"

"Adam!" Bruce got up and rubbed his son's back. "Calm down. No one's going to hurt Marina."

The nurse stared and waited.

"Nurse, believe me when I tell you the police can do nothing," she said with trembling lips. "I was lucky to escape. I am fearful for my life. W-When I feel safe, I want to talk to the police about the other women they kidnapped, but if I get killed, there won't be anyone to help them. Please believe me."

Nurse Ann studied her with furrowed brows. She saw Marina clutching Bruce's hand and using her other hand to grasp her chair. Marina entreated her with pleading eyes to understand.

For a moment, the nurse stared at all of them. Then she

straightened herself in her chair and pressed her forefingers on the keyboard.

"Let's do this," she said. "We'll put you in a room and have a doctor examine you. Then we'll all decide what to do from there." Her eyes nervously darted toward Adam, who tried to walk up right in front of her, but Bruce held a restraining hand on his torso.

"We gotta go wit Marina," Adam insisted.

"I'm sorry, but for the examination she has to go into the room alone," the nurse told him as she crouched back in her chair.

"I won't be long, Adam. I promise," Marina said, letting go of her own fears for a moment.

"No! You can't take Marina away!" Adam yelled, his eyes filling with tears.

Now Bruce stood in front of Adam with his hands on his son's shoulders. "Listen, son, look at me!" he ordered Adam. "The doctor is going to bring Marina into a room to make sure she's not sick. When they're finished, she'll come back to us."

But Adam did not appear to be listening to his father's words. He kept shouting, "Come back, Marina! Come back! Don't leave me too!"

"Is everything OK in here?" A big, burly security guard appeared at the office door.

"No! They're goin' take my friend away!" Adam said. "You've gotta stop 'em!" He turned to his father. "Daddy! Daddy! You can't let 'em do that!"

Face flushed, Bruce tried talking to him again. "Adam, are you listening to what I just said? Marina's coming back! No one's going to hurt . . ."

He didn't get to finish his sentence. Adam suddenly pushed his father against the wall.

Everyone watched in horror. Hearing the heated exchanges, five more security guards ran into the office.

"How could you do that, Daddy? Marina's my friend!" Adam shouted, his face red and tear stained.

"Adam, Adam, these people are here to help. It's OK, son. It's OK," Bruce choked out the words. Barely able to stand, he staggered against the wall so as not to fall. He held out his arm to his son but was unable to catch his attention.

The security guards overpowered Adam, forcing him to the ground but not without a fight. Adam tried pushing them off with all his might. One guard stumbled and fell to the ground. Finally a doctor ran in. The scuttle continued until they were able to hold him down and inject him with a needle. After a few moments, all the fight went out of him.

"Marina! Mommy! Marina! I need my new friend! Where's Mommy?" he wailed before losing consciousness.

His father turned away, his face crumbling, like he was going to burst into tears. Marina clutched her scalp with her hands. Finally she found her voice.

"Please don't hurt him! He's a sweet boy that means no harm," she told the guards. Then she reached for Bruce, putting her hand on his shoulder. "Are you all right? I'm so sorry I caused all this to happen. You must make Adam forget about me if I'm causing so much trouble!" she said and burst into tears.

"No, I'll be all right. Just take care of yourself," he said, trying to catch his breath.

"Miss Dobrin," Nurse Ann said in a shaky voice, "the doctor is here to see you now." A tall, thin, middle-aged man with a white coat and greying brown hair walked in.

Marina glanced over at Adam. "What is going to happen to Adam now? Will he be all right?"

"He'll be fine. He has been put under sedation. He'll sleep for a few hours and then wake up refreshed," the nurse said soothingly.

"I-I can't leave him," she cried.

"Don't worry. I'll take care of him. You go get checked out," Bruce told her. He turned to the nurse, the doctor, and the security guards. "My son has autism. He's only moderately functioning. I should have told you this, but there was too much going on for me to think of it. I apologize." He turned to stare at his son, sleeping peacefully. "He has moments when he's out of control."

The tall doctor cleared his throat. "Hello, Miss Dobrin. My name is Dr. Stein. Please follow me. We'll check you out and take good care of you and the boy."

Marina turned to Bruce, who nodded. She got up and reluctantly followed the doctor. She stared at Adam with eyes huge with fear.

◆ ◆ ◆

With Sergei out of the way, Igor drove along the area where the boy had seen the extremely thin woman who matched Marina's description. He entered a residential neighborhood.

Who could I possibly ask? he wondered.

These houses belonged to the middle class. Small but well-kept homes lined the streets. Residents worked hard to maintain the value of their properties as well as the neighborhood. The problem was there were so many of them!

I can ride around for hours or I can get out of the car and start asking around, he figured. So he parked his car on one of the streets and got out. Tingling with anticipation and clutching his photo of Marina, Igor felt he was close. If only he could find someone who had seen her and would talk. Looking around, he saw a couple riding bikes on the street. Igor held out his hand and they stopped.

"Excuse me. Excuse me, please!" he said in the friendliest tone he could muster. He took out the photo. "I am looking for someone—my sister. Have you seen her, please?"

The man and woman, both wearing helmets and sunglasses, stared at the photo and shook their heads.

"No, sorry, we haven't seen her," the man said.

"A-Are you sure?" Igor asked, almost pleadingly.

They glanced at each other and shook their heads.

Igor slumped his shoulders.

"Sorry. Good luck, buddy," the man said and they rode off.

Igor cursed and continued walking.

Next, a young man with long black hair and wearing a Dead Head T-shirt and torn jeans walked across the street. He was listening to an iPod and appeared to be mouthing the words to a song.

Igor was ready to dismiss him, a kid living in his own world in his head, but he couldn't allow himself to pass by a possible lead. He ran across the street waving to the man, who was so caught up in his own thoughts that he didn't notice Igor approaching until Igor stood right in front of him. The young man jumped upon seeing him and reluctantly removed his earphones.

"Young man, young man, please," Igor said. "I'm very sorry to disturb you, but I am looking for my sister. Have you seen her?" And he whipped out her picture.

The man stared. "Man! She's so thin!" he exclaimed. "Was she in a prison camp or somethin'?"

"No, no! She's sick and I've got to find her!" Igor said, doing his best impression of a caring, protective brother.

"No, man. I've never seen anybody so thin. Only in pictures or on TV," the young man said. And with that, he put on his earphones and continued walking, singing the lyrics of a song. Once again Igor cursed. He was so mad he felt like choking the man. He viewed the street in all directions and didn't see anyone else besides cars driving by. He didn't want to attract too much attention to himself so he didn't try to flag one of them down. He kept on walking.

Twenty minutes later he spotted a convenience store.

Now here I have a chance! he thought.

Walking into the store, he showed the cashier the picture. The woman shook her head.

"God! Is she thin! I wish I could give her some of my weight!" The woman laughed at her own joke, her whole body jiggling.

Igor wasn't amused. He walked to the cold drink section, took out a Coke, and paid for it wordlessly.

Walking out of the store, he drank the Coke and considered this job was a lot harder than he had anticipated. He walked toward his car when in the opposite direction two women in their thirties dressed in sweat clothes passed him. Each one pushed a baby stroller. They were deep in conversation.

"It seems Bruce found another woman fast enough," one

woman told the other. "Gee, I always had the impression he was the sensitive type and would mourn his wife at least a year before he'd start dating again."

"It looks like she moved in with him already! Well, he does need the help with Adam," the other replied.

"Where did she come from? It looks like she hasn't eaten a decent meal in months!" the first one exclaimed.

Igor stopped. This was his chance.

"Excuse me, please!" He called the women who had passed by him.

They turned around.

"You spoke about a very thin woman," he said, looking at them earnestly. "I-I am supposed to visit my sister who's been very sick. She's staying with a man who lives around here. "He quickly pulled out the picture. "Please, ladies, I beg of you. I lost the address and I must give her medication."

The women stared at each other.

"I was in such a hurry to get here I must have dropped the address. Please! She needs the medicine or she will die."

"Sixteen Pine Street," one of the women blurted out.

CHAPTER TWENTY-ONE

BRUCE

Bruce sat, closing his eyes. He felt beaten and confused as hospital staff came in and put Adam on a gurney.

Another doctor came over to him. "I'm Dr. Palmetto," he said, shaking his hand. "Your son will rest comfortably for a while. How are you feeling?"

How do you think I'm feeling, you screwball. My son publicly humiliated me in one of his out-of-control scenes and all I was trying to do was help his friend Marina.

But out loud all he said was, "I've been better."

The doctor chuckled a bit. "You have a lot on your shoulders."

Bruce only nodded but thought, *That has got to be the understatement of the year.*

"Does your son have a mother?"

Bruce shook his head. "She passed away a short time ago. Then he met this young woman who's in trouble and I'm trying to help her."

"The police will be arriving shortly. Let me just check you out quickly. Your son's strong, but I don't think he caused you any damage. He seems to have gotten quite attached to this young woman."

Bruce felt like rolling his eyes but instead said, "He certainly has. She's a very sweet woman."

By now the security guards had dispersed.

"Please follow me. We'll go to my office. The police should be here any minute. We'll all do our best to help," Dr. Palmetto reassured him.

Bruce sat up red-faced, ashamed to leave the office and face all the people who would surely be staring at him, blaming him for his son's strange and disruptive behavior. To his surprise, a woman approached him as he and the doctor left the office and said, "I also have a son with autism. He's real difficult and he sometimes embarrasses me in public. You're not alone in dealing with this."

Bruce tried to smile and nod to this caring, earnest woman. As hurtful and embarrassing as Adam's out-of-control behavior was, her words gave him the courage to follow the doctor with his head held high. The woman walked quickly away, not waiting for a reply.

Once seated in the doctor's office, Dr. Palmetto, now taking a rigid and serious demeanor, faced him behind his desk. "I understand the young woman was kidnapped. The police are on their way. I see she is very afraid and we think it would help if you sat there with her when the police question her." He paused briefly. "Your son is under sedation. He'll be fine. We know you've been through a lot this morning . . ."

Bruce held up his hand. "Sure, I'll be there for Marina. The only thing I request is a cup of coffee."

Dr. Palmetto relaxed and smiled. "I'll do better than that. I'll bring you good coffee and a Danish."

The muscles in Bruce's face relaxed. He sat back and waited for the refreshments, but when the doctor returned, he wore a solemn expression.

"The police have already arrived. I told them to just give you ten minutes to eat and have a short break. First, let me quickly check you."

The doctor felt Bruce's muscles and joints as well as his back. "All's fine," he said. "I'll get you that coffee and Danish now."

He soon returned.

"Thank you, doctor." Bruce gratefully took the coffee and raspberry Danish. "I appreciate this very much."

But as he tried to enjoy the snack, images of a frightened and cowering Marina assailed him. He finished as quickly as he could and, rather than being summoned, Bruce opened the door of the doctor's office and walked over to the nurse's station. Three policemen spoke with Nurse Ann. When she saw him, she lifted a finger to the officers and came over to Bruce.

"How're you feeling?"

"Better, thanks. How's my son?"

"Resting comfortably. These officers have requested that you accompany them when they speak to Miss Dobrin."

Bruce nodded. Taking a deep breath, he walked over to them.

Thoughts and fears hovered over him as he walked with the police officers to Marina's room. Pale and wide-eyed, she lay on the bed in a hospital gown under covers. Her eyes grew wider and her body tensed when she saw the officers, but upon seeing

Bruce walk in, her shoulders relaxed and she almost smiled. Dr. Stein and Nurse Ann were also present.

"Hello, Miss Dobrin, my name is Officer John Lewis." He reached over to shake her hand. "These men are Officers Mark Smith and Joe Miller." They took turns shaking her hand. "We're here to help you and catch the people who kidnapped you. We need to find out your story."

Marina sat up. "They're very vicious, you see. Now that I've escaped from them, I just want to be free of them and not have any of them come after me. Please," she pleaded, "I don't want any more trouble. When I'm sure they're not after me, I-I'll tell you everything. They took many girls. But I know two of the kidnappers are still after me."

Bruce listened to her, but he was confused.

Why does she insist they're still after her?

He answered his own question before he finished the thought.

Marina's trying to protect Adam and me. What am I supposed to do? How can I possibly counsel her if Adam may be in danger?

Lost in his own thoughts, Bruce rubbed his eyes, trying to focus in on the conversation.

"What makes you think they're still after you?" Officer Lewis asked her.

"While I was held captive, there was a man who tried to rape me," Marina said, looking down and reaching for tissues, her hand shaking.

Everyone waited for her to say more, but silence filled the room.

Marina shut her eyes for a moment, opened them, and spoke. "I fought him. Even though I was weak, he was drunk and clumsy. He fell, and I took the knife out of his pocket and slashed him. Another man came into the room, grabbed the knife, and dragged him out. I cried and shook all night. I knew there would be repercussions. Whenever I saw him, he let me know that he would kill me as soon as he got the chance," Marina said, hugging herself. Her lips trembled.

Bruce longed to go over and put his arms around her as she sobbed. But he forced himself to stand there and ache for her suffering.

"He came into the room the next morning and tried to choke me with his bare hands," she continued. "My other captors stopped him and told him he could not lay a hand on me because if he killed me, they would lose money and they'd get rid of him. From then on, every time he saw me, he stared at me with such hatred. I knew he wanted to kill me; he was just waiting for an opportunity. I slashed the side of his face and he has a scar. I remember he frequently touched it."

Marina stopped and stared at the floor. Bruce placed his hands on his mouth and turned his head away. He then glanced at the officers—Officer Miller stared at his feet and Officers Lewis and Smith stared at her with long, withered faces.

"Miss Dobrin," Lewis said quietly. "Where are your captors from?"

"Moldova and Russia," she said, closing her eyes.

"Are they involved in human trafficking?" Miller asked, now looking up at her with piercing eyes. "A month ago, I broke up a small human trafficking ring in Paterson. They were holding six illegal women against their will in a private house—these women were from South America."

"It must be happening all over the world," Bruce interjected.

Everyone in the room looked over at him.

"Yes, it is," Miller responded gravely. "All over the world."

"Miss Dobrin," Lewis turned to her again. "The more information you can tell us about your captors, the better chance we have of punishing them and making sure they never kidnap women again."

After taking a deep breath, Marina continued, "All I remember was the kidnappers kept referring to their boss as Andre and," Marina looked up, her face brightening as she remembered, "they would only mention his name if they thought all the women were asleep. I would pretend I was asleep. But I never heard anything more about him other than his name." She put a hand over her eyes. "He could be from Moldova or Russia. In Moldova, we speak Romanian and Russian. I heard them speak both languages, but mostly Russian." Everyone in the room looked at her and waited. After a few moments she choked back sobs and continued, relating some experiences on the ship that she had already told Bruce. When she finished talking, Dr. Stein spoke up.

"I would like Marina to remain in the hospital. I want to take some tests to find out if she has sustained any lingering damage from her ordeal," he told Bruce and the officers. "It will take a few hours." He then turned to Bruce and said, "Your son will be asleep for a while and you look exhausted. Why don't you go home and get some rest? Come back later and you can pick them up."

"We'll have security guards standing in front of your room, so I guarantee you no one will harm you," Officer Lewis gently informed Marina.

She turned to Bruce.

"I'll stay here if you want me to," he told her.

But he was surprised when she shook her head. "I trust them," she said slowly. She smiled as she said, "I have never seen so much security at a hospital before."

"Are you sure? I have no problem staying," Bruce insisted.

"No," she said. "I can see you're struggling to keep your eyes open and they're right: you need to rest."

"I'll try to check up on Adam in between the tests," she added.

Bruce smiled appreciatively, worrying about his son after all the trauma and fear Marina was experiencing. "I'm going to check up on him myself before I leave. May I have a pen and paper?" he asked, turning to the officers. One of the officers whipped them out, and Bruce jotted down his cell and home numbers. He handed the paper to Marina. "Just call me if you need me. I'll be calling the hospital to make sure the two of you are all right."

Marina took the paper and smiled. "I'll never be able to thank you and Adam enough."

"For now, you just let the doctor examine you and take care of yourself," he answered gently, nodding at the others in the room.

Before leaving, he glanced in his son's room. Adam slept on his back under covers. "Son, don't worry. Everything will be all right. I'm going home to rest, but I'll call the hospital every hour to check up on you . . . and your friend Marina," he said. His eyes starting to mist, he headed for the door, taking one last glance at his son sleeping peacefully.

◆ ◆ ◆

Chewing on a toothpick he took from the hotel lobby, Igor drove to the place where the woman said Marina was now staying. When he came to that place, he saw a small house in the distance.

Could she be in that house now? he wondered.

One advantage about this house is that he could break in with less of a chance of anyone seeing him. He rode up the bumpy dirt road to the house. He saw no car parked outside. Igor parked among some tall oak trees to hide his car while he slowly and carefully made his way to the garage and peeked in one of the windows.

No car! Anyone who lives here must have a car.

Hastily putting on his rubber gloves, he crept to the front door. Locked. He then crept to the side of the house that was farthest from the street and examined the windows.

What luck! A window half open!

Looking around to be reasonably sure no one was looking, he opened the window all the way and jumped inside. Igor stood still a moment, examining the walls for an alarm system. Seeing none, he searched around. Near the front door on a small table he saw a stack of mail. He copied the name and address: everything was addressed to Bruce Hitchens. A few envelopes were addressed to the parents of Adam Hitchens. He did not see any letters with a woman's name on them. Igor proceeded inside the master bedroom and saw women's clothes in the bigger closet. Sitting on one of the dressers was a wedding picture. That bride, of course, was not Marina.

Igor continued searching from room to room, but found no evidence Marina had been there. He was about to give up when he saw the bathroom door ajar and slipped inside. In the wastepaper basket, he spotted the thin, tattered jeans and shirt she had worn when she escaped. Igor had kept the color of her clothes imprinted in his memory because that could be his only clue to locate her whereabouts. An immensely self-satisfied smile curled on his lips.

Finally! Finally I found her, he said to himself triumphantly.

Grinning, he got out his knife, grabbed the clothes, and cut them to shreds. A small vodka bottle dropped out of his coat pocket, but he ignored it, too busy savoring his victory of locating her and anticipating the pleasure of scaring her. Then he slowly opened the front door and surveyed the surroundings. Seeing no one, he got back into his car. As he drove, he saw an elderly lady standing on her front porch watering her plants. She craned her neck and peered at his car. Igor smiled—her efforts to see him were in vain because the Mercedes had tinted windows.

Her eyesight is probably bad so the old bag can't even see my license plate, he thought as he sat back and slightly loosened his grip on the steering wheel. *No worries.*

He made sure he was a few blocks away from the woman's house but still within sight of the small house when he parked. Igor tapped his thumbs against the wheel and waited. His toothpick had disintegrated from his constant biting. Igor wished he had taken some more. Or something to read. In his haste, he didn't think he would be spending so much time in the car waiting. He turned to the passenger seat, almost wishing Sergei was still seated beside him.

"Bah!" he said out loud. Sergei would only be complaining that they were wasting their time. Igor knew Sergei had tried to contact Andre every moment he could. That's why he'd gotten rid of him. His eyes became heavy as he sat waiting, but he refused to allow himself to fall asleep.

Just when he was about to open his car door to walk around and stretch his legs, he saw a car drive by. The old Buick turned into the house's driveway and ground to a halt. Igor wasted no time inching his car slowly toward the front of the path leading up to the house. Taking out his binoculars, he stationed it where he could see who was coming out of the car. It was the man he'd seen in the wedding picture inside the house. No one else was with him.

Damn! Igor said to himself. *She's not with him. Where could she be?*

He jotted down a description of the car and the license plate. Since Marina wasn't with him, Igor decided to wait.

CHAPTER TWENTY-TWO

MARINA

I MADE THE RIGHT DECISION. I KNOW I DID, MARINA kept telling herself. She sat on the bed in her gown and waited for the doctor and nurse to return.

Bruce is keeping Adam here. They have to be trustworthy.

She nearly jumped when she heard a knock at the door.

Dr. Stein and Nurse Ann walked in, smiling.

"Great news," Dr. Stein said. "You test negative for any venereal or infectious diseases. Your two main problems are malnutrition and dehydration. The nutritionist is outlining a diet for you to follow along with vitamins so you'll feel more like yourself again."

Marina's face broke into a smile.

"Oh, that's wonderful. I'm so relieved. You mean there's a chance I could be normal again?" she asked hopefully.

"Physically, yes. Emotionally, we strongly urge you to seek counseling to heal your inner wounds," he told her. "We're going to take a few X-rays to check your bones and muscles to make sure you have a complete overall examination."

Marina was so overcome with gratitude that she felt like hugging the doctor. "And what about Adam?"

"He'll be waking up in an hour or two and you can visit him. His father has been calling about you two. After he gets some rest, he's coming back."

Marina smiled widely, but she noticed the doctor's face turned serious. "Miss Dobrin," he said, "the local police have contacted the FBI. A representative would like to speak to you about your kidnappers. Now don't be afraid," he added upon seeing the terror in her eyes. "They want to capture them just as much as you do. They were particularly alarmed that they got away with landing on American shores."

Marina hugged herself in an effort to contain her fears. Nurse Ann went over to her and lay a hand on her arm. "Believe me, the authorities won't rest until they're caught."

Marina tried to smile but said nothing.

Doctor Stein and Nurse Ann looked at each other.

"We'll be right back as we prepare for the remaining tests," the doctor told her.

"Will you be all right?" the nurse asked anxiously, her eyes filled with warmth and concern.

Marina nodded and said, "While I'm waiting I'll just get some rest."

"Of course," Dr. Stein answered as he and the nurse left the room.

Marina put the covers over her and lay on her pillow. She began thinking about her life in Moldova. True, there was poverty everywhere and many people suffered from alcoholism, but she thought about the happy times: teasing her big brother while eating supper with her family in their small apartment, going out with girlfriends and talking about boys, and attending classes at Moldova State University in Chişinău, the country's capital.

Graduating with a degree in computer science, she was one of the lucky few who had found a job right away, but unlike most of her peers, she rarely had a steady boyfriend. Her mother told her it was because she was exceptionally pretty and smart that some young men felt intimidated by her, but Marina dismissed her mother's assertions. What mother wouldn't think her daughter was exceptionally pretty and smart? Her brother admitted some of his friends asked about her, but then why was she sitting at home alone on weekends?

She would always participate in programs sponsored by her company to help alcoholics recover, and she knew many people in desperate financial situations. She loaned money to friends and would see the money slowly returned back to her; many times their families would perform services for her like making her clothes or cooking meals for her family for a week in repayment of the loan. But lying in the hospital bed now in the States, she never thought much about the burdens and stress her less-fortunate friends and neighbors dealt with on a day-to-day basis. Her mood darkened as she wondered if this was some sort of cosmic payback for being so fortunate. By the time she heard a knock on the door, the sheets covered Marina's whole body and she was too demoralized to respond.

The door opened slightly. "Miss Dobrin?" Dr. Stein's voice inquired.

Marina's hands covered her face under the sheets. "Doctor, please. I need a few more minutes."

"Do you need something or someone to talk to?" he asked while still standing near the door.

"No, I just need some more time . . . ," and Marina began crying uncontrollably.

"I'll have the nurse give you something to calm you down before they . . . ," Dr. Stein began to say.

"No!" Marina screamed in fright, surprising both herself and the doctor. "No . . . I mean, I've had enough drugs put into my body. I don't know what they used, but I can't take any more drugs."

"Miss Dobrin," Dr. Stein said, taking pains to sound patient. "We'll give you some time. Mr. Hitchens's son Adam woke up a few minutes ago, sooner than expected, and he keeps asking for you and his father. We managed to contact his father and he's on his way over, but the son is agitated. If he continues to get more upset, we'll have to inject him with tranquilizers again."

Marina stiffened and stopped sobbing. *You have to pull yourself together for Adam's sake. Where would you be now if not for him? Probably tortured and mangled somewhere undiscovered underneath the ground.*

Out loud she said, "Give me a few minutes to wash up and then I'll visit Adam in his room."

The tone in Dr. Stein's voice was notably relieved. "All right. Very good. Your bathroom should have all the supplies you need. Just ring the nurse if you need anything."

"Ah, there is something," Marina said as she leaned on her elbow in the bed.

Dr. Stein stopped and turned toward her. By this time, Nurse Ann had joined him at the door.

"I-I'd like to take a shower. Is it p-possible for me to have a change of clothes?" Marina asked, biting her lip. She didn't want to be an imposition.

"Oh, of course," Nurse Ann replied. "We have a donation box of clothes. We should have your size, and don't worry, many of the donation clothes are as good as new."

Marina wanted to laugh, but she just smiled. *At this point, I'm just happy to have clothes to wear.*

Once they closed the door, Marina sprang up. No longer overcome with her guilt feelings of karmic payback, she rubbed her eyes and grabbed a tissue to blow her nose. She headed into the bathroom for a quick shower. Marveling for a moment at the modern, brightly colored bathroom with new fixtures and all the amenities, she turned on the shower and kept her head underneath the spray of water while soaping up. As she stood there, Marina imagined herself getting off a plane and returning to Moldova. She wondered what people's reaction to her would be. Would she look broken and demoralized? Would they shun her as damaged? Would even her family look at her in the same way?

She took in deep breaths, gently forcing her mind to think about something pleasant. Her mind settled on images of all the beautiful flowers around the Hitchens' house and that first meal Adam had given her, the slightly burnt toast, the big bowl of Cheerios, and the tallest glass of orange juice she had ever consumed, which finally satisfied the deep physical hunger she had suffered for so long.

Feeling the effects of her relaxed mind and limbs, a refreshed Marina turned off the shower and wrapped her head and body in the towels provided. She took a moment to feel them on her body. She marveled at how soft and sturdy the towels were. She'd never had such quality towels in her home country.

When I go back home, I would love to bring these kinds of towels to my family.

She soon stopped and looked in the mirror.

I don't want to keep Adam waiting. Who knows what state he's in now.

She came out of the bathroom and found black slacks and a blue shirt on the bed, as well as fresh underwear, a bra, and socks. Even though they were all size small, they were slightly big on her.

When she opened the door, she found Nurse Ann waiting for her. She looked at her up and down and said, "Well, I didn't do too badly picking out clothes for you."

"Thank you so much," Marina said gratefully.

The nurse patted her on the back and said, "He's up and he's been asking for you and his father."

"Well, I don't want him to wait," Marina said. "He's a lonely young man who misses his mother terribly," she said, thinking how much she missed her own parents, brother, and friends as well.

Marina stopped and put her arm out to the nurse. When the nurse was facing her, Marina asked, "Is there a way for me to contact my family?"

Nurse Ann gently took her arm and replied, "The police are working on that right now. Don't you worry." And she gently prodded Marina forward to Adam's hospital room.

"Where's my friend?" Adam asked as they approached his room.

"Marina! Marina!" he jumped out of bed in excitement. "You came back!"

Marina noticed his eyes were still cloudy from sleep. Adam's brown wavy hair stuck out in all directions. She longed to pat his strands down so he would appear better-groomed. His shirt had even more holes.

"How are you feeling, Adam?" she asked, her eyes warm and loving.

"Good. Where's my daddy?" he asked, biting his shirt.

"Your father's on his way here now," Nurse Ann told him in a friendly voice.

"Great!" he raised his fists in the air. "I don't want no one leavin' me again."

Marina closed her eyes. *The last thing I'd ever want to do is hurt you, Adam, but I'm in trouble. You don't realize you and your father are better off without me.*

Adam pointed to a chair near his bed. "Sit in the chair, Marina. They're lookin' for a nature tape for me. They even gave me a chocolate bar," he said, bouncing on the bed, unable to contain his excitement.

A hospital staff member knocked on the open door and brought in all kinds of DVDs. He handed them to Adam, who looked through them by their front covers.

"Snakes, whales, fishies, horsies, buffalo—how 'bout we watch the one on snakes, Marina?"

Marina tried to conceal her distaste for snakes and said, "What about horses, Adam? They're so beautiful and I've always dreamed about riding one."

Adam nodded. "OK. We want ta watch the tape 'bout horsies, please." He handed the DVD to the staff worker, who smiled and put the DVD into the hospital TV.

"Do you have popcorn or chips for us while we're watchin' TV?" he asked the man.

Marina blushed, but the man smiled and said, "I don't think we're equipped for that, but let me find out for sure."

"That'll be great," Adam chirped as the man left.

Different horses appeared on the screen. While the narrator explained the different kinds and their histories, anxious thoughts played around in Marina's head. She knew she would be going back to Moldova soon and Adam would be heartbroken, but before she left, she wanted to somehow convey to him that she liked him a lot and would miss him.

Maybe we could e-mail and Skype each other when I go back. I don't want him to feel like he's been abandoned again. He's such a special, sweet boy, and I'll always be indebted to him. She chuckled at the thought that she wished he could come to Moldova and visit.

"You like the horsies, Marina?" Adam turned, upon hearing her chuckle.

"Yes, very much, Adam," she beamed. "But not as much as I like you."

He smiled wide. "I like you much better than the horsies too." Delighted, he turned back to the screen. After a moment he said, "When Daddy gets back, let's have a donut, then go ta the clothes store, take a walk, and what else?" He put his fist under his chin while he thought about it.

Marina tried to hide her smile. *He already had chocolate and now he wants a donut, too.* Aloud she said, "If there's time after supper, maybe we can bake cookies for tomorrow. Would you like that?"

Adam raised his fists in the air. "That'd be great. I usedta bake chocolate chip cookies wit my mommy. Sometimes she would bake 'em while I was at school and she'd save the bowl fer me to lick," he explained to her. Then he raised his arms. "I can't wait."

Marina then realized that since she had suggested it, he would keep bringing it up, putting more stress on his father.

"If there's time. If not tonight, then tomorrow. OK, Adam?"

"Yup," was all he said as he rubbed his stomach and licked his lips.

He certainly likes his sweets, she thought, smiling.

Her thoughts were interrupted when Adam pointed to the TV and exclaimed, "Marina, look at what those horsies are doin'."

"Wow. They're jumping over hurdles. Those horses are specially trained to compete in games."

And they both stared transfixed by the TV for the rest of the program.

◆ ◆ ◆

Not daring to let himself fall asleep, Igor waited two hours while the man was inside the house. Seeing him go back to his car, Igor followed him to the hospital. His eyes grew wide with alarm when he saw police cars there.

So she's going to the police! I knew she'd be trouble! If it weren't for Sergei, I would have gotten rid of her by now, he thought ruefully. *Andre's going to be real upset when he finds out about this.*

Igor tapped his back pocket where he kept his wallet. Running low on money, Igor considered calling Andre, but by the time he reached for his cell phone and was about to punch in his number, he slammed it shut.

No! Let me kill her first and then I'll call Andre. I know what I need to do.

CHAPTER TWENTY-THREE

BRUCE

Bruce called the hospital to check on Adam and Marina. Hearing both were fine, he then practically sleepwalked upon entering his house. He walked into the kitchen to have a quick glass of water and then couldn't wait to tumble into bed. However, the ringing land line telephone interrupted his plans to rest and rejuvenate. Bruce was about to ignore the call until he saw whose name was on the screen.

"Hello?" he said, sitting at the kitchen table and attempting to keep his head up.

"Bruce? I kept trying your cell phone but you weren't picking up," Matt's impatient voice greeted him.

"Oh, really?" he said, fishing in his pocket for his cell phone. The ringer was turned off. "How are you? How was your trip?"

"Everything's fine, Bruce, but what the hell's going on with you?" Matt thundered. Like their father, when he was worried about family, Matt did not mince words.

"Did Judy tell you?"

"Yes, she told me what's going on, but where were you

today? Is Adam all right?"

Bruce tried to sidestep that last question. "Ahh, we brought Marina, the young woman, to the hospital to get her checked out. She's still there."

"And what about Adam?" he demanded.

Bruce rolled his eyes. He really didn't want to get into this with his brother, but he saw no way out of it. "He's at the hospital too," he said quietly. "When they took Marina away to get her checked out, Adam got a little upset. He considers her his friend. So the hospital gave him tranquilizers and he's resting there."

"Bruce! Bruce! How did Adam get involved with her? Judy told me she looked like she was in bad shape, but for heaven's sake, Bruce, you've got enough on your plate! Now Adam's latched on to her, I bet."

"Yes, he has," Bruce conceded.

"I remember you telling me after Adam left the home, everything was, 'Where's Heidi? When's Heidi coming to see me?' You never thought you'd ever hear the end of it. Now another one."

"Matt," Bruce said quietly, hoping his brother would be patient and understanding, "I just came back from the hospital. I want to take a nap before I go back there."

"OK, OK," Matt said, sounding more patient. "Just a minute." It sounded like he was talking to Judy on the other end of the phone. "Bruce, do all of you want to come here for dinner tonight?"

Bruce's shoulders slumped. "No, thank you. You and Judy need some time alone with your kids. I'll take a rain check."

"Are you sure? It's no bother, Bruce. In fact, I want to make sure for myself the two of you are all right."

"We're fine. If there's any problem, we'll call you. Take care of your own family, Matt. Talk to you soon."

"All right. Call me if you need to," Matt said before hanging up.

Bruce decided to slumber on the living room couch since his sheets were already there. A wave of depression overcame him as he pulled the covers over himself. *I'm a failure. Why doesn't anything seem to go right in my life? Dad said I got married too young. I was twenty-two, I had a job, not a great one, but a job. He used to tell me that Matt got married at twenty-five when he was more established, and that made all the difference. What difference? I still held the same job when I was twenty-five. Now I have an eighteen-year-old son with autism and no wife. Just trying to keep everything together and failing at it. And what does Matt expect me to do? Abandon a young woman when she's come into our lives and she's in trouble?*

Bruce fell asleep in the midst of dwelling on these gloomy thoughts.

When he awakened, he jumped out of bed to find out what time it was. He had slept for almost two hours. Sitting on the couch, he called the hospital again and was reassured Adam and Marina were fine. They were watching a DVD in Adam's room and would be ready when he came to pick them up. Marina was not seriously ill but had to regain her strength. However, before he could hang up, Officer Lewis wanted to speak to him.

"Hello, Mr. Hitchens, did you get some rest?" the policeman inquired.

"Yes, I did. I was just going to come over there and pick them up."

"Uh, before you pick them up, I'd like to meet with you for a few minutes at the hospital."

"What's wrong?" Bruce stood up, rigid. He could hear the alarm in his own voice.

"Nothing," Officer Lewis said quickly to calm him. "I just want to keep you abreast of the situation with Miss Dobrin. It's only fair after all you've been through," he added. "But rest assured, there's no terrible news to tell you."

"OK." Bruce took a deep breath and sat back down, no longer alarmed. "I'll be there in about fifteen minutes."

He arrived back to Morristown Memorial Hospital well rested, but his mind was nevertheless in turmoil. Marina did need to go home, but Matt was right: Adam was attached to her now. He said she was a friend, but the truth was he looked at her as a replacement mother figure. Bruce was so worried about his son that he did not even consider his own feelings about Marina.

As soon as he walked into the large building, Officer Lewis was there to greet him. He had already found a private room where they could talk and led Bruce there.

"It's not that we don't believe Miss Dobrin," Lewis mentioned before Bruce even sat down. "It's we have no evidence that anything she told us is true. We're keeping this human trafficking case open, of course, but the majority of these cases we get are from Mexico, Central, and Latin America. Human traffickers from Eastern Europe normally stay in Europe or travel to Asia. We made contact with the FBI, but I want you to know we haven't found information to corroborate her story."

"Not yet," Bruce said.

"No, not yet," Lewis admitted. "But in the meantime, we'd

like to know what you intend to do regarding Miss Dobrin. What we've found out is that she's twenty-seven and she works as a computer programmer in her native country. We made contact with the Moldovan government, and they in turn are trying to contact her family. Hopefully, arrangements will be made to fly her home as soon as possible."

Bruce's heart dropped upon hearing she would leave imminently. "She's welcome to stay with us until she can return home," he said quietly. "I've been sleeping on the couch and it hasn't been a problem."

Officer Lewis remained silent as he regarded Bruce. "But it's going to be a problem for your son when she leaves. He's grown very close with her."

Bruce closed his eyes and nodded. "He has autism, which is quite a challenge in itself. And I'm a widower and he's a lonely boy who needs a mother."

Lewis put his palms up. "I wish there was something we could do to help you. Do you have any relatives that can help?"

"Oh, I have a sister-in-law who's an angel. She's always anxious to help, but she has three children of her own. I hate to bother her, even though I end up doing it anyway," Bruce admitted, staring at his hands. He then grabbed the arms of his chair as he stood up. "But I'll have to make it work out somehow. Marina needs to go home, and I need to take care of my son."

Looking at him sympathetically, Lewis also stood up. "You can check them out now," he said, glancing at his watch. "It's three o'clock. Perhaps you can salvage the rest of this Saturday by doing something fun with your son."

Bruce nodded and put his hands in his pockets. "We're off to Walmart to get Adam some shirts. I'm going to use the rest of the weekend to try impressing upon him that Marina has a family far away and she needs to return to them. Hopefully, he'll start to understand and we can take it from there."

"Sounds like a good plan," Lewis commented. He then added, "You must be a strong individual. I don't know anyone who could handle what you're handling. Alone yet," he shook his head. "A journalist should write about you and everything you're dealing with. People would be amazed."

Bruce did not answer. He put out his hand and shook the policeman's. "Thank you for your help. I better get them now."

He felt Lewis watching him as he turned around and left.

Bruce found Adam and Marina having an animated discussion about horses. Marina sat on a chair near Adam's bed while he bounced up and down,

"Hi, Daddy! Marina and me wanna go horseback riding. Can we, Daddy? Please? Please?"

"Not today, son." Bruce walked in and patted Adam's hair down. "Right now we need to go to Walmart to buy you shirts; hopefully, ones made of iron so you can't bite into them." He turned to Marina. "I understand you checked out OK. That's a big relief."

"Yes it is, certainly," she replied. Bruce noticed her clothes were good quality but were too big on her. "And maybe we'll find some clothes for Marina that she's comfortable in."

Marina opened her mouth to protest, but Adam turned to her and said, "Yeah, Marina. We'll both get clothes. Walmart is a great big store."

"Walmart is reasonably priced. We'll buy you a few things to hold you over. Don't worry," Bruce told her.

"But wait, Daddy! What 'bout the donut?" Adam asked as he was making big rabbit ears to tie his sneaker's laces.

Bruce closed his eyes and slumped his shoulders. When he opened them, Marina led Bruce with her eyes toward the night table. On it was a wrapper from a chocolate bar.

"Ah, Adam, I see you had your chocolate bar. We'll wait on the donut for now," Bruce said, visibly relieved.

"Oh, Daddy. I like both," Adam protested but didn't argue further.

As they walked out, Bruce explained to Marina about the store in Rockaway that was a short distance from the hospital. While in the car, he briefly explained that the police didn't have evidence of the human traffickers from Eastern Europe yet, but they were still digging.

"They're definitely here," Marina said.

"I believe you," he told her with conviction. "We'll talk more about this when we're alone." He moved his head toward the backseat to indicate he did not want to discuss this further with his son present.

Marina nodded and they drove silently the rest of the way. Adam was too busy staring out his window to pay attention to anything else.

Once they parked at the store and got out of the car, Bruce had a sense they were a family walking together. But he sought to banish that thought. *She'll be leaving soon*, he reminded himself.

He pointed in the direction where they had women's clothes. "Look over there," he instructed her. "I'm going to the men's section with Adam."

"OK," Marina said, looking a bit confused. Bruce guessed this was the first American store she had been in. She marveled at all the merchandise.

"You come with me, son." Bruce led him toward the men's section.

But Adam wouldn't budge. "She's coming back to us, right, Daddy? She's my friend."

Bruce rubbed his son's back. "Yes, she is. In fact, we're going to the women's section as soon as we get some shirts for you. Don't worry."

As Bruce started looking through the shirts, he said slowly and carefully to his son, "Adam, you know you have me, right? I'm your father."

"Yeah, I know, Daddy." Adam looked at his father curiously.

"Well, back home in her own country, Marina has a mommy and daddy and even a brother," he began slowly and carefully. "I bet they miss her a lot and she misses them."

Adam brightened and pointed his finger up. "So they can come here too. Then we'll all be together and no one will be alone."

"Bruce," Gwen called him from a few feet away. "Greetings. And this is your handsome son I've heard so much about."

Bruce didn't remember discussing him with Gwen, but he tried to smile. "Hi, Gwen, good to see you. How's your weekend going?"

"I'm still riding high from that presentation," she answered, her eyes sparkling. She turned to Adam. "Do you know how smart your father is?"

"Yeah, my daddy knows a lot. He's buying me shirts because I bite my shirts all the time. My daddy says he wants ta find shirts mada iron," he informed her.

Gwen stopped smiling and noticed for the first time the

holes in his shirt. She looked confused. "How old is he?" she asked Bruce as if Adam weren't even there.

Bruce turned to his son, "How old are you, Adam?"

"I'm eighteen years old," he said proudly, saying it as if he had practiced it. "Do you like horsies?"

Gwen was speechless for a second. When she recovered, she said hastily, "I just came here to buy some cheap socks to knock around in. Oh," she looked at her watch, "I'm running late. Nice to see you, Bruce."

"Take care." Bruce waved his hand limply. He noticed that Gwen did not say good-bye to his son.

He turned back to the shirt rack. "Oh, well. One less problem to worry about."

"Whatdaya mean, Daddy?" Adam stared at his father.

"Nothing, son." He continued looking but thought, *Now Gwen won't be after me as a possible love interest. What a relief!*

Adam searched in every direction. "Daddy, Daddy, where's Marina?"

"I told you she's in the women's section, son. Don't worry."

Bruce chose some shirts and Adam tried them on. All of them had either patterns or deep, rich colors that made him look handsome.

It's a shame they won't last long because he's going to bite into them, he sighed.

Bruce held on to them. "Let's find Marina now . . . Adam, slow down."

His son hurried ahead, calling out, "Marina! Marina!"

"Right here, Adam." Marina waved them over. She held blue jeans, a pink shirt, and white sneakers. Even though they were basic, Bruce figured they'd still look good on her.

"You need proper pajamas, a robe, and slippers," Bruce said. He didn't feel comfortable mentioning underwear and a bra, so all he said was, "Um . . . don't you need a few other things too?"

Marina went to the pajama section and picked out the least expensive pajamas and robe. In the shoes section, she decided to buy a cheap pair of flip flops instead of slippers. She must have realized what Bruce meant by something else because she looked up at him and said, "Yes, um, I'll need a few more things," and walked to the underwear section.

When Marina returned with her chosen items, she met Bruce and Adam in front of a cashier. Marina turned to Bruce and said, "Please, put my clothes on a separate bill so I can pay you back." Bruce started to protest, but Marina said, "I insist. I'm grateful for all you've done, but I'd feel much better if I paid you back." She added, "I had a good job in Moldova, and it gives me dignity to be able to pay for these on my own."

Bruce shrugged his shoulders. "It makes no difference to me, but I'll say it's two separate orders if that'll make you happy."

When Bruce paid and they were on their way out of the store, Adam saw the food section.

"Daddy, I'm getting hungry," Adam said. "Can we have pizza for dinner?"

"Sure, son," Bruce replied. "That'll make it easier."

"You like pizza?" Adam asked Marina.

"Oh, yes, I do, Adam," she smiled.

"Me and my daddy go out for pizza a lot on weekends," he told her.

"Well, let's keep up with your family tradition," she said, and Bruce smiled.

◆ ◆ ◆

Igor didn't have long to wait—he saw Marina coming out with the man and with a younger man he guessed was his son. When they left the hospital and got into their car, he followed them a few cars away. They drove into a town called Rockaway and parked in front of a giant store. Igor watched them go in and thought about when he should grab her. After a few moments in thought, he pounded his fist on the steering wheel. But, as was his habit, he hesitated taking action.

Damn! I can't get her now. She's with those men in a public place! She just spoke to the police. I'll keep following them and I'll choose the right time. When she's most vulnerable and I can easily escape. For now I'll have to bide my time.

So he remained in the car and waited. When he saw them leaving the store, he followed them, again a few cars behind.

CHAPTER TWENTY-FOUR

MARINA

When they reached the car, Adam flapped his hands and cried, "Daddy, Daddy, I'm really hungry."

"Can you call for the pizza so it will be ready by the time we get there?" Marina suggested to Bruce.

"Excellent idea," Bruce agreed and took out his cell phone. He put in the order with Pizza Craze.

Adam flapped his hands excitedly when he saw the Pizza Craze sign. He started getting out of the car while his father still searched for a parking space.

Upon seeing his son open the car door, he stopped the car suddenly. It skidded.

"Adam, are you crazy? You never get out of a moving car!"

"But Daddy, I'm hungry now!"

"Adam, wait!" Marina told him. "Hold my hand, my right hand. You'll be able to stay in the car and sit until your father parks. It's extremely dangerous to jump out of a moving car."

Adam squeezed Marina's hand. She gritted her teeth as he squeezed harder and harder. "H-Hold my h-hand gently, Adam,"

Marina tried to tell him patiently. She didn't want to scream out that he was hurting her. Fortunately, he relaxed his grip as Bruce parked the car. Adam immediately bolted into the restaurant.

"You did a great job calming him down," Bruce said as he got out of the car and jogged to catch up with his son. "Adam sometimes gets irrational when he's hungry."

Bruce paid for the pizza and let Adam and Marina find a seat.

"Adam, let's go to the men's room where you can wash your hands." Bruce indicated for his son to follow him.

When they returned, Marina noticed both men had slightly wet clothes.

"Adam sometimes gets out of hand with the soap and water," Bruce murmured.

"Daddy, that soap did not make alota white bubbles so I had ta use lots," he said. Marina noticed his hands were red and raw.

"That means just a little soap will do the trick, Adam," Marina explained. "You don't need all those white bubbles and water to get your hands clean."

"But I like 'em," he protested in a gentle voice.

Bruce rolled his eyes. "This summer I'll buy you a bottle of liquid bubbles so you can blow your own bubbles. You'll get your bubbles that way."

"When will you get it for me, Daddy? When?"

"As soon as they sell them in the stores," Bruce answered through gritted teeth.

Adam was about to ask more questions, but fortunately the waiter arrived and put the pizza down on their table. Adam grabbed a slice even though it was piping hot, and attempted to devour it.

His father's mouth fell open and he nearly jumped out of

his seat watching him.

"Adam, yikes! The pizza's hot. Slow down and don't stuff your mouth. You'll choke!" Bruce signaled the waiter. "May we have glasses of water, please? We need them right away."

The waiter brought a pitcher of iced water and three glasses. Bruce wasted no time pouring his son a glass. Adam's face had already turned red, but he still chewed the pizza.

"Here, Adam. Drink this," Bruce instructed him.

When everything quieted down, Bruce and Marina took their slices.

"You know, Adam," Marina said, "the pizza tastes much better when you take small bites and chew slowly. Not only that, your stomach feels better after you eat."

"Really?" he asked with a mouthful of food.

"Really. Try it. You'll see."

Adam chewed as she instructed for a few minutes and exclaimed, "Yeah, Marina, you're right. It does taste better."

"And it goes down your stomach easier, too," she added.

"My stomach is feeling better," he told her excitedly as he rubbed his stomach.

He drank his water thirstily. "Daddy, I want lemonade. Aunt Judy's lemonade."

Bruce, who had clearly been sitting relaxed while witnessing their exchange, said, "Son, when we go to Aunt Judy's house, then we can drink her lemonade. She makes it homemade," he explained to Marina. "She loves preparing food, and she obviously has the time. She always makes it when Adam goes over."

"But I wan' her lemonade now, Daddy," Adam said as he flapped his hands in the air and jumped up and down in his seat.

"I like lemonade too, Adam," Marina said. "Do you know how I make my favorite lemonade?"

"How?" Adam immediately calmed down and turned to her, listening expectantly.

"Perhaps the waiter could give us some sliced lemons."

The moment she said this, Bruce wasted no time raising his hand to request sliced lemons. The waiter brought out a dish of them.

Marina took one, squeezed it into her water, and stirred with her straw. Adam watched her and did the same thing.

"Now try it," she instructed him.

"Yum, it taste good," Adam said as he eagerly finished his water. "I wannanother glass, please."

By this time Bruce had dropped all the lemon slices into the remaining pitcher of water. After he poured, he said to Adam, "Marina thinks of everything. And I know this lemonade is very good for you because we didn't add sugar."

Adam didn't seem to understand this. He continued drinking and smacking his lips.

"So," Bruce said, turning his attention to Marina, "are you feeling better about things? Safer?"

She put her hand under her chin as she thought about this. "I feel good about the police and the people at the hospital. I can't wait to talk to my family, but . . ." she said looking down, "I can't stop feeling that someone is watching me. I have no proof, but it's just a feeling. That man—Igor—that's his name. He won't rest until he finds me."

"Maybe he's halfway around the world already," Bruce suggested. "Will his bosses allow him to stay around here looking for you? I'd say they'd be taking a big risk doing that.

If they disappear without a trace, they know there's no way you can prove your story."

"You're right," Marina agreed. "I try to tell myself that. Sometimes I can even convince myself that has happened. Igor can be crazy and unpredictable, and I wouldn't be surprised if they had him killed by now."

"That would certainly be a relief."

Marina shut her eyes and took a deep breath, trying to fight what she thought was her own feelings of paranoia. She smiled as she heard Adam smacking his lips once again. She felt a hand reach for her right hand and she opened her eyes. Bruce was looking at her lovingly.

"We just want you to be safe and happy," he told her.

"Yeah, we're real happy you're gonna live wit us now," Adam looked at her, smiling.

"Ah, Adam, do you need to go to the men's room?" a flushed Bruce turned to his son.

"Yeah, Daddy. I want you ta come wit me."

"Please excuse us," he said to Marina as he led Adam to the men's room again.

"Sure," Marina said as she took the last slice of pizza. As she chewed she tried to convince herself how relieved she would be that she was finally going home. She didn't feel ready to talk about her ordeal, but she would do anything she could to help those other women who were still being held captive. She thought about what she could do now to help them when two men came into the pizzeria speaking Russian.

She dropped the pizza and shivered with fright. Turning her head around slowly with her heart racing, Marina glanced over at them. She put her hand to her chest, relieved that she didn't recognize them. They talked about going to a party later in the evening. She looked all around and was tempted to peek outside to make sure she wouldn't find Igor out there watching and waiting for her. As she was about to rise, Bruce and Adam returned. Adam pouted and looked like he was about to cry. Bruce also looked sullen.

"Marina," he whined, "you've gotta tell your family ta come here."

Marina didn't know what to say to the downcast young man.

Finally, she thought of something. "Adam," she said excitedly, "remember tomorrow we're going to bake chocolate chip cookies—that is, if it's OK with your father."

Bruce shrugged his shoulders. "Sounds good to me."

Before Adam could speak, she said, "And we'll talk while we're making cookies, OK?"

Still serious, Adam nodded.

Looking at him, she thought, *This will be just as hard for me as it will be for you.*

Bruce left four dollars on the table as they rose. Adam stared at the tip.

"That's the tip for the waiter, son," Bruce said, eying him.

"I know," Adam said, his shoulders sagging. "I got no money for candy."

"Candy?" Marina exclaimed, putting her hand on her waist in mock anger. "Why do you need candy when we're making cookies tomorrow?"

Adam brightened. "You're right. I don't need no money for candy when I'm makin' cookies tomorrow wit my friend."

Bruce's tense demeanor relaxed and he broke into a smile, and Marina saw for the first time what a handsome man he really was. His normally worried expression made his features nondescript, but his eyes dancing as he eyed her made him look younger and more appealing. Without thinking, he put his arm around her shoulders and said, "Let's get back home. It's been a long day."

"But Daddy," Adam's stunned expression and loud voice made everyone halt what they were doing, including the restaurant staff and the patrons.

Bruce's eyebrows rose in alarm, and he immediately dropped his arm from Marina's shoulders.

Adam relaxed. "Daddy, you know the rules," he said as if he were an instructor.

Marina laughed and as they left, she discreetly took Bruce's hand and they held hands while Adam rattled on about how much he loved to make and eat cookies.

While walking in the parking lot outside, Marina raised her eyes upward. The sky was filled with stars.

"Adam," Bruce said enthusiastically, "look how many stars are in the night sky. Can you count for me how many you see?"

Adam pointed his finger upward and started counting. Behind them, Bruce quickly gave Marina a kiss on her cheek. Feeling a blush creep up in her face, she looked up at him and wanted to giggle like a teenager. She kissed him back before Adam turned to them.

"Daddy," he said, out of breath in an exasperated voice, "there are so many. I can't count 'em all. I only got ta fourteen stars."

"That's OK, son" he said as he uncharacteristically touched his son's cheek. "The stars are endless. It would be a miracle if anybody could count them all."

"So why try?" he asked, staring at his father.

Bruce shrugged. "I don't know. Maybe miracles can happen."

"No miracle happened tonight," Adam insisted.

I'm not sure about that, Marina thought. She hadn't felt this happy in a long, long time. After all those months on the ship, she never thought she would ever be this happy again.

◆ ◆ ◆

From his black Mercedes twenty feet away, Igor watched them kiss while the younger man was looking up at the sky. He breathed a sigh of relief.

If she weren't distracted, she might have seen my car. So, she's got a boyfriend now, does she? That's why she's staying at his house.

The three of them got into the car and drove off. Igor shifted in his seat. This was a pivotal moment.

If I kill her now right after she's gone to the police, that would be foolish. Wait a day and they'll have other things on their minds. Meanwhile, I'm going back to the hotel. I'll get the silencer for my gun, handcuffs, duct tape, and a Taser. I will take her down and, before she dies, it will be my highest joy to laugh in her face!

Igor rubbed his chin. *That younger man—something about him just doesn't seem right. Like he's not quite normal. He'll most likely not be a problem. The other man I don't know yet. I'll have to figure this won't be an easy operation. Everything must be done carefully.*

Chapter Twenty-Five

BRUCE

Bruce glanced in his rear view mirror. Strapped in his seat belt, Adam sat glued to the window, watching everything. Bruce sat back as he drove, marveling that this was one of the wonders of his son: he was always curious about the world around him. He loved discussing the simplest things as if they were exceedingly fascinating: the cheetah being the fastest animal in the world, his daily quest to shake the orange juice so it tasted just right, and talking about his day when Bruce got home from work. Bruce smiled as he recalled the excited sparkle in his son's eyes when he walked in and turned on the stove so Adam could cook the food he prepared for dinner.

Whenever Judy brought up the subject of her own children, Bruce could never help being envious that she and Matt were lucky enough to have normal children. He never thought much about her concerns, concerns he would never experience: Sarah staying out too late with friends, David trying drugs at parties, and Danielle continually complaining she wasn't pretty, thin, or smart enough. Only now, feeling whole with Marina beside him in the passenger seat of his car, did it dawn on him that families that did not have special needs children could also be fraught with challenges. Perhaps these challenges were only temporary and could be rectified eventually—at least there was always hope the situation would improve. Unfortunately, families with special needs children had little hope for improvement short of a miracle. Bruce realized when his wife Maggie was alive, the hardships were made more bearable because he could count on her love and support. Could the same be possible with Marina?

Bruce's inner critic laughed at his deep longing: Marina would leave the country soon and reunite with her own family in Moldova.

You're dreaming, Bruce. What's wrong with you? Get a reality check, he told himself.

"Bruce?" Marina asked, breaking into his thoughts. He saw her staring at him. "What's wrong, Bruce? You look so sad."

"Oh, nothing." Bruce tried to smile and wave his hand dismissively. "I've got a lot of yard work to do tomorrow and instead of helping, you know who will want my attention every minute." Bruce looked in the back seat. Adam sat back with his eyes now closed.

"Oh, you don't have to worry about that," Marina reassured him, smiling. "Tomorrow we'll make cookies, watch nature shows, and if he wants, we'll take a walk"

"But I'm sure you'll be busy with other things. The police may want to talk to you and you'll probably hear from your parents."

Marina looked out the front window from the passenger seat and sat back. "It's not much, considering all he's done for me," she replied. "I want to show him a good time that, hopefully, we'll both always remember. That reminds me, Bruce," she sat up, raising her head up toward him, "I want to set up Facebook and Skype accounts so we can always see and talk to each other. Adam's a wonderful person who knows the meaning of true mercy." She paused, reflecting. "He saved my life, and I don't want to just disappear from his life or y—," she hesitated. "I want to keep in touch."

Bruce hoped she wanted to add, "or yours" but perhaps felt overcome with shyness. *After all, I'm sure she'll forget about me and find someone else soon enough.*

He brushed these thoughts aside because he did not want to appear melancholy again.

When they reached his house, Bruce concentrated on taking care of his sleepy son, giving him a sponge bath and brushing his teeth. Tomorrow morning he would make sure Adam had a full shower.

After Bruce finished putting Adam to bed, he saw Marina lingering in the bedroom doorway, staring at him and then looking down at the floor.

Does she think I'm going to want to sleep with her? Of course, I do. But she might think she owes it to me. It wouldn't be right because she's leaving soon and she probably needs space after all she's been through.

"Have a good night's sleep, Marina," he said, waving and trying to smile.

"You too. Good night," she said, reaching for the door handle. She faced him again, as if she wanted to say more, but disappeared into the bedroom.

Bruce went into the living room and lay down on the couch. He quickly drifted off to sleep. He must have slept soundly because before he knew it, he opened his eyes and saw Adam standing over him.

"Mornin', Daddy," he said, his hair sticking out in all directions as was usual first thing in the morning. "Is Marina still sleepin'?"

Bruce glanced at his watch. Eight fifteen a.m. "Did you go to the bathroom yet, Adam?"

"Yup," he answered, nodding his head. "Whatawe goin' do today, Daddy?"

Bruce thought about how to answer when the phone rang. He jumped up and ran into the kitchen and picked it up.

Detective Lewis was on the line. "Hello, Mr. Hitchens. I apologize for calling so early on a Sunday morning, but I have Miss Dobrin's parents on the other line and they're anxious to speak to her."

"Of course," Bruce answered. "Give me a moment to knock on her door and wake her up."

"Thank you, Mr. Hitchens."

When Bruce went to knock on her door, Adam took the phone.

"Does this mean Marina and her family will come here and live nearby?" he asked the policeman expectantly.

"Adam," Bruce whispered to his son, "don't bother the policeman." He knocked on the bedroom door.

A groggy Marina came to the door, but her face lit up like a candle upon hearing who was on the line. She ran to the phone with a big smile on her face.

"Thank you, Adam." She took the phone from the speechless young man with his mouth half open.

Tears flowed as she spoke to her family in what Bruce

guessed must be Romanian or Russian. Adam stood near her, staring.

Bruce tried to lead his son away, but he wouldn't move.

"Why's she cryin', Daddy?"

"Marina hasn't spoken to her parents in a long time, son. She's overjoyed to hear from them. Come on," he said, encouraging his son to move away, "let's give her some space."

They headed for the living room. Bruce had to pull Adam's arm because he couldn't take his eyes off Marina.

"Why's Marina talkin' funny? What's she sayin'?"

"She talking in another language. I guess it's Romanian or Russian. She's from a country called Moldova. It's far away from here and that's what they speak there."

Trying to distract him, Bruce faced Adam, put his hands on his shoulders, and tilted his head so he would look directly into his eyes. "I have a lot of work to do around the house today. Why don't you help me with the yard work? I have an extra rake. You can help me rake leaves and put them in big piles. Only Adam," he cautioned, "you can't play in the leaf piles. I've got to shovel them into bags."

Adam responded by pouting and stamping his foot. "But, Daddy, I'm supposedta make chocolate chip cookies wit Marina t'day."

By this time Marina was off the phone. Bruce heard the sink running. Then she entered the living room with a tissue in her hand, her eyes shining.

"They've waited and prayed for months to hear news about me," she said, wiping her eyes. "They never gave up hope that I was still alive." She sat down. "This is so much to take in. I can't believe so much time has gone by since I last saw them."

"Adam," Bruce turned to his son, who flapped his arms and bit his shirt, "I want you to choose your own clothes to wear. Don't forget underwear and socks," he added in a lower tone. "If you can do this all by yourself today, I'll be very proud of you."

Marina, who appeared lost in thought, nodded.

"Then . . . then, we can make cookies?" he asked her.

"Son . . . ," Bruce started to say.

"Yes, yes, of course," she said.

"Now, go on. I know you can do it, Adam. All by yourself," his father said. Once he left the room, Bruce turned to her.

"The police are trying to arrange to get a ticket for me to fly back to Moldova. They can't find any evidence that what I've told them is true yet, but they'll contact me if they do," she mentioned when they were alone. "I want to spend the day with Adam." She covered her face with her hands. "I have so many mixed emotions. I know it sounds crazy, but I'm exhilarated and sad at the same time."

"A lot has happened to you," Bruce said as the phone rang again.

He closed his eyes and his shoulders slouched when he saw who it was on the caller ID.

"Hi, Matt. How're you and the family doing?"

"It's me, Bruce," Judy said. "We're doing fine. How's everything with you?"

"We're fine too," Bruce said, his prepared retorts of telling his brother to mind his own business melting away. *Smart, Matt. You put your wife on the line so you don't hear it from me.*

"Matt and I are wondering whether the three of you can come to dinner tonight. I'm making one of Adam's favorites, southern fried chicken."

That was tempting. Adam went gaga over Judy's chicken, and Bruce loved it too.

"Just one moment," he said.

"Of course," Judy responded.

Bruce walked into the living room. Marina stared out the window, lost in thought. When he coughed, she turned around. "Judy's on the phone. She wants to have us over tonight for dinner. Would you like to go?"

"Oh, that would be fine," she said. "I'd love it."

"Love what, Marina? What would ya love?" Adam walked in wearing formal blue wool pants and an orange shirt full of holes.

"We're going to Aunt Judy's tonight," Bruce said. "But you're not wearing those pants."

"I love goin' ta Aunt Judy's house," he said as he clapped his hands and jumped up and down.

His father stopped listening to Adam's exclamations of delight and headed back into the kitchen. "Ah, thank you, Judy. That sounds great. Can I just talk to Matt for a minute?"

"Sure. We're looking forward to seeing everyone tonight," she said before handing the phone over to her husband.

"Hi, Bruce. Is everything all right?" Matt asked.

"Everything's fine. Believe it or not, I'm handling things on my own. Don't worry about me. You've got your own family to worry about."

"You've gotten the police involved with this woman?" Matt persisted.

Bruce was determined to talk like the confident, in-control older brother, but his resolve soon vanished. An overwhelming depression overcame him, contemplating the return of his lonely life before Marina's arrival. He squeezed his eyes shut to block out the ever-growing sadness at the thought of her leaving. The tremendous weight of loneliness already hung over him.

"She spoke with her parents this morning," he said dolefully.

"That's excellent! I mean, I know this is going to be hard for you, Bruce, but you need a woman with fewer complications. It'll be for the best, you'll see. I'm going to brainstorm with Judy about eligible women we know and . . ."

"I've gotta go. I'll see you tonight." Bruce hung up before he started shouting at his brother. *What gives you the right, little brother, to tell me what's best for me! What the hell do you know about what I've been through and who I should date!*

He didn't want to make a scene in front of Marina. After all, she and Adam were chatting happily about their plans for today. He willed himself to keep his feelings in check until he was alone.

"Excuse me. First of all, Adam," he said, attempting to smile as he walked in on them, "those pants are not right for hanging around the house. Put on jeans. We'll save those pants for special occasions."

"Your father's right," Marina said, smiling. "We don't want you to get chocolate chips all over those fine pants."

Adam's eyes sparkled at the mention of chocolate chips.

"But first, let's all eat breakfast," Bruce said as he led his son back to his bedroom.

After they all ate, Bruce cut the lawn. The grass had grown so tall since he'd last mowed it. The flowers Maggie planted were beginning to bloom. He stopped to look at all the bright, bold colors. His late wife had said it meant new beginnings. His eyes looked down for a moment, and he forced himself to keep working and stop thinking so far ahead.

On his next work break, he spied Marina and Adam in the kitchen pulling out trays of cookies. He saw Adam about to take one but then saw Marina shaking her head, pointing to her tongue, indicating they were too hot. Adam seemed to understand, but he nevertheless kept staring at the cookies. After Bruce had finished with the lawn, he took out his clippers and trimmed the bushes. Adam and Marina came out to tell him they were taking a walk.

He watched them walk away, and in his mind he saw Adam walking with Maggie again. He shook his head, trying to dispel these memories. He clipped the bushes and fought back tears as he remembered how it used to be when his wife was still alive. Life had been challenging, but it was much more manageable and they still had moments to enjoy. Of course, the house was too small and he wanted to go up the company ladder so they would live more comfortably. They had goals. When Maggie died, he'd been bereft and lost but had to keep himself together for Adam's sake.

Then Marina had come into their lives momentarily, but now her departure was imminent. He told himself he had to use this transition period to take care of Adam, who would surely be heartbroken when Marina left, and then set new goals. As always, he needed to impress upon his son that as helpful as women like Heidi and Marina were, neither of them was his mother. But he, as his father, was here to stay and would be here to take care of him as long as he was able.

As he entered the house and showered, his mind returned to what Matt had told him. Apparently, Marina coming into his life was a sign that perhaps he was ready to date again. But it would be awhile before he was ready to do that. At forty-two years old, he certainly wasn't ancient. But before he'd begin dating anyone, he would have to let the woman know he had a son with autism. If a woman had a problem with that, he would know not to pursue her.

By the time he finished showering and changing his clothes, Marina and Adam had returned from their walk. Upon seeing her, his heart melted. *How can I let her go?*

But he couldn't think about that now. Adam looked crestfallen. Marina must have already told him she was leaving.

Before anyone could say anything, the phone rang. Bruce rushed to the kitchen and picked it up.

It was the police. "Mr. Hitchens?"

"Yes. Hi, Detective Lewis."

All formalities were brushed aside. "Mr. Hitchens, I need to speak with Miss Dobrin."

"I'll get her. Have you found a lead to corroborate her story?"

"Possibly," was all the officer would say.

Bruce called Marina to the phone. When she took it, he joined Adam, who enveloped his father, sobbing.

"Marina said she has to go home to her mommy and daddy and brother," Adam said, weeping. "Why won't they come here and live wit us?"

"That's their home, son. Like here is our home," Bruce told him, clutching his son to give himself comfort.

Adam pulled away and faced his father, tears running down his cheeks. "Why can't we go ta her country, Daddy?"

Bruce couldn't help smiling as he brushed away some of Adam's strands from his face. "I don't know their language, son, so I wouldn't be able to make a living. Life would be so much harder for us."

"But we'd have Marina," Adam cried, and Bruce hugged his despondent son.

After a moment, Adam pulled his head back and spoke to his father. "Marina said we could be friends on Facebook and go on Skype. What's that?"

"That would be great, Adam," Bruce said, trying to smile encouragingly. "You can talk to Marina and see her on the computer."

"But it won't be the same, Daddy. It won't be the same," Adam wailed.

Before Bruce could respond, Marina came in. Father and son looked at her.

"The police are going to pick me up. They found a body and they want to know if I can identify it," Marina said, trembling.

"Does that mean you're not leavin', Marina?" Adam asked hopefully.

"I won't be able to go to your Aunt Judy's house tonight, but, Adam, I will come back after dinner. I promise."

"But I want you there wit us," Adam whined.

"Everyone does, son," Bruce told him as he rubbed his back. "But Marina has to be somewhere else tonight, unfortunately." He turned back to her. "Are you all right about this? I could go with you."

Marina shook her head. "Adam needs you." She looked at the younger man tenderly. "I'll be all right. This is something I have to do. Don't worry, I'll be fine." She walked over to them. "All of your help and support have made me stronger. I'm ready for this now. If it is who I think it is, I'll be free to tell the police everything I can remember and perhaps rescue some of the other girls."

◆ ◆ ◆

The morning news was on TV, and Igor was busy making careful preparations to take Marina down. Resisting the temptation to rush over to the Hitchens' house and get it over with by tonight, he wrestled with the chances of being caught if he waited until tomorrow. He was determined to kill her as soon as possible without any more delays. In the midst of his head swirling with plans, he checked his cell phone. The mailbox was full. Igor knew it was Andre. He decided to put off calling him until he had completed what he'd set out to do. As for explaining Sergei's disappearance, Igor would say he drank himself to death at a night club—Andre knew his tendencies: Sergei's first priority was always to spend his money on a good time.

While packing his Taser, a picture slipped out of his suitcase. Igor picked it up and slowly brought it up to his face as he stared at his girlfriend and himself before his jaw and upper neck had been slashed. The memory of her horrified expression when he connected with her on Skype while he was still on the ship reappeared: her face turned away from him in disgust when she saw the ugly scar. She then made a flimsy excuse that she couldn't talk with him that night and she would call him soon. But she never did. Instinctively, he touched his scar. His head throbbed at the memory as he sat down on the bed and massaged his temples. The picture fell to the floor as he reached into the night table for a small bottle. Then he closed his eyes as he felt the vodka go down his throat and awaited the revival of his spirit.

Igor wanted to let go of the past. He wanted to stop thinking about his old girlfriend. Although it never occurred to him that his girlfriend would probably have been aghast at his profession, he never bothered to consider that. He vaguely told her he shipped goods abroad every few weeks. But all he remembered was that their relationship was fine until Marina slashed the side of his face and left him with an ugly scar.

Anxious to clear his head, he got up and continued packing equipment. Igor was about to turn off the TV and go to a nearby restaurant for breakfast when a special news brief came on the screen. A somber-looking newscaster with a dark suit and thick, slicked-backed dark brown hair reported that a body had been found in an old abandoned house in Morristown.

"The man has been identified as Sergei Moskey, originally from Russia. Patrol officers found his body yesterday morning. This is all the information the police have for the public at this time, but they are confident more leads will come in. We will keep our viewers posted as this story develops."

Immediately following the news brief, Igor's cell phone rang incessantly. He checked the phone: it was Andre. Surprising himself, he picked it up.

Andre was unusually calm and personable. "Igor, Igor, where have you been? Don't you know I've been trying to contact you and Sergei?"

"Don't worry." Igor was lulled by his boss's friendly words. "We had a problem. Sergei's dead, but I going to . . ."

"His body was just found, Igor, no?" Andre interrupted him. His tone quickly switched to demanding. "Igor, what happened?"

Igor straightened up. This was a crucial conversation. He knew his future depended on it. "A girl escaped, but don't worry. I already know where she's living and I will dispose of her."

"Tell me where she's staying and I'll bring in some men for backup."

Igor could not believe his good fortune. *Andre was actually willing to help him on his mission to kill that woman.*

He gave Andre the address and described the location.

"Call me if you take care of this on your own, Igor. I'll be sending men over to help you clean up the situation. If needed."

And the phone went dead.

CHAPTER TWENTY-SIX

BRUCE

THE POLICE PICKED UP MARINA. BRUCE COULD SEE tears well up in her eyes as she watched them from the window of the departing patrol car. Officer Lewis, who would escort her to the morgue, said her parents would be making arrangements for her to fly back to Moldova, but if she could identify the body, it would be a significant lead and thereby her departure might be delayed.

All of Bruce's prior rationalizations about accepting Marina leaving no longer consoled him. His emotional side took over. Like his son, he was reluctant to see her go. Facebook and Skype failed to provide the human element he needed: to live with someone, touch that person, and provide companionship in good times as well as in bad.

Bruce tore himself away from the front window. He could not allow himself to succumb to these gloomy thoughts—he had a son to take care of. He turned to Adam, who walked away from the window with his head down. His son also needed a distraction.

"You need to change that shirt, Adam. Put on one of the new ones I bought you with no holes in it."

"I don' wanna, Daddy."

"Don't you want to look nice for your Aunt Judy?"

"I don' care. I want Marina," he whined, stamping his foot and flapping his hands.

Bruce held his arms up and his eyes shot up to the ceiling. "Son, she had to leave. It was urgent. She's going to come back later."

"She can't leave," Adam said, pouting and stubbornly folding his arms in front of him.

"Marina will be back," Bruce pleaded, the energy to argue dissipating from his reserves. But an idea struck him. He turned to his son. "Aunt Judy is making southern fried chicken."

"Southern fried chicken!" he said. His eyes lit up. "Like KFC?"

Bruce nodded. "If you change your shirt now, and also your jeans," he said, noticing their chocolate stains for the first time, "we'll get to Aunt Judy's faster and ask her if we can bring some home for Marina."

"All right," he raised his fist. "Then we'll eat more KFC with Marina later."

"That's right," Bruce answered, relieved he had distracted his son for the moment.

But his spirits sagged again as they got into the car to go. Thoughts of living the solitary life again unnerved him.

He rubbed his temples whenever there was a red light. He blinked his eyes rapidly to make sure a headache wasn't coming on.

"Daddy, when can we see Marina?" Adam asked, sitting in the backseat, pointing his index finger up in the air.

"When *can* we see Marina?" Bruce now repeated his son's own question to him.

"When she finishes talkin' wit the police," Adam replied. He stared out the side window for ten seconds before turning to his father again.

"Daddy, when can we see Marina?" he asked, pointing his index finger in the air again.

"Soon," Bruce replied. He was tired of answering the same question. Attempting to change the subject, he said, "Adam, Daddy's tired."

"Daddy's tired," his son repeated. He flapped his hands as he looked out the side window.

Finally, he stopped. Thank God.

Adam turned to his father, pointing his finger. "When can we see Marina?"

"That's it," Bruce replied with clenched teeth. He pulled into the parking lot of a Quik Check, his tires squealing at the unexpected turn.

Without saying another word, Bruce opened his door and headed into the convenience store.

"Hey, Daddy, wait." Adam speedily joined him at his side.

They approached the candy aisle.

"What do you want?"

Adam's face broke into all smiles upon viewing all the sweet treats.

Bruce lifted his index finger. "Only one, Adam."

His son continued looking around, mesmerized by the chocolates, the bright chewy candy, and the peanut butter-filled treats. His eyes settled on the giant rainbow lollipops.

Without asking him, Bruce grabbed a giant lollipop and

proceeded to the cashier.

"I wonder what all the colors taste like. Do they all taste good, Daddy?"

His father took a bottle of aspirin off the shelf and a bottle of water out of the cooler and paid without answering.

"Come on, Adam. We don't want to keep Aunt Judy waiting," he said, handing him the lollipop as they walked out of the store. Before starting the car's engine, he swallowed two aspirins with the water. He tilted back his head as he felt the aspirins go down his throat and into his bloodstream. He couldn't wait for his head to feel some relief.

"Daddy?" he heard Adam whisper.

When he opened his eyes, the giant multicolored lollipop encompassed his vision. He jerked back, his eyes alarmed.

"Daddy, can you open the lolli for me, please?" he heard his son say.

Bruce grabbed the lollipop and tore the wrapper off, resisting the urge to shove it down his son's throat.

"Here you go, son," he said as he pushed the lollipop away without looking at Adam.

"Thanks, Daddy," Adam said, seemingly oblivious to his father's impatience. "Wow!"

Bruce turned to him.

"It tastes good," Adam said, sticking out his tongue to lick the lollipop. "It tastes like all kinds of different colors."

Bruce turned on the engine without answering. He focused on the road while his son marveled at the taste of the lollipop.

Bruce approached his brother's imposing stucco home with his stomach churning, wondering if this dinner would provide some much-needed relief or if his son would resume his incessant questioning. Adam sat contentedly slurping on the lollipop. Bruce now contemplated what Adam's next dentist visit would be like. He wished he had also brought a toothbrush so he could go over his son's teeth before the sugar set in.

He parked his car in the corner of his brother's circular driveway, the least imposing space he could find for his small Buick. He could see Judy's Mercedes SUV and Matt's Lotus in two of the garages. One of their kids' BMWs was in the third garage while the other two BMWs were parked in the spacious driveway where they could pull out any time they wished. Bruce expected the three kids to do their usual staring at his son and snickering among each other. Adam took off his seat belt and bounced up before the car came to a full stop.

"We're here! We're finally here! I hope Aunt Judy made her lemonade!" Adam chirped as he opened the door.

"Adam! Give me a chance to park the car, will you please?" Bruce snapped, unable to contain his annoyance.

Calm down, Bruce. Get a handle on yourself, he reprimanded himself.

But Adam had already lumbered up the steps of Matt and Judy's McMansion before his father could finish his sentence. Bruce locked up the car when he saw Adam place his thick finger against the doorbell. He was about to yell at him that his aunt didn't need to hear the bell's continuous ringing when she opened the door.

"Hi, Aunt Judy!" He gave her a bear hug.

"Oh no!" Adam pulled away and put his hand over his mouth.

"What's wrong, Adam?" Judy asked, her eyes wide open in alarm.

"Oh, I forgot! You're a woman."

Judy face softened into a loving smile. "That's OK. I'm family."

Adam bumped the corner of his head. "That's right! You're part of my family."

And he embraced her again, this time nearly lifting her off her feet.

"Adam! Don't hug so tight!" Bruce warned as he came up the steps.

Adam let her go. Judy waved away his concerns. "I live for hugs," she said, squeezing his cheeks.

She turned to Bruce. "Nice to see you, too. Welcome," she beamed. She looked over at the car. "Where's Marina?"

"She couldn't come. The police needed to question her."

Before Judy could ask another question, Adam asked, "Can we bring some KFC for her when she gets home, Aunt Judy? Please, please?"

"Of course," she said, looking at Bruce for an explanation.

"They may have a lead," was all he said.

"That would be great! I hope so." She turned to lead them inside and called into the house, "Matt! Kids! They're here!"

Bruce braced himself. He was determined to put everything behind him—Marina, his job, Adam's future—but his stomach was still tied up in knots. He hoped the aspirins would soon take effect.

As Judy ushered them in to her long marble dining room table, Adam raised his fists as in victory, "Yay! Aunt Judy made her lemonade!"

"Hi, guys." Matt came down the stairs to greet them. Before he realized what was happening, Matt was enveloped in Adam's arms for a quick hug. He patted him on the back while his mouth hung open in an attempt to breathe.

Once Adam released him and he could speak again, Matt glanced around. "Where is she?"

"Being questioned again by police," Bruce answered grimly.

Matt waved his hand. "Bruce, you don't need this. Hope this is over with as soon as possible."

Bruce felt his anger building inside, but he did not respond.

"My friend Marina couldn't come," Adam said.

"That's all right, buddy," Matt said, rumpling his hair. Matt whispered to his brother, "Getting too attached" and shook his head.

Bruce changed the subject. "Where're the kids?"

"Oh, I don't know," Judy said, taking plates out of the cupboard. "They're either texting their friends, watching TV, or a combination of both."

"Let me go upstairs to see if I can find them," Matt said, rolling his eyes. As he went up the steps, he called out, "Earth to Sarah, David, and Danielle. Your relatives are here!"

Judy ushered them to the dining room table. "Come sit and eat. It takes awhile to get them down."

"When are we goin' see Marina, Daddy?" Adam asked as he looked at his father expectantly.

But he was distracted when Judy served the chicken and side dishes. The savory-looking crispness of the chicken cooked to perfection and the inviting, freshly made cooking smells of the Spanish rice made even Bruce temporarily forget everything else. But as he was about to take a bite of chicken, Bruce glanced over at his son's anxious, gloomy eyes and wondered how long he could put off the inevitable: he didn't know how much longer

Marina would be in their lives.

Judy raised her eyebrows in surprise, but Bruce was used to his son's dramatic sulking.

"That poor young woman," Judy said in a low voice, shaking her head. "I wonder how she's doing." She then turned to her nephew. "I bet she'll be so happy to see you tonight, Adam."

"When can I see Marina again? It's takin' too long," Adam exclaimed, slapping his palm on his knee.

"How, how did David do with the science experiment he was working on?" Bruce asked Judy.

"He won first place," she said proudly, her eyes glowing. "I had to go shopping for days to get all the supplies he needed. He and his sisters were too busy to help me. Finally, I got everything and he put it all together and won."

"Congratulations," Bruce said a little too enthusiastically. "You hear that, Adam? Your cousin is a top science student."

Leaning on his elbow and picking at his chicken, Adam said nothing.

"Maybe David will show you his science experiment. Won't that be cool?" Bruce persisted. "Adam, have some of your aunt's lemonade."

His son chugged down half a glass and Bruce appreciated the break.

He heard Matt knocking on doors and calling his kids.

"I don't care if you're texting the president of the United States. Come down. You're being rude!" Matt's voice could be heard from the second floor.

Bruce looked at Judy. "What's Sarah up to? Isn't she graduating high school this year?"

"Sarah's looking at more colleges this week," Judy answered, pouring lemonade for herself.

"Oh really? She's a great student. She must have a lot of colleges to choose from."

"We've been running around visiting campuses everywhere."

Bruce noticed she looked introspective, her eyes tired.

"She goin' go to Columbus?" Adam asked, reaching for a chicken breast.

"Columbus, Ohio?" Judy asked.

Bruce relaxed his shoulders while he ate, hoping his son was finally off the Marina subject.

"Columbus University? I dunno," Adam bit into a large chicken breast.

"Oh, you mean, Columbia University! We went there, but Sarah said she doesn't want to live in New York City. It's too busy."

With his mouth full, Adam turned to his father. "Daddy, I wanna live in New York City. So many people I won't be alone. We can go to New York City. Can we, Daddy? Can we, please? Marina'll like it too."

How about the Fairmount Home, Adam? You'll never be alone there, Bruce yearned to say out loud.

"Adam, if you move to New York City, I won't get to see you much. And then I'll be sad," his aunt took a bite of her chicken wing.

Adam raised his index finger. "We can have a room for Aunt Judy in New York City, Daddy. A room for Aunt Judy and a room for Marina. We'll have a good time."

"Adam, honey, you think of everything," Judy giggled, bringing her napkin to her mouth. "But, you know, I have to see Uncle Matt and my kids sometimes."

Bruce put his drumstick down. He was no longer hungry. His head began pounding and the chicken he ate now formed a pain in the pit of his stomach.

"I'm going to use the restroom," he said as he rose.

"Of course," his sister-in-law said. "Adam, can I pour you some more lemonade?"

Adam reached out his glass. "Yeah. You make the best lemonade, Aunt Judy."

Bruce tried to shut out his son's chatter. He walked into the restroom and locked the door. He splashed cold water on his face and studied his reflection in the mirror. He stared at himself, wondering if he was looking more grey. He was forty-two years old, but was life turning him into a prematurely old man? He couldn't focus on this now—he had to attend to his son, particularly since he was so anxious to see Marina again.

By the time he left the bathroom, Matt and his three kids were at the table.

"Hi, Uncle Bruce," Sarah said. "Sorry I didn't come down right away. I just had to finish up an essay."

Matt nudged his other two kids. "It's hard for them to hear when they have their iPods on full blast."

Putting on his social face, Bruce smiled at them. "Hi, kids. Good to see you again. How's it going?"

"Great!" David waved, giving a thumbs-up while failing to conceal a smirk.

Bruce went over and shook David's hand. David then went to shake Adam's hand. "Don't squeeze too hard, buddy," he said gently. "We all know you're a tough guy."

"I've been waitin' all day for your mommy's KFC and lemonade," Adam declared loudly as he gave his cousin a quick shake. "I wish my friend was here."

"Hi, Sarah and Danielle. You girls are looking well," Bruce walked over to them.

Danielle looked like she was ready to bolt. Sarah wore a weak smile and waved unenthusiastically. Bruce realized instinctively not to come too close. *They want to stay away from their weird uncle and his even weirder son*, he thought glumly.

"Daddy, Sarah and Danielle are my family. Can I give them a hug too?"

Both girls' eyes widened in sheer terror, but Bruce told him he could only shake their hands gently.

"Why not, Daddy? Isn't Sarah and Danielle my family too?" Adam whined, oblivious to both girls tensing up and shaking slightly.

"Yeah, Uncle Bruce, they're family too," David said, snickering.

His sisters glared at him.

"It wouldn't be appropriate to hug them, son. The girls are close to your age," Bruce fumbled with an explanation.

"But David would certainly love a hug from his favorite cousin!" Danielle said as she smiled wickedly.

David glared at her and before he had a chance to reply, he was engulfed in Adam's arms. David lost his balance but fortunately, both landed on the leather couch close to the dining room table and not on the hardwood floor.

"Adam, what're you doing?" Bruce exhorted him stridently with his eyes bulging and his jaw down.

Sarah and Danielle giggled. David struggled to free himself from Adam's arms, which still enclosed him. Also laughing, Matt walked over to help his son free himself.

Judy turned to Bruce. "Calm down. No big deal." She then told her husband and kids to sit down and eat dinner.

Embarrassed, Bruce wanted to leave but realized he was trapped. He didn't feel like hanging around after his son's antics, but he knew Adam would refuse to leave, and Judy and Matt would insist they stay. So he slinked back into his chair with the others. When he got there, he felt a tap on his shoulder.

"We'll talk privately in the office after dinner's finished, Bruce. Just hang in there," whispered his brother.

Bruce felt like rolling his eyes. *Great! Now I'm really ready to make my escape.*

Judy poured Adam some more lemonade and offered him salad and corn on the cob. David steered clear of his cousin and sat as far away from him as possible, his leg shaking, continually glancing at the stairs as if he couldn't wait to eat and be excused from the table. Grinning widely, Danielle sat next to him with Sarah sitting next to her. Bruce noticed they were all at a fairly safe distance from his son.

"Help yourself to Caesar salad, corn on the cob, and lemonade, everyone," Judy announced. "I'll get some more chicken from the kitchen. Danielle and Sarah, you girls will help me serve."

"Certainly, mother," Danielle said. She was clearly being entertained. Sarah just stood up with a scowl on her face.

◆ ◆ ◆

The time was well past midnight. Andre's face was taut with anger. His tightened fist slammed his desk. He had finally gotten in touch with Igor and his worst fear had been realized:

his employee's instability could jeopardize his operations. The American police could be on to them. "Damn that Igor! Sergei's dead, and he's after that one woman who escaped! He's threatening my empire with his obsession!" He looked around his office. "That girl will end up dead anyway if she's wandering in America with no passport and she can't speak English! Who cares if we lose just one!" He sat back and gritted his teeth. "I must know what's going on there and what he's doing. I don't believe Igor's story. Sergei would have had the sense to contact me!" He directed his eyes toward Vladimir, who was seated quietly across from him. "What do you have for me? You were telling me about this man you found." He waved his hand and said, "Go on."

Vladimir continued telling Andre about him. Andre was about to question the veracity of the story but was cut short.

Vladimir's cell phone rang.

"Yes," Vladimir answered the cell. His eyebrows perked up and he nodded to Andre.

"Yes, Mr. Standu, I've been waiting for your call." He mouthed to Andre, "It's him."

"Yes, you are free now?" Vladimir said, looking at Andre for a response. When Andre nodded, Vladimir spoke into the phone, "Yes, let's not waste any time. If you come to my office. I can meet you in ten minutes."

Vladimir gave the caller his address and hung up.

"I'll set up my camera to view your office," Andre told him. "Hopefully, he will be the one and we just have to find him a partner."

"I have a good feeling about this one, but we will see," Vladimir said, his eyes bright and his mouth displaying a self-satisfied smug. He called two of his assistants to be ready for the interview.

His enthusiasm quelled any nagging questions Andre considered asking.

Wasting no time, Vladimir bowed slightly to Andre and departed from the basement office. His own office, only six blocks away, was in a building with many of the region's best doctors, attorneys, and business people. The tenants had an unspoken understanding that Vladimir was known as the "superintendent's assistant." He occupied an office in the basement and the other tenants rarely saw him. Vladimir did most of his work after midnight until the early morning hours. Truth be told, no one gave him much thought. He remained a shadowy figure whom they were told was supposedly vital to the maintenance of the upscale office building. On rare occasions when the other tenants saw him walking through the building, Vladimir stared straight ahead and ignored the others whenever he crossed their paths. This bothered no one because these professionals were far too busy with their own businesses and making as much money as they could to be concerned about him. The building was far enough away from Andre's to be thought of as a whole different world, despite being only six blocks away.

Vladimir's office was spartan, consisting of a solid steel desk and a faux leather chair. Across the desk were two fabric-covered wooden chairs in a rich, dark blue. The vast majority entering his office were low-level prospective employees who were sufficiently impressed with its clean and well-maintained appearance.

As instructed, two of Vladimir's assistants led a blindfolded, muscular man into his office. He knew his men had already patted the man down. Wordlessly, they sat him down across from Vladimir, and when Vladimir nodded, they exited the room. The man, Victor Standu, sat silently, still blindfolded.

This is a good sign, thought Vladimir. *The man has patience.*

"Please, remove your blindfold," Vladimir instructed.

As he did so, he saw a man with blue eyes and blondish-brown wavy hair. Victor was in peak physical shape, not an ounce of fat. Vladimir could see the muscles bulging out of his arms underneath his black shirt. His clothes were tailored but inexpensive. Victor had an oval face and a small nose. His steely eyes looked like they could see inside another person's soul. When he grinned, he was particularly handsome, and his expression took on a hint of softness.

"Nice to meet you, Mr. Standu." Vladimir reached out his hand without getting up.

He noticed that Victor's hand was as hard as steel.

"So," Vladimir said, anxious to get down to business, "Do you normally work with a partner?"

"No, I work by myself. A partner would just get in the way and if he doesn't follow directions exactly, he could undermine the whole operation."

Vladimir nodded, thinking of the Igor-Sergei catastrophe.

"Do you have experience in sex slavery?" Vladimir asked, turning a bit red because he sounded like any ordinary job interviewer.

"I've done some small operations, but in my experience, I find them too often badly managed," he explained while seated with his hands calmly on his knees. "Operations rarely go as planned and police are usually on to them fast."

"How do you feel when you see young women crying and begging to escape?" Vladimir's facial muscles tensed when he asked this question.

"I believe life is a constant war, and in wars, people get hurt, sometimes even get killed, no?" Victor answered without flinching. "There are plenty of homes in Russia and Moldova where people live without any fight left in them. Men are docile and they drown their troubles in drink. Women become old and embittered. Many of these families are impoverished. They can't afford basic necessities like food and medicine. People live miserably and all is for nothing. I call them the walking dead. If one has any advantage or ability to break out of these conditions, he shouldn't hesitate to utilize it for his own survival. Otherwise, he will inevitably go down himself."

Upon hearing Victor's words, Vladimir nodded and sat back, clearly impressed.

He questioned Victor about his background.

"I originally come from Moldova, but we moved to Russia when my father got a job working in the mines. He wasn't around much, but whenever he came home he was drunk and violent. He beat my mother and two sisters." He paused for a moment. "My sisters told me he even raped them when he was drunk. When he was killed in a mine under suspicious circumstances, I was a teenager and we were left with nothing. My mother couldn't pay the rent and the landlord threw us out on the street."

"What happened to your family?" Vladimir asked, leaning forward.

"My mother lost her mind so I put her in an asylum. I haven't seen her in three years. My sisters were unable to find jobs or husbands so I keep them in a small apartment. They do exactly what I say or I will cut them off. I tried prostituting them, but they look like two frightened old hags. They assist me if I ever need them. They're both hooked on heroin now and I give them money for their habit and basic necessities."

"And what kind of women have you handled in previous sex slavery rings?"

"Mostly Moldovan, Ukrainian, and Russian women, but I'm open to doing all women," Victor smiled briefly. His whole body remained rigid but composed. He was clearly a man who had control over himself.

Vladimir finally smiled with a calm feeling of satisfaction and certainty. "And when can you begin?"

"Immediately," Victor replied. "I cannot work in any more half-cocked operations because the police are cracking down. But I know this operation is a strong, solid one. Plus," he raised his forefinger, "I have bigger aspirations and I want to make more money on a steady basis."

The phone rang.

"Excuse me," Vladimir said. He knew who was on the other line.

"He's good. Hire him," Andre said. Vladimir could imagine Andre now wore a self-satisfied, smug expression.

"Very good," Vladimir said as he hung up the phone, believing that with the hiring of Victor, things were finally going to turn around.

"We will give you an opportunity to prove yourself." Vladimir's lips curled slightly but his eyes were solemn.

Victor added. "However, my services don't come cheap. I expect to be paid handsomely for the time I put in."

My, quite confident. Vladimir thought.

Vladimir nodded his head and said, "Don't worry. We were

expecting that. Just do your assignments superbly." He added, "There's an American expression, 'You get what you pay for.'"

Victor smiled. "There's another American expression. 'It looks like we're on the same page.'"

After negotiating, mostly on Victor's terms, for an exorbitant salary and an open expense account, Vladimir gave him instructions to depart for Newark right away.

"Eliminate Igor Agapov immediately. Also the young woman, if she isn't dead already. One of my employees will meet you at the airport and give you their photographs and information."

The two men rose and shook hands, each one sizing the other one up.

We're anxious to see you prove your worth, Vladimir thought as he watched the man depart.

CHAPTER TWENTY-SEVEN

MARINA

Officer Lewis escorted Marina to the Morris County Medical Examiner in a nondescript red brick building set back behind the police station. No outside sign was visible except the chief medical examiner's name at the top of the stairs to the left of the door. A large, round generator buzzed on the right side of the building. Nothing could be seen from the old windows. Walking up the steps, an ominous feeling swept over Marina. Pale-faced, she braced herself as the officer opened the door for her.

They entered a still, quiet room with a strong antiseptic odor. Marina winced, fighting the urge to flee. Overhead fluorescent lights shined down in the windowless room. Dark tiled walls and doors added to the dull, lifeless atmosphere. Marina saw all kinds of equipment like an electric saw and face shields that she had never seen before, nor did she even want to know their use. Steel sinks sat behind rows of autopsy tables.

"I know this is going to be difficult," he told her as she slowly walked in, her eyes darting around looking for an escape.

"But if you can identify the body, it may be the evidence we need to prove the existence of this human trafficking ring you told us about."

"This man could be from Russia or Moldova," he continued. "We found loose papers in his pockets in both Russian and Romanian. So far there have been no witnesses or anyone who has any knowledge of who he is." He led Marina to another room with his hand on her back. They stopped at the door. "Are you ready, or do you need a few more minutes?"

Having too much trouble breathing to answer, she could only nod her head. She knew there was no way she could avoid viewing the dead body.

Lewis opened the door, and Marina saw a slab with a stiff horizontal body underneath white sheets. Marina shut her eyes and tried to breathe normally but couldn't.

Just think! If this is Igor, your problems may be over, she thought.

Opening her eyes, she nodded to the officer that she was ready. Her body was so tense and her legs quivered so much that she was afraid she would collapse, unable to carry her own weight.

Getting the signal from Lewis, the stony-faced mortician uncovered the face of the dead body.

Marina gasped and her whole body shuddered at the sight. Lewis had to grab her to prevent her from falling. Her eyes were wide with terror. She couldn't find her breath to scream. She clung to the officer as if her life depended on it.

"Easy, easy," Lewis said as he supported Marina. "He can't do anything to hurt you ever again. He's gone."

Yes, I know this man, but unfortunately, he isn't Igor, Marina wanted to say.

The man lying on the slab had cuts and abrasions.

"What are those marks on his face?" Marina asked.

Lewis looked at her, his brows furrowed, clearly surprised by her question.

He shrugged. "Animals, probably rats, pecking at his flesh."

Marina trembled and stared at the face. "His name is Sergei. I-I don't know h-his last name." She turned to Lewis. "I don't feel bad at all for him. He got what he deserved. He was one of the kidnappers. He brutalized the women and enjoyed it."

"Well, now," Lewis's eyes brightened, "we're making progress here."

Marina nodded slowly but didn't look relieved. Finally she said, "There's another one, even more vicious. I just hope and pray he's dead as well."

"Weren't there more of them?" he asked.

"Yes, but Sergei and the other one," it was distasteful for Marina to even utter his name. She cast her eyes to the ground. "Igor. Those were the two who mainly dealt with the women."

"So we have to find Igor," Lewis said gravely. "I'm going to contact the FBI and see what they can come up with. Now that we have some solid evidence." He glanced back at the cadaver. "An identified body."

Marina struggled to stand on her own. She stared at Sergei with contempt. One of the two men responsible for her nightmare.

I hope the rats pecked at him while he was dying and he was helpless to do anything about it. It's exactly what he deserved after what he did to us, she thought.

She felt like vomiting, relieved she hadn't eaten for a while. The mortician covered Sergei's face as Lewis slowly led her out of the room. When he closed the door, Marina found she was able to breathe and walk on her own again.

"How do you feel?" Lewis asked her.

She closed her eyes for a moment. "If you don't mind, could I have a few minutes to sit down and digest all of this?"

"Certainly," Lewis told her. "I'll bring you to a room where you can have peace and quiet. I have to make some calls." He led her to a room down the hall. "Would you like anything?"

"Not yet, thanks," Marina replied.

Lewis pointed to the next room. "I'll be in there. Don't hesitate to come and knock if you need anything at all."

Marina sat on a comfortable cloth chair with her hand resting on her chin. She wondered how Sergei had gotten killed. Had Igor killed him? Had Igor been killed too? Was she safe now? These questions swirled around in her mind. Of course, she had no answers. She wondered how long it would take to reunite with her family. She sat back with her arms resting on the arms of the chair. Her tenseness gave way to lethargy. She felt safe here, but the stress made her tired. Images of the brutality done to her and the other women on the ship competed with those of her time with Bruce and Adam. Her sluggish mind quieted and she struggled to keep her eyes open. All Marina could think of was that she was tired of being scared and afraid. Her body yearned to let go of all the anxieties twisting inside of her. She fought sleep, but her eyelids wouldn't stay open. Occasionally she would hear footsteps or voices in the hallway, but she drifted off. Her dreams were not dark and frightening—instead she saw a scene she had often begun thinking about at night before she drifted off to sleep but would suppress as soon as it began.

She dreamed of taking a walk on a calm, picturesque beach. As she strolled, she felt a man's hands on her shoulders. She looked behind her and saw Bruce smiling and laughing, happy to see her. They were both totally relaxed without a care in the world. The beach was on the ocean, the water a deep blue, with waves that fell with white foam only a few feet from where they strolled on the sparkling sand. Other than an occasional seashell lying in the sand, the beach was spotless. They had the beach all to themselves. Marina had never experienced such perfect weather, not too hot and not too cold. She felt a light breeze that made her hair fly in the wind. An inner happiness glowed inside of her when Bruce admired how beautiful she looked.

Marina pictured herself and Bruce stopping in the middle of the beach. All of their problems slipped into the ocean and the water dragged them away into oblivion. They embraced and kissed passionately. Finally they had the freedom to enjoy each other.

They held each other urgently. They didn't want anyone to tear them apart and spoil this perfect moment. But then they heard a familiar voice in the distance calling, "Daddy! Marina!"

Neither one was willing to loosen their hold on the other. They just wanted to taste and explore each other and have this moment last for eternity.

Both Marina and Bruce recognized that innocent, loving voice. It made the forced interruption with lovemaking a bit gentler because they loved the person this voice belonged to. They both felt confident there would be other opportunities to join together. They continued to hug until they heard the voice come closer. Marina put her head on Bruce's shoulder as they saw Adam approaching. Her mind and body were awash in contentment and relaxation.

But when Adam finally met them, his jaw dropped and he became unsteady on his feet.

"What's wrong, son?" Bruce reluctantly took his arm off Marina's shoulder, but he was too calm and happy to panic.

"Daddy," Adam said with his eyes so wide they took over his whole face. "You're not supposed to touch a woman. You can only shake her hand!"

"Miss Dobrin. Excuse me, Miss Dobrin."

Marina's eyes popped open. She jumped and turned to Officer Lewis. She then surveyed her unfamiliar surroundings, finally recognizing where she was and why she was there.

"I'm sorry to startle you." Lewis cocked his head, wanting her to know it was him but not getting too close to scare her.

"That's OK." She held her hand to her heart in an effort to make it stop beating frantically. She then blushed and turned downwards, hoping her expression did not reveal the contents of her dream. "I just fell asleep once I got a little relaxed."

"That's all right, don't worry about it," he said as he ran his hand through his closely cropped hair. "I just got off the phone with the FBI. They are definitely interested in this case. I gave them your information and they submitted it to the National Crime Information Center, or the NCIC for short. The NCIC contains information about, among other things, wanted persons. They found this man, Sergei Moskey, in their files. He has been a person of interest in connection with kidnappings in Eastern Europe and he has been spotted in this country before." Lewis took a seat near but not right next to her. "They want to get a plane ready to bring you back to Moldova. I just spoke with Deputy Assistant Director Agent Louis Baron. He's in charge of the Criminal Investigative Division of the FBI. He gave me some history about what's been going on in Moldova and other countries in Eastern Europe." Lewis sat forward, facing Marina with his hands on his knees. "Unfortunately, this isn't just happening in Eastern Europe but it is a worldwide problem. Baron explained to me how this crime has become particularly widespread in Eastern Europe since the 1990s."

Before he continued, he sat up and asked, "First of all, before we go on, is there something I can get you? Would you like something to drink? We just have water, coffee, or tea here."

Marina found she did want something warm to hold in her hand. "Tea would be good," she said, attempting to smile but only able to purse her lips.

"Sure, I'll be right back." He got out of his chair. When he came back, he handed her a cup of tea, and he held a cup of coffee in his other hand for himself. "I could use a drink too after hearing all of this," he admitted as he sat down.

He took a sip of his coffee and said, "Here's what I've found out." He stopped a moment and added, "This all happened when you were just a little child, maybe even before you were born. I don't know how much history you've learned, but do you remember hearing about the collapse of the Soviet Union in 1989?"

Marina nodded. "I learned about it in school. My country Moldova used to be a satellite country of the communist Soviet Union."

"That's right," Lewis affirmed before continuing. "When the former Soviet Union broke up, it opened up a Pandora's Box of crime and economic hardship. In all of Eastern Europe, particularly in a very poor country like Moldova, displaced workers had no means to support themselves, and vicious opportunists took advantage of the situation by luring women into jobs abroad, claiming they were going to be nannies, but they were actually sex slavery schemes. Their subsequent disappearances left families devastated, young women traumatized, and communities shattered.

"Now, unfortunately, these operations are sprouting up everywhere, even in the United States."

Marina sat back while she digested this information. She was glad to have a warm drink with her—she took sips to warm her chilled body after hearing these brutalities occurred much more often than she realized. It was a growing, profitable worldwide business that damaged and ruined countless lives. She clutched her hand on the arm of the chair to hold herself steady. She willed herself to be strong. *I am one of the lucky ones*, she told herself. *I can't fall apart now*. Recalling her normal, everyday life before the kidnapping when she worked at a good job, had friends and family, and dated, Lewis interrupted her thoughts.

"Miss Dobrin, could you give me the background of what happened to you?" He took out a small cassette recorder. "I have to record this for other law enforcement officials to hear. The more we know, the more we can help you and other young women who are victims and are still out there." Lewis then spoke his name, the date, and time into the recorder.

Marina did not need prompting to speak. Taking a long, anguished breath, she began, "I was in Chişinău, the capital of Moldova, visiting my boyfriend, who originally came from Moscow. We had broken up but thought we'd try again. It wasn't working out." She gave a mirthless smile. She recapped to Officer Lewis exactly what she had told Bruce: from leaving her boyfriend's apartment early in the morning to her encounter with the two men and then finding herself chained to a bed on a ship.

"Sergei and Igor came in periodically and checked on us. They carted off the dead women like they were trash. They'd bring pails and brown toilet paper to use when we had to go to the bathroom. Whenever somebody had an accident, the men would slap that woman so much that she rarely ever had another one. There'd always be a foul odor in the room." Marina's eyes teared up and Lewis handed her some tissues. She blew her nose and continued about her experience when the ship docked in Turkey. Lewis couldn't conceal his horror as his eyes bulged as she continued her story.

Marina choked up and had to stop. Her head throbbed, and Lewis was afraid she was going to get sick. He asked Marina if there was anything else she needed.

"I need a few minutes," she whispered.

Lewis nodded and said, "I'll go out and give you some privacy." While he was gone, Marina practiced deep breathing until she felt more normal. After a few minutes Lewis stuck his head inside and she nodded, signaling she was ready to continue.

"Like all the women, I was so weak that I could barely talk; we just went through the motions of life totally powerless to what was happening to us and did everything we could to avoid more pain. One day I couldn't go on this way and begged them to let us go; they responded by injecting me with even more drugs. By then I didn't even know if it was day or night.

"One day Sergei came in to unchain me and I resisted. He carried me to a small, dirty room that had mice running around and ordered me to stay standing up. He would check on me from time to time, and if he caught me sitting or lying down,

I wouldn't be fed for days and beaten. Finally, when Sergei and Igor thought I wouldn't make any more trouble, they led me by my hair back to the wooden table and chained me. It was actually less horrible than being in that small room.

"I don't know how long I lived like this. It got to the point where I was so weak I couldn't lift my head. I lost control of my body. They put me in diapers. They talked about not allowing me to die or else they would not make any more money off me, so they gave me extra food, loosened my chains a little, and let me walk around the ship once a day so I wouldn't wither away and die on them."

Lewis leaned forward and asked quietly, "So what did they do?"

Marina turned to him with a grave expression. "They gave me more food. A lot more food. They made sure I brushed my teeth and fixed up my hair and face to look presentable. There was one man, I guess you'd call him a client, who kept requesting me, and they wanted to make sure they could still make money off of me."

Lewis gazed steadily at her with a solemn expression.

"The ship left Turkey and we were at sea for weeks. I don't know for how long. The Russian and Moldovan kidnappers would rape us, but it wasn't as constant as it was when we were raped by many different men who boarded the ship in Turkey. At that point I got very sick again, so they left me alone."

Tears streamed down Marina's cheeks. Lewis handed her some more tissues. She blotted her eyes, trying to conclude her story.

"I got stronger. I overheard the men talking that they finally reached the shores. I didn't know what shores they were talking about. The ship slowed down to a creep. Then and there I decided I was going to escape, even if I was going to get killed trying."

By the time Marina finished her accounting, her hands shook as she struggled to steady herself and finish drinking her tea. She sat back, emotionally exhausted from recalling the past. Officer Lewis turned off his cassette tape and put it away in his shirt pocket.

"Let me get you something to eat," he said. "You look drained. I realize this is extremely painful to talk about, but we need this information in order to capture these human traffickers."

He took out his cell phone. "What would you like to eat? Would a hamburger and fries be all right?"

"Yes, that would be fine," Marina agreed.

After he called in an order from a nearby restaurant, he said, "Miss Dobrin, there are safe houses for individuals who may be in danger. Would you feel safer staying in one of these?" Not waiting for her answer, he continued, "Let me call the nearest ones and see if they have a bed for you. I'll go to the office and see what I can do." The officer stood up and left without waiting for her to reply.

Marina raised her eyebrows and stared. Her first thought was, *What about Adam? How would he react if I don't go back? I promised I would return.* She was speechless as she waited for Lewis.

When he came back, he shook his head and said, "Unfortunately, none of them has an empty bed. Would it be all right if you return to the Hitchens' house tonight? Mr. Hitchens indicated to me that you were welcome to stay there."

Marina brightened. "Oh, yes. That would be fine."

"And we'll have a police car drive by the house every hour just to make sure everything's all right." After a moment, he chuckled and said, "I know Mr. Hitchens's son will be glad to have you back." His face grew more serious. "Now that we have proof about this human trafficking ring, we have to make sure you're safe."

◆ ◆ ◆

Victor arrived at the Domodedovo International Airport in Moscow within a matter of hours. As Vladimir promised, his employee met Victor at the airport and gave him a passport as well as pictures, maps, and other necessary documents. Victor gazed at the photograph of Igor for a while, studying every feature until he could easily conjure up the face in his mind.

Sitting on the plane, he stared out the window. Victor always had a liberated feeling being on the same level as the clouds, feeling like he could break free from all troubles and begin anew. But this time was different. He concentrated on his mission because the thought of failure was too unbearable to contemplate.

What is awaiting me there? he asked himself. *Will I be successful or get captured and killed? Will all be lost then?* Victor closed his eyes and forced himself to stop thinking. His seat was unusually comfortable. He stretched his legs out. Plenty of leg room. He took his glass and sipped his wine. If he were on holiday, Victor would delight in these first-class accommodations.

"Would you like a pillow, sir?" a young, fresh-faced blonde stewardess walking by asked him.

"Yes, that would be perfect," Victor answered with a slight smile.

The stewardess disappeared and a few moments later came back with a soft pillow with a puffy, high-cotton content.

"Thank you." Victor took the pillow from her.

"And is your one blanket enough? I could bring you a second one if you'd like?" she asked.

"No, thanks. That won't be necessary," he answered. He then closed his eyes as a means of dismissing her.

"Enjoy your flight," she said as she walked away.

CHAPTER TWENTY-EIGHT

MARINA

MARINA STARED OUT THE WINDOW SILENTLY as Officer Lewis drove her back to the Hitchens' house. She was disappointed to hear that the government had encountered delays in preparing to find an airplane to fly her home. She suspected the reason was that they still needed her for more evidence and information. Marina couldn't shake off the feeling that her situation now had become more dangerous. She worried not only about herself but about Adam and Bruce as well.

"Remember, we're going to have a police car drive by the house every hour tonight," Officer Lewis told her, as if reading her thoughts.

Marina nodded and gazed downward. *Bruce and Adam are better off without me. I need to return to my own country,* she thought, clutching her arms around herself. She felt damaged and depressed after going over her ordeal with Officer Lewis. He gave no indication, but she imagined he couldn't wait to be rid of her—a person that had gone through so much trauma and abuse could never be whole or productive again.

Marina thought she heard the officer's voice but was too absorbed in her own thoughts to hear what he said. Finally, they pulled near Bruce's house. His old Buick was parked near the house and the outside light was on.

"Miss Dobrin," Lewis said, staring at her until she turned her head to face him. "Are you sure you're going to be all right?"

She tried to smile, but her eyes were so grave and sad. "I'll be OK," was all she said. They both left the police car and approached the front door.

Adam appeared at the front window, anxiously biting his shirt. His questioning expression broke into a wide grin as they heard him say, "Daddy! Daddy! Marina's here!" He ran to the door and opened it quickly. "We got some KFC for you from Aunt Judy's house. I saw Uncle Matt and all my cousins. It was a blast!"

By then, Bruce was at the door. "Come on in," he said, smiling, clearly happy to see her, too.

Even Marina brightened upon seeing them. The only one that didn't look happy was Officer Lewis.

"May I speak to you, Mr. Hitchens?" Officer Lewis took Bruce aside and walked into the kitchen with him without waiting for an answer. Marina stared at them while Lewis spoke to him in a hushed voice. She knew Lewis was informing Bruce of all he had learned. She wasn't able to watch and try to make out what they were saying for long; Adam wanted her attention.

"Tomorrow I gotta go ta work," he told her in a disappointed voice. "But then I'll come home and we can watch a nature show. You wanna watch 'bout monkeys? They love ta eat bananas and hang on the trees."

Marina forced herself to smile and said, "That would be great, Adam. Monkeys are fun to watch."

"Adam," Bruce said in a loud voice, startling them both, "for a few days, whenever you see anyone, don't open the door. Do you understand, son?"

"Why not, Daddy?" Adam said, staring at his father with his eyebrows up.

Marina looked down. She felt deflated and heartbroken, wishing now a shelter had an extra bed for her. *He's probably regretting he ever met me.*

Bruce sighed and turned his head upward toward the ceiling. "A very, very bad man wants to hurt Marina. We want to make sure we don't let him in the house."

Adam moved his head slightly as if he hadn't heard his father right. "Why would anyone wanna hurt Marina?"

"Because there's a very bad man out there, a man who belongs in jail, and the police have to catch him so Marina will be safe and he won't hurt anyone else."

Adam kept turning his gaze from his father to Marina as he took in his father's words. Bruce interrupted his thoughts by asking him, "Son, what can't we do for the next few days?"

Adam thought for a moment. "Open the door."

Bruce heaved a sigh of relief. His shoulders relaxed. "That's right."

"Well, I gotta go now," Officer Lewis said, looking more relaxed himself. He proceeded to the door, but Adam blocked his exit.

"Adam, what are you doing?" Bruce demanded.

"We can't open the door," Adam said, shaking his head and putting his body against the door to prevent Lewis from leaving.

"Adam, we know Officer Lewis. He's trying to help us. We can open the door to let him out," Marina said, smiling now.

To everyone's relief, he listened to her. He moved aside and said, "You can leave this time," he said with the utmost seriousness.

Lewis nodded and tried to conceal a smile. "Good night, everyone. Call me if you need me."

As soon as he left, Bruce said to his son, "It's time to get ready for bed now, Adam."

Adam stomped his foot. "But I wanna eat KFC wit Marina. It'll taste even better if I eat wit Marina."

"Oh, I already ate, Adam. I'm full," she said, patting her stomach.

"And you already ate some more chicken when we came home, Adam. We've got to get up early tomorrow morning for work."

Adam's jaw fell open and he jumped back. "But we can't leave Marina here all alone, Daddy."

"Officer Lewis will be here tomorrow morning to pick her up. Don't you worry," Bruce told him soothingly.

"And she'll be here when I git home?" Adam asked anxiously, flapping his hands.

"Yes!" Bruce and Marina said at the same time.

"Adam," Marina said gently, "it's time to go to bed now. I'll see you tomorrow. Good night," she said brightly.

"We're all tired, Adam. We all have to go to bed." Bruce gently tugged at his son's arm to get him into bed. "And don't forget, you need to take out the garbage tomorrow night. But I'll walk with you outside."

"Aww, Daddy. I hate to do that. I want to be wit Marina."

She could hear the exasperation in his father's voice. "Collecting and taking out the garbage only takes a few minutes, son. Nobody likes to do it, but it has to be done."

"I still wanna watch a whole nature show wit Marina," he insisted.

"Taking out the garbage will not take you away from watching a nature show with her. I promise you that," Bruce told him slowly with increasing impatience.

Marina brushed her teeth in the bathroom while Adam's father got his son's pajamas ready so he could give him a shower. She could overhear Adam chatting happily about monkeys and eating more of Aunt Judy's chicken. She slipped into the bedroom, not knowing what more she could say to them. She knew it would take time, but eventually Adam would get used to her being out of his life. As she heard Bruce turning the shower nozzle on, her thoughts grew morbid: she pictured herself living the rest of her life alone because no one wanted her after all she'd been through. She imagined Bruce must want her out of their lives by now.

She blinked back tears as she fell asleep. At one point, she thought she heard Bruce call her while she dozed, but her eyelids were too heavy to open.

She woke in the morning to the whispered voices of Bruce and Adam. Adam would occasionally talk too loud and his father would tell him to speak more quietly. She sat up in bed as Adam shouted, "Bye, Marina. See ya later."

"Have a nice day, Adam," she called as she got up and put on her robe.

Adam was already boarding his bus outside by the time she opened the bedroom door. Upon hearing the door open, his father unexpectedly came out of the kitchen, wiping his hands on a dish towel.

"Good morning. How are you?" he asked, his tone serious.

"Good morning. I'm fine. How are you?"

"Now that Adam is off to work, I'm a lot better," he said. "I hope we didn't wake you up."

"No, no. I need to get up anyway."

"I'm going into work a little later. I wanted to make sure Adam caught his bus."

"I meant it when I said I would like to keep in touch with Adam through Facebook and Skype unless . . . ," she began.

Bruce's eyes furrowed together. "Unless what?"

She looked down. "I'm sure you and Adam are anxious to make a new start once I leave." She shrugged. "No one should be put in danger because of me."

Bruce looked at her with sympathetic eyes. "Marina, we don't feel that way at all," he said, throwing the dish towel on a chair. He looked like he was going to walk up and embrace her but stopped himself. "Officer Lewis said he was confident that body was going to provide more leads and the other man won't dare come near here now. He was just being cautious. We love—I mean—Adam loves having you here. Don't feel like you're unwelcome."

When she looked up and met his eyes, he said, "If you want to go back to Moldova, we understand. It's your home. But please don't feel like we're pushing you out."

Marina's eyes welled with tears upon hearing him say this. She put a few strands of hair behind her ear and said, "Thank you. I know Officer Lewis will pick me up soon . . ."

"And I'm also leaving work early so I'll be here when Adam gets home. Don't worry about us. Just worry about yourself. Hopefully this will all be over with soon. We'll all be thrilled.

If you're able, we'd love to see you tonight," he added with a grin as he put on his jacket and picked up his briefcase. "Adam won't rest until you try his aunt's southern fried chicken. I have to say it's delicious."

Marina laughed. "He's so lovable and gentle." She wanted to add, "and so are you," but the words refused to come out.

Bruce stared at her for a moment like there were words he longed to say but couldn't. So he walked toward the door and said, "You have my number, right?"

She nodded.

"Officer Lewis also has my number. Call me if there's anything you need." He touched the doorknob but didn't turn it. "I can wait here until the policeman comes. I'll tell them at work I'll come in a little later," he said, putting down his briefcase. "Since I had such a good presentation on Friday, they'll let me come in anytime I want."

"Oh no," Marina said, shaking her head and looking at the clock. "Officer Lewis will be here in less than half an hour. I'll be fine. Please don't let me keep you."

"Are you sure? It would be no problem."

Happiness welled up inside her. *I was too tough on myself last night,* she thought. *Maybe people can still care about me.*

"I'm sure. Drive carefully and have a good day. I'll be looking forward to seeing you tonight. And Adam," she quickly added.

"You too." Bruce slowly turned the knob on the door. He stood for a moment before leaving. Finally, he said, "You can give me a call when Officer Lewis comes."

"OK," she agreed, nodding.

"In fact, I would prefer it if you gave me a call that he came and you're all right."

Marina felt herself blushing. "I'll give you a call. I promise."

With that reassurance, Bruce smiled, waved, and was on his way.

Marina took a quick shower, ate a light breakfast, and put on her new clothes. While sitting in the living room waiting for Officer Lewis to come, she remembered Bruce reminding his son to take out the garbage tonight. She decided she would start collecting it in the house to help him out. She walked into the kitchen and wrapped up that garbage first. Then she walked into the bathroom. As she tied the bag, she immediately released it and jumped back in horror. Inside the bag she saw the old tattered clothes she had worn when she came here. But now they were cut up in shreds.

Who did that? she wondered, shivering. Marina had a hard time picturing Bruce or Adam cutting up her old clothes.

Th-There must be a simple explanation for this. But she was at a loss to think of one. Marina took a deep breath and decided to dismiss her fears, convinced she was safe now. With trembling hands, she slowly lifted the garbage bag. From the outside of the clear plastic garbage, she saw a small, familiar-looking bottle inside.

Her jaw dropped in disbelief. She instantly turned pale and couldn't control her shaking hands as she rifled through the garbage bag and took out the small bottle. It was the same vodka bottle she had seen Igor drink the whole time she was on the ship.

Marina fell back against the wall and sank down into a sitting position before screaming.

He found me!

She clutched her hair, and her whole body shook. She

recalled images of Igor coming after her with a knife, ready to slash her up. Closing her eyes, Marina imagined him descending on her, chains dangling in his arms, ready to lock her on a bed in the Hitchens' house and torture her, cutting her up until she died a slow, agonizing death. While Igor left her to her fate, he would prepare a similar fate for Adam and Bruce.

No!

She pictured Adam's terrified expression, not even comprehending the existence of such evil. And Igor would arrange it that Bruce would be powerless to protect his son. Vowing to prevent this from ever happening, Marina listened to her first instinct: she had to run. Run away as far from here as she could. Igor had found her and would kill her for certain. On impulse, she ran to the front door and bolted, but not before checking it had slammed shut for Adam and Bruce's protection. She hurried away as if someone was chasing after her. Paranoia set in as Igor's threats played over and over in her mind. Her thoughts turned more foreboding as she began thinking that some police officers could've been paid off by the human trafficking ring and were shielding their operations. She knew the traffickers made a lot of money and would not hesitate to pay off officials handsomely for help. Other than Lewis and the others she had met, she didn't know if there were others working on the case who were potential informers.

Amid these fears, she asked herself what made her so valuable that they spent time and manpower looking for her, when they kidnapped so many young women in their organization.

Igor would find a way to prove they had to kill me.

In the faint distance, she thought she heard police sirens. Should she run back, or was a corrupt officer among them waiting to shoot her at the scene?

Instinctively, she kept running, thinking the farther away she was, the safer she and Bruce and Adam were. Not knowing where father and son worked and having no idea how she could possibly contact them now, she didn't know what else to do but run. Marina knew there were areas of Morristown filled with stores and office buildings, but most other parts contained large stretches of private homes, most average-sized but some sections with sprawling estates. She had seen no cars in the homes she had run past so far. They could be in the garages, but she did not want to slow down and waste time peeking in to see if someone was at home to contact Officer Lewis. Lewis had handed her his phone number, but it was lying on Bruce's dresser.

That would be no help now, she thought ruefully.

◆ ◆ ◆

Igor was parked on the street and sipping from a small bottle of vodka when he saw the Buick drive away. He drove around the block a few times in case someone spotted him watching the house. People all over the neighborhood left their homes to go to work, school, and other activities. He didn't want to be noticed or remembered. After his last round of driving around the block, he had driven directly to the Hitchens' house and hidden the car behind a cluster of trees on the property. He scrutinized the house—he was sure she was still in there. Getting quietly out of the car and opening the trunk, he put on gloves and a mask and gathered his equipment together in a carry-on so he'd be ready.

At the sound of screaming piercing the air, he dropped his bag and hid behind the car. Igor looked up and saw her, wild-eyed and shaking, running out of the house, not even looking in his direction. Igor took out his silencer, preparing to shoot her leg. He would take delight in torturing her before he killed her. But then he heard a car door close and a yellow school bus stopping on the street. Igor spotted neighbors and school children leaving their homes. Since the Hitchens' house was so far away from all the other houses, he doubted they had heard her screams.

He hid behind his car, paralyzed by indecision. He was afraid people would see the mask and the gun, so he tore off the mask and instead of firing, placed the gun inside his jacket and tried to walk as nonchalantly as he could after her, not caring if people walking by saw him coming from the Hitchens' property. They might think he was a friend of hers. But by this time Marina had run across the street, and the yellow school bus blocked his view of her. Neighbors stopped and stared at her for a moment but shrugged their shoulders. They didn't know who she was, and everyone was in a hurry to get where they needed to go this morning. Igor cursed loudly, not caring who heard him, and scurried back into his car to pursue her.

CHAPTER TWENTY-NINE

BRUCE

Getting out of his car, Bruce looked up at the sky. It was a clear, crisp, cloudless spring day. This bolstered his upbeat feelings that his life was improving: Adam was at work, Marina was with the police, and he could focus on his job. The weekend was hectic and he would have to tell his boss Steve that he hadn't found the technology manuscript he wrote in his last year of college. He was certain his boss would understand and give him a few more days to search. His boss even mentioning his talent last week continued to buoy his spirits. Entering the building and pressing the elevator button, he recalled Maggie frequently praising his writing talent.

When the elevator doors opened and he walked inside carrying his briefcase, he promptly pressed the button to the ninth floor, wondering if he would ever find someone like Maggie again. He told himself Marina would want to return home after all the trauma she had experienced. Bruce was ready to begin a relationship, but he kept telling himself that she most likely needed a lot more time and would almost certainly no longer be in their lives once she boarded the plane to Moldova.

He stepped out of the elevator and walked to his office. Everyone was busy with work but managed to smile and wish him a good morning. But he came to a stop upon seeing Gwen and Dave seated on a desk near his office going through stacks of papers.

They looked up. "Hey, Bruce," said Dave, sitting up straight and grinning. "We knew you were coming in a little late," he said glancing at his watch, "but a lot of work came in this morning. Gwen and I wanted to give you the heads-up about what's going on."

Bruce made sure his favorite tie was in place as he nodded. He noticed Dave's hair was shorter and neater than usual. It also looked like he was wearing a more expensive suit.

Now just what are you trying to do, Davey boy?

Gwen smiled slightly, looking at Bruce as if she now realized he led a double life.

No, my life is not perfect, he wanted to tell her. *Life doesn't always go your way. Perhaps someday you'll also find that out when you start a family.*

"More work?" Bruce said, trying to sound cheerful. "Well, that's great."

"But it's more complicated than what we've handled in the past," Gwen said, handing him a packet. "Look at this and see what you think." Impeccably dressed, her nails painted blood red with white stripes, she did not flirt when she spoke to him anymore, for which Bruce was grateful.

"We'll handle it, Gwen. I remember some of this stuff from college." Dave sat up even more erect in his chair. "Just give me a chance to study it and we'll have no problem."

"Of course we'll have no problem. With Bruce's technology background and presentation skills, we'll be in good shape," Steve said as he approached and shook Bruce's hand.

Bruce held his breath, hoping Steve wouldn't mention his old manuscript.

"Bruce, this is an even bigger project than the one we tackled last week," Steve said in a serious tone as he stared steadily into his eyes. "All of us will have to work overtime to make a killing on this." He gestured toward Dave. "Dave graduated from college only three years ago. He said he's learned some of this." He nodded and smiled at Dave, who looked up briefly while he appeared to studiously go over the information in one of the packets. Steve turned back to Bruce. "I assume you got plenty of rest this weekend."

"Yes," Bruce said a little too quickly.

"Good. Take a seat in your office and begin looking over the information and what they want us to do," Steve instructed.

Gwen handed him a stack of more packets, and Bruce headed wordlessly into his office. He put the cell phone on his desk, praying that everything was going well for Adam and Marina. As he read, he glanced at the phone from time to time. Marina promised she would call. He shrugged. *Maybe she forgot.* He tried to keep reading but couldn't get through more than a sentence. He stopped and looked up.

Marina wouldn't forget. That's not like her.

His hands shook as he tentatively reached for his cell phone. But before he could press a button, it rang.

"H-Hello, Marina? Are you making out all right?"

But it wasn't Marina. Officer Lewis's voice came on the phone. Bruce sat straight up and his mouth fell open in alarm.

"Mr. Hitchens, have you seen Miss Dobrin?"

His face turning pale, Bruce shot up from his chair. "Not since I left the house this morning. Didn't you pick her up?"

"She wasn't there."

His heart fell and his eyes grew wide as he clutched his head with his hand.

"Where is she? Has anyone seen her?" he asked, barely containing the panic in his voice.

"No, but we'll call you as soon as we hear something. You stay where you are so we know where to find you in case we need you." Lewis gave him his phone number again and hung up.

Bruce slumped in his chair. He barely had a chance to take in the news before another fear seized him: Adam. Where was he? Was he all right? Within ten seconds he dialed Adam's workplace.

"The Hutton Factory," a voice said.

"Is Adam Hitchens there?" he demanded.

"Let me transfer you to his department."

Bruce's knees buckled at the thought of his son in danger.

"Good morning. Production."

Bruce recognized Mr. Price's English accent.

"Mr. Price, this is Adam's father. Is Adam there?"

"Why, yes, Mr. Hitchens is here. I think he now understands the responsibility he has to come into work every day so he will have a much greater chance of holding onto this job," Mr. Price said, clearing his throat. "However, he keeps asking when work will be finished. So apparently, he still has a ways to go on learning the importance of staying on task and being focused at work."

"So he's all right?" Bruce said, not even hearing anything Price mentioned.

Mr. Price said nothing for a moment, clearly annoyed that Adam's father had ignored his assessment of his son's job performance.

"Mr. Hitchens," he said in a clipped voice. "You will receive my evaluation of your son's work performance promptly at the end of the month."

"Great," Bruce said. "Call me please, Mr. Price, if anything is amiss."

"Very well," Mr. Price answered and then added, "and if Mr. Hitchens keeps asking when the day will end, I will give you a call. Good day now." And he hung up.

Bruce stared at the phone as the line went dead, deciding what he should do. He turned to the packets on the desk. Out of the corner of his eye, he saw Gwen and Dave glancing up at him. He sighed and picked up a random packet and attempted to read. He could only read individual words but failed to connect them into sentences.

Focus, Bruce! You've got to focus! he told himself. He tried to read again when his phone rang.

"Mr. Hitchens?" he heard Officer Lewis's wary voice on the other line.

Bruce's stomach tightened. "What's going on?"

"Your son went to work today?"

"Yes, I just called his job. He's there."

"Good. A neighbor of yours reported that she saw a woman who fits the description of Miss Dobrin running away from your property and a car driving after her. Where does your son work? There's no reason to believe the driver of that car knows where he is, but we want to pick him up to be sure he's safe."

Bruce's hand trembled as he held the phone. He closed his eyes in an effort to think clearly instead of giving in to sheer panic. "He works at the Hutton Factory in Dover," he said. "I'm going to pick him up now."

"We could pick him up and bring him to the police station for you," Officer Lewis offered.

"No, no. He'll be too agitated if you pick him up and bring him there without me," Bruce said, shaking his head vigorously.

"We really don't know the scope of this operation and how many people are involved. It's best if you two stay with us," Lewis admitted. He gave Bruce the address of the police station and hung up.

Bruce felt hot as he closed his cell phone. He felt his forehead perspiring as he rose. Gwen and Dave, who were glimpsing over at him the whole time he was on the phone, exchanged glances.

"What's up, Bruce?" Gwen asked as she rifled through one of the packets of papers on her desk.

"I-I have to go," was all he managed to sputter out.

"Bruce," Gwen said, heaving a sigh, "we all know you have a special needs kid, but we're counting on you."

"We know your kid's demanding," Dave chimed in as he threw a new packet on top of the stack on his desk, "but this is a demanding assignment and we need *somebody* who has the time for this."

Bruce looked at the two of them, single, with only themselves to worry about. He was afraid whatever he would say he would later regret, so he simply walked away.

Steve rubbed his eyes and shifted in his seat when he saw Bruce approaching his office.

"I'm sorry, Steve, but there's another emergency," Bruce said as he grabbed the door knob.

Steve slammed his own packet on his desk. "Again, Bruce! It's one crisis after another with you." He looked at his employee with tired, hooded eyes. "I know you have it rough, but we've got a lot going on here, too." His hands tapped on the stacks of papers on his desk. "The shareholders are on my back. They're pressuring me to get this new account. There's a lot of money at stake here!"

"The police are involved. They called me . . ."

Steve raised his hand, not giving him a chance to finish. "Gwen saw him." He directed his eyes at Bruce. "He's a little boy in the body of a man," Steve said. "Did he get himself in trouble? Bruce, you've got to put that kid in an institution. That's where he belongs." He stopped himself, staring at the ground, trying to calm down.

"Look, Bruce. We're under the gun here," he said quietly. "Because you did such a great job on the last presentation, you've attracted more clients for us, higher-level clients. But you've got to be here full time and then some for us to show everyone we can get this project done," Steve said in a pleading tone. "Let the police deal with your son, Bruce. I need you here now."

Bruce looked at his boss as if he were a stranger. "You don't understand, Steve. My son didn't do anything wrong. Someone is after him. I can't risk anyone harming him . . ."

Steve's fist fell on his lap and he looked away, resigned. "OK, Bruce. I'm sorry for ripping into you. Just go. Do what you need to do." He shook his head and waved him away. "If we don't get this project done, it will permanently damage our reputation . . . we all need our jobs. Maybe Dave can take over this project. He can certainly commit to the time . . ."

Bruce didn't stay in Steve's office to hear any more. He turned around and marched straight to his own office. Gwen and Dave stared at him and then at each other as he packed his briefcase, got his coat, and walked out.

When Bruce got outside, he ripped off his necktie, unwittingly tearing it. Sweat trickled down his scalp all the way to his neck. He leaned on his car and gripped his head. He stood there a moment.

The car alarm went off, startling him from dwelling on the precarious situation and forcing him to return to what he must do now. While searching for his car key, Bruce saw it fall to the ground. Hands shaking, he struggled to pick it up and silence the alarm.

He dared not look up at the office building. He could imagine everyone watching him, particularly the people he worked with, shaking their heads and thinking what a pathetic life he had.

And that Steve must surely be thinking about replacing him.

He pictured Dave smirking, casting his eyes filled with malice down on him from the window.

Keeping his head down, Bruce started his car. He was so befuddled he had to consciously review in his head how to travel to Adam's job. He willed himself to concentrate on doing that and getting there as soon as possible.

◆ ◆ ◆

Igor stepped on the gas. He didn't care who saw him now. He was yards away from his prey and was determined to catch her before she got away again. When he saw her fleeing in between houses, he got out of his Mercedes to catch up with her on foot. As he chased her and edged closer and closer to her brown flowing hair dancing on her back and her skeletal body moving as quickly as she could, he yearned to squash her dead with his foot like a defenseless bug. When he reached her, he grabbed her arm and wrestled her fragile body to the ground. Once she lost her balance and fell, he grabbed her neck and cut off her breathing.

"Thought you could run away, eh?" he growled as her eyes grew wide in terror and her lips trembled, unable to speak. "You're getting exactly what you deserve! More of my men are out there, and they're going to get the two men you've been living and sleeping with." He gave her a wickedly delighted grin as he reached for his gun from inside his belt.

"Get away from her!"

Igor turned around. He saw a tiny, grey-haired elderly lady standing and peering at him with a bulldog on a leash only two feet away on the sidewalk. "Get away from her, you monster!"

At that moment, Igor loosened his grasp and Marina kicked him in the balls. She struggled to catch her breath. The dog growled menacingly. She looked over and saw foam hanging out of his mouth as he ran toward Igor.

Unfortunately, her kick was not hard enough to paralyze him. He aimed his gun with the silencer and shot the dog. He was about to turn his gun on the lady, but her scream piercing through the whole neighborhood unnerved him. Cars stopped, and neighbors peered out of their windows. Igor grabbed Marina by the hair and wrapped his arm around her neck, putting his gun to her forehead. "Anyone move or come near and she'll be dead too!" he shouted to all the witnesses. Pale and taut with fright, she couldn't think and allowed him to manipulate her like a puppet.

"I'd let you go back to being a prostitute. We raked in a lot of money with you," he snarled in her ear, "but that would be too kind for you." As he forced her to move with him, he stumbled on one of the dog's legs. The dog lay on the ground, its body shaking in its death throes. Caught completely off guard, he let her go, and his gun fell to the ground. Marina ran away as fast as she could without turning back. When she was almost out of sight of Igor, she heard shots fired in her direction. When a tree close to her was hit, she ducked and continued running, neither stopping nor glancing back. Igor must have taken off his gun's silencer.

Igor regained his bearings and dashed back to his car while everyone gaped at him, motionless. Hearing police sirens in the distance, he slammed down on the gas so fast he almost hit a tree. He slowed down a little but remained undeterred.

Marina's efforts to escape Igor were in vain. She breathed heavily and her legs barely held her up as she tried to run away.

Back in his car, Igor sped up and he swerved right by her side and jumped out of his car. He then grabbed her shoulder and pointed the gun at her head. He proceeded to drag her away from the growing congregation of neighbors and pedestrians only a few yards away. The sirens in the distance grew louder, but Igor was reluctant to shoot her execution-style in public. He had always operated in the shadows. Besides, escape would prove impossible if he did not keep her alive as his hostage. In his ruthless pursuit of killing Marina, Igor decided risking his own life was not worth his vengeance.

Have to get back to my car. No other way out!

He jerked her arm so hard she was afraid it would break. He led her toward his Mercedes, clutching his arm around her throat and his gun at her head so no one would dare attempt to rescue her. Opening the back passenger side door, he shoved Marina inside. After he closed the door, he fired shots at the distant crowd. Everyone fell to the ground to avoid the bullets as he ran to the driver's side. Determined that Marina would have no chance to escape, he punched her in the face and then turned on the engine. The squeal of his tires pierced the air as Igor drove full speed away.

He drove his unconscious victim, whose body kept moving as he turned each corner. He arrived in an upscale neighborhood in a spacious parking lot of an enormous, modern, state-of-the-art medical building on James Street. A large, paved stone in front of the building read 261 The Medical Center at James Street. It was a large three-story building made of white concrete with aqua windows. He parked his car among the many other cars in the lot and glared at her body slumped in the backseat. Igor yearned to break her neck, but his cautious nature took over. He studied his surroundings and saw nobody but decided to take out a needle and inject her in the arm with a tranquilizer while he planned how he would kill her.

That should keep her out for about an hour.

CHAPTER THIRTY

ADAM

ADAM KEPT LOOKING AT THE DOOR, HOPING MR. Price would tell him to work on something else. He was busy licking envelopes, but he constantly had to run to the men's room to spit out the seals' metallic taste. He even positioned his tongue under the running water for a moment. The manager came into the men's room and saw Adam washing his tongue. His eyes crinkled and his lips turned down when he saw Adam. The manager immediately left the men's room.

When Adam finally returned to his worktable, Mr. Price stood rigidly over the table, inspecting the sealed envelopes.

"Mr. Hitchens, is this all the work you've done in the last hour? Surely you've been busy doing other things, God knows what, all this time?"

"This is hard ta do, Mr. Price . . . ," Adam began.

"Right, and stamping hurts your hand." Mr. Price put his hands behind his back and lifted his head to stare at him through his spectacles. "What, may I inquire, is so hard about this?"

Adam wasn't sure what Mr. Price meant by "inquire," but

he tried to explain, "Mr. Price, the envelopes taste terrible!"

Mr. Price just stared at him. Finally, he said, "What?"

"I gotta keep washin' my tongue 'cause it tastes so bad!"

Mr. Price closed his eyes and tightened his jaw. "Someone just told me you were washing your tongue under running water in the men's room. I couldn't for the life of me figure out why you needed to do that."

"My tongue hurts now. I think it got cuts," Adam said as he stuck it out for added emphasis. Mr. Price gasped in horror and shrank back in revulsion at the sight of Adam's black tongue. Face turning red, Mr. Price grabbed the glue from Adam's worktable and held it up.

"Young man, what do you have this glue for? Is it supposed to serve as a decoration on the table?"

"B-But, Mr. Price," Adam said, stuttering to get the words out, "ya d-don't understand. I-I kept spillin' the glue by accident and it makes my hands sticky."

Mr. Price looked aghast. "Don't you already know that to use glue properly to seal envelopes you just need to put on a dab or two? Mr. Hitchens, is this work too challenging for you? It doesn't take a lot of brainpower to glue envelopes!" He pounded on the envelopes, causing some to fall on the floor.

Bending down and hurrying to retrieve them, Adam said, "But, Mr. Price, these here envelopes can't go on the floor. They'll get all dirty!" Adam stacked them together back on the table. Most of them had dirt and dust spots now.

Mr. Price wiped his hand over his forehead, turned back, and walked a few paces back and forth, continually loosening his necktie and swallowing. Adam overheard him muttering that perhaps collecting unemployment for a while was a better option than supervising special needs workers like this young man.

Adam scratched his head, observing his boss. He didn't understand what he was talking about, but he figured Mr. Price had a headache.

"Mr. Price, what's wrong? You gotta headache? My daddy gets headaches sometimes." Sensing Mr. Price's anger, Adam nervously started flapping his hands in the air. He put a foot forward and leaned on one and then the other, causing his whole body to sway back and forth.

Mr. Price took his hand away from his face and looked askance at Adam's jerky movements. He said emphatically, "Now does he really?"

Adam nodded his head vigorously. "Oh yes! And he takes pills after the suppas I make for him too!"

Mr. Price stopped and stared at him with his mouth hanging open. Unexpectedly, he fell into a chair near Adam's worktable. "You cook too?"

Adam stood up taller and held his head up proudly. "Even when food gets burned, my daddy says it's real good! He says he jist needs a pill ta settle his stomach or somethin'."

"So saints do still exist in the world," Mr. Price mumbled, turning his face heavenward.

Adam leaned his head forward and gaped at his boss with wrinkled eyebrows. "Huh?"

Mr. Price closed his eyes and shook his head. He then turned to the glue bottle in his hand. "Mr. Hitchens, this is how you properly seal envelopes. Watch me."

Mr. Price grabbed an envelope and dabbed the glue sponge a few times on the top seams of the back of the envelope. In his haste he pressed too hard and extra glue came squirting out beyond the seal of the envelope and on to his fingers. However, he failed to notice.

"See. This is how it's done. Do you understand now, Mr. Hitchens?" When he looked up and smiled triumphantly at Adam, Mr. Price noticed his fingers stuck together. Examining them in dismay, he whipped out a handkerchief from his jacket pocket and started rubbing the glue spots on his fingers. To his horror, he saw that not only were the glue spots stubbornly clinging to his fingers, but his jacket also now had a few glue spots. In anger, Mr. Price threw the handkerchief on the table and stood up.

"I get that problem, too, Mr. Price. Sticky fingers!" Adam waved his fingers around in the air as he swayed from side to side.

Mr. Price's eyes bored into Adam's while his nostrils flared.

"Would it be too much for you to do some stamping while I find another job for you today? I can arrange to have the cards brought in here so you can stamp."

"Yeah, I'll do that!" Adam brightened considerably. Showing that his tongue couldn't take any more licking envelopes, he stuck it out again.

"All right, then. I've already seen your tongue," Mr. Price said as he stood up. He quickly turned his head toward the door and was about to leave, when he stopped and looked at Adam again.

"Oh, and by the way," Mr. Price coughed, "your father called to say that he was going to pick you up in forty-five minutes." He hesitated, twitching his fingers at his sides but finally asked, "Do you have plans today?"

Adam scratched his head. "I dunno. Guess police wanna talk again."

Mr. Price froze. "Did you say the police?" he whispered. He looked toward the door and back at the young man. "Mr. Hitchens, are you in some kind of trouble? Is the manager of this business aware of this?"

Adam saw a growing smile forming on Mr. Price's face, but he quickly concealed it as he asked, "D-Does this mean you will no longer be working here?"

Adam shook his head vigorously and said, "Oh no, Mr. Price. I'm a good boy! A very mean man wanna hurt my friend. We can't let that happen, Mr. Price, no way!" Adam shook his head somberly. "And my daddy don't want 'im ta come and hurt me."

Mr. Price's hands shook. His felt his pockets for his pain pills. Realizing he was just getting more glue on his clothing, he muttered, "Damn" under his breath. Catching himself, he saw Adam staring at him quizzically. Mr. Price cleared his throat and quickly said, "I wish you a good day, Mr. Hitchens," and abruptly walked out of the room.

Five minutes later, Mr. Price returned. "Unfortunately, the stacks of cards are not yet ready for stamping, so I have another job for you," he informed Adam.

He entered carrying rags and a soapy water bucket and instructed him to clean the extra glue off his worktable, and the dirt and dust off the other tables and seats in the workroom. His boss left abruptly with no further instructions, so Adam dumped the rags in the bucket. Since he had not been directed to squeeze out the extra water, he covered the tables in the soapy water, spilling it onto the chairs and floor.

Ten minutes later, Mr. Price poked his face into the room, and Adam looked up and waved as his boss opened his mouth to speak. His eyes bulged upon seeing soapy water everywhere—on the tables, the chairs, and the floors. Mr. Price shook his fists at his sides and his mouth tightened into a grimace.

"Well, what doya think, Mr. Price? I clean great. I use lotsa soap and water 'cause I want ta make the place squeaky clean! Ever see it look this way?"

"It looks like the Second Deluge, Mr. Hitchens!" Mr. Price said sharply.

"What's that?" Adam asked.

"Mr. Hitchens, I'm going to get some clean, dry rags, and we're going to dry up this room before we both lose our jobs!" Seeing the question on Adam's face, Mr. Price added sharply, "Then it will in fact be clean." His face turned red as he spoke.

When he returned carrying a handful of clean rags, he added, "Oh, by the way, Mr. Hitchens, let's clean this quickly because your father is coming to pick you up."

"Ohhh, that's right. I forgot," Adam said, bumping his hand on his head.

Mr. Price gritted his teeth as he said, "I only told you a short time ago and you've already forgotten?" Adam shrugged and Mr. Price shook his head.

So the two quickly soaked up the soapy water with rags. Adam got on his hands and knees to wipe the floor while his boss went over the floor with a clean rag under his shoe. All the while, Mr. Price mumbled that when he went home this afternoon, he would shower and drink a cup of his favorite English tea, the same tea that the queen drinks. He then noticed that the bottom of his pants had gotten wet. He cursed under his breath.

Adam heard Mr. Price mumbling to himself, "I've got to get another job. A real job, not this nonsense. Dealing with an overgrown child is beneath me!" He didn't understand what his boss meant and continued cleaning, thinking that his boss was so smart he didn't always understand what he was talking about. He came to the conclusion that his boss must have felt like talking to him.

"We maka good team, right, Mr. Price?" Adam smiled cheerfully at him.

His boss shot him a look. By this time the chairs and tables were fairly dry. Only the floor was still damp in a few spots.

His boss stood up and stated, "Well then, Mr. Hitchens, I'll see you when I'll see you," but slipped and fell on a soapy puddle on the floor neither one had noticed before they finished. He screamed out in pain.

"Careful, Mr. Price! Gotta be careful! I'll get someone for ya!"

Mr. Price howled in pain as he grabbed his left leg. As Adam rushed out the door for help, he heard his boss yelling, "This job is distasteful to me! A graduate of Oxford supervising a man with such limited intelligence. How did I ever end up here?" He screamed to no one in particular. Adam heard him as he ran down the hall but shrugged his shoulders, not understanding.

As Mr. Price moaned how fate had been so unkind to him, Adam returned with the maintenance man and the manager, who was Mr. Price's boss.

"What happened in here, Price?" the manager remarked loudly as he hurried into the room. Seeing him on the floor, he added, "And what happened to you?"

"Mr. Hitchens spilled water all over," he sputtered, clutching his leg.

The manager looked around and then at Mr. Price. "You're supposed to be checking on him from time to time. Remember? That's your job."

The maintenance man rolled his eyes and tried to conceal his smile.

Before Mr. Price could answer, Bruce walked in. "What happened here?" he asked and saw his son's boss on the ground. "Mr. Price, are you all right?"

"Daddy, we were cleanin' up in here and Mr. Price slipped on the floor," Adam said, waving his hands in the air and biting his shirt.

The manager, who looked at Adam's father warily, asked, "Did you break your leg, Mr. Price?"

"I think so," Mr. Price said as he tried to get in a more comfortable position to ease the pain.

"I'm going to call an ambulance, Price. You hang on."

Bruce wanted to leave, but he went over to Mr. Price. "Do you need anything? Is there something I can do, Mr. Price?"

Red-faced, Mr. Price gritted his teeth and said quietly, "I'll be fine. You and Mr. Hitchens can go on your way!"

"Hope it's just a pull and you won't need a cast," Bruce said.

Adam walked up to his boss and squatted down as he said, "Mr. Price, if you need a cast, can I sign my name on it?"

Mr. Price cradled his leg, writhing in pain even more at the sound of Adam's voice. He stared at the young man with contempt.

"When my cousin David had a cast, I was the first one ta sign it," Adam explained, putting his shoulders up high as if that were a real achievement.

"We need to go, son." Bruce tapped Adam on the shoulder when he saw Mr. Price's hooded eyes glowering at his son.

"Feel better," Bruce said as he led his son out the door. Adam stared back at his boss.

"I want to visit ya, Mr. Price," called Adam as they neared the door.

The maintenance man held back a smile while Mr. Price lay shaking his head and gripping his knee. The manager returned, announcing an ambulance was on its way.

◆ ◆ ◆

Victor ignored his grogginess as he departed from the plane at Newark International Airport. The bright sunny day with moderate temperatures made no impact on him. His mind was focused solely on his mission.

While walking through the airport, his cell phone rang insistently. It was Vladimir.

"Get a taxi to the Hitchens' house in Morristown. You have the address," he instructed. "Igor is already there. If the girl isn't dead by now, kill her. And then kill Igor. Be extra careful there are no witnesses."

"Right," Victor answered and hung up. He was seized with a new spurt of energy as he sprinted out of the building and ran to the nearest taxi. The driver blew on a cup of hot coffee, but when Victor jumped into the back of his car and threw two one-hundred-dollar bills at him, he tossed the coffee out the window.

Victor shoved a piece of paper in front of him. "Please. Get to this address as soon as you can."

Making a quick call to his company, the driver entered the address in his GPS and stepped on the gas.

CHAPTER THIRTY-ONE

BRUCE

As Bruce led his son out the door, he turned back and said, "I hope Mr. Price will be all right." His gaze then fell on Adam. "I hope you were doing good listening, son."

"Oh, yeah, Daddy, I was," he said, nodding his head vigorously. "I helped Mr. Price clean the tables, chairs, and floor. We both had problems wit the glue."

"Glue?" Bruce said as he opened the car on the driver's side. "What were you doing with glue?"

"Sealing envelopes," he said as he settled into the car through the passenger door. He looked at his father and asked, "Daddy, why does glue have to be so sticky?"

Despite all the danger they were in, Bruce had to smile. "That's what glue's for, son. To stick things together and keep them in place." He stared at his son's mouth. "Adam, how did your tongue get all black. What've you been eating?"

"It's from lickin', Daddy. Lickin' the black line on the envelopes."

Bruce was about to start the car but stopped and asked,

"Adam, that's stuff's gross. So you were having problems with glue and you were licking the envelopes instead. Oh boy." He shook his head. "When we get to the police station, I want you to clean out your mouth right away." He started the car. "How could Mr. Price let you lick all those envelopes? Wasn't he watching you? What's he doing all day if he's not keeping an eye on you?"

"Whenever I go to Mr. Price's office, he's readin' books and drinkin' tea," Adam replied. "Once he pointed to a fancy piece of paper on the wall. He said he finished from a school to teach history. He's from a faraway place, I think. He tells people he was an ex'lent student."

"An excellent student," Bruce corrected him as he pulled his car out of the parking lot. "But not such a good boss, apparently."

"I betta visit Mr. Price if he needs a cast. I'll sign it. I know he'll miss me. He's always talkin' to hisself 'cause he needs me to be his friend."

They came to a red light. Bruce studied his son—his brown hair standing in all directions, holes dotting the top front of his shirt, and his hands waving in the air. He also glanced at those large, innocent eyes and his sweet smile. Adam had only the most innocent thoughts and feelings. He sought love and companionship and wanted to make other people happy. As much as Maggie used to complain how hard it was to take care of him, Bruce knew she adored their son. He reached over and touched Adam's cheek.

"I love you, son," he said, his eyes moistening.

"I love you too, Daddy." He smiled.

"I know Mommy used to say that to you all the time," he said as he brought his hand back to the wheel and sighed in regret.

"Yeah," Adam said. He stared ahead. "I usedta ask her why you never said that, but Mommy said you loved me too but you didn't say it 'cause you're a man and you forget."

"Son, I promise you, I won't forget from now on, OK?"

Adam raised his fists in the air and said, "Yay! I wanna hear that. I miss Mommy telling me that. She usedta say it all the time."

"I know," Bruce acknowledged quietly. "Mommy was a great Mommy and a great wife. People need to hear they're loved."

"OK, Daddy. I'll tell you I love you every day," Adam said. Bruce turned and saw his son examining him earnestly.

Bruce noticed the light just changed to green when he heard his son ask, "Daddy?"

He turned to Adam, whose eyes were sparkling and his grin was wide. "Yes, son? I need to drive now." His gaze kept switching from the road to his son.

Adam leaned forward. "Can I smell your feet when we get ta the police station?"

"Absolutely not!" Bruce barked. Adam crouched away, startled by his father's sudden temper. In a calmer, more pleasant voice, he said, "Adam, we've got to help Marina."

"Yeah, Daddy, she's a good friend," Adam said, nodding solemnly, seemingly forgetting his father's bout of temper.

"You're right, son. I agree."

A moment later, Adam, who was still waving both his hands, told his father, "Music. Daddy, I wanna hear music."

Bruce turned on the local radio. Carrie Underwood and Miranda Lambert were belting out "Somethin' Bad." Adam sang along, waving his hands and rocking back and forth. As he always did, his father glanced around to see if anyone saw his son. Two little kids in the backseat of a passing car stared at Adam with their mouths hanging open. As the car drove off, the kids then looked at each other and burst out laughing, pointing at Adam. Bruce blinked hard in an effort to block out the sight of those kids making fun of his son. Fortunately, it didn't take him long, for he had more pressing concerns. He was minutes away from turning into downtown Morristown, where the police station was located. He braced himself for the usual onslaught of traffic when a news brief interrupted the music:

"A woman is reported missing in the Morristown area. She is described as being a white female, five feet, four inches tall and approximately one hundred pounds. The woman has brown hair and blue eyes. She was last seen in a pink shirt and blue jeans with white sneakers. Please call this number immediately if you have seen her."

Bruce gripped the steering wheel as this announcement was read. He looked over at Adam.

"What was that all about, Daddy? I wanna hear 'Somethin' Bad,'" he said as he folded his arms in front of him and pouted. His father was speechless. Adam stared at him, waiting for an answer.

Fortunately, Miley Cyrus's "Wrecking Ball" began playing and Adam again waved his hands and rocked back and forth again as he tried to sing the words.

Bruce used this opportunity to focus on his driving and getting to the police station as quickly and as safely as possible.

"Ice cream!" Adam pointed out when the song finished and they were about to pass the ice cream parlor. "Daddy, let's stop for ice cream. I want choc'late."

Bruce's eyes grew wide. *We don't know if Marina is alive or dead right now and you're bothering me about ice cream,* he was tempted to shout. He glanced at his son. *You don't have a clue what's going on.*

He shook his head and refused to answer. "No, Daddy," Adam said. "We'll eat choc'late ice cream when we get Marina. I want to see Marina."

"So do I," he agreed and he parked in the parking lot of the Morristown police station on South Street. Fighting his rising panic, he turned off the engine without shifting his car into park first. He realized it when he opened his car door.

"Wait a minute," he told his son as he turned on the ignition and shifted his car into park. Adam was already out of the car.

"Stay right there," Bruce ordered him, wiping his perspiring forehead with his sleeve. "We're walking in together, son."

Bruce grabbed Adam's hand. South Street was always busy and he had to keep him close. Bruce considered from time to time how strange it must look for an adult male to be holding a teenage boy's hand, but he didn't have the luxury to be self-conscious. Any keen observer watching Adam closely would realize there was something wrong with him: the waving of the hands; the empty, innocent look in his eyes; the holes at the top of his shirt; and the grip on his father's hand indicating his dependency.

Let people think what they want. I've got too many problems to worry about how odd we look. My main concerns are finding Marina and keeping Adam safe. He glanced at his son, who chewed on his shirt while clutching his father's hand. *I wish Adam would stop biting away at his shirts. I can't even think about going to the store to buy him more shirts.*

He led Adam carefully on the congested street full of cars and pedestrians. They entered the police station.

He gave their names at the desk. They were immediately escorted to Officer Lewis's office.

"Mr. Hitchens." Lewis came from behind his desk to greet him. He turned to Adam and held out his hand. "How are you holding up, Adam?"

"Where's my friend Marina?" he asked, grabbing on to the officer's hand.

Lewis grunted and with his left hand extricated his right from Adam's strong grasp. "We're looking for her," he told him, rubbing his hand. "We won't stop until we find her."

"Who'd wanna hurt my friend anyway?" he asked, failing to pay attention to the officer stretching out and rubbing his hand. Bruce stared at the officer, waiting for more information and too distracted to reprimand his son for his tight grasp.

Detective Lewis's phone rang. As he listened to the person on the other line, the officer's eyebrows arched and a small smile formed on his face.

"Get some more patrols to follow them, and call me if there are any further developments," Lewis said as he hung up. He turned to Bruce, "Witnesses saw an elderly lady walking her dog and yelling at a man who was attacking a woman fitting Miss Dobrin's description a few blocks from your house. She ordered the man to let her go and he shot the dog with his gun that had a silencer," he told Bruce. "But the lady's screams alerted the neighbors. Police and ambulances are on their way over."

Visibly shaken, Bruce grabbed Adam and covered his ears. As he digested what Lewis had told him, his son pulled away and asked, "Daddy, Daddy, where's Marina?"

His father could only stare at him, his eyes wide open and his lips trembling. Lewis cleared his throat and responded, "We think we found her and we're going to bring her back as soon as we can."

"Will she be home for suppa tonight? I wanna take a walk with Marina and we can all watch my new tape 'bout whales," he told Lewis excitedly as he waved his hands, seemingly oblivious to his father's panic. He turned to him, "Daddy, can we order a pizza again? When I go ta work tomorra, will Mr. Price be there? I gotta get a marker and put my name on his cast."

Seeing Adam's father still silent, Officer Miller, who had walked in and overheard Adam's chatter, said, "Hey Adam, there's hot chocolate in the coffee machine. Do you want a hot chocolate?"

Adam's face brightened. "Wit marshmallows too?"

"Yeah, you can get marshmallows in there if you want them," Miller replied.

Adam raised his fists in the air as in victory, and said, "Yeah! I love hot choc'late wit marshmallows."

"Come with me." Miller waved him over with his hand. Bruce and Lewis nodded their thanks as Adam lumbered over to him, hands waving in excitement.

"Have a seat, Mr. Hitchens. I know this is a lot to take in, especially with your son," Lewis said, putting his hand on Bruce's shoulder and directing him to a seat.

"Call me Bruce," he said as he plopped down on the chair. "I think we're more than a little acquainted by now."

"And you can call me John. Tell me, how do you manage taking care of your son all by yourself. He has autism, right?"

Bruce nodded and then shook his head and shrugged.

As pale as a piece of chalk, Bruce felt as if his brain was about to explode. He barely heard Lewis talking to him. "Bruce," Officer Lewis said. When Bruce finally managed to focus his eyes on him, Lewis said, "I have three kids, elementary-school aged, and my wife and I refer to taking care of them as 'mission impossible.' But Adam is even more of a handful. And good God, you're worrying about Miss Dobrin too. Not to mention holding down a job."

Bruce closed his eyes at the mention of his job. He wished Lewis would stop talking and he could escape from all the harsh realities of his life.

I wish I would've left it as him calling me Mr. Hitchens.

He opened his eyes. "So what are you going to do now, Officer?" he asked, eager to change the subject.

The detective appeared to understand Bruce's desire not to delve into how he handled his many responsibilities and returned to his more professional demeanor. "Well, the good news is they can run a check on that license plate. Then we can find out whose name that car is registered under," he told him. "What we're going to do now is, after Adam finishes his hot chocolate, you and your son'll go home with a police escort, and we'll have officers watching your house all night because there's always the possibility the man may turn up there with Marina since they obviously know that's where she's been staying." He paused and leaned his head forward. "Unless you two would prefer to stay at a safe house. An undisclosed location for now until they're caught."

"A safe house?" Bruce looked at Lewis, perplexed. "It's Marina they're after, not us."

Lewis breathed in before responding. "Yes, they're after her. But we don't know why they want her so badly. Could she have information that will bring their operation down?"

"Marina's said nothing about that."

Officer Lewis leaned forward and held up his hands. "But, Mr. Hitchens, there must be a reason they're pursuing her so aggressively."

"What could she know? She's just one of the many girls they trafficked."

Lewis leaned back. "Mr. Hitchens, she's not their typical trafficking victim. They always kidnap unsuspecting young women who answer ads to work as a nanny or housekeeper overseas. These unsuspecting women answer these ads out of sheer desperation because they're impoverished. But Miss Dobrin is educated, had a good job and prospects to move ahead. They kidnapped her off the streets of Moldova in the early morning hours. She speaks English as well as Russian and Romanian. Unfortunately, at this time, we know as much as you do what's going on."

Lewis's phone rang. "Officer Lewis," he said. His expression perked up. "That's great news. Keep me informed." He hung up.

Bruce eyebrows lifted and he asked the detective eagerly, "What did you find out?"

Lewis faced Bruce with his hands folded on his desk. "They ran a check of the license plate number. The car is being rented by a TAV Company. They operate out of Moldova. They're going to run a check on the company to find out if they're legitimate."

"It's great you're making progress. I only wish there was something I could do to help."

Lewis lowered his face slightly and said, "Mr. Hitchens, you've already been a tremendous help. We'll keep you informed of any further developments." He nodded toward the hallway where Adam had gone to get his hot chocolate. "Take care of your son. Do you want to pursue the safe house option?"

Bruce lowered his gaze, contemplating. Finally he shook his head. "I think the police protection will be enough." He paused. "Adam gets out-of-sorts when he stays in a new place. I would say not yet."

Officer Lewis nodded, seeming to agree. "Well then, go home and get some rest."

Bruce would much rather have stayed at the police station to find out what was happening with Marina, but he knew the police could not spend their manpower babysitting his son. He rose and was about to shake Lewis's hand when his cell phone went off.

"Bruce?" he recognized Matt's voice right away. "That woman's missing now?"

"Yes," Bruce answered, feeling guilty and annoyed at the same time. He should have let his brother know but knew he would only worry.

"Listen, I'm supposed to go to China tomorrow. I can delay this trip if there's an emergency."

Bruce waved his hand. "Oh, you go on your trip, Matt. There's nothing you can do."

"I know that, Bruce," Matt said in his "duh" voice, "but I want you and Adam to stay out of it. I don't know who she's connected with and it looks like they're a dangerous bunch. Do you have police protection?"

Bruce looked at his phone. He wanted to hang up on his brother. "Yes, we do have police protection. Marina was kidnapped, you know."

Matt sighed, and Bruce could tell he was trying to keep his temper in check. "I know. Judy's also worried about her, but my main concern is you and Adam. Please just stay away from trouble. Will you do that for me?"

"Matt, do you think for one minute I'm looking for trouble?" he almost shouted, then glanced up to find Lewis and others staring at him, so he walked away to a corner. "The police are doing the investigation. I'm going to take Adam home and rest."

"Where are you?" Matt demanded.

"At the police station right now. With Adam."

"The police called you from work?"

"The police wanted us to come to the station," Bruce answered, clenching and unclenching his fist. He wanted more than anything to tell his brother to butt out of his problems and just stay in his perfect life. He didn't trust himself to say anything further so he just said, "I'm going home now. Bye." He hung up.

Bruce ignored Lewis's stare. Fortunately, Adam walked in. He had brown all over his mouth with a few white spots on his upper lip.

"I had a big cuppa hot choc'late wit marshmallows, Daddy," he said, not noticing his father's angry expression.

"That's great, Adam," he said. "Let's wash your mouth in the bathroom and then we're going home."

"What 'bout Marina?" he protested. "I want Marina."

His father closed his eyes. "Hopefully later, son. She'll be home later." He put his weary hand on his son's back and asked Lewis where the men's room was.

"Down the hall. Second left," Lewis told him. Bruce

imagined the detective and everyone else within earshot shaking their heads at his miserable, pathetic lot in life.

"Lewis, I found him." Officer Smith was almost running toward the office as Bruce and Adam were about to depart. Bruce held his son's arm as he waited for the officer to tell them what he had found out.

"The man who has Miss Dobrin." He waved the paper and placed it on Lewis's desk. "His name is Igor Agapov! Been in sex trafficking for years and has been described as 'unstable and needs to be under a tight leash.'" Smith shook his head and said, "Somebody made the mistake of allowing him to take the reins."

The skin on Bruce's neck broke out in an immediate sweat. He felt himself perspiring all over and had to lean on his son to keep from falling.

"Whatsthemadder, Daddy?" Adam said as his father grasped his shoulders.

Bruce could not even attempt a response. He closed his eyes and fought to restore his balance.

◆ ◆ ◆

Igor took out his carry-on and rummaged through his instruments, tempted to drive away and devise a method of killing Marina that would give her the slowest, most painful death possible.

Then the phone rang. Cursing under his breath, he reluctantly picked it up.

"Where are you, Igor?" Andre barked.

Igor told him about the large medical building on James Street.

"I'm sending backup now," he ordered.

"What?" Igor almost shouted, perplexed. "I'm going to drive to an abandoned area and kill her already!"

"No!" Andre screamed.

"This is what I need to do if it's the last thing I ever do," Igor told him, speaking recklessly to his powerful boss.

Seeing there was no dissuading him, Andre tried another tactic. "My backup will help you kill her and then she will disappear forever. Then we're all getting out of America!"

"No! I cannot wait any longer!" he protested.

"Give the backup an hour!" Andre's voice was almost pleading. "You'll see the backup has tools so that she will die a very cruel death. You'll see. You won't be sorry. In fact, I will richly reward you."

This gave Igor pause. He decided his plan of torturing her was not as painful as he thought she deserved. He heard footsteps behind him and saw a pregnant woman with an older woman accompanying her. His cautious nature took over.

"I will wait," he conceded to Andre. "But only an hour."

CHAPTER THIRTY-TWO

BRUCE

Bruce drove home with Adam. A police car followed them.

"Daddy?" Adam said looking at his father. "I gotta go to the batroom."

Bruce hit his hand on the steering wheel. "Damn! You should have told me you had to use the bathroom before we left the police station. I've got to think of everything, Adam!" He concentrated on the road as he tightened his grip on the steering wheel. With gritted teeth, he asked his son, "So how many hot chocolates did you drink?"

His son tilted his head a bit. "Mmmm, I think two or three."

Bruce closed his eyes. "Two or three giant cups of hot chocolate."

"Yeah, Daddy. I gotta pee."

Bruce waved his hand at the police car behind him. Then he pulled into a diner. Looking quizzically, the policeman followed and parked his car beside his.

"He has to go to the bathroom. Sorry," he said, his eyes

downcast and his face slightly pink.

"It's all right," the policeman said as Bruce rushed Adam into the restaurant.

"My son needs to use the restroom," he said to the woman at the register.

"There's a sign on the front door," she pointed gruffly. "You can't use the restroom unless you make a purchase."

Bruce slumped his shoulders and rubbed his hand over his face. Adam said, "Daddy, I wanna get somethin'."

"OK, son. How about a donut?" Bruce asked, his eyes scanning the desserts in the front window under the cash register.

"Yeah!" Adam said, nodding his head and waving his arms.

"I'll buy a donut after we leave the bathroom," Bruce assured the woman as he searched around for where it was located.

But the woman remained unmoved by Bruce's predicament. "You gotta make a purchase before using the men's room."

Bruce put his hands through his hair and squeezed his eyes shut. He leaned close to the woman and said, "Miss, my son has autism. He can't hold it in. Do you want him to pee all over the floor?"

The woman glanced at Adam, who was now holding himself and jumping from one foot to another.

"For God's sakes, Alice. Let the kid use the bathroom," another woman who had the title Manager attached to her name clip said, scowling at her employee. She pointed to her left and said, "It's all the way down the hall where you see the exit sign."

"Thank you," Bruce said emphatically as he put his hands on Adam's shoulders and led him in that direction. He noticed the woman named Alice wrinkling her nose as she watched them go.

"I wanna donut," Adam said with glee after he peed into the urinal.

Bruce couldn't help staring at Adam's waistline. He saw the beginnings of a potbelly. "Just this time, Adam," he said. "After all this is over, I'm going to put you on a diet." He rubbed his chin and nodded. "You're due for a checkup soon. I'm sure the doctor will agree with me."

"What's a diet?" Adam asked. Then he turned quickly to his father, his pants still down. "Daddy, I don' wanna go to the doctor for a checkup," he wailed, waving his hands. "I don' wanna shot! No checkup." He shook his head.

"Adam! Adam, pull up your pants," Bruce said as he glanced toward the door.

Adam then ambled over to the sink and squirted five shots of liquid soap into his hands and worked up enough lather for a sink full of dishes.

"Adam, rinse your hands and let's go," Bruce said, his hands on his hips.

He clutched Adam's shoulder as they made their way out of the restroom. Alice sat behind the register but turned away upon seeing them.

Bruce cleared his throat and turned to his son. "Son, what kind of donut would you like?"

Alice turned toward them grudgingly.

"Choc'late," Adam said, waving his hands. His eyes were bright with anticipation. Bruce and Alice couldn't help smiling on seeing the spark of excitement in his eyes.

She opened the pastry window and pulled out the chocolate donut with parchment paper. "Manager said it's on the house."

Adam surveyed the place. "What house?"

Bruce grinned and took the donut. "Tell her thank you."

Alice gave up being angry and was all smiles as she turned to help another customer. "Come on, let's go now," Bruce told Adam, who licked the chocolate frosting on top of the donut. As they headed out, the manager spotted them.

Bruce turned to his son. "What do you say, Adam?"

"Tank you." He smiled widely as his mouth was again covered in chocolate.

The manager waved her hand. "No problem. Don't mind Alice. She's such a stickler for rules."

As Bruce waved good-bye, he suddenly remembered what had happened at the Fairmount Home. The staff member Heidi would break the rules and walk with Adam individually. He recalled his son speaking about her endlessly once he left the home, telling him how much he missed her.

"Sometimes rules need to be broken," he heard himself say out loud.

"What, Daddy?" Adam said, his mouth full.

"Nothing, son," he replied, shaking his head. He stared at his son taking generous bites of his donut. "But one rule that's going to have to be followed is no more sweets for you." But Adam was too busy gobbling up his donut to pay attention.

The policeman had been leaning on his car. He nodded when he saw them and got back into his vehicle.

When they reached Bruce's house, they saw another car parked there: a Lotus. As soon as he parked, Matt and Judy hopped out of their car. Matt hurried over to them, his eyes filled with fear while Judy's mouth was a straight line.

"Bruce," he said as he nodded to the policeman, "I don't want you involved in this mess. I put off my China trip for a week. Please, please come over to our house and let the police deal with this."

Bruce was about to respond, but Adam spoke first. "Hi, Uncle Matt. You're comin' to suppa wit us. We're waiting for Marina. I love havin' company."

Matt tilted his head when he saw Adam. Chocolate covered his mouth, and he had chocolate stains on his jacket and pants. He turned to his brother, focusing on him instead.

"Go to my vacation house in Newport," Matt pleaded with his older brother. "Adam will like the ocean. There are tons of places to visit up in Rhode Island. Go there until the police straighten everything out with that woman."

"You mean Marina," Judy said, putting her hands on her hips and eying her husband angrily.

"But I have to go to work . . . ," Bruce started to say, then stared down, his face visibly pained. A lump formed in his throat and his body tensed.

"What's wrong, Bruce?" Judy asked quietly, trying to meet his eyes.

Bruce ran a hand over his eyes and looked up at her. "Judy, I really can't discuss this right now. Please understand." His eyes pleaded with her.

"See!" Matt said, raising his eyebrows and pointing his finger at his brother as if in validation. "That woman has caused him nothing but trouble. Oww!" Matt yelped when Judy poked her husband hard in the ribs.

"Daddy, I gotta go ta the bathroom 'gain," Adam said, waving his hands and shifting his weight from one foot to the other.

The policeman, who had been drumming his fingers in front

of his car, interrupted them. "Bring your son to the bathroom. Then you'll go inside and talk," he said in a commanding tone. He then stared at Matt and Judy and appeared as if he wanted to speak to them privately, but his cell phone rang.

Looking resigned, Bruce tapped his son. "Let's go in, Adam. He took out his house key and headed up the gravel path to their front door. Inviting images of Newport, Rhode Island, came into his mind. The last time he had been there was with Maggie. They had visited Matt and his family in the summer. Sailboats, beaches, mansions, and restaurants swirled in his head as he opened the door and watched Adam hurry to the bathroom. It seemed like a lifetime ago. He couldn't believe he would ever be able to enjoy good times like that again. Morbid thoughts ensued: he convinced himself he had lost his job and therefore had no means to support himself and Adam. He worried that something terrible had happened to Marina, and he knew both he and Adam would be shattered if she were dead.

Bruce heard the toilet flush. "Did you wipe yourself, Adam?"

"Yup," was the reply as he heard the water turn on.

"Just a little soap," he called out.

Adam came bustling out of the bathroom. "Is Marina here, Daddy?"

Not able to even address the question, he said, "Let's go outside with Uncle Matt and Aunt Judy."

The policeman, Matt, and Judy were talking outside. They abruptly stopped upon seeing Bruce and Adam.

The policeman whispered in Bruce's ear, "That man Igor took her away in his car."

"How?" he asked, staring open-mouthed.

The policeman glanced at Adam and hesitated to speak.

"Kidnapped her," he said.

"Judy, take Adam inside, please," Bruce managed to sputter, leaning against the police car as he imagined what was now happening to Marina.

"Of course," Judy said, her face stricken. "Come on in, Adam."

"But where's Marina?" Adam whined, looking from one adult to another.

Bruce said the first thing that popped into his mind. "M-Marina's c-coming, Adam. Set the table for a meal."

"All right!" Adam raised his fist in the air and ran to the front door, his arms flapping in excitement. Judy morosely followed him in.

"All we can do now is sit tight while we wait for more news," the policeman told Bruce and Matt.

"Sit tight!" Bruce shouted. "Marina's in danger, maybe even dead, and you're telling me to sit tight!"

"Bruce," Matt said, putting his hand on his brother's shoulder, "there's nothing we can do. We've got to leave it to the professionals." He pointed to the house. "Let's go in and sit."

Bruce groaned inwardly. He hoped his younger brother would stop lecturing him. At least Judy was here to watch Adam.

◆ ◆ ◆

While Victor made his way to the Hitchens' house, Vladimir called Victor and gave him the new address where he could meet up with Igor. When they arrived, Victor instructed the taxi driver to drop him off ten feet away from the black Mercedes in the parking lot of the medical building. He walked determinedly to the driver's side of the car. Igor carefully observed him through the rear view mirror. *The backup?*

Victor saw her slumped on the passenger side, looking like she was sleeping peacefully. His whole body tightened and he willed himself to look at Igor.

When Igor rolled his window down slightly, Victor stated simply, "Andre sent me."

"Goodt. Let's go," Igor replied. "We waste no time."

Victor wordlessly opened the passenger's side door. He needed all his willpower to refrain from the killing urge that consumed him.

"We go to abandoned area. I know where," Igor said as he started the car. He had seen another abandoned field for sale near his hotel. Why not there? They were leaving the country and no one would likely see or hear them.

CHAPTER THIRTY-THREE

MARINA

Marina's head throbbed as she struggled to open her eyes. She thought she heard a familiar voice but figured she must be dreaming. As she attempted to lift her head, she heard Igor telling someone, "Here. Put this on. This girl keeps escaping when you least expect it! She'll be even more afraid when she sees the masks."

After a moment, she heard Igor ask in a menacing voice, "What's wrong with you? Why don't you put on mask?"

The other must have put it on because she heard Igor make a satisfied grunt and say, "Now!"

Her mouth was parched and her limbs throbbed in pain. There was little chance of escape in her condition. When she finally managed to open her eyes, she heard Igor coaxing the man to get his knife ready. She feared getting up and turning around, for she knew the end was coming.

"I said a knife, not a gun!" Igor shouted at the man.

She heard both men dash out of the car.

Whack!

It sounded like one man had punched the other. Marina turned her head and saw both masked men wrestling on the ground. Each fought the other for the gun.

Marina coaxed her body to move. Although her head still felt hazy, she forced herself to limp out of the car, and fear propelled her to move. She didn't know where she was, but she crawled as far away from these men as possible without daring to turn back.

As she moved, she heard a gunshot, then Igor cursing.

Marina lifted herself to her feet but feared to look back. She made her way to the nearest neighborhood. She whispered a prayer of thanks as she saw familiar-looking houses. She entered the neighborhood where the Hitchens lived.

Just when she thought she could breathe easy for a moment, she heard the squeal of tires behind her. Igor's Mercedes rolled right in front of her as she stumbled on someone's lawn. Unfortunately, many backyards were fenced in and it forced her to make her escape out in the open. He had obviously overcome the other man. Pointing a gun at her, Igor wore a smug expression on his bloodied face. Marina was so shocked she nearly collapsed.

No! No! This can't be happening! I'll never be rid of him until he kills me!

She stopped in her tracks and struggled to prevent herself from falling over, unwilling to allow him his final victory without a fight. She screamed, "You can't kill me in a neighborhood full of people! It's over!"

"Shut up! I don't care what happens to me. You've ruined my life anyway! You're not getting out of here alive," Igor hissed. But even as he told her this, he surveyed his surroundings, and when he spotted someone, he hid his gun.

Out of the corner of her eye, Marina saw a young girl with flowing brown hair leaving one of the nearby houses. She carried a backpack and was only a few yards away. She was about to turn the corner and disappear out of sight. Marina closed her eyes, said a brief prayer, and did the only thing she could think of to escape. Igor raised his gun while searching in all directions for possible witnesses. Surprising both of them, she headed for Igor's car, opened and closed the passenger door and yelled at the top of her lungs, "Thanks for the ride! See you later!" The girl with the backpack turned around.

"Hi, Irene! Wait up!" Marina yelled to the girl, who looked back startled and stared hard at Marina, trying to recognize her. Marina's body was numb and working on automatic. She forced her legs to jog toward her, but the girl trembled, quickened her steps, and sped away.

"Irene, I have to talk to you!" Marina yelled, undeterred.

Soon a few people popped their heads out of windows of nearby houses and pointed and stared at her. Igor's gun, which had been aimed toward her, quickly disappeared under his jacket when he saw people watching.

"You've been staying at the Hitchens' house, haven't you?" An elderly lady wearing an old, faded robe came out and stood on her front porch with her arms folded. Marina and Igor turned to her. The woman shook her head in consternation. "His wife just died and already he's invited another woman to come live with him."

The woman was about to go back into her house when Marina surprised her by yelling, "So what are you trying to say?" She had never made such a loud scene in public, but the mortal danger brought out a boldness she had never experienced before. She didn't dare glimpse back to see what Igor was doing.

The elderly lady stared hard at her with hooded eyes and said, "People today got no feelings! His wife just died and is still warm in the ground and he goes out and takes up with a much younger woman! It's a disgrace!" She spat out, "When my husband passed away, I mourned him for years. He was a good man. I would never have dreamed of desecrating his memory by carrying on with another man so soon after he passed! People today have no respect!" She gesticulated with her arms. "Out with the old and in with the new!"

"Actually, I agree with you," Igor said behind Marina. She turned. He had hurried out of his car and came up from behind to clutch Marina's trembling arm. He told the woman, "I'm trying to bring her back home and to stop dating a man who just lost his wife." Marina was speechless. Her mind and body froze.

"Now you give me hope," the elderly lady said, folding her arms and nodding approvingly. "It's so good to see a young person show some respect when a loved one has just departed."

Even though Marina couldn't think, she found herself blurting out sarcastically, "Oh, Igor has a lot of respect for women! He believes in keeping them chained to beds and injecting them with drugs."

Igor glared at her and tightened his grasp on her arm, squeezing it. The elderly woman glared at Marina strangely and said, "This woman speaks nonsense."

"I agree," Igor said with gritted teeth. "The sooner I get her back to the hospital, the better." Marina turned white, and her efforts to break free from his grasp were in vain; he held her with an iron grip.

"Come, let's go now!" He pulled her toward the car. Marina couldn't breathe. Her effort to escape had backfired.

When Igor turned his face, the woman stared. "How did you get that terrible scar, young man?" she asked, unconsciously putting her own hand on her jaw.

Igor ignored her and, holding Marina tight, he growled in her ear, "Talk and I'll break your arm!"

"Wait a minute!" shouted a woman in her early thirties pushing a baby stroller. Everyone turned toward her, not realizing she had been there listening.

"I caught a few snippets about what you've been talking about," she said, looking at all of them. At the sound of his mother's voice, the toddler squealed and shook his rattle up and down. "I wouldn't call myself a nosy person," she said, straightening up and attempting to appear more dignified, "but I'm always pushing my son around and I've seen this woman walking with Bruce Hitchens's son the way he used to with his mother." She turned her head and regarded both the elderly woman and Igor as she spoke. "The son is handicapped. I think you're judging her too harshly."

Marina smiled and tears welled up in her eyes. Igor banged his fist in his leg and muttered curses under his breath. In the process, his grip loosened from her arm.

The elderly lady stood with her mouth open.

"Thank you for your kind words." Marina could barely speak, her heart filled with gratitude. "I do love Adam." She loosened her arm from Igor's grasp and said to him, "If you'll excuse me, I'll be on my way."

"Are you going to the Hitchens' house?" the woman asked. "We can walk there together."

Marina's smile encompassed her entire face. "That would be lovely."

She smiled sweetly at Igor and wrangled free from his grasp. Igor blanched and reluctantly released her arm. More people stared from windows. A few even ventured out and stood in front of their houses to witness the exchange.

As Marina walked with the woman pushing her baby in the stroller toward the Hitchens' house, she felt many eyes following them. She quickly glanced back and caught Igor seething, tightening his fists, and letting out a string of curses in Russian. She saw the elderly lady eying Igor in shock at his angry outburst. Then the woman fled back into her house, closing the door with a definitive bang.

Marina tensed when she heard Igor slam his car door and start his engine. The woman glanced back and asked her, "Who's that guy?"

"We've got to get out of here," Marina whispered. Touching the woman's back, she prodded the woman to walk faster. The woman's face turned ashen and her movements were wooden as she kept hushing her toddler, who started crying. Consumed with guilt for involving them, Marina told the woman, "Turn the next block. Smile and wave like you know nothing."

"I don't know anything," the woman said. Her hand gripped the stroller so hard that her knuckles were white.

"Exactly," Marina said.

At the next block they parted, and Marina ran. The Mercedes picked up speed behind her. She ran on people's properties, going through yards and in between trees in order to dodge Igor. Her path confused him; he had to stop the car a few times and get out to search for her. She continued running, hoping to stay alive and reach her destination for help.

◆ ◆ ◆

His plans also foiled, Victor ran in their direction. Fortunately, he always kept handkerchiefs in his pocket. He needed them now to stem the bleeding on his arm. He was prepared to shoot Igor when out of the corner of his eye, he saw a pregnant woman and another who looked like her mother leave the medical building. They recoiled in terror as the mother pushed her pregnant daughter back into the building. That distraction allowed Igor to get the upper hand and slash Victor's arm. Igor then took out his gun and shot him in the chest, not knowing he wore a bulletproof vest. Victor had to pretend he was dead for a few moments while Igor turned his gun to shoot Marina. Obviously missing his target, he cursed loudly and scrambled into his car in hot pursuit of her.

Victor knew it was only a matter of time before the police were called. He had to find Igor before the evil man captured Marina. His cell phone buzzed insistently; he knew it was Andre, but his boss would have to wait. Despite his arm bleeding anew, he had to catch up with them. Victor followed the path where people were outside talking about a strange incident with a man in a Mercedes chasing a woman and he heard murmurings of hearing a gun shot.

CHAPTER THIRTY-FOUR

BRUCE

"Where's Marina, Daddy? Where's Marina?" Adam asked endlessly as he stared out the front window, his hands waving. The more he asked, the more vigorously his hands waved, signaling his growing impatience.

Bruce paced the room helplessly while Judy and Matt, sitting on the couch, tried to calm his restless son.

"She'll come. Don't worry, Adam," Matt said, turning to Judy and shaking his head.

"Sit down with us, Adam," Judy said as she patted the seat next to her.

But Adam would only respond by asking, "Where's Marina?"

The officer stood by, waiting for further instructions, when his phone rang.

His eyebrows rose, and he nodded upon hearing the voice on the other line.

The moment he hung up, Bruce asked, "What's happening?"

"Backup's coming," the officer announced. "Lewis told me the FBI found out who these two Russians are working for.

They just contacted the Moscow police. They were delighted we gave them this lead and they've now connected the dots."

Before anyone could say more, Adam squealed in delight. "Marina!" he shouted, pointing to the window, jumping up and down. "I see Marina!"

Everyone headed to the window. But in a flash, before anyone knew it, Adam was out the door.

"Adam! Adam! Get back here!" Bruce called out.

But Adam, racing at full speed, was halfway off the property by then.

Bruce chased after him.

"Mr. Hitchens, stay inside, please! I'll get your son!" the officer called, but Bruce kept running.

"Bruce! Adam! Come back!" Judy shouted, but to no avail.

"You stay here!" the officer instructed Judy and Matt.

Bruce briefly glanced back and saw the officer taking his gun out of his holster and crouching low, running to his police car, but the father's first instinct was to protect his son. He turned forward. Adam was already twenty feet ahead of him.

"Adam! Come back! Please!" he shouted as he ran.

From a distance he saw Marina running toward them. Although she was tired and scared, her expression brightened considerably upon seeing Adam. Behind her a black Mercedes crept in the distance. When the driver spotted her running on the sidewalk, he hit the gas and drove right at her. Turning around, Marina paled and her expression froze in fear, her eyes wild with terror and her mouth opening wide. She yelled, "Adam! Adam! Run away!"

Adam didn't understand. Instead, he held his arms out wide, face beaming, "Marina! You came back! I knew you wouldn't leave me."

Bruce caught up with Adam and Marina. As they came together, Adam was about to hug her, but remembering he couldn't do that, he held out his right hand.

"A policeman's here at my house," Adam proclaimed, smiling and pointing his finger at his small house tucked away from the rest of the neighborhood. He appeared oblivious to the roaring car approaching. "But Marina," he said, his face all smiles, "we can have suppa and go for a walk and watch my new tape 'bout whales and . . ."

His father didn't let him finish. He grabbed Adam and Marina and pushed them away as the car raced toward them. Bruce pushed them even lower to the ground toward a parked car on the neighbor's front lawn when he heard shots fired from the vehicle, shielding them with his body. Finally aware of the danger, Adam screamed and blocked his ears. Marina, trembling, lay still. Shots came from the other direction. When Bruce looked up, he saw the policeman's body slumped to the ground.

He heard Igor reloading his gun. Police sirens screamed in the distance, but the danger still lurked close at hand.

"Come on!" he grasped his son and Marina and dragged them behind a parked car. Still screaming, Adam jerked his hands in all directions, and Marina grasped and held his right hand.

"Adam, we're here for you," Marina told him, but Adam kept flailing on the ground.

The car was now parallel to the parked car. Igor was ready, aiming his gun at Marina, when Bruce found a large stone and hurled it at the car and ducked. The glass in the front window shattered, startling Igor. Before he had a chance to recover, the approaching police cars surrounded him.

Igor snapped. Face red with rage, he ignored Officer Lewis's command to drop the gun and put his hands up. Instead, he crawled around his car, aiming his gun at Marina, who was holding Adam's hand and talking soothing words to him. Igor fired his gun, but Bruce, following Igor's movements around the car, intercepted, jerking his arm down. The bullet hit the trunk of a nearby oak tree.

◆ ◆ ◆

Andre paced his office. His normally cool and calm demeanor was gone; instead, he kept wiping a handkerchief across his forehead. Andre never remembered getting so nervous about an operation—they always ran so smoothly. He punched his fist in his hand: operations almost always went according to plan, that is, until he hired Igor Agapov.

Why hadn't Victor called? He was supposed to be independent and super reliable—another James Bond.

The phone rang. When he saw it was Victor, he charged to the phone, nearly dropping it. "What's going on?" Andre demanded.

"I'm heading to the house where the girl is. Igor just got there and is facing the police."

Andre nearly gagged when he tried to speak. "He cannot be taken alive! You must kill them both! Now!"

"Don't worry. Each one will meet the fate they deserve," Victor replied.

"See to it and phone me immediately when they're both disposed of," Andre replied, fighting to remain calm. Still, he was unnerved by Victor's cryptic reply.

He paced the room again and then stopped a moment.

Each will meet the fate they deserve? What the hell does that mean?

But Andre tried again to resist the nagging fears swirling around his head. *I am the boss. I must return to my usual unflappable demeanor like a strong leader.* He focused on the statement 'all is not lost' like a mantra.

Andre glanced at his watch. Vladimir had had an appointment with him a half hour ago and he was uncharacteristically late. In fact, he was never late.

Now what's happening with Vladimir? he wondered, attempting to stifle his increasing panic growing within.

Andre again tried to will himself to keep calm. He was a leader, after all.

◆ ◆ ◆

The game was up and he knew it.

Vladimir was pale and drained. He had lost twenty pounds and his hands shook. His normally small frame had shriveled to almost a stick figure. He climbed up the stairs of a basement that resembled a cold, dark dungeon. After raping a kidnapped eighteen-year-old, he had slapped her until she lost consciousness. The other women looking on were forbidden by their armed guards to scream out so they huddled together, weeping quietly.

Vladimir had mistakenly thought a rape would calm him, but just the opposite had occurred. His stomach remained queasy and his throbbing headache returned.

One of the perks of working for Andre was raping the newly captured, assuming this would get the women used to the idea of what fate had in store for them. Andre referred to it as "breaking them in," but Vladimir knew what it really was: an added benefit to satisfy his employees' lust. But this rape would be his last, at least while working for Andre. Now he needed to disappear. Vladimir had it all planned out: he would have plastic surgery tonight and then head to Monaco. He would hire bodyguards who would protect him for the rest of his life. Listening to his gut feeling, over the years he had saved an enormous sum of money in case he fell into disfavor.

That moment had inevitably arrived.

Vladimir had promised Andre that Victor Standu would deliver. Despite his carefully obtained background checks, Victor was not who he said he was. His background information had turned out to be fake.

The previous night, Vladimir had gone through a sleepless night racking his brains, trying to figure out how he had been so badly deceived. Who was Victor really working for? Giving up on sleep, he had gotten out of bed and spent hours on the phone and computer from after midnight into the early morning hours trying to contact the people who had given him Victor's references. These contacts had mysteriously disappeared.

Wearing a bulletproof vest, he bolted from the basement and, upon leaving the building, kept his eyes and ears attuned to any unusual people and sounds. Even though he was armed with guns and knives, he kept turning around to make sure no one was about to creep up behind him and kill him.

Andre must suspect something. I didn't keep my appointment. He's probably so distracted now by what's going on in America that he could've forgotten about me. I'd better disappear before he remembers.

Vladimir had promised Andre that Victor would deliver.

He walked a mile and waited for a public bus to arrive. A

nagging fear that Andre's men may have wired explosives to his car prevented him from driving himself.

It is wiser to stay in public—Andre always carries out his operations as discreetly as possible.

CHAPTER THIRTY-FIVE

MARINA

Now it was Bruce and Igor wrestling to the ground. For once Igor threw caution to the wind; he fought wildly, for he was in the battle of his life. He managed to grab the gun and shoot Bruce, aiming for his heart but only grazing his shoulder. The police kept trying to aim their guns at Igor, but the men moved around too quickly to safely shoot Igor. Igor began covering Bruce's face with his hand, cutting off his breathing. At this point, he scrambled over and pointed his gun at Adam, who lay in a fetal position, his right hand holding Marina's.

"Igor! Don't do this. It's me you want," Marina shouted, trembling and trying to extricate her hand from Adam's, whose eyes remained shut tight. She covered his body in her efforts to shield him.

A victorious smile crept over Igor's face.

Grabbing his shoulder to stem the bleeding and finally extricating himself from Igor's clutches, Bruce managed to shout hoarsely, "You hurt him and Marina and I'll spend the rest of my life hunting you down!"

Igor aimed his gun and was about to shoot Marina when they all heard a voice call out, "Stop, Igor! I have a message for you from Andre!"

Igor hesitated upon hearing his boss's name from a familiar-sounding voice. He couldn't help turning his attention away, the aim of the gun wavering despite his utmost desire to finish off Marina. Two shots rang out seconds apart: the first hit Igor's jagged scar on the side of his face, and the other landed smack between his eyes. He staggered like an out-of-control puppet on strings before falling to the ground.

Everyone stood frozen in place, staring at Igor.

"What the hell!" Lewis muttered as he stared in shock at the man approaching from between two houses. "Who is that man?"

Adam got up slowly, reaching for Marina's right hand. He wailed, "Marina! Marina!"

Despite the intense pain, Bruce managed to wobble over to Adam and Marina. But her attention was on the man who had shot Igor. Her mouth hung open and soon her face was radiant and her mouth curled into a delighted smile as she shouted, "Victor!"

Everyone, from the police to the growing number of spectators watching safely from their windows to Matt and Judy slowly approaching, turned toward Victor.

Marina's taut features softened. Her heart melted and she wept softly. Everyone stared, baffled by her reaction. Victor had dropped his gun, broke into a smile, and ran over to her.

"Victor!" she shouted again, holding her arms out wide.

"Marina, are you all right?" He reached out and gently embraced her. He kissed her forehead. She held onto him, ignoring everyone who gathered and gaped in confusion. But after a few moments, she turned to the crowd.

"Victor is my brother," Marina told everyone as she laughed and cried at the same time.

No one moved except Adam. "Hey!" he ran over and tried tearing Victor away from Marina. "You can't do that!" he thrust out his right hand. "You can only shake a woman's hand. That's it!" He pointed his finger for emphasis.

Victor looked at the young man quizzically. Overcome with emotion, Marina could not form words to protest. She touched Victor's arm and gazed lovingly at Adam.

"Adam, this is my brother, Victor."

"Ohhh, that's different." Adam moved the finger near his mouth.

"Do you remember I told you I had a brother?" She then faced Victor. "This is Adam. He and his father saved me. I stayed with them while they were looking for me."

Meanwhile, Matt ran over and reached Bruce. "Are you OK?" he asked as he helped him stand. "Man, were you brave! You're nobody to mess with, big brother!" He hugged Bruce as he allowed his tears to flow. Bruce cradled him like a big brother.

◆ ◆ ◆

After an eight-hour bus ride, a weary Vladimir staggered off, still looking at everything around him. He walked into a restaurant and collapsed into a chair. He required nourishment before walking two miles to the doctor's. He felt his bulging front pocket. Vladimir carried a bundle of cash in his wallet for the doctor to perform the surgery tonight. After his meal, he was sorely tempted to catch a taxi, but he couldn't take the chance.

Walking slowly, taking many breaks to catch his breath, he finally made it to the doctor's building and knocked on the door.

"Come in, come in." A tall man with a wide, balding head ushered him in.

"Everything all set?" Vladimir asked as he stepped in and kept looking around.

"Yes, yes. Don't worry," the doctor assured him.

"As you know, I am giving you half the payment now," Vladimir told him, counting the cash he had in his wallet, "but I'm leaving immediately, so I will send you the rest by tomorrow afternoon. You have my word."

"I'm not worried," the doctor said. "Get undressed and put on this gown and I'll give you the anesthesia."

Vladimir did as he was told. The doctor beckoned him to lie down on the operating table to await the anesthesia.

"Remember, I want to be better looking after the operation," Vladimir reminded him as he struggled to move his tired body to lie down on the table.

My goal is to actually bed women without having to rape them, he thought, chuckling.

"Don't worry. As I told you, women won't be able to resist you when I'm all done with you," the doctor said with shifty eyes and a too-wide grin.

"You do anesthesia too?" Vladimir asked. He was looking around for someone else. "I thought a special doctor does that."

"No need for another doctor," he said, placing the mask onto Vladimir's face. "I have expertise in anesthesiology as well."

Vladimir watched the doctor push a button. He noticed the doctor's eyes narrow and a smirk play on his lips.

"What is it?" Vladimir asked, seeing his expression and

trying to take off the mask. "Don't forget you're being paid handsomely."

The doctor raised his eyebrows and snarled, "I know you're paying me handsomely. I don't think you remember me from a few years ago when I was on television and in the newspapers. I met a man named Victor Standu. He told me you were responsible for kidnapping my teenage daughter who ran away from home five years ago."

Vladimir's eyes bulged and he quickly scrambled to take off the mask. But it was too late. The poison rendered him helpless. His throat closed and tears welled up in his eyes. It took half a minute for the poison to kill him, but for Vladimir, it felt like an eternity. The last image he saw was the sad eyes and triumphant smile on the doctor's face.

CHAPTER THIRTY-SIX

JOSEPH

EIGHT-YEAR-OLD JOSEPH WOULD OFTEN WAKE UP in the middle of the night in his tenth-floor apartment that he shared with his family in Port Elizabeth. They had only arrived from Puerto Rico a few months ago. His mother's brother, who had lived in New Jersey for years, had helped to arrange their passage to the United States.

Joseph found the move a difficult transition; he was already a light sleeper, but now he often woke up in the night and couldn't drift off to sleep again. His parents were concerned because his teachers told them Joseph would often fall asleep during school.

He had particular trouble falling asleep on two consecutive nights at two o'clock in the morning each week. Joseph claimed he would wake up and hear a ship lapping in the waves as it came into port. The ship's engine made enough noise to wake him out of his light sleep.

But one night he heard wailing police cars and fire trucks and shouts emanating from the port at two o'clock in the morning. Joseph jumped out of bed and stared out of his window, curious to see what was going on, but the gates and trucks obstructed his view. Not knowing what else to do, he ran into his parents' bedroom.

He shook his father. "Daddy! Mommy! There's lots and lots of noise outside! All kinds of police cars! Come quick! Come quick!" His father Manuel, who was not a light sleeper, woke up instantly upon hearing his son. He, too, heard all the loud noises. He sat straight up with his eyes bulging and his hands shaking. Manuel grabbed his son. "What's going on?"

"I don't know! It's coming from outside my window," Joseph said, putting his thumb in his mouth.

In addition to lack of sleep, ever since they had arrived to Port Elizabeth, Joseph had also begun putting his thumb in his mouth like he had done when he was a baby. Manuel and his wife Ana had recently spoken with the school counselor, and they decided this was due to Joseph adjusting to his new environment. They were now looking into a child psychologist they could afford while trying to adjust to this move themselves. Ana feared that she was neglecting her son by working on her own homework from her ESL class in the evenings after she came home from work during the day. Both parents felt guilty they were unable to help Joseph with his English homework. Ana forced herself to get up when her son entered the bedroom. Her eyes remained half closed while she and Manuel practically sleepwalked to Joseph's room to peer out the window, Joseph following behind, clutching his father's arm.

All their eyes opened wide as they saw the swirling red-colored lights all over the port. Screeching sirens filled the air. The family had never heard such loud noises as the night came alive with frenzied activity: police, ambulance workers, and others speeding onto the scene. Ana grabbed her husband's arm and moved a protective arm around Joseph, making sure he stayed behind them. She could feel his little body trembling as he hid his face. But Joseph couldn't help peeking every now and then. The three of them stared out the window, trying to make sense of what was going on.

Soon they saw about ten men in handcuffs being hauled into police cars while disheveled, skinny, shaking young women, some crying and others with faces frozen in shock, huddled under heavy blankets. Medics led each woman into ambulances. Joseph, Manuel, and Ana kept turning their stares from the window to each other.

"Did you hear things at night from here, Joseph?" Manuel asked as he turned to his son.

"Yes, Daddy. I've told you and Mommy and the school counselor that I would hear things at night. I got so used to it that I would get up every night even though it was quiet," Joseph smiled, feeling vindicated at last.

"So, you weren't dreaming about noises then." Turning to his wife, Manuel said, "Ana, Let's cancel that appointment with the child psychologist tomorrow morning." Putting his arm on his son's shoulder, he said, "There's nothing wrong with our son."

Ana nodded as she watched one young woman after another leave in an ambulance with police, and firemen scurrying all around the port and the ship.

◆ ◆ ◆

Finally! thought Ivan Denisov, head of the central police in Moscow. *The lead we've been waiting for.*

At this point he no longer cared the American FBI had given them the lead. The police had been searching for Andre and his human trafficking organization for years. No matter how hard they tried, they kept coming up empty-handed. Andre and his organization had remained elusive. Until now.

◆ ◆ ◆

Inside his basement office, Andre sat as still as a mannequin. He had been left stunned and deflated when one of his men had informed him that Victor had fabricated his whole life story. He was, in fact, the girl's brother. Andre couldn't move as he sought to process this revelation.

How could I have been so completely duped? How could this have possibly happened?

If Vladimir weren't already dead, Andre would have choked him to death with his bare hands. On his desk was the e-mail with the headline of Vladimir's mysterious demise. His body had been found in a garbage dump. No witnesses.

Rivulets of sweat formed around Andre's forehead. He had to hunt for a dry handkerchief in his desk to wipe his brow. His organization, as well as his mind, was falling apart at the seams.

We had a solid, air-tight operation, he ruminated.

He decided then and there he could no longer afford to wait to find out what happened or what was going to happen next. Escape was the only option. Who knew? Maybe someday he could reemerge with another enormously profitable sex slavery ring. As long as he had his life and freedom, all was not lost.

He stood up, rushed to his safe, and took out enough money to disappear. Ever the careful planner, Andre had already formulated his foolproof escape plan. Leaning his hands on the desk, he found the key underneath his pen holder and rummaged in his locked drawer for the ax. Time to execute the emergency escape.

It was at this moment he heard someone pounding on his door.

This gave Andre a start. He nearly collapsed back in his chair. He told himself not to panic, he was going to get through this. Hands and legs involuntarily trembling, he limped to his coat closet. Closing the door from the inside, he turned on the closet light switch. With shortness of breath he slowly sank to the floor and tried pulling out one of the large tiles with the ax. He kept trying to open the tile, but in his panic, he continually lost his grip. By the time he finally opened it, he dropped the ax and loose tile with loud thuds.

I'm always prepared, he tried to reassure himself, despite sweating profusely.

"Police! Open up now!" A commanding voice yelled from outside the door.

Andre was so anxious he couldn't waste a second to calm himself down. By that time the police would have broken in and invaded his office.

Andre moved his tense muscles as fast as he could. When he finally fitted his body down the opening to the secret tunnel in the ground, he clumsily tried to fit the tile back in place. Hearing the police breaking his door down, he sloppily put the tile back half open. It sounded like an army of police officers charging into his office.

Andre didn't fool them. They immediately saw the closet light on, and when they hurled it open, saw the hastily placed tile covering only part of the opening to his now not-so-secret tunnel.

Ivan and his police team wasted no time drawing their guns down the tunnel and calling after him, "Stop right there! You're under arrest!"

Andre stood on a rung in the middle of the ladder. He attempted to pull out his Luger, but his trembling hands made him drop it down into the darkness. He heard it land with a loud thud. Foolishly, he reached down to make a grab for it, lost his balance on the rung, and fell headfirst into the void. The last the policemen saw of him were his bulging, doomed eyes and his piercing scream that echoed throughout the tunnel.

Ivan's shoulders dropped down, relaxed. He turned to his fellow officers and said, "This man finally got what was coming to him." He shook his head. "Thank God Victor got involved. And thank God for the Americans! One operation finally eliminated, but so many more to go!"

CHAPTER THIRTY-SEVEN

BRUCE

Both Hitchens families relaxed in Matt and Judy's living room.

"So how does it feel being a muscleman hero now?" Matt teased, winking at his brother as he reclined back on his easy chair.

Before all this, Bruce would have waved his hand at Matt whenever his brother teased him. But now he broke into a grin. His shoulder was bandaged and the doctor said it would fully heal in a matter of weeks.

"Bruce," Judy exclaimed, "I'm glad to see you're developing a sense of humor."

"After all I went through—after all we went through—you gotta laugh over the little things," he admitted. He sat back and put his feet up on the ottoman.

"You're finally loosening up, Bruce! I'm proud of you!" Matt beamed.

Judy stopped smiling and looked down. "But don't forget what all those young women like Marina go through," she reminded them.

"An absolute nightmare," Bruce agreed soberly. He shook his head. "It's still hard for me to believe people could be capable of such evil." He sighed. "I really shouldn't be so surprised after what Hitler and Stalin did to millions of people."

Everyone nodded and sat in silence for a moment.

"The police are still trying to locate all the girls and their families from that last ship that came into port," added Matt. "I hope all the people involved in the sex slavery ring die slow, painful deaths!"

"And their torture should only continue for them in hell!" Judy added vehemently.

There was a gloomy silence in the room as everyone's minds turned to the victims, including Marina.

Adam gazed around the whole time, biting his shirt, seemingly perplexed by their somber conversation, not understanding the sad faces everyone wore.

David finally spoke up to lighten the moment. "Don't forget Danielle is bringing home a movie for you to watch, Adam."

"A movie!" Adam shouted gleefully. He sat on the couch next to his father. "What kinda movie? Does it have animals in it?"

Sarah smiled warmly at her cousin in a love seat next to her brother. "It sure does! And after we watch the movie, I'm going to teach you how to Skype, Adam. I want to know how you and Uncle Bruce are doing when I'm in college!"

"That's after the ice cream," David corrected her.

"Ice cream. All right!" Adam jumped out of his seat, waving his fists in the air.

"And after the ice cream, we'll hopefully start your diet," Bruce said with his eyes closed but still smiling. He opened them to look at his nephew and niece in wonder, never believing he would see the day when they finally welcomed his son into their lives.

"Can I still eat ice cream when I'm on a dying?" his huge, innocent eyes stared intently at his father.

"It's called a diet, son," Bruce said, sitting forward. "And no, there's no ice cream when you're on a diet."

"No! No, Daddy. I don't lika diet." Adam shook his head vigorously. His ever-growing cheeks jiggled from side to side.

David glided on the seat next to Adam and put his arm around his shoulders. "Today, buddy, don't worry about a diet," he said as he ruffled his cousin's hair. "Today we're going to eat ice cream with hot fudge and whipped cream."

At that, Danielle walked through the front door, asking, "Who's ready for *Dr. Doolittle*?" She turned to her cousin. "Adam, do you know there are talking animals in *Dr. Doolittle*?"

"Really?" he sat up and bounced on the sofa in excitement, forgetting all about the diet.

But before his cousins got up to prepare for the movie, Adam stopped. "What 'bout Marina, Daddy?" Adam asked, turning to his father. "Is she goin' come over and watch *Dr. Doolittle* wit me?"

Bruce had a pensive expression and said nothing.

"Marina's certainly welcome to come over and watch it with us, isn't she, Matt?" Judy said, turning to her husband.

"Of course. It's fine with me," Matt answered, looking a bit shamefaced. He had seen how devoted she was to Adam and Bruce and had finally come to accept her.

Bruce stood up. "I'm going to go out for a bit. Is it OK if Adam stays here?"

"No problem. We're going to watch the movie," David said as he gestured to Adam and his sisters. "Come on, let's go into the TV room."

"Daddy, where you goin'?" Adam asked as Bruce went to the closet to get his jacket.

"I'm just going to meet with a friend. I won't be long," Bruce told him.

After he left the house, Sarah smiled. "I bet I know who the friend is."

"And why not?" Judy asked. "He's been living like a monk ever since Aunt Maggie passed away."

"We wish him the best, whatever's going to happen with them," Matt declared. He gestured to his wife. "Come on, Judy. Let's watch the movie. We could use a few laughs."

CHAPTER THIRTY-EIGHT

MARINA

MARINA AND VICTOR'S PARENTS WERE ON THEIR way to America. They would meet them at Newark Airport that evening.

"Must feel good to finally be going back home, yes?" Victor asked her, taking her hand. They were seated by the window of her hotel room, taking in a bird's-eye view of downtown Newark, viewing the pedestrians, the cars, and the many businesses. The hotel had a clean, breezy scent that permeated the air. That and the spacious, tidy rooms with plants adorning the hotel lobby made the atmosphere calm and relaxed.

Marina smiled. "I can't wait to see Mom and Dad." Shaking her head, she stared at her brother. "I still can't believe all we went through. My God, I'm so glad it's finally over." She bowed her head and covered her eyes with her hands. When she opened them and faced her brother, she said, "Victor, do you still want to be an undercover policeman? I remember you discussing it with Mom and Dad."

He nodded without hesitation. "If I could carry on

the mission with my sister's life in danger, I must be pretty good at it."

She reached over and touched his shoulder gently, away from his bandage. "I think so. You always did look out for me."

Victor held his breath a moment before he asked, "So that man who helped you, do you have feelings for him? His son seems very attached to you."

"They're wonderful," she said solemnly. "I wouldn't be alive without them." She opened her hands wide. "Adam lost his mother a few months ago. He misses her so much." She paused and said, "So much has happened that I don't know where things stand with any of us, to be honest."

"You've gone through so much, Marina," he said. "Don't feel rushed." He turned to stare out the window. "I've always wanted to visit America. Life seems easier here than in Moldova." He turned back to her and said wistfully, "Perhaps I can return here someday and enjoy it like a tourist, no?"

"I know just how you feel, Victor," Marina agreed, smiling. "And I'm going to save up money to pay for that vacation. You deserve it!"

The Moscow police had wired Victor that they were impressed with his investigative skills while still at the beginning stages of his training. They waived his remaining tuition to continue school before officially entering the police force. Victor had agreed with delight, although he stipulated that he wanted to continue hunting down criminals in sex slavery rings. His life goal was to free all the victims and bring those responsible to justice.

Marina had decided she would stay with her parents at first and save up enough money to find her own apartment. She tried to think about her old life in Moldova, but her thoughts kept returning to Bruce and Adam.

While they both sat in silence, contemplating their futures, the room phone startled them out of their reverie.

Marina ran to the phone. "Hello?"

"Hello, this is the front desk of the hotel. A man named Bruce Hitchens would like to know if you could come down to the lobby."

Marina's face broke into a big smile. "Oh, yes. I'll go down."

When she hung up, Victor rose from his chair. He said with a twinkle in his eye, "That must be the father, judging from your smile. Would it be better if I went to my own room?"

"No, no. I'm going down." Marina hurried to the bathroom to make sure her hair, clothes, and makeup were just right.

"I should have known he was coming, the way you're dressed this morning," Victor said teasingly as he sat back down.

"I didn't know he was coming," Marina protested as she headed toward the door.

"But you had a feeling." Victor gave her a sidelong look.

Marina had her hand on the doorknob and faced him. "I had a feeling he might want to say good-bye."

"Marina," he said with a serious expression, "do what your heart tells you is right. And good luck."

Whatever happens, I still have my family. And the future.

"Hi! You're looking great!" Bruce rose from his seat in the lobby when he saw her.

Marina wore bangs in a sleek hairstyle. She had gotten a haircut, and wisps of shiny, layered hair flew around her shoulders. She wore a tailored green shirt and black spandex pants. She had on mascara, blush, and lipstick. She even had a French manicure, which made her feel particularly feminine and elegant.

"Thank you," she answered, blushing slightly. "You look good too."

Bruce wore dark blue cotton pants and a crisp plaid shirt. The dark blue, green, and red tones of the shirt complemented his dark eyes. For the first time, Marina noted there were no dark circles under his eyes. His expression was relaxed, and he had a ready smile.

When they met, he discreetly kissed her on the cheek. *Always a gentleman.*

Marina looked around. "Where's Adam?"

"He's with Matt and Judy and the kids," he said. "They insisted on him staying with them." He smiled contentedly. "The kids wanted him to watch *Dr. Doolittle* with them."

"Sorry?" Marina shook her head.

"A movie with talking animals," he explained. "Then they were going to make ice cream sundaes with him." He shook his head, but he looked pleased. "Judy didn't even have to convince her kids. It was their idea."

He glimpsed out the tall windows with the stylish ivory drapes. "It's a beautiful day. Why don't we take a walk?"

"Sure," Marina said. She longed to take his hand in hers but did not want to rush him. Pleasantly surprised, he reached for her hand and she clasped his.

Outside the weather was perfect. There was a lot of traffic, but they were blissfully unaware of the fast cars and drivers honking their horns. Since it was between the breakfast and lunch hours, fewer pedestrians were outside. Bruce and Marina concentrated mainly on each other.

Bruce cleared his throat. "I didn't tell you that my boss at work was a little upset when I had to leave when I found out you and Adam were in danger."

"Oh no!" Marina said and stopped, cupping her hand on her mouth.

"But it's OK," he assured her, and they continued walking. "He was under stress and said things he didn't mean. He apologized and promoted me to the position I've been working for for years."

"Congratulations!" Marina stopped. She hugged him and kissed his cheek.

Bruce radiated a calm happiness she had never seen.

"Actually, the few days I wasn't there, Steve—my boss—said business took a nosedive. Clients were actually threatening to do business elsewhere if I didn't come back." His eyes became distant, and he spoke as if he were talking to himself. "I never thought I would be appreciated and needed so much at work." He chuckled. "I thought they barely tolerated me and I was always hanging on by a thread." He stared into the distance. "Sometimes I thought the idea of getting promoted was a only a silly fantasy of mine."

"Well, you know now that isn't true," Marina said as he turned to her. She placed both her hands in his. "And you've done a phenomenal job taking care of Adam. You should be proud of yourself for accomplishing that, too. I don't know any other man who could take on all you've had to handle."

Bruce faced her. "And I see that he really is a good kid." He glanced down and faced her again, smiling. "I must admit it even though he's my son."

"And he's crazy about you," she said and added softly,

"So am I."

He gazed into her eyes. "Now that this is all over," he said carefully, "what are your plans?"

"I'll probably go back to Moldova and live with my parents until I can find my way again."

Bruce squeezed her hand. "I'd ask you to stay, but I don't want to rush you." He gazed deeply into her eyes. "I haven't felt this way about another woman since my wife died. But I don't want to be selfish. I want you to do what's best for you."

Marina was speechless; she realized that he felt the same way about her that she felt about him.

"If you need to go back home for a while, I'll understand. But if you want to come and visit, I'll pay for your ticket," Bruce said and smiled shyly. "I'm hoping you'll only need a one-way ticket."

Marina gazed into his eyes. "I love you and Adam so much."

"And we love you. We'd be crushed if we never saw you again."

"And I couldn't bear to leave the two of you for long. He's a very special young man," she said and added, "and so is his father."

"We could give it a chance, you know," Bruce said. "Hopefully, in a more regular environment."

Marina's face glowed and her eyes sparkled. "I would like nothing better."